"Piper's internal battles between familial duty and a desire for independence are sensitively rendered, and readers will cheer her on as she tackles the racial stereotypes baked into the overwhelmingly white world of horse racing. Shiloh's fans will speed through this sweet, satisfying romance."

—*Publishers Weekly* on *A Run at Love*

"Shiloh radiates wisdom and sincerity. . . . *A Run at Love* is an inspiring friends-to-lovers modern romance about breaking barriers of ethnicity and gender and the importance of representation in non-diverse spaces. She brilliantly captures the drama of the equestrian world and the road to the Kentucky Derby while illuminating the emotional and experiential complexities of transracial adoption and identity."

—*Booklist* starred review of *A Run at Love*

"With faith and pop culture references from page one, Shiloh excels at growing multidimensional characters into friends, with a little help from family and God."

—*Library Journal* starred review of
The Love Script

"Shiloh offers a sweet romance with a strong dose of spiritual truth."

—Pepper Basham, award-winning author of
Authentically, Izzy, on *The Love Script*

"Toni Shiloh delivers another soulful, uplifting romance. . . . A swoon-worthy romance readers will adore."

—Belle Calhoune, bestselling author of *An Alaskan Christmas Promise*, on *The Love Script*

"I love a romance populated with characters you can truly root for. And this one has that and more. Coupled with Toni Shiloh's winning voice, it's a story not to be missed."

—Oprah Daily on *In Search of a Prince*

"This romance with a touch of mystery will stay with you long after The End."

—Rachel Hauck, *New York Times* bestselling author, on *In Search of a Prince*

"Toni Shiloh brilliantly weaves a romantic tale."

—Vanessa Riley, bestselling author of *Island Queen*, on *In Search of a Prince*

"Shiloh has penned yet another adorable and charming royal romance!"

—Melissa Ferguson, bestselling author of *Meet Me in the Margins*, on *To Win a Prince*

"Another winner that readers will enjoy from start to finish."

—Vanessa Miller, author of *Something Good*, on *To Win a Prince*

"Readers are going to be delighted by this endearing and adorable romance."

—Sarah Monzon, author of the SEWING IN SOCAL series, on *The Love Script*

the
NATURE
of
LOVE

the NATURE of LOVE

Toni Shiloh

BETHANYHOUSE

a division of Baker Publishing Group
Minneapolis, Minnesota

Published by Bethany House Publishers
Minneapolis, Minnesota
BethanyHouse.com

Bethany House Publishers is a division of
Baker Publishing Group, Grand Rapids, Michigan

Printed in the United States of America

Library of Congress Cataloging-in-Publication Data
Names: Shiloh, Toni, author.
Title: The nature of love / Toni Shiloh.
Description: Minneapolis, Minnesota : Bethany House Publishers, a division
  of Baker Publishing Group, 2025. | Series: Love in the Spotlight
Identifiers: LCCN 2024039012 | ISBN 9780764241529 (paper) | ISBN 9780764244605
  (casebound) | ISBN 9781493448999 (ebook)
Subjects: LCGFT: Christian fiction. | Romance fiction. | Novels.
Classification: LCC PS3619.H548 N38 2025 | DDC 813/.6—dc23/eng/20240828
LC record available at https://lccn.loc.gov/2024039012

Cover design and illustration by Sarah Kvam

Author is represented by Rachel McMillan.

Baker Publishing Group publications use paper produced from sustainable forestry practices and postconsumer waste whenever possible.

25 26 27 28 29 30 31   7 6 5 4 3 2 1

To the Author and Finisher of my faith.

One

Drilling a hole in the middle of a person's femur was my least favorite thing to do. Not because I wasn't capable. Technology had made a way for me to drill a precise hole exactly where I needed to insert a metal rod and screws to repair the midshaft femoral break. However, I couldn't do anything to stop the intense pain this sweet woman would feel when she woke up. A broken femur was one of the hardest injuries to overcome. Couple that with the woman's occupation—an Olympic ski jumper—and she'd have an uphill battle.

I would do everything in my power to ensure she'd return to the slopes.

"Ready for the rod," I murmured, now that the sound of the drill had stopped overtaking the classical music floating through the operating room speakers.

I'd been listening to classical composers in the OR since the very first time I'd scrubbed in on a surgery. One of my med school professors had insisted that listening to the music while learning would guarantee a good grade. I played it while studying, when learning new procedures, and in the operating room. Classical music represented my career. On the other hand, my at-home playlist consisted of '70s music that would help me unwind from the long day of surgeries.

"Rod," the second-year student replied.

I slid the rod right down the middle of the femur and into the broken piece. Next, I inserted the screws to ensure a close bond to allow the healing process to begin. I gestured for the fourth-year resident to suture the incision. "Close up, Dr. Bryner."

"Yes, Dr. Kennedy."

I walked out of the operating room, breathing a sigh of relief that nothing had gone wrong. Besides working here, I was on call at the nation's Olympic sports injury clinic up in Vail, so I'd done this procedure multiple times before. But I still couldn't perform one of these surgeries without my gut twisting like a gymnast during a floor routine.

I removed my surgical gown, placing it into the dirty bin, then washed up before heading into the hall. A glance at my smartwatch told me I'd have about thirty minutes to look at my email and answer any phone calls that were urgent before I clocked out.

Today had been a good day.

"Have a good evening, Dr. Kennedy," Nurse Jones said as she passed me.

"You too." My throat constricted.

Whenever I interacted with my colleagues, my mouth dried out. My throat seemed to get tighter as my mind grappled for words. What should I say to them? Did they expect more than simple small talk? I'd heard whispers behind my back. Most of my colleagues found me stuck up and abrasive. Just because I didn't share what I did on the weekend or gossip about the other hospital workers didn't mean that I was silently judging them.

I simply had no idea how to respond.

You'd think a world-class doctor would be able to navigate

the basics of small talk, but I didn't earn my accolades by making friends. No, I obtained my status by working my tail off until the only person I knew, *really* knew, was my baby sister. And even that relationship had changed. Not that we were at odds, but she'd built a life separate from me. One that I had to get weekly phone call updates on because she lived in Kentucky, and I was happy in Colorado.

Or at least satisfied.

After making the last follow-up call of the day, I turned off my office computer, grabbed my purse, and headed to the employee parking lot. I'd already changed from scrubs into jeans and a sweater. My peacoat would give added protection against the cold temps October had brought. Though the calendar said fall, the freshly fallen snow spoke of something else. Regardless, I was here for it.

I started my white Range Rover, inhaling the scent of the leather seats. Turning on the seat warmer, I took a moment to settle in, letting the weight of today's surgeries fall from me. Now wasn't the time to analyze what had gone right or wrong, but to simply empty my mind.

My stomach rumbled, and I glanced at the dashboard. *6:07 p.m.* Time for some dinner. I was ravenous and knew just the place to grab a bite.

Colorado Springs could be walkable, depending on where you lived. It just so happened that my work (Peak University Hospital), my home (right on West Pikes Peak Avenue in Old Colorado City), and food (a stop at Skirted Heifer was a must) were all within four miles of each other. I could be at the hospital in a jiffy by car, but on my off days a car wasn't necessary unless I wanted to stay warm.

I slid into an empty parking spot, then climbed out of my Rover. A cool breeze fluttered the trees, and I peered up into the clear sky. The sky was making its way to sunset, but I didn't care that I'd missed the sunshine by being in the OR all day. It was enough to feel the breeze on my face and know I had a show to binge when I got home.

I made my way to the front door just as a man reached for the handle. I paused, and he stared at me, a hesitant look on his handsome face.

"Um, would you like to go in first?" he asked in a smooth tenor.

For some reason, the question made tiny goose bumps pebble my arms. Was it the thoughtful request or the tone of his voice?

"If you don't mind."

"Please." He gestured me forward.

I walked ahead of him, conscious of his stare behind me. *Don't be ridiculous. He's not staring.* But *I* wanted to.

I wanted to turn around and stare at his warm blue eyes once more. I'd never seen a Black man with eyes that particular shade, unless you counted the movie star Michael Ealy. Now that I thought of it, the guy behind me had similar features, but he was more handsome in my opinion.

Erykah, what's gotten into you?

I didn't stare at men. I didn't note their voices or their eye color, and I certainly didn't try to talk to them. I was the woman who couldn't carry a conversation in a bucket.

Ignoring his presence, I placed my order for a naked heifer, adding my favorite toppings—this girl couldn't live without bacon, guac, and pepper jack on her burger—and requested a side of fries with their handcrafted soda.

I moved on, finding a spot to wait in the dining area. A spot that earned me a portrait view of the man's face. His beard was on the scraggly side, as if he'd just come down from camping in the mountains and enjoying all that Colorado had to offer. Or maybe that was his style.

He wore a black beanie and black-frame glasses. He looked studious but masculine at the same time. I watched as he placed his order and then scanned the area as if searching for some-one. Shock coursed through me when his gaze landed on mine. A small smile lifted his full lips, and he walked to my table.

"Hi," he said.

"Hello." I straightened in my seat.

"May I sit for a moment?"

I nodded, not sure what else to do.

"So I don't normally do this."

"Order food?"

He chuckled. "Sit at a stranger's table."

"Then why mine?" I winced inwardly. Had that sounded rude?

"Because you ordered your burger just like I order mine."

Okay, a little surprising but considering the odds—not that I knew them—not totally stunning. "And that made you want to sit here?"

"It made me want to introduce myself."

"Fair enough." I held out my hand. "Erykah Kennedy."

"Christian Gamble, but my friends call me Chris."

"Nice to meet you, Christian."

His eyes twinkled. I wasn't sure if I'd said something funny, or if he was just one of those happy guys.

"What do you do, Erykah?"

I swallowed. *Here it goes.* When I'd encountered similar lines of questioning with men in the past, they often got defensive when I said I was a surgeon. Or they treated me as if it was so cute I tried to be more than just a homemaker.

My shoulders tensed. "I'm an orthopedic surgeon." My breath caught in my chest as I waited for his reaction.

He let out a low whistle. "So you're unbelievably smart and talented."

"Uh . . ." Why were my cheeks heating? "I am." It was the one thing in life I was sure about. The rest was freestyling. Remembering niceties, I replied, "What do you do?"

"Official title: wildlife conservationist."

"Unofficial?" I asked, curiosity piqued.

"Animal wrangler."

My lips curved upward. "What kinds of animals?"

"Whichever are in-house."

"Erykah," an employee called out.

"Oh, um, my order's ready."

"I hope you enjoy that burger," Christian said.

"You too." I stood, fidgeting with my purse strap. Was I supposed to say anything more? Invite him to dine with me even though I had placed a to-go order?

I opened my mouth, then promptly shut it and headed for the counter. Sitting at my table didn't mean anything. I'd go home, eat my dinner, and watch another episode of *Nadiya Bakes*. Her accent soothed me, and in another life, I imagined myself baking everything she did.

As I grabbed my food, I glanced over at Christian Gamble one last time, marking every single feature of his face in my mind. A sigh tore from my lips as I pushed the door open and headed to my car.

Erykah Kennedy, you are *a coward.*

Two

Lamont

Nevaeh wants to know if you need a good dating app recommendation.

Chris Gamble stared at the text in the group chat with his two friends, searching for the right reply. Normally his brain had a comeback in a matter of seconds, but lately, all he could think about was how alone he felt. He couldn't help but blame the reason on the fellas' recent relationship status changes.

Lamont had fallen in love with the woman he'd fake dated to save his movie-star reputation, and Tuck had finally caved and admitted he loved his best friend. Now both couples were putting all their efforts into getting Chris to hop on the love train. *Great, now the O'Jays will be singing in my head.*

Only he wasn't so sure jumping into the dating pool was the right thing to do.

Not because he liked being the fifth and oldest wheel—how he ended up friends with guys a decade younger than him was all God—but because he couldn't forget what had happened the last time he'd been in a relationship. He didn't want to be alone, but at the moment, those were the cards in his hand.

Even so, he couldn't get the woman he'd met the week before out of his head. Something told him Dr. Erykah Kennedy was the type to cherish the coveted title and didn't often introduce herself without first mentioning she was a surgeon. There had been a quiet steadiness about her that made him want to take the time to get to know her, but something sad also lurked in her dark brown eyes.

Or maybe he was simply projecting.

"Chris, production wants to know if you can get them access so they can film parts of the gray wolf reintroduction."

Colorado citizens had voted for the reintroduction of the gray wolf to the Colorado ecosystems. The news was huge, and it was no wonder that PathLight wanted access to the monumental event come this December.

Chris glanced up from his phone. His project manager, Cameron, stared at him expectantly, foot tapping against the tile. Her sky-blue shirt with their company logo on it was tucked into her high-waisted jeans. He'd made the mistake once of calling them mom jeans and had been quickly corrected.

"Tell them it's not as simple as a yes or no. I need to reach out to someone on the team to verify that'll be okay." He rubbed the bridge of his nose.

Why had he agreed to a documentary, again?

When he'd first mulled over the idea of hosting a docuseries, *yes* had been the obvious response. A bigger platform to discuss wildlife conservation and the many ways the everyday person could care for God's creation? *Yes*. Being filmed around Chris's own schedule? *Definite yes*.

But that's where the yeses stopped.

Chris had never thought of a camera in his face as annoying. Then again, maybe it was just PathLight's director, whose constant demands made Chris question whether the docuseries would actually impact society for the greater good. Uploading YouTube videos and shorts to share what he knew about animals and simple ways to make sustainable changes in the home was easy, but this was a production of a whole different magnitude.

But he'd already signed on the dotted line—figuratively since he'd signed online with the suggested software signature —and filming had begun.

PathLight was calling the docuseries *This Is Colorado*, with Chris being the host. He was supposed to show the audience how great Colorado was and teach them how to be good stewards of the earth. If the series did well, PathLight would go on to create additional seasons, featuring each state and hosted by a different conservationist in each location.

They had started by shooting at Chris's nonprofit—a combination of a nature center with educational outreach programs and an emergency rehab facility. His employees had all agreed to being filmed, jumping at a chance to get their fifteen minutes of fame.

Despite the help of his staff, his work efforts had doubled. YouTube and the docuseries both vied for his time, along with the other demands the nonprofit board required of him. Two weeks in, and Chris already wished the constant *turn here*, *let's do that again*, and *one more time* would leave his vocabulary so he could work in peace.

It's for a good cause, remember that. People won't completely understand the importance of being good stewards if no one ever shows them.

The verse "So then faith comes by hearing, and hearing by the word of God" filtered through his thoughts. The same premise for faith fit conservation efforts. People wouldn't know why they should change their ways if no one spoke the truth to listening ears.

So Chris would tough it out and get through the heavy demand of filming a docuseries. No wonder Lamont was always exhausted after making a movie. A YouTube video was nothing compared to that.

His phone chimed again, reminding him of the text he never responded to. Chris read the other texts that had come in.

Tuck
Don't do it, man. I've heard horror stories.

Lamont
Same.

Tuck
If you want to meet a girl the old-fashioned way, go to the grocery store.

Lamont
What? The store?

Tuck
You can tell a lot about a woman by the way she shops.

Lamont
Don't listen to him, Chris. Find a woman at church.

Tuck
🙂

Tuck
Yeah, because dropping a church pickup line will win major points.

Lamont
You might have a point. Plus, did they even have church pickup lines when Chris was young?

Okay, time for him to interject before his friends became even more ridiculous.

> Chris
> I won't do an app, but I will definitely consider the old-fashioned way.

Once more his thoughts strayed toward Dr. Kennedy. An image of how her beautiful brown skin glowed came to mind. Her braids had been shoulder length and somehow looked different from regular braids, but how, he couldn't put into words. All he knew was the full cheeks that had curved into a prominent chin made his heart soften a little. He wouldn't mind getting to know her. Too bad she had left the restaurant before he could attempt to exchange numbers.

That was a foolish move. And an obvious reminder of how long he'd been out of the dating game.

> Lamont
> Good luck to you.

> Tuck
> I can always do some digging and try to find out that info on my surgeon.

> Chris
> Don't bother. God'll figure it all out.

At least, Chris assumed that God was on the same wavelength as he was. Chris had made it down the aisle before and faced the biggest humiliation of his life. He'd figured God was sparing him from a repeat embarrassment. Why else had no other woman sparked his interest?

Except Erykah Kennedy.

He sighed. Enough of that. He'd push past the distraction and start checking off items on his to-do list before he went for a hike.

He stood, left his office, and entered the hallway of his nonprofit.

On a daily basis, Chris's team took care of various wildlife that'd been injured in the regional area until they could be turned over to a long-term rehab center. They also had a few animals that remained with them on a permanent basis for educational programs.

Right now, he needed to prepare the kit fox and the black-footed ferret for the second-grade class coming in for a field trip. The ferret had made his home at Gamble on Nature a couple of years after retiring from a breeding facility that was trying to prevent the species from becoming extinct. Students usually enjoyed meeting him. Maybe Chris could even see if their injured beaver would want to meet the kids. A temporary resident, the beaver would be picked up by a rehab facility on Friday. Surely the kids would love to get a look at him up close.

"How are we coming along for the field trip?" Chris asked Cameron.

She pulled out one of the many pencils keeping her bun on top of her head. "Zach put Nick into the small cage, so he's ready. Kimble stills need to be prepared."

"I'll take care of him." Chris headed down the hall to where the ferret's cage was. Kimble was about as close to a pet as Chris could get. Not because he didn't want a domesticated animal in his home. He did. In a perfect world, he'd have a Bernese mountain dog named Bernie. But the travel he did for educational outreaches, animal rescues, board events, and now the docuseries meant he wasn't home much to give a dog attention. Then again, there was always the option of bringing the dog along as a travel companion.

In a different world. Not now. You're too busy.

"Kimble, wanna play?" he murmured.

The ferret happily began dooking. The chuckling sound often happened when Kimble played. Just offering the invitation had Kimble coming out of the cubby he liked to snuggle in. Chris put out a tray of food for the guy so he could eat before engaging with six- and seven-year-olds. He moved on to the beaver, checking on the little guy. He seemed content in the sleeping area, so Chris allowed him to rest.

When Kimble finished his snack, Chris brought him out into the instructional classroom. The kids filed in quietly, their teacher praising them for their good behavior.

"Mr. Gamble is going to talk to us now. Please give him your best Raven behavior."

Chris held back a smirk as the kids immediately sat ram-rod straight in the chairs. "Good morning, everyone."

"Good morning," they called back.

"I'm Mr. Gamble, and I run Gamble on Nature with my colleagues, Cameron"—he pointed to the project manager, who waved—"and Zach." The intern waved.

"Sometimes we have a couple more people in-house, but right now, they're out in the wild tracking animals."

"Ohhh," the kids chorused.

Chris clucked his tongue, and Kimble scurried from the little cat carrier to his shoulder. He instinctively slipped his arm through the short leash he'd fashioned for the ferret. Kids loved seeing animals, but ones that weren't leashed always unnerved a few students. In fact, a couple of the girls' eyes widened in horrified fascination.

"Does anyone know what kind of animal Kimble is?"

Hands shot up around the room. Chris pointed to a little boy with the straightest cowlick he'd ever seen.

"A cat!"

"No!" some of the others groaned.

Chris pointed to a little girl with pigtails in the front row. She motioned toward herself in question, so he nodded.

"Um, a ferret?" she said.

"That's right. Kimble is a black-footed ferret. Does anyone know what he likes to eat?"

"Berries!" a kid shouted.

"Try again."

Someone correctly guessed Kimble to be a carnivore, making the transition to how Kimble ate in the wild and how they fed him here. Once his introduction of the ferret was over, Chris asked the most popular question in the educational outreaches.

"Would anyone like to pet Kimble?"

Hands shot up, but not as many as when they were trying to answer the questions. Chris showed the students exactly how Kimble liked to be touched, making sure they understood him.

"Did everyone get that?" the teacher asked. She glanced around the room, waiting for the kids to make eye contact. "Kimble likes to be touched gently. If you do not obey Mr. Gamble's rules, there will be consequences when we return to school."

"Yes, ma'am," the class acknowledged.

Chris let them touch the ferret, thankful for the teacher backing him up.

After the kids finished petting the ferret, Chris motioned for Zach to step to the front. The intern began teaching the kids about the fox. When he was done, Cameron came up to show off one of their birds. She was an excellent handler when she wasn't busy ensuring their operation ran smoothly. Chris prayed she planned on staying long-term at Gamble on Nature. He couldn't imagine finding anyone else so competent, but since she was engaged, it was always possible her plans would change with the I dos.

Finally, the class left, and the building quieted. Chris blew out a breath as he washed his hands in the mudroom.

"You heading to the governor's dinner?" Cameron asked, coming to stand beside him.

Chris squinted his eyes in an attempt to visualize his calendar. "That's today?"

"Yes, sir."

He let out a low moan. *Lord, I don't wanna.*

"Don't whine. The ladies will fawn all over you in your tux, and you'll get the funding we need to continue running efficiently."

"I hate these dinners. They're so pretentious." Why did the board always make him attend? Oh, sure, some of them would go to make sure he played well with others, but that didn't make networking any more tolerable. *But you said you would go, so man up.*

"Says the man who's friends with a movie star and Derby winner. I feel so sorry for your plight."

He snorted at Cameron's dry tone. "You don't know what it's like having to schmooze."

"Because I don't talk to people."

"You just talked to a bunch of second graders."

"Kids don't become people until they hit fifth grade and lose their lovely innocence." She placed a hand on her hip. "Then they're monsters until high school."

Chris chuckled. "Tell me how you really feel."

"I really feel that you should leave ASAP, so you have enough time to do something to that nest growing on your face. And maybe wash the animal stink off of you before you don the tux."

"You nag so much, Cameron." He headed for the exit.

"It's what you pay me for!"

Three

I stared at my reflection in the full-length mirror. The black evening gown was my go-to for events such as this. The lace top created a whimsical impression while the satin skirt—complete with pockets—maintained a professional look. Adding some black drop earrings completed the picture. I could now attend the governor's dinner.

Why the man called it a dinner when the event was more of a who's who and a scratch-your-back networking association was beyond me. Then again, titling the event a dinner gave an idea of what was to come. Over a four-course meal, Governor Jankowski would thank people and honor them by handing out certificates for various accomplishments—volunteering, model citizen, best business, et cetera. Attendees would network around the dinner tables before and after the awards ceremony.

It was utterly exhausting.

Still, I had sent in my RSVP, which meant I had to paste on a fake smile and prepare to sob internally while the night dragged on.

I grabbed my black-glitter clutch, checking to ensure my ID, credit card, and lipstick were inside. The small canister of mace was a just-in-case precaution I'd yet to use but always carried with me. Flicking the light off, I strode out of my bedroom, down the wood-floor hall, and out the front door of my condo building.

The governor's house was in Denver, so I had about an hour and a half—depending on traffic—before I arrived. A mindfulness podcast would help keep my mind in a serene state. It didn't do me any good to get anxious as I drove north to the capital city.

Halfway there, I turned off the podcast and selected my '90s diva playlist. It held songs from powerhouses like Janet Jackson, Mariah Carey, and En Vogue. Maybe listening to the artists belt out songs about love would empower me to walk into the mansion confidently, without fear that someone would recognize me as a fraud.

Because did I, an orthopedic surgeon, really deserve an invitation? Yes, I'd saved the governor's son's leg, but any doctor would have done the same thing in my position. I just happened to be the one assigned to his case. That didn't mean that I was any more deserving of recognition than the next surgeon.

Plus, I really hated schmoozing with the elite. I simply wanted to sit on my chaise lounge with a glass of red wine— keeps the doctor away—and talk to my sister on the phone. I hadn't spoken to Ellynn in a couple of days. Since Ellynn had had her youngest in March, my niece's evening nap time had become when we had our talk sessions. Our calls coincided perfectly with my work schedule. If Ellynn failed to connect, then it was most likely because her oldest daughter or husband vied for her attention.

I couldn't complain, but at times, loneliness made me want to speak into the void, *"What about me?"*

Again, I couldn't complain. I'd set myself on this course.

My focus had been on getting into med school, becoming an orthopedic surgeon, then becoming the best. Now that I'd won a few awards implying as much, my life seemed to be . . . adrift.

I sighed and shook my head. No melancholy when Mariah was singing "Always Be My Baby." I pushed my thoughts aside and attempted to match my voice to Mariah's higher octave. Yeah, good thing I was the only one in the car.

After I entered the driveway that ran alongside the governor's mansion, I exited my car in the full demureness that hid my internal shaking. The valet nodded, and I followed the other well-dressed visitors entering the brick home.

I gave my name to the gatekeeper, who, unfortunately, let me proceed. I scanned the premises, searching for someone I recognized. Correction, *knew*. I recognized many of the faces—an actor from *Yellowstone* and a country star who sang "Settle for a Slowdown"—but didn't actually *know* them.

Remember to breathe deeply and center yourself. You put bones back together and occasionally save lives. Surely you can chitchat with celebrities.

Instead of taking the words to heart, my mind's eye searched for exits and potential rooms in which to hide to gather my breath and escape the noise.

"Erykah?" Disbelief coated a man's voice.

A familiar voice.

I turned to my right, and a slight gasp escaped me. It was the man from the Skirted Heifer.

"Christian?"

"Chris," he reminded while sliding his hands into his tux pockets.

My mouth dried as he stepped closer. How did his blue eyes shine brighter? He'd cleaned up his facial hair and turned his beard into a goatee. Without the beanie on his head, I could see the thick, perfectly groomed hair on top. My pulse skittered.

"I thought *Chris* was only used by your friends." I swallowed. Did my voice hold a breathless quality?

"I could use a local friend."

Heat filled my cheeks, and I glanced away. "How do you know I'm local?"

"You live in Colorado, right?"

My gaze found his once more. "Yes."

"Then you've got a leg up on my other friends. They're out-of-staters."

"Oh." *Oh? That's all you've got, Erykah?* But considering my clammy palms, *oh* was a step up from silence.

Christian tilted his head. "What are you doing here?"

"I was invited. You?"

"Same."

"Oh." I groaned inwardly. I needed to learn how to talk without using medical jargon or barking out instructions.

"Can I get you something to drink? Do you know what table you're sitting at?"

I shook my head. "I don't." I blinked. "I mean, I would like something to drink, and I have no idea where I'm sitting."

"Well, let's solve both problems, huh?"

"Okay." Was it sad I wanted to applaud myself for not saying *oh* once more?

I followed Chris toward the bar, where he ordered a club soda and lime—*yuck*—and then turned my way. "What would you like?"

"A Roy Rogers, please."

Chris chuckled. "No Shirley Temple?"

"I'm not a lemon-lime fan." I'd much prefer adding Coke to any mixed virgin drinks than a Sprite.

"So first we meet at the Skirted Heifer and now the governor's mansion." He stared into my eyes. "What are the odds?"

"Wild, right?" I forced a laugh even though my emotions were stuck in my throat.

Because seriously, what *were* the odds? I'd never seen Christian Gamble before in my life, and in a matter of a week, I'd run into him twice. *And in the most random places!*

"How did you enjoy your burger?"

"It was perfection." I smiled. Burgers were neck and neck with mountain pie. No one could beat Colorado-style pizza.

"How often do you go there?"

I arched a brow. "Were you looking for me?"

"Maybe." Chris glanced away, taking a sip of his club soda.

A thrill shot through my middle, my curiosity piqued. "How many times have you gone back?"

"I plead the fifth." His lips curved.

Oh. My. Word!

Were we flirting? It felt like flirting, but I was solely judging this moment on the movies I'd watched. I almost felt like Sanaa Lathan in *Something New.* Though Chris wasn't a white guy like the hero in the movie, something told me we were still opposites in every other way.

"Maybe the restaurant is a guilty pleasure and I don't go that often."

"But something tells me that's not true."

I pursed my lips, hoping to stay the grin threatening to form. "What if I like mountain pies more?"

"Do you go to Molly's Mountain Pies?"

"Are you from Colorado Springs?" He knew the spots, but now he was here in Denver.

So are you, girl. Right. We were both out of our natural environments.

"Answering a question with a question?" Chris smirked. "Okay. I was born there but don't currently reside in the city."

"Then what made you choose the Skirted Heifer?"

"My work is in Colorado Springs, but I live in Woodland Park."

"Oh." That was a thirty-minute drive. "You commute in every day?"

Chris shook his head. "No. I'm a wildlife conservationist and run a nonprofit. Sometimes that means I'm in-house doing admin work or educational outreaches. Other times, I'm out in the wild for a variety of reasons."

"Clever use of words." I didn't know what else to say.

"What about yourself? You said you're a surgeon. Do you have more days in the OR, or do you have to do admin work equally as much?"

"It varies as well. I have days devoted to paperwork, days when I'm visiting a patient before surgery or after if they require a follow-up, then there are the OR days."

"Do you work a lot?"

I took a moment to think. "Not really. I'm an attending, so my time of staying in a hospital all hours of the day and night are over. I'm on a pretty regulated schedule now."

"Do you like routine?"

"Yes." I studied him. "You don't?"

"Not at all. I don't like to be still."

Another personal tidbit of his filed itself away in my mind. There was something about Chris that made me comfortable. Sure, I'd started out awkward, but the more we talked, the more relaxed I became. Was it because he'd asked about work, or did something about the man himself put me at ease?

"What's an average day look like for you?" I asked.

"Average, huh?"

I nodded.

"It looks like me going into the center and checking on the animals that live with us either permanently or temporarily. Usually, I feed them breakfast unless a staff member has beaten me to the office. Then I answer emails, make phone calls, fill out grant paperwork or whatever funding details I need to. Then we do classes with schools and homeschooling co-ops."

"Really? What kind of animals permanently reside with you?" His job fascinated me. I couldn't imagine hanging out with animals all day long. The longest amount of time I'd spent with an animal was dissecting animal cadavers in college. *Make sure you keep that to yourself.*

"Well, there's Kimble, the ferret."

I chuckled. "A *Kindergarten Cop* fan?"

"Yes!" His eyes lit up. "My staff is too young to catch the reference."

I groaned. "When did we become middle-aged?" At least I assumed he was around the same age as me.

"Probably around the time we stopped listening to current music."

"It's trash," we said simultaneously.

The sound of our laughter mixed so harmoniously I stopped, breath catching. When had I ever had a moment like this with a man? My stomach clenched, and I stepped backward.

"Uh, I think I'll go find my seat now."

Chris glanced around the place. "Good idea. Maybe we'll be seated next to each other."

Please no. I couldn't sit next to this man and attempt to schmooze whomever else was at the table. My mind would be too focused on cataloging how his eyes crinkled with delight or the way he smelled. If I said *mountain man*, would every woman on the planet understand that was a total swoon-worthy scent? How could I sit next to Christian Gamble and keep my wits about me?

Erykah, you're an award-winning surgeon. Of course you can keep your cool. Remember the self-control that envelops you in the OR? Focus on that for the dinner. Surely one man won't weaken your resolve as you network.

Except I'd been talking to him nonstop from the moment we caught eyes.

Sounds like the perfect meet twice. Because our meet cute was officially over the love of burgers.

Too bad I couldn't text Ellynn and have her save me from myself. But like all the times before, I would gather my inner strength and do what needed to be done. And right now, Operation Stay Away had commenced. Satisfied with my plan, I walked around the round tables until I found my name . . . right next to Chris's own placard.

We were seated right next to each other.

Four

Someone had turned down the temperature.

It took everything within Chris not to show his confusion. One minute he was having a great conversation with Erykah, the next minute she looked like she wanted to be seated anywhere but right next to him.

He'd thought their shared laughter meant the dinner would go by quicker. But the one-word answers coupled with her avoiding eye contact meant something completely different.

Had he upset her?

Chris mentally rolled back their conversation, searching for an offensive remark, but found none. He cleared his throat and leaned toward Erykah, careful to make sure he still maintained a proper distance.

"Did I say something wrong?" he whispered.

Her gaze flicked to his, softened for a moment, then darted away once more. "No." She matched his low tone.

"Okay. Then why the cold shoulder all of a sudden?" Maybe he shouldn't have asked, but the not knowing pricked under his skin worse than any splinter.

She sighed. "Could you please drop it?"

He wanted to say no. He wanted to argue about whatever he'd done. Instead, he straightened and stabbed his fork into the salad greens. Guess he'd been right thinking this dinner would be a waste of his time, just for different reasons than he first imagined.

This is why you don't date. Dealing with a woman's conflicting emotions was too much for his own to handle with the scars he still bore from giving his all the last time. Was being lonely really so bad?

Sure, he was always the odd man out among couples, but he didn't have to worry about going all in on a relationship only for the woman to decide Chris wasn't the man for her. It saved him from a lot of heartache, because he couldn't handle the seesaw of emotions that came from dating.

The next few minutes were spent silently as everyone at the table made quick work of their salads. Slowly, chatter made its way around the circular table as the waitstaff came around to remove their plates.

"So, Chris." Mr. Jackson dabbed at his lips. "I hear you persuaded the powers that be that reintroducing the gray wolf species would be the best thing for the environment." He arched a brow. "How did you manage that?"

Chris's face heated as all eyes landed on him. "The initiative wasn't a one-person effort, and I certainly wasn't running lead."

"You really think another predator is the best thing for our livestock?"

Chris's elbows clenched to his sides. Unfortunately, Jackson owned a large herd of cattle and was a known supplier of beef in Colorado. Situations like this made Chris tense, as if poised for a physical threat. He had to make sure his mind stayed sharp, but his heart needed to remain compassionate. "If you have any questions or concerns, I'd be happy to talk to you afterward. Or I can give you my card so we could meet one-on-one." Anything but incite a debate at the governor's mansion.

With Erykah looking on.

Chris pushed that thought aside. She'd already shut him down and made it clear she didn't want to talk, so what did it matter what she thought of the whole conversation?

"Trying to evade the subject?"

"Not at all. I just figured we'd all benefit from getting a chance to mingle and get to know one another." He flashed a smile, hoping the gesture seemed sincere. "I'd hate to hog the conversation when I know the rest of you hold such important positions in your fields."

"Right, like you care about the citizens of our state. If you did, you wouldn't have been part of this initiative."

Chris bit back a sigh. "Mr. Jackson, as a professed believer, don't you think it's our duty to do the best we can to look after the earth? After all, God left humans in charge. Not to be dictators, but good stewards."

"That's rich." Jackson scoffed. "Let's use the Bible to bring predators into our state."

"I think Mr. Gamble has a point," Erykah interjected.

Chris wanted to turn and stare at her, but the shock surging through him at her sudden support meant the emotion probably showed on his face.

"You do?" Mrs. Flowers leaned forward. "Why?"

"Humans have made a mess in many areas. Even when science and experience show us a better way, some are hesitant to correct course. But what I've seen over the last decade or so is a new desire for people to right their wrongs. If Mr. Gamble and other scientists believe that reintroducing the wolves will do more good than harm to our environment, then who are we to discount their expert opinion?"

"Quite easily." Jackson huffed. "He hasn't lived a farmer's life. He hasn't had to rescue his livestock or domesticated animals from the jaws of those beasts."

"And you have?" Chris asked. "The gray wolf hasn't been in Colorado since 1940. I doubt you were alive to rescue your animals from one of their kind."

Jackson sputtered, and his face turned bright red.

Chris held up a hand. "Like I said earlier, I'm more than happy to discuss this with you at a different time, but let's change the subject for now." Chris turned to Erykah. "Dr. Kennedy, surely there is something innovative happening in the orthopedic world you can regale us with."

A light flickered in her eyes, and she nodded.

Chris kept quiet while she spoke, listening to the sound of her voice. Her words came out confidently, but there was this softness to her tone that almost lulled Chris to sleep. Instead of submitting to the feeling, he watched the rest of their tablemates lean in as she shared about new equipment that would make amputations easier for the patient.

The more she talked, the more Chris realized the depth of care she felt for her patients. She wasn't excited to use a new tool for the tool's sake or even for how it could benefit a surgeon. No, she simply wanted to help patients experience less pain.

"You sound like a great doctor," he murmured at the end of her speech. The others at the table turned to their own conversations, so Chris continued speaking. "If I ever break a bone, I hope you'll be the one doing the surgery."

"I don't know. It's difficult for a surgeon to perform on someone they know. Sometimes there can be a conflict of interest."

He gazed into her warm brown eyes. "For the patient or the doctor?"

"The doctor, obviously." A little smile lifted one corner of her mouth. "You want a surgeon with steady hands, not one that will shake because of who's on the operating table."

"As long as you don't treat me like a game of Operation, I think I'll have the best chances with you holding the scalpel."

She laughed. "My sister hated that game, but I found it fascinating. Plus, I always won."

"Sounds like you're definitely the one with the steady hands." He took a deep breath, plunging ahead with a more personal line of questioning. "How many sisters do you have?"

"Just one. She's younger."

"Makes sense. You definitely have that oldest-sibling vibe going on."

She chuckled. "Okay, only child."

He let out a low whistle. "Calling me out like that, huh?"

"You started it."

"Oh, you mean when I said oldest-sibling vibe?" He blinked innocently. "Obviously, I was talking about those wonderful, goal-oriented, independent skills you have. What did you think I meant?"

A blush filled her cheeks. "I'm not falling for your innocent act, Mr. Gamble."

"Can we please drop the mister? I know I'm older. Believe me, my friends never let me forget. However, I feel like we're within the same age range."

"That's a dangerous assumption," Erykah's lips twitched.

Probably. He'd already annoyed her once before, but their repartee had him continuing despite the warning going off in his head. "I'm going off Operation and nothing else. You're gorgeous, so I'd totally guess early thirties except I doubt my friends in that age group know what that game is."

She chuckled. "Fine. I'm a member of the forties club."

"As am I." Two years in, in fact. But being forty-two didn't feel much different from forty in his opinion.

"What year?" She arched a brow.

"Now who's asking indecent questions?"

Why did he love making her blush like that? *You know why.*

"Do you joke this much with your friends?"

While eating his salad, he'd been ready to throw in the towel. But now with her studying him so guilelessly, he wanted to take the plunge into dangerous territories.

"Only with them. I'm a little bit more serious with everyone else."

A beam filled her face. "I'm glad to be included in that club . . . *Chris.*"

That smile on her face made her absolutely breathtaking. Couple that with the use of his nickname, and his breath stuck in his chest.

"Chris?"

He blinked. "I'm sorry. Did you say something?"

"Yes." Amusement lightened her eyes. "I asked about your friends. You said they were younger. How did you guys meet?"

"Uh, interesting enough, one I met through a . . . consultation." A movie one at that. Lamont Booker had been named *People*'s "Sexiest Man Alive" one year, and Chris and Tuck never let him forget it.

"The other I met through the friend I made on the consulting job."

"What does a wildlife conservationist do in a consulting job?" She tilted her head.

"Just that. I talked to him about what I do on a daily basis. Helped him get into character—" Chris coughed. "I mean, really understand the heart behind what I do." Because Lamont was somewhat of a method actor.

Her brow bent slightly. "What do your friends do?"

"One's an entertainer, and the other works with horses." Lord forgive him for making light of his friends' occupations. Tucker Hale was a Kentucky Derby–winning trainer, and Lamont had won countless awards for his movies. But Chris didn't want to name drop when Erykah was opening up to him.

Perhaps his earlier concern had been a knee-jerk reaction at the memory of dating. It was obvious that Erykah wasn't as open as some other women. He had to keep reminding himself that other people's reactions might not have anything to do with him. They could be thinking of their own past or just having an off day.

It's not you, it's me was quite accurate at times.

"What about you? What do your closest friends do?"

Immediately a detached expression replaced the friendly façade she'd presented. "I work a lot," she muttered.

Did that mean she didn't have any friends? He took a deep breath. "Well, don't forget one of them hangs around animals all day."

She peered at him through a lidded gaze. "You're right, Chris."

"You know, I think I accidentally lost my friend's number." He unlocked his cell and slid it her way. "You should add yourself to my contacts, so I won't lose it again."

Her shoulders shook as if holding back suppressed laughter. She added her number, then slid his phone back to him. "Points for cleverness."

"Do I get points for charm as well?"

"Jury's still out."

He laughed. Getting to know Erykah Kennedy was going to be interesting.

Five

Work had seemed to drag, and my usual joy at doing something I was extremely competent in had waned with each passing hour. Finally, I was able to clock out. Now at the sight of the double doors showcasing the entrance to my condo, I was tempted to whimper in relief, but then a noise that sounded very real—and not coming from me—reached my ears. The pathetic nature of the whine told me it was an injured or fairly young animal. Seeing as the sun had already set, I wasn't keen on searching the bushes for the culprit of said noise.

If this were a movie, I'd hightail it inside and pretend I'd never heard so much as a whisper. But the whimper sounded like the soft cries of a dog, and that made me think of Chris. What would he do in this situation?

I may have gone down the YouTube rabbit trail after the governor's dinner, watching Chris's many wildlife shorts. He was always respectful and cautious when nearing a wild animal. Should I do the same?

No, Erykah. We do not investigate noises. This could be a trap.

But I'd seen *Lady and the Tramp* one too many times as

a kid and couldn't ignore the pleas of the mystery howler. I squatted down, peering into the bushes just in time to see two eyes blinking at me.

"Are you okay?" I whispered.

The irony of that being a leading question taught at CPR classes was not lost on me. However, I doubted there was a scripted question to ask potentially injured mammals.

The creature's nose poked out, so I held my hand toward it like I'd seen done in countless movies. His nose twitched, and then a small paw came out of the bushes.

"It's okay. I'm friendly." Well, as friendly as I knew how to be.

Just because I didn't talk to everyone I passed or sing "Kumbaya" with my coworkers didn't mean that I was as bad as Miranda Priestly in *The Devil Wears Prada* either.

A second paw appeared, then the animal's whole face. *Yep.* Definitely a dog. "Are you hurt?"

The dog whined but moved forward. I held still until the little one rubbed his head under my hand. Gingerly, I scooped him up and immediately saw the issue. His back paw was red from blood or inflammation. I couldn't tell which in the dark.

"We need to get you fixed up, huh?"

The dog nuzzled his snout into my neck. He licked my hand, and I laughed at the tickling sensation.

"Can we get a puppy, Erykah?"

"We can barely feed ourselves, Ellynn. How are we going to feed a dog?"

"But they're so fluffy."

I blinked away the memory and stared at the fluffball in my arms. His muzzle was white, but he had brown patches around his eyes. The rest of his coat held a mixture of brown, black, and white. Was he a runaway? Had he been abandoned? There was no collar. I had no idea if he'd been chipped.

If this little guy didn't already have a family, maybe I could ship him to Ellynn. Surely she and her family would enjoy him. Then again, my niece hadn't even turned one, so dealing with a baby, a five-year-old, and a puppy at the same time might not be a good mix.

I walked into the building and went to the bulletin board. There was no advertisement for a missing dog, so he was either newly missing or hadn't come from here. I turned toward the elevators. I could doctor up the puppy's foot. It couldn't be that complicated, right?

Why don't you just call Chris and get his help?

My cheeks heated.

Operation Stay Away proved to be harder than I'd imagined. I'd lasted a few minutes at the governor's dinner before I ended up talking to Chris and flirting. *Flirting!* At least, it seemed like flirting. But he was very clear to call me a *friend*, so maybe not. Or maybe our interaction was just a getting-to-know-you period that I didn't understand because dating and I didn't go hand in hand.

Are you trying to date him?

No. . . . Right?

I shook my head, then unlocked my front door. Warmth enveloped me. I'd set the timer on the thermostat to heat the room to seventy-five a little before my arrival. There was nothing like walking into a warm home. Who cared if it was empty?

You, you ninny.

I shrugged out of my coat, holding on to the cutie, who was content to curl up against me. After disposing of my coat and purse, I walked down the hall and into the one and only bedroom. The first aid kit stayed under my bathroom sink. There should be gauze and something to clean abrasions with inside.

After looking at the puppy's paw, I could finally admit

41

I knew nothing about veterinary care. I snapped a picture, then sent the photo along with a message to Chris. We'd texted here and there since our second meeting a few days ago. I couldn't get over the feeling of having a friend to text and ask questions of. That was usually reserved for Ellynn.

Erykah
I found an injured pup. How can I tend to this?

Chris
Is he friendly? It's really not a good idea to get close to an injured animal.

Erykah
So your YouTube video said. However, he's been snuggled next to me since I found him in the bushes. I think I'm okay.

Chris
It looks free of debris so use some mild antibacterial soap on it. Then dry it carefully, and if it's still bleeding, wrap it in gauze.

Erykah
That's it?

Chris
Yep

Erykah
Then what do I do with him?

Chris
Take him to an animal shelter. They can see if he's chipped to locate the owners. I've got numbers for a couple of good ones in the area.

The puppy made a low rumble as if he were sleeping. I stared at our reflection, him content, me looking a little panicked. I couldn't take him to an animal shelter. What if he didn't have people? Everyone knew what happened to those animals. Unfortunately, I also knew what it felt like to be cast aside. Someone had ditched him, and he was injured. How could I just turn around and abandon him all over again?

Chris
Do you want the numbers?

Erykah
I can't just abandon him.

Chris
You can at least see if he's chipped. If he isn't, are you willing to take responsibility? Raising a puppy takes a lot of time. What will you do when you're at work?

Erykah
I hate that you're right. Still, if he doesn't have a home, I want to give him one. When I go to work, can I leave him in a crate or something?

Chris
He'd be lonely.

The ellipsis danced across the screen.

Chris
If you want, you can drop him off at my nonprofit during the day. If I'm not there, one of my associates can watch him.

I bit my lip. Agreeing to this plan did not sound like it would fall under Operation Stay Away. But the thought of turning the pup over to the pound sounded worse.

Erykah
Okay. Thank you.

Chris
Sure. I like helping my friends out.

Why did being called a friend burn just a little? Still, his words were comforting and made me smile, even if I didn't feel like doing so right that moment.

43

> **Erykah**
> Thanks. Send me the address, and I'll see you Monday.

> **Chris**
> Will do.

> **Erykah**
> Oh, and what should I buy him until then?

> **Chris**
> Give me your address. I'll pick you up. We'll see if he's chipped, and if not, go supply shopping.

My heart thumped. First my number, now my address? But the trepidation didn't come, and soon my thumbs were sending a pin of my location.

> **Chris**
> I can be there in twenty.

> **Erykah**
> We'll be ready.

I got some soap and gently washed the wound. The puppy licked my hand occasionally as I murmured nonsensical noises that hopefully sounded reassuring. He didn't seem to be afraid of me. *Thank goodness.*

"I'm going to have to give you a name." I tilted my head, studying him. He copied my movements.

"Mime?"

He whined.

"Okay. Obviously that was a paltry attempt at a name." It would help if I knew what kind of dog he was. His coat was longish. Colorful. Um . . . I was *terrible* at this.

"I can't call you Dog."

He whined.

"See? Even you know that's an awful name."

"Marlowe?" I waited for a response, but he didn't do anything. "Does that mean you like the name, or should I keep trying?"

He barked.

Okay. I'd keep thinking. Maybe Chris would have some suggestions when he arrived.

I gathered up the pup and headed down the hall. For once, my small condo didn't feel so quiet or so isolating. The puppy was keeping me company and preventing me from sitting in the dark and staring at the skyline for hours on end.

I was actually going to meet up with a *friend* and go hang out. Granted, we were going pet supply shopping—hopefully. I couldn't explain why I was so attached already. I didn't want the dog to have a home and leave me too. I winced.

"Let's take a selfie," I said to the pup. "This is something my little sister will find newsworthy."

Ellynn
Oh my word. I thought old ladies were supposed to buy cats.

Erykah
Har har. I'm forty-one. That's not old.

Ellynn
Do you have gray hair?

Erykah
A strand or two doesn't count.

Ellynn
Did your twenty-year high school reunion already pass?

Erykah
Girl, bye!

I locked my door and took the elevator to the lobby. As I arrived, an old Jeep-like vehicle pulled up to the curb. A man jumped out from the driver's side and came around.

My mouth dropped.

What was Chris doing driving a jalopy? That thing was ancient. I pushed through the front door and left the warmth of the building.

"What on earth is that?" I pointed toward the blue sports utility vehicle.

"A Bronco."

"A what now?"

Chris's lips quirked into a half smile. "It's vintage." He held the door open, motioning me in.

I buckled up, then held on to the puppy. Once Chris sat down, I asked him my burning question. "How old is something before you can label it vintage?"

"It's a 1975 Ford Bronco. It could get collector license plates if I promised not to drive it above collector limits."

"I'm stunned. I thought you'd be driving some ecofriendly vehicle, not a gas guzzler."

"It is ecofriendly."

I looked around the vehicle, trying to see what I was missing. Spotting no obvious clues, I turned to Chris. "Explain."

"Some people think, 'Oh no, my car is harming the planet.' Then they go buy a hybrid or electric vehicle that has all the eco bells and whistles. They don't take into account the carbon footprint it cost to make a brand-new vehicle or what will happen to the so-called planet-harming car they just ditched."

"So you're saying driving an older car that probably couldn't pass emissions testing is better?"

"If it still runs well. I'm not creating more waste by purchasing a new vehicle, and I get all the standard maintenance completed so that it *doesn't* fail emissions testing. Though it is older, so technically it doesn't have to take the test."

"And the gas you're buying?"

"This car runs on unleaded, so it's no different than yours."

"I'm kind of shocked."

He chuckled. "I make up for it with my house."

"Is that vintage too?"

"It's a log cabin. I collect rainwater to use and live in a way that astonishes most people."

"Including your friends?" I wondered about them. Chris had been so vague describing his friends. Maybe he was waiting to see if I would be a good friend before sharing more information. That, I could understand.

"Not in a horrifying way, but it does provide fodder for them to tease me with. In fact, they were just texting me about it. You can read for yourself. Nothing incriminating."

He handed me his cell phone.

Giddiness flowed through me at the trust he was extending. "Oh, you have to unlock it."

"Right." He stopped at the light and typed in his password. He scrolled through and grinned. "Start at 'It's going to rain tomorrow' and read on down."

"You sure?" I asked, though eagerness already filled me.

"Yep. Go ahead."

> **Chris**
> It's going to rain tomorrow.

> **Tuck**
> Whoo boy. I bet you're happy your little aquifer is gonna fill up.

> **Lamont**
> I still can't believe you live like a person off-grid. You may as well ditch the smartphone and delete your YouTube account.

> **Chris**
> Ha. I'll have you know those items are beneficial. Lead by example. How else will others learn how to help the planet?

Lamont

'90s cartoons on streaming. I'm sure Captain Planet can be found.

I snickered softly to myself.

Chris

What do you know about that cartoon?

Tuck

"By your powers combined . . ."

Lamont had sent an "I am Captain Planet" GIF.

Tuck

😂

Chris

So y'all got jokes.

Lamont

All day, every day.

Six

O h my word. Your friends are hilarious," Erykah said.
"They have their moments." He glanced at her,
trying not to notice just how beautiful she was when
her guard was down and laughter brightened her eyes. "Every
now and again, Lamont and Tuck's fiancées take over our
thread and then the jokes really roll in."

"Have either set wedding dates?" She passed back his cell.

Chris made a left onto a street that ran right in front of
an animal shelter. "Yep."

He sighed. The thought of going to two weddings so close
together made him slightly antsy. "Tuck and Piper are getting
married in November. Lamont and Nevaeh have decided on
a New Year's wedding."

Chris hopped out of the vehicle and rounded the front to
assist Erykah, but she was already shutting the door. Of course
she wouldn't have waited for him. It's not like this was a date
or anything. Going into an animal shelter wasn't romantic.

An associate greeted them when they walked in. He'd
already called ahead and let her know the situation, so she
took the pup right back behind the double doors. In a matter
of moments, she informed them the dog wasn't registered.

"Have you seen any wanted posters with his face?" Chris asked.

"Nope."

"Thanks." He waved, then escorted Erykah out of the building. "You checked your own condo for wanted posters, right?"

"Yeah. I talked to the front desk as well. No one has a missing pet."

"Then it looks like he's all yours."

The happiness shining in her brown eyes almost did him in. They got back in the car, and he drove until they reached his favorite pet store.

Silence filled the cab until Erykah broke it. "You know, when you said Lamont and Nevaeh, it made me think of that Hollywood couple. Remember that one actor who starred in *Troubled* and admitted to starting a fake relationship?"

Placing the vehicle in park, Chris faced her. "Might be because they're one and the same."

She blinked. "Are you trying to say the Lamont in your phone is *the Lamont Booker*? Like, the Sexiest Man Alive Lamont?"

"That's what I'm saying." Would she start fangirling?

Nevaeh had shared with him and Tuck how she'd fangirled in the early parts of her relationship to the actor. Chris was secure enough to admit that Lamont could catch any woman's eye. But there was a part of Chris—he'd ignore just how great a part—that didn't want Erykah to react in the same way.

"You *know* him?"

"I do."

"And Tuck? Is he someone famous too?"

He rubbed the back of his neck. "If you follow the world of horse racing."

"The trainer of this year's Derby winner?"

Huh. Not many people knew Derby trainers. "Yep."

Her mouth dropped, then closed. "Who are you, Chris Gamble?"

"I'm just a man."

"Likely story," she muttered, unbuckling her seat belt. She snuggled the puppy close to her. "Puppy's ready to go inside."

His brows raised. "You're not naming him that, are you?"

"No, but he doesn't like any of my choices."

"Which were?"

"Mime," she whispered, then speaking louder, "but he liked Marlowe better."

Chris winced. "Poor guy. Can't say I blame him for not wanting to answer to Mime or Marlowe."

"True, but what *do* I call him?"

"Let me see him."

Erykah handed the dog over, and Chris studied the little guy, confirming he was indeed a boy.

"I think he's one of those Tibetan terriers. Maybe you could name him Chewy or Bear."

The look on her face said she wasn't amused, and the pitiful whine that came from the dog said he sided with Erykah.

"Okay. I'm not usually bad at this."

"Oh really? You named your ferret Kimble. That's terrible."

"But you got the reference."

She laughed. "Fine. Maybe Chewbacca wouldn't be so bad, but he doesn't like the name."

Just then, her phone chimed. She pulled it out and smiled. "I sent a pic of him to my sister. She says my niece likes Charlie as a name."

The dog's tail wagged with excitement.

Chris passed the pup back to Erykah. "Looks like he likes the name too."

"Is that right?" she asked the pup softly. "Should I call you Charlie?"

He barked, and his tongue lolled out.

"I guess Charlie it is."

"Let's head inside and get Charlie some supplies."

He had to remind himself that this outing was just between two friends. Still, he couldn't deny the way his heart thumped in his chest every time she spoke to Charlie or smiled at his antics. Soon they were at the checkout with dog food, a collar, a leash, and other supplies.

"Hey, Chris. Didn't think I'd see the day you came in here with a normal pet." The salesclerk's eyes twinkled as she scanned a squeaky toy.

He chuckled. "Norma, this is Erykah. Erykah, this is Norma. And Norma, that's Charlie, Erykah's pet."

"Phooey. I thought you'd joined the domesticated world for a second."

"Nope. I'm still hanging out with the wild ones for now."

Norma looked at Erykah. "You need to convince this man to get a normal pet."

"You don't like Kimble?" Erykah threw a smirk his way.

"You've met the ferret?"

Erykah's laugh floated around him and skittered goose bumps across his arms. Thank goodness no one could see under his fleece hoodie.

"I haven't, but Chris has told me about him."

"I suppose it's a good thing he saved him, but that man goes home to an empty house. No pets, no people, nothing."

Ouch, Norma. Way to twist the knife.

Only she wasn't wrong. Chris didn't have anyone to keep him company. He used to believe it was better that way, but lately, other thoughts were trying to creep into his mind. He wanted more, wanted someone. A person. Not the same type of woman he'd chosen in the past. No, he had to ensure he never made that foolish mistake again.

Was Erykah like *her*, or was she different? Erykah's smile was different, seemingly genuine and pure kindness. The subtle honey scent of her perfume—or was it some type of body wash?—was enough to entice his senses but not overwhelm them.

Observation told him Erykah was different in other ways too, but Chris wouldn't go past friendship until the idea felt right in his spirit. Being friends was a good move in his opinion. He could get to know her in a non-pressurized environment and discover her character and who she was as a person.

Despite telling his friends he'd jump back into the dating ring, Chris opted for extreme caution and was merely dipping a toe in the tepid waters.

Erykah peered up at him before returning her gaze to Norma. "I'll make sure he does better."

"Sounds like he finally found the right woman."

The problem with well-meaning people was that they never knew when to be quiet. Chris said nothing, merely loaded the cart with the filled reusable bags.

"Have a good evening, Norma," he said quietly.

"You too, hon. Come back again, Erykah. We'll make sure that pup grows up strong."

"Thank you."

Chris pushed the cart outside. He unloaded the items while Erykah settled Charlie in the car.

"So how will this exchange work?" Erykah asked as Chris climbed into the driver's side. "I just drive to your work on Monday and hand Charlie over?"

"Basically." He thought for a moment. "If you don't have time to feed him beforehand, I've got a bag of the same feed at the center. We'll take care of him and make sure he stays out of trouble." Cameron, Zach, and the others would enjoy having the little guy around.

"Are you *sure* you don't mind?"

Chris glanced at Erykah. A chance to see her every day and see if she was as special as he hoped she was? "Positive."

Relief relaxed the lines in the middle of her forehead until they disappeared completely. "Thank you so much, Chris."

"Happy to help."

By the time he pulled up to Erykah's condo, Charlie had fallen asleep. "I'll grab the bags."

"You sure? I can grab some."

"Nah. I've got them. Just get the little guy." Besides, he could put some of the items in the kennel and then carry that and anything else into her place. He carried heavier items at the center than this.

Thankfully, her building had an elevator, which made moving everything from his car to her condo a lot easier. Erykah darted a nervous glance over her shoulder as she twisted the key into the lock. Was she worried about his thoughts on her place? Or worried the dog wouldn't fare well?

Chris schooled his features. The least he could do was maintain a neutral expression instead of the one burning with curiosity at entering her domain.

She set Charlie down. The dog's gaze roamed the halls, still looking a little sleepy.

Erykah had her place unlocked and door held wide open in seconds. "Come on, boy." Charlie sniffed his way across the wood floors.

Chris took a step, then another as he examined his surroundings. The exposed red brick in her living room went all the way into the kitchen, giving off an industrial vibe. The neutral brown décor fit the modern look, along with the African American–style paintings hanging on the walls. Her taste ran a lot richer than his.

"Nice place."

She smiled. "Thank you. It's only one bedroom, but I don't need much."

"You don't feel claustrophobic in here?" No office or anything? This place could only be about nine hundred square feet, though he had no idea how large the bedroom was.

"No. Why? Is your place big?"

"Yep." He popped his lips.

"Really? For one person?" An amazed expression filled her face.

"I'll show you one day." Chris blew out a breath. *Or maybe not.* He wasn't ready to show her his place or even ask her on a date. For now, he'd continue texting her, watch over Charlie while she worked, and see what happened from there.

He clapped his hands. "Well, I better let you get all settled."

"Thanks again for your help."

"No problem." He headed out the door, not sure how else to make a charming exit. He pressed the down button next to the elevator and let out a sigh, going over the evening's events in his head.

The fact that she'd asked him for help was a good thing, right? He wasn't certain if he wanted her to be interested in him or have the same idea of strictly friendship. But he couldn't deny the pleasure that hit his chest from knowing she'd asked him for assistance and no one else.

You do work with animals. You're a no-brainer. Don't jump for joy so soon.

Right. He needed to keep logic at the forefront so he

wouldn't cause any issues in getting to know her. His heart needed him to remain cautious.

His phone chimed, and he checked the text notifications.

Erykah
Charlie says thank you.

She sent a picture of the pup lying in his new bed and looking very pleased with his surroundings.

Chris
Tell him he's welcome.

He grinned and put his Bronco in drive. Yeah, he was thankful they were friends.

Seven

Why couldn't I drag myself out of my car and hand Charlie over to Chris?

Maybe the idea that his coworkers would think there was more to our relationship than what was actually there kept me in the comfort of my own car? (That's friendship, by the way. Nothing else. Nothing more.) I would keep repeating that until my heart stopped having these ridiculous palpitations—*not* romantic flutters—that started every time I saw Chris.

But in order to hand over Charlie, I had to walk into Gamble on Nature. *Ugh*. Even the name of his business was as charming and cute as the man himself.

"I can do this. He's just a man. Nothing special about him."

Except I really loved his blue eyes. The way they crinkled when he laughed. And, oh, his laugh. The sound draped over me like a warm blanket, inviting me to burrow deeper. Not to mention he always put me at ease. There was no one on earth who made me feel so comfortable, except for my sister. To find that same quality in another person, a man at that, floored me.

I groaned. "You're pathetic. You're just friends. That's what he wants. That's what *you* want. That's what you have time for."

Charlie whined. I wasn't sure if he was agreeing about my pathetic nature or the word-hemorrhage falling from my mouth.

"You'll be my little spy, right, Charlie?"

He stared at me.

"What? We need more intel on Chris. How is he friends with an actor and a Derby-winning trainer?" Who I was ninety-nine percent certain I'd operated on earlier in the year.

Charlie stared.

"Right, you can't talk. Still." Was there a way to sneak a video cam on his collar? Surely there was a way Charlie could let me know if Chris was genuinely a good guy.

I hoped he was. He *seemed* to be. But what did I know? My knowledge of men was purely anatomical in nature. I'd never dated. Never had one befriend me before. The whole thing was surreal and kept me up late at night wondering what was going on. People weren't dependable. The hard knocks of life had taught me that. But part of me wanted to believe Chris was who he said he was.

Gathering up my courage, I grabbed the kennel and slid out of my car. Chris hadn't told me to bring it—he probably had a bunch in his office—but all the pet forums I'd poured over convinced me I couldn't just hold Charlie in my lap while driving and hope for the best. If I did and I got in a car accident, Charlie's chances of survival lessened. Since I'd already saved him once, I really wanted to prevent anything bad from happening to him again.

Sometimes I wished I believed in prayer and a God who listened. I could use the help right about now. But the past had shown me there was no God looking out for me, let alone listening to any prayers. It was up to me to practice my deep breathing and hope that I wouldn't have to talk to anyone but the man I came here for. *You got this.*

I pushed the double door, and my sure steps immediately faltered. The place smelled like a menagerie of animals, and that was *not* a pleasant scent. I ventured farther, and a scuffle of noise down one of the halls drew my attention. Chris and his colleagues had created a makeshift Soul Train line.

Laughter bubbled up from within me and spilled out as Chris did the Running Man. He must have heard my giggles, because he stopped and stared right at me. I bit my lip trying to contain my amusement, but instead of being embarrassed, he winked. Winked!

He started doing the Cabbage Patch and ended with the Hammer dance. I was in tears by the time the last strands of the song played over the speakers. When was the last time I'd laughed so hard? *Never, girl. Never.*

"All right, all right. Get back to work." Chris turned off the music and headed my way. "Morning." His voice sounded husky from exertion.

"Good morning." I tilted my head. "Do that often?"

"Every Monday. They need a reason not to dread the week."

"I thought you guys loved what you do?"

He smirked. "Of course we do, but it's still a Monday."

That, I could understand. Mondays were my fill-out-all-the-paperwork and back-to-back-appointments days. How the hospital expected me to get my paperwork finished in the midst of endless meetings, which created more paperwork, was beyond me. Not to mention other doctors occasionally liked to throw an emergency consultation my way. So yeah, I knew exactly what he meant about loving your job in the context of Mondays.

"I don't think I can pull off a Soul Train line at work, but maybe I can change my playlist." My coworkers would probably appreciate a mix-up in my constant classical choices.

"Do you listen to Spotify? If so, I can send you my Monday list. It's full of late '80s and '90s throwbacks."

"It's my most-used app." Why did my cheeks feel so heated?

Was it the way his attention focused solely on me? His kindness? Or perhaps just those good looks?

"Not Facebook?" he asked.

I shook my head. "Social media isn't my thing."

"Well, you have to at least get a YouTube account. How else can you subscribe to our videos?" He winked.

Again.

I wanted to clutch my heart, but the palpitations were a normal reaction. I *knew* that, but my heart acted like this was new information. Good thing a person couldn't go into shock from an influx of serotonin.

Pay attention to the conversation. You two are talking about YouTube. Right.

"I've seen your videos. I particularly like your blooper reels." I grinned, remembering the last one I watched.

Chris groaned. "Those seem to be everyone's favorite."

"Keep it up." I held out the kennel with Charlie inside. "Here's my new friend."

"Morning, Charlie." Chris peered into the kennel, and Charlie's nose poked through the grate. "We're going to have fun. Wait until you meet Kimble."

"Oh brother," I murmured.

Chris chuckled. "Don't worry, Dr. Kennedy. When you come pick Charlie back up, I'll be sure to introduce you."

"I can't wait," I drolled.

"You'll love him."

Remembering Chris dealt with animals all day should pull

some of the shine off him, but that only emphasized his goodness. Someone who cared about the planet, animals, and other conservation efforts was a man worth knowing.

Yeah, as a friend. *Get it together, girl.*

I stepped back. "I'm going to go. Don't want to be late." At this point, was Operation Stay Away still in play?

"Have a good day."

"Mm-hmm. You do the same." I whirled around and raced toward the exit.

You do the same? What kind of response is that, Erykah Kennedy?

A normal one, I hoped. Yet dropping off my puppy and having a man tell me to have a good day was *not* my norm. Chris Gamble needed to come with a warning label because every time I neared him, my stomach quivered, and my hormones spiked above functional levels.

I pulled into my assigned hospital parking spot, then walked down the long hall toward my office. I'd already taken a glimpse at today's schedule before leaving my condo this morning in preparation. Keeping the day's events in the forefront of my mind—which meant taking multiple looks at my calendar throughout the day—made the day run smoother. I had about a half hour to answer emails and start on paperwork before my first appointment.

By lunch my stomach growled fiercely, and the edges of irritability pressed in. I left the patient room, ducking my head to avoid talking to other staff in the hall, then made my escape into my office. I leaned against the door, inhaling for a count of four and exhaling for a count of six. The deep breathing continued until my head cleared and my pulse beat at a steady pace. Talking to patients wasn't difficult because it was all medical procedure, but I didn't want to be pulled into gossip by the staff.

I had just taken out my insulated lunchbox from the bottom drawer when my phone chimed. A video message from Chris appeared, and I watched enraptured as he attempted to teach Charlie how to sit. No matter how many times he repeated the word and pushed Charlie's rump down, the puppy refused to cooperate. Instead, he insisted on sniffing Chris's hand.

> Erykah
> Did you give him the treat?

> Chris
> No! Well, yeah. He finally sat after the twentieth try.

> Erykah
> You were counting?

> Chris
> No, but Cameron was.

I chuckled. Chris seemed like he had a good group of people around him. More than that, they actually seemed to like one another.

My mind turned to my colleagues. They were the people I worked with closely—sometimes hours on end—but I wouldn't call them friends or even anything more than acquaintances. How sad was that?

Degrees from prestigious universities hung on my office walls alongside accolades and awards I'd received in the medical field. But the only two personal pictures I owned featured me and my sister in one and her and her family in the other. I picked up my cell, feeling the need to talk to Ellynn.

> Erykah
> How are you? How are the kiddos?

> Ellynn
> I'm exhausted. I need a break from the crying and Cheyenne's whining.

I chuckled. Cheyenne wanted everyone's attention on her all the time and whined when she didn't get what she wanted.

> **Erykah**
> Maybe I can FaceTime you later and occupy Cheyenne for a bit.

> **Ellynn**
> I would love that. I'd also love to go out with Asher again. I miss date nights.

> **Erykah**
> Call your babysitter.

My newest niece had been born in March. A seven-month-old could be entrusted to a babysitter, right?

Then again, what did I know? I had no children. Back in my residency days, I'd delivered a few babies, but that was so long ago I wouldn't feel comfortable performing a delivery today. Not to mention, all I'd done was hand off the baby to the nurses, who'd done the rest of the work.

> **Ellynn**
> Maybe. But if you call tonight, we'd love to see your face.

I stared in shock at the teardrop that plinked against the screen on my phone. Wiping my hand across my face, I was surprised to discover I was legit crying. I thought for a moment, trying to figure out what was wrong. Then it hit me.

I was lonely *and* homesick. It had been so long since I'd had that feeling. But how did you explain to your emotions that you had no home to return to? Ellynn had been my home growing up, but now she had her own family, and I was all alone.

You've been alone for decades. Now's not the time to cry.

But seeing how Chris interacted with those around him, knowing how he had close friends, it seemed to break something in me. Chris's presence showed me what I'd been missing, a home, a community. Apparently, my body wanted to commiserate the sad state of my relationships, or rather lack thereof.

Chalk it up to perimenopause. All women in their forties cry excessively.

That would be my story, and I'd stick to it.

I slid my phone into my lab coat and finished my lunch. All too soon I'd be back in the fray of surgery consults and post-op follow-ups.

After packing my food containers back into my lunchbox, I grabbed a mint and the hospital iPad. There were more patients to see before I could pick up Charlie and resume my solitary life. *You have Charlie now, so not completely solitary.*

My heart warmed. I'd be able to go home to a dog tonight and talk to Ellynn and the girls through video chat. I wasn't completely alone, no matter how my thoughts wanted me to believe otherwise. Just because I didn't do a Soul Train line with colleagues didn't make Chris's world better than mine. I'd done my job by my sister, and now I was living how I wanted, sort of.

A home was what I made of it, and adding a pet would surely chase some of the blues away. I just had to remind myself of that until I could see my pup once more. Until then, it was time to be the doctor the hospital staff expected and the patients needed.

Eight

This little guy is known as the greenback cutthroat trout."
Chris held up the fish for the cameraman. "He's the
Colorado state fish and currently classified as *threat-
ened* for the state and federal listings."

Chris let the fish go, then stood to his full height, the
camera blinking red as it recorded.

"The greenback territory historically ranged all the way
from southern Wyoming and down the Front Range Mountains into Colorado. Now their territory is mostly restricted
to the Colorado Springs area, which is our current source of
conservation efforts. Follow me as we discuss ways to help
our animals thrive in the wild and coexist with humanity.
This . . . is Colorado."

"Cut."

Chris blew out a sigh as David called for an end of the
taping. They'd been filming since sunup. That had been two
coffees and a full stainless-steel bottle ago, so Chris headed
for the portable toilet near the trailers.

"Chris, a moment." David tapped his clipboard.

When filming for the series finally completed, Chris would
hunt that clipboard down and break it in two right in front of
David's face. The immense satisfaction would overcome any

guilt that might come from the action. The director tapped the clipboard to insinuate he was in control of the project instead of Chris, despite the fact the production company would be capitalizing on Chris's brand for the docuseries. *Is this how famous actors develop egos?*

He cleared his throat. "Can it wait? I need to use the restroom."

"It'll only be a sec."

Chris arched a brow.

"Any updates on the additional sites you've been working on getting us access to?"

Chris bit back a sigh. "Yes, but sharing that info will take longer than a second, and I *really* need to use the restroom." He pointed behind him. "Give me a moment."

"Fine."

He wanted to roll his eyes at the younger man, but that would make Chris just as petulant as PathLight's director. David was in his late twenties but sometimes acted much younger. Besides, what he truly wanted to know was if they'd be allowed to film the gray wolf reintroduction. That would be a boon to the director, but the last thing Chris wanted was to ruin the reintroduction.

Could he actually trust the PathLight team to keep a respectful distance when needed? They probably had cameras that would allow them to zoom in and still capture the majesty of the wolves, but they also had a lot of outlying staff members who were always in the way. Or at least being crowded was a feeling Chris dealt with each time they were on set. If you could call the great outdoors a set.

After cleaning his hands, Chris pulled out his phone to check his notifications. He made a couple of comments on social media, saw one of his YouTube shorts had gone viral, then opened his text messages.

Erykah
How's Charlie?

Chris
The gang is watching him today while I'm out filming. Want me to check in with them?

Erykah
No. I'll find out when I pick him up. Hope filming is going well.

Chris
About as well as removing ticks from animals.

Erykah
😂

Erykah
Hang in there!

He slid his phone into his back pocket. Chris wanted to be happy that Erykah texted him, but the message was merely for her new friend, as she referred to Charlie. Though Chris had admitted to Lamont and Tuck he wanted a relationship, he still felt hesitant when it came to acknowledging any sort of romantic interest in Erykah. If he did, would she give him the cold shoulder like she'd done at the governor's mansion? Or would she be willing to go on a date and see what could happen between them? The fact that he didn't know kept him quiet.

"Chris! You got a moment now?" David stared him down.

"Uh, yeah." He blinked, trying to remember the last email update he'd gotten on the wildlife they were actively tracking. He paired that information with areas where they could see animals roaming freely. "We can go to Mueller State Park and see the bears. They're packing on their calories to get ready for the winter season."

David nodded. "Good. Good. And the wolves?"

There it is. "Still waiting on a reply."

"Can you nudge them?"

Chris thought about it. "I don't know. Their schedule is usually packed, so if I bug them again it might just get deleted versus being seen as an urgent request."

"Fine. If there's no response by Friday, email or call them. We need to get the rest of the schedule fleshed out."

"Understood."

"And you're good for the hike tomorrow?"

They'd already done Crowe Gulch, but the director had a few more trails he wanted to get to. Good thing Chris did this for a living. "I'll be ready."

The guy turned, and Chris watched him walk away. Relief flooded him. It wasn't that he didn't like David, but the director put him on edge. Every day Chris woke up wanting to be a good steward because he believed that was what God wanted. But since he'd been working for PathLight, he'd gotten nothing but headache after headache, along with the increased workload. Something had to give, or he'd reach burnout before he knew it.

By the time they were done filming for the day, Chris wanted nothing more than to crawl into his bed and sleep for a week. Only he couldn't let his staff continue taking care of Charlie when he'd promised Erykah he'd be the one to help. He prided himself on being a man of his word. He knew what it was like when people went back on their promises. *I refuse to be like that.*

Soon he pulled up to Gamble on Nature and parked the Bronco. Just as he entered the building, his phone chimed.

Erykah
I have an emergency I have to handle. I'll be late.

He groaned. He didn't want to be here any longer than he had to be. *But you promised.* He ran a hand across his beard.

Chris

If it's okay with you, I'll just take him home for the night.

Erykah

Yes! Thank you so much. I owe you.

Chris

Nah. Be safe.

He slid his cell into his pocket and went searching for the pup. The little guy barked happily when he saw Chris.

"Thanks for watching him, Cam."

"Happy to." She smiled. "Now to convince Felix we need a pup."

Chris smiled. "Not a bird?"

"He doesn't like birds, but he does like dogs."

She was going to marry a guy who didn't like birds? How? Birds were her thing. Then again, it wasn't his relationship. Cam's eyes practically glowed when she talked about her fiancé. Even now, she didn't seem fazed.

He put Charlie in his kennel. "Everything all good here?"

"Yeah. We'll be fine. Go home."

Thank You, Lord. "Great. See you tomorrow."

"Night, Boss."

Chris carried the kennel out to his vehicle. He opened up his streaming app and set the music to Anthony Brown & group therAPy. Music all set, he took the turn that would take him home to Woodland Park. After navigating through traffic, Chris turned onto his dirt driveway. He stopped the car, then leaned his head back against the headrest.

The stress of the day slowly eked out of his body in the stillness. He pushed thoughts of the day away and tried to empty his mind completely.

His stomach growled. Charlie barked.

Maybe now wasn't the time to rest in silence. "Okay, let's

get out of the car, bud." Chris grabbed the kennel and headed inside.

He walked up the stone steps that led to the front door. His place was open concept, so there wasn't a foyer. The living room immediately opened up in front of him, with stairs leading up and down situated to the left. A side table sat against the wall. He placed his keys on top and slid his backpack off, pushing it under the console table as he set the kennel down.

"Want to come out?" He unlocked the gate and watched as Charlie emerged, taking in his surroundings.

"Do you need to go?" Probably should've done that before they walked inside.

Chris went right back out the front door, Charlie following. They stood out there until the pup found a patch of grass to water.

"Good boy." He'd grabbed a bag of treats from work before leaving. Once inside, he pulled one out of his backpack and gave it to him. "You're a good boy." He ruffled his head. "My turn for a treat, Charlie. I'm starved."

The dog barked.

Normally it was just the walls listening to his voice. It was nice having someone else in the home. It made talking out loud more pleasurable, versus a necessity to avoid being encased in hard silence.

Chris walked past the living room and into the kitchen on the left. There was a dining area to the right with a table that held two chairs. Chris technically didn't need the second one, but not having the extra seating would make him feel the loss of company even more.

Why do you keep thinking about your single status?

He shook off the morose feeling and opened the fridge. He'd left some trout inside to defrost before heading out this morning. He grabbed the fish, a sweet potato, and red and yellow bell peppers. After chopping the vegetables, he made a bed with the sweet potato and peppers on top of a cedar wrap before adding the filet on top. He made two cedar wraps, ignoring the twinge in his chest. Typically, when people cooked a meal for two, it was literally for two people. His meals for two were always in prep for the next day's lunch.

"Well, isn't that a depressing thought."

Charlie barked. Chris didn't know if that meant the dog agreed with him or was embarrassed for him.

"Probably the latter," he mumbled to himself.

He opened the back door that stood nestled between the kitchen space and dining area. There was a gas grill right outside. Soon, his meal and the ground chicken he added for Charlie were finished.

Chris didn't have a dog bowl, so he piled Charlie's food onto a plate. He'd just have to make sure to never eat off it again or bring the dishware into work and make it property of the Gamble on Nature animals so they could use it.

After they ate, Chris went for a walk in the wooded area behind his home. The pup needed exercise, and Chris needed to push away the thoughts of loneliness that had slowly been invading his mind day by day. Hopefully the mountain air would clear his mind and help him sleep peacefully tonight. And maybe the reason God had given Erykah an emergency to handle was so Chris didn't have to be alone tonight.

Maybe . . .

Nine

"Auntie Erykah, look at my drawing." Cheyenne held up a stick-figure family.

There was one with a hat. That had to be my brother-in-law, Asher. The stick figure wearing a circle had to be Ellynn. Then there came a third figure with wild hair. Definitely Cheyenne. She preferred to wear her natural hair without constraint and fought Ellynn every time my sister attempted to braid it. There was also a little circle that more than likely represented the newest addition, Ashlynn.

"What a great picture, Cheyenne. You did an amazing job."

She beamed. "Mama said I could put it on the fridge."

"Oh, that's the place of honor."

She nodded, then skipped away.

"Hurry and tell me what you need to say before she gets back," Ellynn rushed out. "You know she'll take over this video call if you give an inch."

I laughed. She wasn't wrong. "There's not much to say."

"Well, what about the dog? Did you keep him? Actually name him Charlie?"

"I did." I grinned. "He's so sweet and likes to be near me."

"How's the potty training going?"

"Actually not bad. My friend"—my voice cracked—"is helping with that."

"Friend?" Ellynn's eyebrows rose. "Female friend or . . . ?"

My cheeks heated.

"You're blushing!"

I rolled my eyes. "I'm not so light you can tell that." At least I didn't think I was.

"Of course I can tell. You're my *sister*." Ellynn leaned forward, eyes glittering with excitement. "How did you meet him? When did you start hanging out with other people? Is there more than friendship there?"

Her rapid questions made me want to hide, but this was Ellynn. We didn't hide stuff from each other. Plus, she was probably trying to get as much in as she could before Cheyenne decided to come back. "We met by accident at a restaurant, then at the governor's dinner. Since he called me friend. And, no, I'm not girlfriend material."

Ellynn snorted. "Whatever. Anyone can be a girlfriend. You just have to meet your person."

"Ell, I'm not like you. I'm not friendly. People don't strike up random conversations with me."

"Yet you connected with a stranger enough to now call him a friend." She stared at me pointedly through the phone lens. "Obviously someone struck up a random conversation and thought you were friendly enough to add to their collection of people."

"I hate that you're right."

She laughed. "Is there chemistry between you? Do you think there's something more to the friendly feeling?"

"On whose part?"

"I knew it!" Ellynn pumped a fist in the air. "You *like* him."

"What's not to like? He looks good in a tux but is perfectly comfortable in his log cabin and working with animals all day. The guy is actually somewhat of a celebrity."

"Who is he?" My sister's brow furrowed.

"Chris Gamble."

"From Gamble on Nature? The YouTube guy?"

I nodded.

Her mouth dropped. "Girl! He *is* cute."

"Who's cute? Are you looking at another man?" Asher's face came into view, and he waved. "Hey, sis."

"Hey, Asher." Asher was the perfect guy for my sister. I wouldn't have wanted to lose her to anyone else.

She's not lost. She's still your sister.

"Erykah's new friend is Chris Gamble."

"The YouTube guy?" Asher asked.

Ell nodded, and I could feel my cheeks heating. Why was this so embarrassing?

"How did you meet him?" he asked.

"Ordering a burger. He's nice."

"Good for you. You need people."

Unease filtered through me. Did I seem so cut off from others? So alone?

You are *cut off. Don't act like this is a surprise.*

I stifled a sigh.

"When will you see him again?" Ellynn asked.

"When he brings Charlie home."

Her eyes widened. "Girl, you're not giving me enough information."

"Oh, Ell. He's a really great guy. We'd been texting here and there before I got Charlie. Now that he's helping me while I work, we talk more. He'll send me random texts during the day, and it's just so . . ." I searched for the right word. "Wonderful having a friend. I've never had a relationship like this."

Ellynn's eyes watered. "You deserve friendship and more." She bit her lip. "I know you worry about being in a relationship as a doctor because of your hours, but your person is out there. Promise me if it looks like this could be more that you'll stay open to something new. 'Kay?"

Before I could respond, Cheyenne came back. This time she brought her favorite doll and told me all about her and why she was treasured. Cheye dominated the rest of the phone call, but it was so good to chat with her. I loved my niece, and talking to her was one of my favorite things.

"You're my best friend, Auntie Erykah."

My heart filled to bursting. "And you're mine, sweetie." Now I had two friends.

I wanted to stick my tongue out at Asher and his "you need people" comment. But he'd long since left the room. Too soon I said good-bye to my family and sat quietly on my couch in my empty condo.

Chris wouldn't be coming until tomorrow to drop off Charlie, which meant two nights in a row without my new companion. Chris had had something conflicting on his schedule today, and I'd dealt with another emergency, but since we'd already made plans for Chris to bring Charlie back in the morning, I hadn't worried.

Maybe I'd distract myself by putting on Chris's Spotify playlist and tidying the place up a bit before heading to bed.

The next morning, I opened the door to let Chris and Charlie in. "Hey, thanks for bringing him by."

"Happy to help."

A fissure of pleasure unfurled in my middle at the sound of his voice. Having a visit with someone outside of the hospital was huge. Did I get bonus points that my guest fell on the friendly relationship spectrum instead of professional?

Friendly, huh? Keep telling yourself that when you keep wondering about more.

Oh, I would. A friendship was all this could ever be. Sure, Chris watched my puppy while I worked. Yes, I was attracted to him—I did have eyes. No, nothing would go past the thoughts in my mind. They couldn't, because I couldn't even be relied upon to pick up my own dog on time. What kind of girlfriend would I make as a doctor? Ell's words echoed in my head, but I ignored them. I hadn't actually promised, so I would stick to my friendship mantra.

"How are you?" Chris asked. The crinkles alongside his eyes became prominent. "Everything okay?"

I nodded. "Yeah. There was another emergency surgery, but that happens sometimes." I'd given the patient the best outcome toward recovery. His rehab would be extensive but not insurmountable.

"Then I'm glad. I'll pray for their speedy recovery."

"What?" I blinked. "You don't even know him." Who *was* this man?

"God does." He shrugged. "I'm just adding a prayer to the ones I'm sure his loved ones are already saying."

Who did that? Who prayed for someone they'd never met? I eyed Chris. "You'll really pray for him?"

"Yes. I'll do it right now if you want to join me." He smiled.

"Uh . . ." I pointed toward my living room, and we went to sit. I'm not sure my *uh* was really assent, but Chris bowed his head, nevertheless.

"Dear Lord, we come to You today thanking You for the talent You've blessed Erykah with. That talent was able to help save a couple of people these past two nights." Chris cracked an eye open and looked at me. "Is that right?"

"Yes," I croaked. Was this really happening?

His eye closed once more. "Thank You for sending Erykah

to save them. We ask that You bring full healing to their bodies. Please help them through any rehab they go through, and continue equipping Erykah to be Your hands and feet. In Jesus's name, amen."

I'd never heard anyone pray before, and it wasn't at all what I'd imagined. Not that I'd necessarily imagined people praying. Still, I couldn't believe Chris would pray for a perfect stranger. Part of me was in awe. This man exuded kindness in a way that made me want to get closer. Only now I knew beyond a shadow of a doubt we weren't meant to be. How could someone pray to an invisible being and believe wholeheartedly that he was heard and that God would answer him? That was *not* possible.

You're too opposite. Friendship is all this could be.

Charlie wagged his tail and lay down on my shoes. As I looked down into his black eyes, his tongue lolled out. He seemed to be smiling.

"Can dogs smile?"

Chris glanced at him. "Sure looks like it."

"That can't be possible, right?"

Chris shrugged. He ran a hand down his face, and I suddenly realized he looked tired. But also . . .

"Your glasses are gone," I whispered.

"Oh, yeah, put my contacts in today." He smiled.

His eyes were so blue, almost matching the clear azure color of the sky from my earlier peek outside. Why did I have to notice everything about Chris Gamble?

I cleared my throat. "Guess I should let you get back to your day."

"You want to grab lunch first?" Chris offered. "There's a barbecue place nearby that's phenomenal."

Before I could decline, the doorbell rang. "Sorry. Let me see who this is. I'm not expecting visitors."

"Sure thing." He sat back down.

A squint through the peephole showed someone in a uniform, but I couldn't make out what kind. "Hey, Chris? Could you stand nearby just in case?" I wasn't comfortable opening my door to a stranger. No one ever knocked on my door, well, except for Chris.

"Sure." He moved off to the side and motioned for me to go ahead and answer the door.

As soon as it swung open, the Colorado Springs Police Department uniform became obvious.

"Oh, I'm sorry. Do you have the wrong door?"

"Are you Dr. Erykah Kennedy?" the police officer asked me.

"Yes, I'm Dr. Kennedy." What did they want with me? Had something happened to my car? Was this related to the emergency last night?

"I'm Officer Pratt. May I come in?"

I nodded, too dumbfounded to do otherwise. Vaguely, I became aware of Chris introducing himself until I found all of us seated in my living room. *Focus.*

I cleared my throat. "I'm sorry, what's this about?"

"Dr. Kennedy, I have some bad news for you." His eyes were full of sympathy.

Already my head was shaking. I didn't like where this was going. I reached for Chris, who instinctively wrapped his hand around mine.

"Unfortunately, there was a tragic car accident that led to the death of your sister, Ellynn Charles, and her husband, Asher."

"What?" I scoffed. "That's not possible. I just talked to her yesterday." I turned to Chris. "We FaceTimed yesterday. I spoke to both of them." My voice shook as I tried to get them to understand.

"Dr. Kennedy, I'm sorry to say the Lexington Police Department confirmed their deaths. They were in an accident at eight this morning, eastern time. The LPD asked us to notify you."

It was already nine mountain time. Was he saying they'd been dead for three hours? My breath hitched. How could that be true? I'd talked to them yesterday! "No. It can't be true." I squeezed Chris's hand harder, my own hands shaking. "It's not true."

"Dr. Kennedy . . ." the officer started, but I shook my head. "No. No. *No!*"

Strong arms wrapped around me. I was vaguely aware of Chris's presence, but everything else faded as the roaring in my ears took over. I curled my face into his chest and sobbed.

Ten

L *ord God, no. . . .*
   Chris turned to the officer as he held Erykah and kept his voice low. "What about her nieces? Were they in the car too?"

"Her sister had children?" Officer Pratt's face reddened. "I'm sorry. I didn't even ask the detective on the case. I have his number and can find out."

"Please. She has two nieces." Chris thought back to what Erykah had shared with him. "Um, Cheyenne and Ashlynn are their names, I believe."

Officer Pratt took out a cell, then dialed a number. "Yes, this is Officer Pratt with the Colorado Springs PD. May I speak to Detective Harold Spence?"

Chris listened as Officer Pratt relayed the information to the detective.

"Hold on." The officer turned to Chris. "There were no kids in the car. They're going to send an officer to their house to look for them. Do you know if Dr. Kennedy can fly out there and head to the police station?"

"I'll make sure she's on the first plane out." Even if Chris had to buy the plane ticket himself.

Erykah's cries hadn't stopped, but they had gone down in volume. She probably wasn't even aware of what was going on around her.

The officer conveyed the new info, then hung up. "They'll have to notify CPS but will note that Dr. Kennedy will be out there as soon as possible. Detective Spence asked me to pass along his number."

Chris pulled out his cell from his inside jacket pocket. "I'm ready." He typed in the number, then put the phone away.

Sympathy crossed the officer's face. "I'm sorry to come with such tragic news. I'm glad she has you with her."

Chris closed his eyes. She was going to have to bury two of her family members. His breath stuck in his chest as he tried to formulate a prayer. *Help her, Lord. Please just help her.*

"Will they be giving her any further updates, or will she have to wait until we get there?"

"I can pass along your number, but more than likely, they'll reach out to Dr. Kennedy only."

Chris gave Officer Pratt his contact info just in case.

"I'll see myself out."

After locking the door behind the officer, Chris pulled Erykah back into his arms. She turned her face into his shirt, wetting it with tears. Charlie jumped up on the couch and placed his head on her lap.

"I know, boy. It's up to us to be here for her."

He couldn't see how she would get through this. As far as Chris was aware, Ellynn had been Erykah's only family. Now she was gone. He had no idea whether her brother-in-law had family. That would be something he'd have to find out and help her navigate.

Chris rubbed Erykah's back until her cries finally subsided, and she shifted in his arms.

"Please tell me it was a dream." Her bottom lip trembled.

"I wish I could," he spoke softly. "But I'm here for you. Whatever you need."

"I don't even know where to begin." She shot up, almost slamming the bottom of his chin with the top of her head in the process.

"What about the girls?" she cried. "Were they in the car?"

"The detective said no one else was in the car. They're sending someone to the house to get them." Chris gave her the Lexington police officer's information.

"I need to go." She wiped her face, then pulled her cell from the end table, unlocking the device with facial recognition. "I need a plane ticket out of here."

Actually . . . he did know a man who owned a plane. Grier was associated with one of the board members at Gamble on Nature. Sometimes he flew them around Colorado or other areas if needed. Chris would call him and ask for a favor, but first, he needed to get some prayers going.

Chris
My friend just received some tragic news. Pray for her.

Tuck
Wait *her*?

Chris
Not now. I'll fill you in later.

Lamont
Praying.

Tuck
Sorry, man. Praying.

Chris got up from the couch and found Grier in his contacts. He spoke low into the receiver.

"Gamble, what's up, man?"

"Hey, Grier. Listen, I need a favor. Any way you can fly

a friend out to Lexington, Kentucky, today? Her sister and brother-in-law were killed in a car accident, and now her nieces are without their parents."

"Oh my word. I'm so sorry, Gamble. Let me check today's schedule."

Chris glanced at Erykah, who had tears streaming down her cheeks while she maintained an intense focus on her phone.

"I can fly out at noon. How's that?"

A quick look at his watch showed *10:00 a.m.* "Give me a sec." He muted the phone and walked toward Erykah. "Any luck with flights?"

"No. There's nothing going out until midnight." She bit her bottom lip.

"So I know a guy." Her gaze fixed on him. "He can fly you out in a couple of hours."

"Yes. I'll take it." Desperation shone in her eyes.

He hated this for her. "Then I'll get everything handled for you."

"Thank you so much. Just let me know how much it is."

Chris nodded, but he had no plans of making her pay for the flight. "Hey, Grier, she'll be there. Put it on my tab."

"Nah, man. This is on the house. I'm sorry it's under such difficult circumstances."

Chris glanced at Erykah. "Do you have room for one more and a dog?" Could he really let her go by herself? What kind of friend would he be if he let her walk into darkness all alone?

"You coming along?"

"Yes."

"Don't be late."

"We won't." Chris hung up and walked to Erykah. "Okay, here's the plan. Go get packed, and I'll get Charlie's stuff ready. Then we'll make our way to my friend Grier. He can fly us out at noon. By the time you're packed, and we drive there, we should be right on time. We'll be in Kentucky about five thirty eastern time."

She blinked. "We?"

"Is that okay?" Chris held out a hand. "I just want to be a support system for you. I won't be a nuisance. I promise."

Fresh tears fell, and she squeezed his hand. "I can't ask that of you."

"You're not. I'm offering. No strings. Just a friend being there for another friend."

She threw herself into his arms, body shuddering from another wave of tears. "I've never had a friend like you before," she whispered, then withdrew.

"I'm so sorry, Erykah. I don't want to give you any platitudes, any clichés, because you'll quickly grow tired of them." And how he hated that he knew that. "But I'll be here. I'll listen to you vent. Let you cry in peace. Whatever you need. I promise I'll be there."

She gave a wobbly nod.

His mind scrambled to think of everything they needed. "I hate to ask, but did your sister have a will? Any kind of guardianship paperwork for the girls? I wasn't sure of the situation with your brother-in-law's family."

"Um . . ." Erykah's voice trailed off. "I don't know, but if she did, they'd probably be in her home office. And Asher didn't have family. His parents were pretty old and died when he was in college. One from a heart attack, I believe, and the other from a stroke."

So much tragedy all around. "I see."

She rose to her feet. "Are we driving to your house first, so you can pack?"

"I actually have a go bag in the trunk of the Bronco. Never

know when I'm going to have an animal crisis that requires a change of clothes. Sometimes you get sprayed." He made a face like *What can you do?*

A ghost of a smile crossed her lips. "You can't live on one change of clothes. There must be time for you to go home and back."

He shook his head. "Grier said not to be late. I don't want to be responsible for you missing that flight. Besides, I have at least two outfits in there, and I'm sure there are stores in Kentucky."

He thought about Tuck. Maybe there was a possibility he'd be able to see his friend in person. Though they'd last seen each other in May for the Kentucky Derby, it felt a lot longer than five months.

"I'll take Charlie for a bathroom break, then be back up." He motioned to the pup.

"'Kay."

Chris headed for the elevator, out the front doors, then to the grassy knoll. The pup nosed around the area. "Charlie, you'll need to be on your best behavior. Erykah needs us. We gotta be there for her."

The dog watered the leaves and looked at Chris as if saying *Duh*. Chris cracked a smile.

He pulled out his cell and dialed Tuck.

"Hey, man, what's going on?"

"Where do I start?" He blew out a breath. "My friend's sister and brother-in-law were killed in a car accident. We're flying into Lexington around five thirty your time. Is it possible you could give us a ride to the police station? At least, I'm assuming that's the first place she needs to go."

"Absolutely. How is she handling the news?"

"About as well as can be expected."

"I'm really sorry, man. I'll be praying. See you later."

"Thanks, Tuck." He pocketed his cell, then looked up into the sky, picturing the Lord watching over him and Erykah. He'd need the Lord's guidance over the next few days, weeks even, if Chris had to guess. *Please help her. Please guide us and see us safely to her nieces.*

While Charlie continued to snoop around the bushes, Chris took a moment to let his own emotions out. By the time he composed himself, Charlie was ready to head back up.

Erykah had tears running down her face once more. He rushed to her. "What happened?"

"Detective Spence called. Cheyenne and Ash were at home with a babysitter." She sniffed. "I know you said they weren't in the car, but it was such a relief for him to confirm it."

"Are they staying with the babysitter?"

She shook her head. "They're calling in a social worker and bringing them to the station. I told him we'd be landing about five thirty. He said he'll make sure social services knows that."

"Did they find a will?" Chris asked.

"They won't search their house for it. We'll have to do that and file with the court and show any documents to CPS."

He nodded. "Are you all packed?"

"Almost."

"All right. Let me get Charlie ready, and we'll be there for your nieces as soon as possible."

"I can't thank you enough."

"Please, I wouldn't be able to rest if I didn't help you. It's my honor."

A tremulous smile covered her lips, but the sadness in her eyes nearly undid him. The quicker they could get to Kentucky, the better.

Eleven

My mind had now become a place of torment. Every single precious memory I had with Ellynn blazed like Technicolor and the best CGI framework. Along with each memory came the glaring gap of time that spanned between each visit with my baby sister. Why did she have to move to Kentucky? Why couldn't I have seen her on a daily basis?

I'd been too focused on my job. What had started as a childhood dream to keep us from starving had turned into a path I never allowed myself to deviate from. Too much had ridden on my success. Becoming a doctor had meant a better life for myself as well as Ellynn. Sure, I'd become a doctor, had cared for my sister, but at what cost?

How could my sweet sister be dead? My poor, precious nieces. Once more, two sisters had been orphaned.

Not true. They have you. You care when no one else will.

I had to remind myself that my nieces wouldn't suffer the same fate Ellynn and I had. Though we hadn't been true orphans, our parents' absence still remained a daily reality. They'd been too busy chasing the next high to care whether we were fed or clothed. I'd been the one to make breakfast for us, get us to the bus on time, and make sure we had food to eat come dinnertime.

When I'd graduated from high school, my parents had agreed to let Ellynn come live with me. She'd only been twelve, but I made sure I had a job to pay for an apartment for the both of us. We flourished away from our childhood home—a shack that should've been condemned years before.

Ellynn graduated from high school six years later and went to culinary school, where she met Asher. They'd fallen in love and were married by the time she turned twenty. Only Ellynn didn't start the family she'd dreamed of right away. She suffered with infertility issues for years. Cheyenne was the gift Ellynn had been waiting nine years for, and Ashlynn an added bonus.

I'd always imagined I'd have kids of my own. Yet my chances dwindled with every birthday. I hadn't hit menopause yet, but my biological clock seemed to shout at me with every passing day. However, I'd never imagined caring for two kids through the act of guardianship.

"Dr. Kennedy, do you understand?"

I blinked, my eyes bringing the social worker into focus. Linda Simmons—as she'd introduced herself—had said a whole lot, but not much registered in my brain. I turned to Chris, who squeezed my hand, then let go.

"Ms. Simmons stated that Ellynn and Asher previously filed paperwork stating you would be the girls' guardian if both of them passed away." Chris's Adam's apple bobbed. "She said you can take the girls back to Colorado, but the family courts will set a date to confirm the guardianship as permanent."

"Okay." I grimaced. My voice sounded so weak, so feeble.

"You'll need new car seats. The current ones are no longer

viable since they were in the car at the time of the accident," Ms. Simmons continued. "If your young man wants to go buy them, there's a store just up the road."

My hand gripped Chris's arm. He couldn't leave. How could I talk to the girls by myself? And sweet Ashlynn. A baby had no real understanding of death.

"I can ask Tuck to go to the store, if you need me here," Chris said.

"Please." I still hadn't come to grips with how he knew Tucker Hale, the same man I had operated on earlier in the year when I'd visited Ellynn to celebrate Ashlynn's birth. Kentucky really was a small world.

Chris pulled out his cell and texted a message, then slipped the phone back into his pocket. "He's on it."

"Are you ready to see the girls?" the social worker asked.

No. I was not ready, but I couldn't let them just stay in the next room, confused as to where Ellynn and Asher were.

"You can do this," Chris murmured in my ear.

I slowly nodded.

The social worker smiled at me. "You'll be just what they need."

Tears pricked my eyelids once more. How could I look at my nieces and tell them their mom and dad wouldn't be coming home?

We stood, and I wrapped my hand around Chris's. "Chris?"

"Yeah?" He studied me.

I gathered some courage. "Will you pray? I . . . I don't know how. I don't even know if it works, but when you did it the last time, I felt something." And something was better than nothing at this point. I was falling apart, but if Chris's strength and even his faith in an unknown deity could see me through, then I needed whatever it took.

"Of course." He bowed his head.

Like last time, I watched. I listened.

The pressure across my chest eased just enough for me to take in a breath. To exhale as Chris's calm voice washed over me, strengthened me, prepared me somewhat.

"Amen."

"Thank you."

Ms. Simmons led the way down the hall. Each step felt like a walk along the green mile.

I can't do this. I can't do this. I can't.

You've got no choice, Erykah. Lean on Chris.

Could I tighten my fingers around his any more without restricting his blood flow? Would he even speak up if I crushed his hand? Not once since I received that awful visit from Officer Pratt had Chris faltered. He'd gotten us on the plane, into Tuck's truck, and in front of the police and then the social worker.

He'll be with you in front of the girls as well.

Ms. Simmons quietly opened the door. Cheyenne popped up from the mat, where she had sat quietly with her doll. "Auntie Erykah!"

She ran to me, arms wide. I let go of Chris's hand and scooped her up, cradling her close to me. Tears welled in my eyes as I pushed against the need to cry. She reminded me so much of Ellynn when she was this age.

"Where's Mama? Daddy?"

Cheye's hair had been tamed into two twin braids. I smoothed my hand down the plaits, imagining Ellynn braiding her daughter's hair. What would've been a normal routine would now be one of the last moments Cheyenne had with her mom. My throat ached with unshed tears.

"I have to tell you something, sweetie."

Cheyenne's big brown eyes stared into my very soul. "What happened? Something bad?"

"Yes. I'm so sorry. But your mommy and daddy got hurt." *Please don't cry, please don't cry.*

"Can you make them all better? You're a doctor."

Break my heart. I wished I could. "I can't, Cheye. They're in heaven now." Oh goodness. I was telling an impressionable child Ellynn resided in a place I wasn't sure existed. But if it did . . .

I stared at Chris, and he dipped his head as if to say, *You're doing just fine.* I hoped he was right. I didn't want to scar Cheyenne. I had no idea how you were supposed to tell a child their parents were both dead.

Agony filled every fiber of my being.

"What do you mean?" Her brow wrinkled.

"They died, sweetie." I said the words gently. Spoke the horrifying words that my own mind was still wrestling with.

"You're lying." A storm cloud rose on her face. "Mama and Daddy wouldn't leave me. You're a meanie."

"Cheyenne . . ."

She shoved against me, bucking in my arms. I set her down, hoping to avoid any injuries to her small body.

"Mommy!" she wailed.

The social worker stepped forward. Had she been standing there the whole time?

She lowered herself to her knees, looking Cheyenne right in the eyes. "Cheyenne, I'm afraid your aunt isn't lying."

Cheyenne sniffed while staring at the social worker.

"Remember what I said my job was when I first met you?"

"To help kids like me?"

I glanced at the crib in the room, surprised Ashlynn could stay asleep through her big sister's tears.

"That's right. When parents can no longer take care of their children, they call me to make sure the kids will be okay."

Confusion covered Cheye's little face. "Aunt Erykah isn't lying?"

"No. She got on a plane and came out here as soon as she could to make sure you were safe too. She wants to take you home with her."

"But home is with my mommy and daddy." Her little lip poked out.

I wholeheartedly agreed with her statement, but I was powerless to change reality.

"I know it's hard to believe, but they're in heaven just like your aunt said."

"They can't be. They're not old like you."

I winced. In any other circumstances, this might pull some type of chuckle from me, but all I felt was an ache deep in my soul.

"Sometimes people get hurt even if they're young."

Cheyenne's bottom lip began to quiver again.

"What about my room?"

This time, I was the one to move closer. Taking a page out of Ms. Simmons's book, I sat on the floor. "We can take whatever you want back to my place."

"You really flew on a plane?"

I nodded and pointed to Chris. "My friend, Chris, made sure I got here as soon as possible."

"Thank you, Mr. Chris." Cheyenne stepped closer to me. "Will Ashlynn come too?"

"Of course she will."

She nodded as if accepting her fate. I hated this for her, but I was thankful she had calmed quickly, though I was sure the tears would be here for a while. "Are you ready to leave?"

"Go home with you right now?" Her eyes widened.

I shook my head. "No, sorry, sweetie. We'll go to your house first. I have to know what you want to bring to Colorado, right?"

Relief pooled in her eyes. "Okay." She slipped her hand into mine. "Don't forget the baby."

Ms. Simmons picked up my sleeping niece and placed her into my arm. I had one arm wrapped around Ashlynn, and the other hand held Cheyenne. My gaze met Chris's. "We're ready." But the staccato rhythm of my heart said otherwise.

"All right. Tuck just pulled up."

Ms. Simmons followed behind us to ensure we'd obtained the appropriate car seats for the girls. After watching me buckle them in to make sure I had an understanding, she nodded. "I'll contact you once the courts set the date."

"Thank you for watching over them."

"It was my pleasure." She squeezed my hand. "I'm so sorry for your loss. Take care of those dear girls."

"I will." I maneuvered around one of the car seats until I sat in the middle between the girls.

Chris and Tuck kept quiet all the way to my sister's place. There seemed to be an unspoken agreement that everyone would be left to their thoughts, but I couldn't wait to be alone. There was a storm of tears waiting for release, but until then, I'd put on a brave front for my nieces. I was no stranger to hardship, but not having Ellynn by my side had rocked my very foundation. How was I supposed to move forward?

Twelve

They said new mercies came in the morning. Today, they came in the form of Tuck and Piper, who arrived on the doorstep with a donut box and Charlie. When Chris and Erykah had landed yesterday, Tuck agreed to watch the pup until they got the girls and were settled.

"Thanks for watching him." Chris clapped Tuck on the back.

"It was fun."

"Good to see you, Piper." He gave her a side hug.

Her arm squeezed his neck. "I'm so sorry. I couldn't believe it when Tuck told me." She pulled back and studied him. "Are you resting? It's hard to be the pillar someone else leans on."

Why did that statement choke him up? He nodded, waiting for the opportune time to clear his throat and effectively rid himself of emotions that he needed to keep locked inside.

"Come on in. The girls are sleeping. Erykah's been awake for a while." Chris grimaced.

She'd woken at five in the morning, which was even earlier for them considering their bodies were running on mountain time and not eastern. Despite that, Chris had heard her movements and gotten up to be with her. All she'd done was sit in the living room, clutching a photo of her and Ellynn.

He set the kennel down. "I'll be back, boy." He stood and gestured for his friends to follow him into the kitchen.

"What's the plan?" Tuck asked as he set the donut box on the island.

Chris ran a hand across his beard. "We need to get a funeral planned, then head back to Colorado. We're actually thinking of a road trip back home versus flying with a bunch of stuff we'd most likely have to ship. We could make the trip in two days, but it's probably best for the girls and the puppy if we do the drive in three."

"So what's that going to entail?" Piper asked. "Will you have to rent a moving truck or something?"

Chris nodded. "That's on today's to-do list. We'll pick it up tomorrow so we can start loading and packing." He sighed. "It's a lot. I found a list on the internet to guide us because Erykah is . . ." *A zombie?* That sounded so callous, but she definitely wasn't herself.

Not being present was to be suspected, or maybe it was more of a brain fog. Regardless, Chris wanted to ease her burden, hence the internet checklist.

"We want to help," Piper said. "Tuck and I will pack or do whatever y'all need."

"Thanks, guys." Once again, Chris thanked the Lord for their friendship.

Footsteps sounded, and Chris turned, already anticipating Erykah's arrival. What did it say that he knew the sound of her footfalls? Or that his senses were already anticipating that soothing scent she wore? The smell reminded him of vanilla and honey. Whatever the fragrance was, it made him want to nuzzle his nose right into the curve of her neck.

Get it together. She needs a friend, not someone cataloging how she smells, Gamble.

He blew out a breath just as she walked into the kitchen.

Erykah blinked, noticing Tuck and Piper, then her face softened. "Hi." Her gaze cleared as if seeing Tuck for the first time, despite meeting him yesterday. "Mr. Hale, how's the shoulder?"

"It's all right. Some top-notch surgeon performed the surgery, so rehab could've been worse." Tuck smirked.

Erykah laughed. *Laughed.*

Chris hated that slight fissure of jealousy that shot through him.

"I was so shocked when Tuck said you were the Erykah Chris has been talking about." Piper walked up to her. "Can I give you a hug?"

"Please," Erykah rasped. The two women embraced, and after a long moment, broke apart. "I was surprised as well when Chris first mentioned you two, but then thought how small the world really is."

"So wait," Chris interrupted. "You guys all know each other?"

Tuck nodded. "She's the doctor I told you about at the gala in May. Remember?" Tuck arched a brow.

Why did Chris's neck have to heat at the memory of the conversation? His friends had wanted to set him up with the surgeon who had operated on Tuck's broken shoulder. But they'd remembered she'd only been in town for vacation, and they didn't know where she lived. Chris had thought he'd dodged a messy setup and had been relieved. Now, well, he didn't know how to feel.

How was Tuck's doctor the person Chris now called friend?

"Small world, right?" Erykah smiled at him.

"Very. But that's a good thing."

She bit her lip. "Um, the girls are awake. Cheyenne is getting dressed on her own because she didn't want my help." Her shoulders sagged. "I came in here to find some milk for the baby."

Uh-oh.

"Was Ellynn breastfeeding?" Piper asked.

"She was, but I'm worried about what happens when we run out." Erykah turned an uncertain gaze his way.

"We'll find the right formula. Promise." Chris didn't know how they'd do it. He'd never taken care of a kid before, but he wouldn't leave Erykah alone to flounder.

"Erykah," Piper said gently. "Do you have any boxes for packing? How can we help?"

Chris watched Erykah, waiting for any telltale sign of tears or anything else that meant he needed to step in and help her.

"Um, we do need something to pack their stuff in." She tugged at a twist of hair as if thinking. "I'm bringing all of their bedding and clothes. Plus anything else they want and is reasonable to fit into the moving truck."

"Remember," Chris said, "we can come back for other stuff. We don't have to bring everything now, and we can certainly buy anything else we need."

She nodded. "Right. I'll definitely have to come back to go through the rest of the stuff. I took two weeks of leave, but any more than that and my schedule of surgeries becomes more difficult to rearrange."

Wow. She'd have to go back to work in two weeks? That seemed cruel. But time waited for no one and no thing—including grief.

"I'm so sorry, Erykah," Piper said. There was a brief silence, then she motioned to the food boxes. "We brought breakfast, so fuel up. Tuck and I will go get supplies to pack everything."

"I appreciate that."

"Of course." Piper hugged Erykah again. Then she and Tuck left the house.

"Your friends are really great."

Chris nodded. "I was thinking that earlier." He turned to the cabinet and removed two plates. "What kind of donuts do you like?"

Her nose wrinkled. "I don't eat a lot of food like this normally."

"I don't think calories count right now." His gaze skimmed her body. "And you definitely don't have to worry about a thing."

She looked downward. Chris wanted to give himself a kick in the pants. She was grieving. This wasn't the time for flirting—even unintentional flirting.

"I'll have one." She added a glazed donut to her plate.

Chris added another one. "Or two."

Erykah threw him a look.

"If you warm it up, you'll see two is the correct choice."

"Warm what up?" Cheyenne walked into the kitchen looking very . . . *Disgruntled? Annoyed?*

Her hair, no longer in braids, fanned out like a lion's mane. She wore a pink polka dot shirt with purple-and-yellow-striped pants. Obviously the girl loved patterns and didn't care about matching.

"My friends bought us donuts."

Her eyes widened. "Are there any with sprinkles?" she whispered.

"Pink ones," Chris said just as quietly.

"And you warm donuts up?" The skeptical look she threw Chris's way resembled a royal looking down her nose at a peasant.

"I promise it's delicious."

"Okay. Warm one up." She held up her pointer. "If it tastes okay, I'll eat the rest warm too."

"The rest?"

"Cheyenne, you can have two donuts, and that's it," Erykah interjected.

"But why?" she whined. "How many have you had?"

"Two." Erykah pointed to her plate. "That's all we need."

Cheyenne swung her head in Chris's direction. "How many are you having?"

He pointed at the two donuts on his plate. They were jelly filled, and he couldn't wait to eat them.

"Fine." She crossed her arms.

She was going to keep Erykah on her toes for sure.

Chris heated up her donut and watched expectantly. "Well?"

"You're right. It's the best. Please heat up another one." She waved a hand.

It was all he could do not to laugh, but he did as directed.

Cheyenne looked up at her aunt, then glanced at Chris before speaking. "What are we doing today?"

"We're going to pack some." Erykah kept her gaze on her plate.

"And then?"

"We'll take each moment one at a time," Chris answered. Probably wasn't his place to speak, but they both looked like they needed saving.

"Are you sure you can't fix them?" Cheyenne's voice quivered.

"I would if I could. You know I would," Erykah said.

Cheyenne bobbed her head, then stuffed the rest of the donut in her mouth. Was it bad if comfort eating started at five?

A cry filled the house.

"Oh no." Erykah slapped her forehead. "Bottle."

She went to the fridge, grabbed a bottle, then left the room. Chris watched Cheyenne as she polished off the second donut.

"Hey, Cheyenne, do you want to meet my friend?" Charlie was probably itching to get out of the kennel.

"I already know her. She's *my* aunt."

"No, I have another friend." He grinned. "Come on."

She hopped off the bar stool and followed him. "Who's that?" she gasped.

"This is Charlie." He unlocked the kennel. "I believe you named him."

"The puppy? Auntie Erykah brought him?"

He nodded and held on to the pup as his tail wagged enthusiastically.

"Aww." Cheyenne petted him and grinned. "Can I hold him?"

"Just be gentle." That's what he always told kids her age. They had a tendency not to realize how strong they were.

Speaking of, he needed to call Cameron and let her know what was going on. Probably needed to speak to someone at PathLight as well. They needed to know he wouldn't be back until next week. Could he take two weeks off too?

Cheyenne sat on the floor, then Chris placed Charlie into her lap. She giggled as the puppy licked her chin. As he watched them, Chris couldn't help but think of God's provision. The Lord knew what Erykah would be facing and had sent Charlie to her just in time to help comfort her and her niece.

God was good even when living in the world felt very bad.

Thirteen

Some sights would always be unnatural.

Two coffins being lowered into the ground topped that list when I considered my baby sister and her husband lay at rest within. I held Ashlynn to me while Cheyenne sobbed into Chris's arms.

But we weren't alone.

Ellynn and Asher's friends had come out in support. They'd expressed their sorrow and shared stories with me at the visitation the day before. When the fog lifted, I'd appreciate the anecdotes and company, but right then, I couldn't process anything other than the fact that my sweet nieces had been robbed, and having me as a guardian was barely a consolation to their grief.

I'm not equipped to raise these precious children.

Ashlynn was so fussy, and I knew it was because I wasn't her mother. She hated the bottle, hated how I smelled, and hated that my voice wasn't Ellynn's. Cheyenne helped, but she needed me to allow her to grieve and not to become a little mother to her baby sister. I knew that hardship, and I wanted to spare her.

But I also wanted to crawl back into bed, burrow under the covers, and hope I'd wake up from this nightmare.

My sister's pastor said something about heaven, and my breath stayed trapped in my chest. There it was again. That word. That place. I'd never believed in such things, but Asher had introduced religion to Ellynn. She'd sent me a Bible and sermon or two (more like too many to count) in hopes I'd be converted. Honestly, I'd never watched any of the videos she sent nor cracked open the book. Guilt pierced me. My sister had wanted to share something with me, and I'd ignored her.

What else had I ignored, thinking I'd have time to do it later or simply that it was too unrealistic to spend my time on?

Chris believed in a heaven. He had to with the way he prayed. As if some being truly listened to him, truly cared what he said. The idea seemed unfathomable. If there was a God, why hadn't He helped us when we were children? Why hadn't He saved Ellynn and Asher? Saved their kids from being raised by me and carted off to Colorado?

Cheyenne probably thought our upcoming move cruel, but my life was in Colorado. I had commitments and couldn't just abandon those even though my only sister had passed. I was fortunate my contract with the hospital even had bereavement leave.

And I was more than fortunate Chris had stayed with me through all of this. I'd never had a friend like him. I didn't even really know how to make friends, so seeing him help me care for my nieces and helping me pack meant the world.

I still couldn't believe that Tucker and Piper were here to help as well. They'd brought breakfast every day this week as well as boxes for us to load items into. Now the moving trailer was all ready for us to start the road trip back home. Chris had rented a truck with the perfect back seat for the girls. He'd also bought a cooler for us to store the breast milk and any snacks Cheyenne and I would need.

He was a . . . *godsend*.

I'd heard that word before. Had been praised with it by patients' family members after I performed particularly harrowing surgeries. I'd always shrugged the compliments off, but now I wondered . . . could it be true? If God existed, did He really send me to help those families? And more importantly, had I met Chris at a time God knew I'd need a friend the most?

My head spun with too many questions and not enough answers.

An arm came around my shoulders. "Anything I can do?" Chris whispered.

"You're doing it," I murmured back. I leaned my head against his shoulder and closed my eyes.

Though I felt comforted, tears welled in my eyes. I couldn't cry now. Not with so many people around me. Tears were for the dark of night when all slept and I gave myself permission to unleash the floodgates.

As if he understood, Chris withdrew his arm but offered a gentle smile.

A different time, maybe even a different place, I'd allow the feelings inside me to have free rein. Chris was one of those guys who made a woman reconsider her priorities. But now . . . now I was a caregiver for two treasures. I didn't have time to entertain romance. Not that he was actually offering that. We'd agreed to be friends, nothing more.

The service ended, and Chris turned to walk to the car. We'd decided against a repast after the funeral service. I didn't want the girls to be overwhelmed. I'd had enough peopling and just wanted to be alone with my grief. Well, except for Tucker and Piper. They were supposed to come over and bring dinner—their offer.

Piper had found a management company who would look

over the house for me until I figured out whether it would be sold. Ellynn's lawyer confirmed they had a mortgage, which meant I should probably sell the place. I didn't want to take over payments while also paying for my own condo in Colorado. But I didn't know what to do with all their things. *Worry about that in the future*. For now, I'd pay their mortgage until I could figure everything else out, which meant I would definitely keep my leave to two weeks.

After settling Ashlynn in the Pack 'n Play, I went to find Cheyenne. Her room stood empty, so I moved on to the bathroom. *Empty*. Finally, I found her in Ellynn's room, curled up in a ball on the bed, Charlie curled up right next to her. She had an arm around him, and her sniffles reached my ears and settled straight into my heart.

"Hey, Cheye, do you want some company?"

"I have Charlie," she mumbled.

"Would you like me too?"

"Okay," she said softly.

I climbed onto the bed and spooned her, rubbing a hand down her arm. She'd let me braid her hair this morning, and I had never been more thankful for all the practice I'd had on Ellynn's hair. If I hadn't, Cheyenne's hair would closely resemble that of the '80s singer Chaka Khan.

"Why'd they have to die?" Cheyenne's small voice broke the silence.

"I wish I knew. I miss them so much."

"Me too." Cheyenne sniffed. "I don't want to move."

"I know, sweetie. I'm so sorry I live in a different state." Was there anything I could do to help her through this? Should I consider moving to Kentucky? *You have a contract to fulfill in Colorado*. I bit my lip.

"Can't you move to Kentucky?"

"Not today I can't." I had previously tried to explain

about my work obligations, but how much did a five-year-old understand about contracts?

"Will I have my own room?"

I winced. *Oh great*. I hadn't even given two thoughts to our living situation. I'd been so focused on packing and getting back home. Where would I put a kid's bed? A crib?

"I'm not sure. We'll figure it out together, Cheye. I promise. I'll be here for you."

She turned and threw her arms around my neck, tears soaking my shirt. And because it was just the two of us, I let mine run down my face as I comforted my niece and she comforted me.

Sometime later, Chris leaned against the doorframe. Cheyenne had long since fallen asleep, but I hadn't wanted to leave the comfort of her presence.

"Do you need me?" I asked.

"Just wanted to let you know I fed Ashlynn."

"Really?" I slid myself away from my oldest niece and walked to Chris. "You didn't have to do that."

He pointed toward the bed with his head. "You two needed a reprieve."

"Thank you." I slid my fingers through Chris's and pulled him away from the room. We needed to talk. Or rather, I needed to profusely thank him for all he'd done.

When we made it to the living room, I faced him. "I just wanted to say thank you."

"Don't." He shook his head. "Any friend would do the same."

My nose wrinkled. "I don't think so, Chris Gamble. You are one of a kind, and I'm so glad I met you. I'm so glad you decided to be my friend. That doesn't happen easily."

"That's because people are intimidated by your brains and beauty."

My cheeks heated under his sincerity. "How come you aren't?"

"Who said I'm not?" he asked softly.

Goose bumps pricked my flesh, and I found myself leaning toward him. *Girl, get it together.* Somehow, I managed to step back and collect myself. I pulled my twists up into a bun on top of my head and slid the hair tie I kept on my wrist onto my hair.

Whew. It was warm in here.

"I have a question," Chris started.

"Yes?"

"What are you going to do with the girls' things? Are you going to get a bigger place?"

I winced. "Cheyenne asked me if she would have her own room, and it hit me that I don't have space for them." I bit my lip. "Is it bad that I want to solve that problem at another date? I know it's foolish seeing as we're driving out tomorrow, but I just . . ." I placed a hand on top of my head. "It's all so much."

Chris nodded thoughtfully. "I can see that, and I certainly don't want to stress you." He studied me. "I have an idea, if you want to hear it."

I nodded.

"What if you moved in with me?"

My eyes widened.

"I mean, temporarily," he rushed out. "You could either sleep upstairs on the second floor or in the basement. The second floor has a bedroom and a little sitting area. The bedroom is certainly big enough for all three of you. Or the basement has two bedrooms. Well, one is an office, but I can move all that stuff out to another area. Um, the main floor has one bedroom, but it's a little smaller so I could stay in that space depending on what floor you choose. Just know

I'd make sure not to be in your way. Then you'd have time to find a place for all three of you without the stress of feeling rushed." He blew out a breath.

Was it sad that I loved how nervous he looked? Did that make me mean or just battling feelings that were more than friendly?

"Can I think about it?"

"Of course. I just want to help."

"You have in ways you'll never realize." I cupped the side of his face, loving the warmth there and the feel of his beard. "You're an amazing friend, Chris."

Something flickered in his eyes, and then he kissed the inside of my palm before stepping back. "I'll be whatever you need, Erykah. Help in any way I can. I hope you know that."

"I'm starting to," I whispered. And now I feared I just might lose my heart to Christian Gamble.

Fourteen

Chris
I'm not sure there are enough prayers in the world to get me through this road trip.

Tuck
A baby and a five-year-old keeping you on your toes?

Chris
Ashlynn hasn't stopped crying.

Lamont
A crying baby would have me jumping out of the vehicle and taking chances with the other cars.

Tuck
It's that serious?

Chris
YES!

Lamont
Have you never heard a baby crying?

Tuck
My bad. I'll double up my prayers.

"Why are we stopped again?" Cheyenne asked from the back seat.

Chris put his cell down and turned to look at her. "Your aunt is trying to get Ashlynn comfortable enough to stop crying."

They'd fed her, changed her diaper, and attempted to rock her to sleep. Chris had even found a kids' playlist on Spotify to try to soothe the little one. Nothing worked. Nothing.

Lord God, despite what I said about prayers in my text, I know they work. But I'm so exhausted from the noise. I can only imagine how Erykah feels. Please help us.

He blew out a breath. "Do you need to use the bathroom?"

"I went last time." Cheyenne rolled her eyes.

"That was thirty minutes ago."

"I haven't drank anything."

"Drunk."

"Huh?"

He sighed. It didn't matter if she spoke properly. All that mattered was getting Ashlynn through this first leg of travel. They still had six more hours of driving before they reached their hotel for the night. Chris didn't think they'd make it.

"Can you play 'Baby Shark' again? Maybe that will help her."

Absolutely not. If he had to hear that song one more time . . .

Chris's phone pinged. "I think we'll try a different song when they get back in the car." He picked up his phone, glancing outside toward where Erykah had disappeared. They'd stopped at a coffee shop for her to grab some liquid fuel and take Ashlynn to the restroom.

Lamont

Nevaeh says try white noise. You can find a video on YouTube to play.

Tuck

My mom also said try hanging a mirror in the back.

Chris checked Ashlynn's car seat. There wasn't a mirror. "Hey, Cheyenne, does your sister have a car seat mirror?"

"Yes."

He blinked. "Where?"

The little girl reached over and pulled a mirror that was tucked at the top. "It's supposed to go here." She tried to put it across from where Ashlynn would lie but couldn't reach. "I need out."

"I'll do it." Chris unbuckled himself, then came around to the back seat and set the mirror on the empty Velcro spot. "Will that help her not cry?"

"Probably. That and Mama always plays *Frozen* songs to keep Ashlynn from crying." Her eyes welled. "I want my mommy," she wailed.

Tears ran down her face. Chris glanced out the car, but there was still no sign of Erykah, which meant he had to calm Cheyenne himself. "I know I'm not your mommy, but I can give you a hug. Would that help any?" *Lord, I don't know what to do. How do you help a five-year-old recover from the loss of her parents?* Chris felt so ill-equipped.

"I want Charlie," she whimpered.

As if understanding he was needed, the dog whined from his crate. Chris unlocked the kennel at Cheyenne's feet and took the guy out. He immediately settled in the little girl's lap, and her cries slowly subsided.

A minute later, Erykah returned to the car, looking harried and close to weeping herself. She settled Ashlynn into the car seat. Her tears stopped when she noticed the mirror.

"What just happened?"

Chris pointed to the mirror. "Cheyenne also said we need to play the *Frozen* soundtrack."

"One or two?" she asked.

110

"There's more than one?"

"Yes," she and Cheyenne spoke simultaneously.

"Mama plays them all."

Chris didn't know if *Frozen* was better than "Baby Shark," but he'd take anything else at this point.

"Hey, Cheyenne, I need to put Charlie back in his crate. Will you be okay?"

She brushed the tears away. "Yes."

He settled Charlie back in, then walked around to where Erykah stood outside the truck. "You okay?" He lowered his voice, hoping the kids couldn't hear him through the closed doors.

"I'm tired." She sounded so defeated.

"Hang in there. You're doing great."

"Am I?" A lone tear slid down her cheek, but she quickly wiped it away, averting her gaze.

Saying nothing, Chris tugged her into a hug. She wrapped her arms around his waist, laying her head against his chest. She fit so perfectly. A sigh left her lips, and she burrowed closer. He wasn't sure how long they stood out there, but it was enough that Ashlynn started crying again.

"I'll go turn on some music. Let's see if we can keep driving."

"All right," Erykah murmured.

Chris opened the door for her, then rounded the front. He quickly found the soundtrack and pressed play. Ashlynn's cries settled to a whimper, then stopped altogether. Blessed relief filled his heart as his mind cleared of her cries. He quickly put the gear in drive and headed for the freeway. If the music worked, they could drive another hour or two before the baby would need to be fed again.

Cheyenne soon fell asleep, and after her, Ashlynn did too.

Erykah reached over and squeezed his arm. "Have I thanked you yet?"

"Pretty sure you did that yesterday."

"It's a new day, and you deserve more thanks," she said.

"I'm not sure that's true. You're the one who needs to be thanked." He glanced at her and winked.

"No, sir. I'm this close"—she held up her thumb and pointer close together—"to losing it. I want to cry constantly. I feel like a failure because I can't get my niece to stop crying. I have no idea what I'm doing."

"But you're doing it. You've given all of your attention to them and made sure they're clothed, fed, and not alone. They know you love them and want nothing more than to take care of them. You're amazing."

"I'm a terrible aunt. Maybe if I'd lived closer, this wouldn't be so hard." She sniffed, staring out of the passenger side window.

"Erykah." He laid his palm on top of her hand. "You're grieving. Give yourself grace."

"I have a question for you." She shifted to face him.

"Sure, what's up?" He glanced at her, then returned his gaze to the road.

"You believe in a higher power, right?"

"Well, not just a higher power. I believe in the one true God and His Son, Jesus." And now he was just getting the idea that she didn't. Sadness filled his heart. How could she go through this loss without knowing the Lord? No wonder she felt all the things with such a heaviness. "Your sister believed in Him, right?"

Her pastor had officiated the ceremony, and a lot of the visitors had known Ellynn and Asher from church. Hopefully that meant they'd accepted the salvation of Jesus before and had the comfort of eternal life.

"She did. Even sent me a Bible, though I never read it." Erykah blew out a breath. "I regret that. I regret not giving her faith more thought simply because she asked me to consider it."

"Are you considering it now?" Hope lit in him like the smallest of flames.

"Yes, but I know nothing. I don't know where to start. The Bible is huge. But you keep praying and . . ." She sighed. "Something happens inside of me. I don't know how to explain it, but I want to know more. The thought that heaven could be real, that I could potentially see Ellynn again . . ."

Chris glanced over in time to see her shrug. "I'll help." He'd do anything to ease her burden. He wasn't sure what that meant in the long run, but Chris knew he couldn't leave her to deal with life's lemons all alone. He'd once been abandoned, and he never wanted anyone to feel the burden of being forsaken.

"Thank you . . . *again*." She chuckled.

"Well, here's what we'll do. You read the Bible, and I'll answer your questions."

"Where do I start? And I don't have it with me."

"That's not a problem. I have an app on my phone you could read from, or you could download one on your phone."

"Okay."

He gave her an app suggestion, which she immediately downloaded.

"Now what?"

"Start at the book of John. It's the fourth book in the New Testament." He explained the difference between the Old and the New Testaments, then how the first four books in the New Testament were known as the Gospels. "John is a good place to start because he loved explaining who Jesus was and why He's so important to the faith."

"All right."

Silence filled the cab. As she read, Chris prayed. He prayed that Erykah would come to know Jesus and accept the gift of His sacrifice. He wanted nothing more than for her to live a life with God. Chris had been through a lot in his forty-two years, and he couldn't imagine getting through any of it without having God on his side.

When Tracey left him standing at the altar alone, something had cracked in his chest. Chris had felt a little less-than ever since. After that day, his self-worth had plummeted. Out of all the years he'd been single, that had been the worst. The one that had him questioning everything. But one thing he knew for certain: God had been with him. Bit by bit, He'd healed Chris and helped him learn forgiveness. Even so, Chris had never wanted to dive back into a relationship until he saw how happy Lamont and Tuck were with their fiancées. Now Chris knew Erykah, could call her friend, and a small part of him wanted more with her.

But he didn't need a psychology degree to know the timing was awful. She was going through something traumatic, which meant he needed to remain firmly in the friend zone. Erykah needed Chris in that role more than a romantic relationship.

This morning she took up his offer of a place to stay with the kids and mentioned moving into his basement with the girls while looking for a more suitable family home. Her condo building had some larger apartments, but she wasn't sure that a condo was the best place to raise two girls. She wanted a yard for Charlie and the girls to play in.

If she was moving in, that meant there was no way he could ask her out on a date.

Timing is everything, Gamble. She needs to heal. She needs Jesus. Quite literally, in fact.

So yeah. As much as it stunk, he could logically see the friend zone was the only place for him to be. Now he just had to accept the fact.

Fifteen

In the beginning was the Word, and the Word was with God, and the Word was God. He was in the beginning with God. All things were made through Him, and without Him nothing was made that was made. In Him was life, and the life was the light of men. And the light shines in the darkness, and the darkness did not comprehend it.

The beginning paragraph of John captivated me. It read lyrically, but at the same time, I couldn't make sense of it. I didn't necessarily want to admit that to Chris, but then again, he did say I could ask him anything.

But I didn't want to. If I read this over and over again, wouldn't I be able to make sense of the words for myself? Only, why was *Word* capitalized? Did it have a bigger meaning than *word*?

And why were tears pricking my eyelids once more? Couldn't I go a day without crying? Ashlynn finally slept soundly, and Cheyenne wasn't giving me pitiful looks with every mile Chris drove away from Kentucky.

Then again, maybe it was the pressing sense of failure

that weighed heavy on me. I couldn't make my nieces happy. I'd failed my sister in more ways than I cared to count. And nothing in this Bible made sense.

I let out a low sigh. "I don't understand this," I said quietly. I could feel Chris's gaze on me, and my cheeks heated with embarrassment. "Will you please help me make sense of it?"

"I'd be happy to. Read the part that you don't understand."

My voice wavered as I reread the paragraph.

"Okay, now give me your questions," Chris said.

"Why are there numbers after some of the sentences? Why is *Word* capitalized?" I read it again. "Is it a person, and if so, do they have a name other than the Word?" I could feel wrinkles popping up in my forehead. "I thought this would be easier to read."

"You know, your questions make a lot of sense."

"They do?" I looked at Chris.

"Yes. I've read it with understanding for a while, but when I think back, John confused me in the beginning of my faith journey as well."

A bit of the pressure eased. So it wasn't uncommon not to understand. Somehow that comforted me. But . . . "You're not just saying that?"

He chuckled. "I'm not. I promise." He paused, then continued. "The Word is Jesus. He's the one who was with God in the beginning, along with the Holy Spirit, but we'll get to that later. Jesus is the light of the world, which is cool when you consider the first thing God created was light. There are so many connections between the Old Testament and New Testament, and they all point to the hope of Jesus as our Savior."

Okay, some of that made the paragraph make more sense. "If the New Testament talks about the Old, shouldn't I read that first?" Why go out of order? That triggered me.

"Some people find the Old Testament tedious. They don't like the genealogies or reading about wars and death. It's historical in nature, but also prophetic because it foretold Jesus's birth and what He'd do on earth and in heaven."

"What's the first book in the Old Testament?"

"Genesis."

I told my app to go to that spot. I didn't want to read out of order, though history had never been my favorite subject. Too many dates and facts to remember. But I wanted to get this right.

In the beginning God created the heavens and the earth. The earth was without form, and void; and darkness was on the face of the deep. And the Spirit of God was hovering over the face of the waters.

Then God said, "Let there be light"; and there was light.

"Okay, so in Genesis it talks about the Spirit of God."

"Yep. The Holy Spirit, or Holy Ghost, as some people say."

This was much easier to read. I could understand each day as life slowly formed on earth. I'm not sure the scientific part of my brain could accept creation theory as truth, but I could read the passage and understand it in a logical sense.

As we drove in silence, I read. I continued chapter after chapter, stopping only when I needed to ask a question. Chris never treated me like my doubts were absurd. He never sighed or huffed like the constant interruptions of his quiet time were bothersome. In fact, I got the feeling he was *happy* I kept asking questions.

This openness and lack of judgment wasn't something I'd ever experienced in my life. My mom tired of my questions when I was young and would make me sit in my room until I learned to keep my mouth shut. In school, kids ridiculed me for asking questions, while my teachers always praised me for them. Still, I learned as I grew and matured that people resented inquiries. It made me seem like a try-hard, as some of the new residents would say whenever another inquisitive resident was in their pool. Questions put people on guard.

Not Chris.

He sat in the driver's seat completely relaxed. I'd glance his way occasionally because I liked looking at the person I was talking to. Okay, fine. Chris was extremely good-looking, and peeking at his handsome profile while asking questions was a great way to kill two birds.

Plus, I was in awe of this man. I had never met someone who would put their life on hold to help another. Surely that wasn't normal, no matter how many times he professed otherwise.

"I have a personal question," I said.

"Yeah? Shoot."

"Why did you put your life on hold? Why are you here?" I bit my lip. There probably was a better way to ask that, but I couldn't properly formulate all the thoughts running through my mind.

"I've been alone, and I've also grieved. I believe no matter what a person is facing, they should never face it alone." He paused. "I couldn't help but notice there wasn't any family at the funeral." He glanced my way, then at the road. "How come?" he asked softly.

"I have no idea where my parents are." I cleared my throat. That was a subject I didn't want to talk about. "And you know about Asher's family."

"I'm sorry."

"What about you? What's your family like?"

118

"Small." He ran a hand across his chin. "My dad died when I was ten."

"What?" I breathed. "From what?"

"Car accident. Icy roads and not a good ending."

Could my heart break any more? That explained why he was so empathetic. He knew exactly what I was going through. Though icy roads hadn't claimed Ellynn and Asher, a driver who'd had a heart attack had caused the same outcome.

"My mom entered the workforce after that. She'd been a stay-at-home mom but ended up working her fingers to the bone until I graduated from high school. After that, she decided to take it easy."

Understandable. Raising Ellynn after I graduated from high school had taken a toll, one I didn't speak of because it had been worth it. We both had a better life because of my hard work. Call it vanity, but I was proud I'd given that to her.

I shifted in my seat to face Chris. "What does your mom do now?"

"Nothing. I bought her a home when I could afford it. Her retirement pays the rest of her bills, and she lives the social life in her fifty-five-and-up community."

"Do you see her often?"

He shook his head. "Mom wasn't very . . . nurturing. I think Dad's death flipped off that switch, and all she could focus on was putting food on the table and clothes on my back. When I successfully graduated from college, she considered her job done. She retired and moved to Denver. I see her if I make it up that way."

"She doesn't come down to visit you?"

He shook his head again.

Why? He was such a good man. I'd had more joy in my life since he befriended me than I'd had in a really long time. My heart ached for him. I couldn't imagine him not wanting a better relationship with his mom . . . the way I used to with mine. But there was also one other thing I didn't understand.

"How are you so . . . joyful, then? I've never seen you upset or even sad. You seem to live a solitary life like me and . . ." I didn't want to admit that I was lonely. That sometimes sadness gripped me and all I wanted to do was climb in my bed and stay there. But I had a job that gave me a reason to get up every morning and not give in.

Ugh. You should've moved closer to Ellynn.

"Honestly, Jesus is the reason I can smile. He's the reason I normally don't feel lonely or abandoned."

"Normally?" Did he have days like I did?

He rubbed the back of his neck. "Lately, I've felt a bit isolated." He glanced at me. "My friends are engaged." He shrugged. "It's hard not to feel like the odd man out."

"But that still means you aren't alone." I grimaced. Did that sound as pathetic and attention grabbing to him as it did to me?

But Chris merely reached over and grasped my hand. "You're not alone anymore."

Something fluttered in my middle and warmth spread through my entire being.

Just then, Ashlynn whimpered. I turned and saw her shifting in her car seat. The mirror also showed her eyelids fluttering.

"I think it's mealtime." I faced forward. "Are we near a stop? Cheyenne could probably use a bathroom break too."

"Yeah. Let's just stop for dinner. Then we can all fuel up and make it the rest of the way to our hotel."

We stopped at a fast-food restaurant just as Ashlynn's whimpers turned to full-fledged cries. I unbuckled her from the car seat, holding her close to me as I grabbed the diaper bag. I probably needed to figure out how to use one of those wraps Ellynn used.

Chris helped Cheyenne out of her seat and held her hand as we walked inside.

"I'm going to change Ash's diaper."

"Want me to order food for you?"

I glanced at the menu. "Yes, a number five, please."

"On it."

"Thanks, Chris." I offered a smile that I hoped showed my fullest gratitude for all he was doing.

"No problem."

He and Cheyenne went to stand in line, and I headed for the bathroom. Ash's cries settled as I got her into a fresh diaper. I grabbed the bottle I'd pulled from the cooler and popped it into her mouth. Greedy sounds of sucking came as she attempted to wrap her pudgy hands around the bottle.

"She's darling. How old is she?" A woman asked as I made my way toward our table.

I stopped and looked at the older woman. "Seven months." Tears sprang to my eyes. Ellynn wouldn't be here for Ashlynn's first birthday. My breath shuddered as I attempted to take a steady breath.

"She looks just like you."

My breath hitched. "O-oh. Th-thank you." *Do not cry, do not cry. Do. Not. Cry.*

But I could feel the tears coming. I speed-walked away from the woman. Chris must have noticed something, because he stood and met me partway.

"What's wrong? Did someone hurt you?" His gaze scanned the premises.

"A lady thought Ashlynn looked just like me." My voice sounded scratchy to my ears.

Chris pulled me into a hug, and my chin quivered as I struggled to gain control. The last thing I wanted was to break down in the middle of this place and have people wonder what was wrong with me. Ash continued to eat undisturbed by Chris and me hugging with her nestled between us.

"Auntie Erykah, you okay?" Cheyenne tugged at the hem of my shirt.

I stepped out of Chris's embrace and smiled at her. "I am now."

"Do you miss Mommy?" she whispered.

I nodded vigorously as another bout of tears tried to creep up on me. Cheyenne wrapped her small arms around me, and something shifted in my chest. No matter what, I was going to be here for these girls. No matter if Ashlynn continued crying incessantly or if Cheyenne hated Colorado. I would show up every single day just to make sure they knew they were loved and not alone.

Sixteen

Chris stared at his home from the comfort of his truck. Late October had brought another snowfall, which had canceled his latest film day with PathLight. David wasn't happy with the delay, so Chris needed to come up with something to appease the director.

For Gamble on Nature's channel, he'd been able to upload some YouTube shorts of animals who didn't hibernate that he'd spotted in the wild. Before he'd left work this evening, Cameron said they already had tens of thousands of views. Sometimes he couldn't believe this was his life.

The center had been noisy as the elementary students would've rather been outside instead of inside learning about animal habitats and how to help the environment. His head still rang despite the pain reliever he'd swallowed midday. Now he had to gather up his courage to go into his former sanctuary, where Cheyenne and Ashlynn had done nothing but wail since they'd arrived yesterday. God forgive him, for the very thought drained Chris.

Cheyenne thought his house was ugly and didn't want to live in the basement. She'd made her feelings quite clear in a tantrum Chris would have expected from someone younger.

Ashlynn simply cried. She probably picked up on the emotions of everyone else and reacted in the only way she knew how.

Frustration from Erykah, anger from Cheyenne, and sadness from the baby. Chris wanted to be a light to them all, but right now his well was dry.

He leaned his forehead against the steering wheel. "Lord, help me, help them."

The words echoed in the cab and settled in his heart. All he wanted to do for Erykah and her nieces was ease their burden. He wanted to make the transition of care for Erykah as easy as possible. Maybe he should've encouraged her to just set the kids up in her living room until she purchased a larger place. Had he made a mistake by moving them to Woodland Park?

Yesterday he'd unloaded the trailer that carried the girls' items and stored them all in the basement. He'd moved furniture around until it actually looked like a separate apartment. Granted, they came up to use the kitchen or sit in the living room. Cheyenne hated that he didn't have her favorite streaming apps, but last night, Erykah managed to appease her with the use of a tablet. Cheyenne had watched his blooper reels and actually laughed a few times. Chris only had one streaming app, but he'd have to talk to Erykah today and find out which additional ones he needed to purchase. He wasn't a huge TV show or movie watcher.

He sat back and looked up at the cloth ceiling. He should go in. See if Erykah needed help with the girls.

Just another minute. Sit in peace, and let the Lord fill you up.

Instead, all his mind could think of were the ways he could continue helping his new friend and her new charges. Man, life had a way of uppercutting you to the chin and knocking you out flat. He honestly didn't know how Erykah still stood. She was incredible.

His phone chimed.

Lamont
How you holding up?

Tuck
That's what I wanted to know. You back at work or hanging with Erykah and the kids?

Chris
I'm hiding in my car. Maybe in a minute I'll get the nerve to go inside.

Lamont
Whoa. You okay? Mentally, I mean?

Chris
Just tired. So tired.

Tuck
Man, sounds like you need to just be still and rest in the fullness of God.

Chris
Hence the hiding in the truck.

Lamont
Wherever it's quiet, right? We'll leave you to your peace. Know I'm praying.

Tuck
Same. You're a good man and doing a good thing. Let your light shine, but make sure you have enough fuel to do so.

Chris
Appreciate you guys.

Lamont
Same. You two have been a huge influence in my life.

Tuck
Agreed. Y'all make me more mature.

Chris
I take full credit as the oldest in the group.

Lamont

Have at it, grandpa.

Tuck

Chris slid the phone back into the inner pocket of his puffer jacket. Now he didn't feel so bad for sitting here in the silence. He'd take another few minutes and just be still like Tuck advised. Let his heart empty out his worries to the Lord and go inside better equipped to lend a helping hand.

Ten minutes later, he exited the truck and trudged up the snowy sidewalk. *Don't forget to shovel after dinner.*

He stomped on the outdoor mat while unlocking the door, then walked in. A heavenly aroma greeted him. The smells of a pot roast and bread welcomed him. Had Erykah really cooked while watching after her two nieces? That was so not what he'd expected. He'd fully intended to cook for them all when he arrived. He'd have to mention that he could pull his weight in household chores when he saw her.

But the toys littered around the living floor momentarily distracted him. As did Cheyenne lying in the middle of the floor with a doll in her hand, held up high before her.

"Hey, Cheyenne."

She tilted her chin up to look at him. "Hi, Chris."

He'd gotten her to drop the mister on the road trip out here. "Where's Charlie?"

She sat up and peered around the room, a frown marring her smooth forehead. "He was just here."

Great. Was Chris about to find something shredded, or had the pup done his business somewhere?

"Charlie?" He whistled low, something he'd started doing when he'd first begun watching the pup.

A tinkle that sounded like a dog collar met his ears. Chris watched for the dog and realized he was coming up the stairs. He trotted over, tongue lolling out.

"Hey, boy. Need to go out?"

Charlie barked.

"All right. It's cold outside, but I think you'll like it."

"He doesn't," Cheyenne said. "He cried when I took him to the backyard earlier."

"Did he go?"

She nodded.

"Then he'll get used to it. I'll grab a ball and let him get some exercise."

Chris spent the next fifteen minutes outside with the pup until Charlie trotted close to him and plopped on the concrete deck.

"Tired, huh?"

Charlie panted.

"Let's go inside and hang out with the girls." Chris let him inside the back door.

Erykah stood in the kitchen and glanced over at him. "Oh, you're home."

"Yeah. Took the dog outside for a bit."

"I made dinner." She bit her lip.

"You know you don't have to do that, right?"

A shadow fell over her face, and she turned away.

Crap. He reached for her arm. "Erykah."

"Hmm?"

He wove his fingers through hers and squeezed. "I'm so grateful for the meal, but I meant, you have a lot going on. I'm more than happy to handle cooking dinner." She'd been a machine since they arrived yesterday. If she stayed so busy, when would she have time to grieve?

She turned and faced him, arms folded across her chest.

"You've done so much, Chris. So. Much." Her voice shook. "The least I can do is make dinner for you. The *very* least."

He wanted to pull her to him, to give her another hug, but the folded arms were a neon sign he wouldn't ignore. Chris slid his hands into his pockets and nodded. "Okay, thank you for dinner."

A choked laugh fell from her lips. "You're welcome. It's ready. Let me get Cheyenne to wash her hands."

"I'll wash up in here."

Thank goodness he'd managed to remove his foot from his mouth. After washing his hands, he dished up a bowl for him and Erykah. Then he found one of Cheyenne's bright orange kid-sized plates and scooped up some roast for the girl. He had no idea if she'd eat it. Supposedly kids were picky eaters. He could only pray she wouldn't give Erykah any grief. She'd doled out enough theatrics during that tantrum yesterday. Apparently basements were the stuff of nightmares. He'd blame Macaulay Culkin for that one, though Cheyenne may have never watched any of the movies in the *Home Alone* franchise.

He didn't understand her concern considering he had a finished basement. Maybe Cheye just nitpicked because of the unfamiliar surroundings. She had to get her heartache out somehow, and that had showcased in a fit that lasted for-ev-er while she pounded the carpet and cried about life being unfair.

Chris placed the dinnerware at the table, then came with the rolls Erykah had heated up. He'd bought the rolls at the farmers' market and frozen them before they left for Kentucky. Thankfully they warmed up well in the oven. He breathed in the yeasty smell now permeating the house.

"I don't want to eat this." Cheyenne pouted as she came to stand by the table. "It looks like poop."

"Cheye, don't say *poop* at dinner." Exhaustion filled Erykah's voice.

"When *can* I say it? At breakfast? When I need to use the bathroom?" She glared at her aunt.

"Are you hungry?"

"Not for poop." Cheyenne gave Erykah a pointed look.

Chris would have laughed if not for the frustrated look on Erykah's face. "Hey, Cheyenne."

"Huh?" She studied him warily.

"Have you read the book *Green Eggs and Ham*?"

Her lower lip poked out. "Maybe."

"Remember how he didn't want to try the eggs, but in the end, he really liked them?"

She nodded slowly.

"Then consider that this could be a really good meal you're missing out on because you don't like the way it looks."

"All right," she whined.

Cheyenne sat down, and Erykah followed suit.

"May I say grace?" he asked.

Both of them nodded.

Chris bowed his head. "Lord, thank You for this meal. Please bless the hands that prepared it, and may the food nourish our bodies. Amen."

"Amen," Cheyenne said loudly. She tilted her head. "What happened to 'God is great, God is good'? Didn't your mom teach you that one?"

He stifled a laugh. "She did. When I got older, I started saying different prayers. Did you like this one?"

"Sure, but I don't know what *nourish* is. Sounds gross." She scrunched up her face as if physically affronted by the word.

Erykah's shoulders shook, and her lips twitched, but somehow she didn't laugh. "He meant he wanted the food to give us all the good stuff we need to keep growing healthy. Sort of like taking a vitamin."

"Oh. I eat the gummy ones. They taste like candy, but Daddy says they aren't." She froze, then sniffed, looking down at her plate. "Why did they leave me?"

Big fat tears rolled down her cheeks, and Chris felt like his heart would split. There was so much heartache here, and he couldn't do anything to make the passage of time go any faster or to make the grief be any less. All he could do was let them cry in comfort and peace.

He moved, picking up Cheyenne as she wiped at her face. But it was no use. The tears came faster than her little hands could make them disappear.

"They'll always be in your heart, Cheyenne. Always," Chris murmured.

"Really?" she stuttered.

"He's right, Cheye." Erykah pointed to her heart. "They'll live in our memories forever."

"I don't want a memory. I want them here. Now."

Frustration and despair warred for her attention, but in the end Cheyenne settled against him and hiccupped until her tears were gone. He and Erykah said nothing. She merely got up, reheated all of their plates, and then they attempted round two of eating.

Silence filled the table, and for once, Chris couldn't think of anything lighthearted to say. And maybe that was a good thing. Maybe you didn't have to always fill silence with platitudes or attempt well wishes. After all, the Bible did say, "Rejoice with those who rejoice, and weep with those who weep."

So Chris would sit in silence and mourn with the two women who had lost two important people in the blink of an eye.

Seventeen

The music wasn't working.

Normally when I came into the operating room, my classical playlist bolstered me. The soothing music reminded me that I knew how to do the current surgical procedure. But today, the sound failed to bring comfort.

The room was filled with tension, and I feared the source stemmed from my own misery. From the moment I entered the hospital, I'd received condolence after condolence. I might have even snapped at Dr. Bryner when he told me he was sorry for my loss.

Chris said I'd come to hate that phrase, and he wasn't wrong. Relegating Ellynn's and Asher's deaths to a loss seemed heartless. They weren't lost. They were dead. I couldn't imagine the dread they must have felt when that car crossed over the median and headed straight for them. A lump formed in my throat.

Angry tears threatened to blur my vision, so I cleared my throat. "Scalpel," I said in my most stern voice.

Unfortunately, this surgery couldn't be performed laparoscopically, since the bone had broken through the skin. I needed to widen the opening and get in there to set the bone. I pushed thoughts of my family out of my head and concentrated on the patient in front of me. He deserved my full attention no matter what the others in the room were thinking. I didn't know if they were pitying me, and frankly, that didn't matter at the moment.

Focus. You've done this surgery hundreds of times. You've got this.

By the time the patient was ready for stitches, sweat dripped down my back despite the freezing temperature in the room. I stepped back. "Suture and send him to recovery."

"Yes, Dr. Kennedy," Dr. Collier replied.

I left the room and removed my gloves and gown, tossing them in the correct bins. Then I scrubbed my hands and arms clean. Drying them, I left the OR and took in a deep breath, leaning against the nearest wall.

"Are you all right, Dr. Kennedy?"

I bit back a groan as my superior came to stand by me. "Just a little warm."

"Ah yes, they never have the rooms cold enough, do they?" Dr. Cook's brown eyes twinkled.

I'd always thought of him as fatherly. He had a perfect white beard that shone against his brown skin. He was a little portly in the middle. Not enough to have a true gut but noticeable against his lean frame. Still, his eyes always seemed to glint with merriment, and his tone was always kind.

"Not today." I slipped off my cap, letting air hit my twists. Still, I felt too warm.

"I appreciate you returning to work." He paused, as if gathering his thoughts. "But perhaps it's too soon."

I bit the inside of my cheek. "Bereavement leave is only two weeks."

"True, true. But upon further discussion with HR, you actually qualify for the Family Leave Act since you are now guardian to your nieces. We can give you twelve weeks of unpaid leave to adjust."

Twelve weeks? My blood pressure must've tanked, for I felt the color drain out of my face. I couldn't stay home for twelve weeks with Cheye and Ash. I loved them dearly, but twelve weeks of proof that I was a failure as a caretaker was too much. I needed to stay busy. I had to provide for them and pay for two mortgages. I just couldn't stay home for three months.

"I need to work," I stammered out.

Dr. Cook studied me. "Perhaps, but I think at least another week at home with your nieces would do you some good."

Cheyenne would certainly appreciate the time. She'd hated it when I'd left for work this morning. I hadn't yet enrolled her in a school because I was still looking for the right place to live. So until then, she wasn't in school, but fortunately, Chris offered to bring Cheyenne and Charlie to work with him. The hospital had a nursery available to staff employees, so Ashlynn was there now. But remembering Cheyenne's glare when I'd walked out the door this morning still pierced my soul.

Why does every decision I make regarding the kids seem wrong?

"How about you submit the paperwork for another week, hm? Your team can handle things in your absence."

I opened my mouth, then shut it. He wasn't wrong. "Okay. You'll need to get another surgeon to fill in for those patients who can't wait any longer for treatment," I said. Those people didn't deserve to be rescheduled again. Three weeks was a lot of time to wait when you were in pain.

"Understood. I'll take care of them myself if it comes to it."

"I appreciate that, Dr. Cook."

"Then off you go."

I swallowed past the lump in my throat and headed for my office. I'd submit my paperwork, then drive home, well, to Chris's house. Maybe having another week would give me some time to find a decent place for the girls and me. They needed a stable environment, especially considering how their world had upended. I'd contacted a real estate agent last week, but the first batch of houses she'd shown me were too far from work. Not to mention Ashlynn had cried the entire time we were viewing the homes.

After I picked her up from the nursery, Ashlynn blissfully fell asleep in her car seat as I drove back to Woodland Park. When I pulled up the gravel road, I took in Chris's home. The place suited him perfectly. When he'd first mentioned a log cabin, I was thinking a one-story place backed into the woods. But this was three stories with wooded land standing like a backdrop.

I also wasn't expecting just how much he lived a sustainable life. Sure, he'd mentioned collecting water, but I hadn't considered how regular rolls of paper towels would be switched out with reusable terrycloth. Or how cloth napkins could be used in place of paper ones. Not to mention, he owned a compost bin and several recycle bins that made me pause any time I needed to throw something away to figure out which receptacle the item belonged in. And though he said I didn't have to follow his lifestyle, what kind of person would I be if I just threw away a plastic bottle if he was collecting them for recycling purposes?

I was learning a lot from him and reexamining my own habits. I blew out a breath. I was tired of thinking. Tired of not feeling like my life was mine any longer. Everything had changed. I wasn't resentful so much as . . . hurt.

I thought about Chris's prayers, how much they comforted

me. Could I try doing that on my own? Try reaching out to Someone I wasn't sure was there? That seemed . . . offensive, but at the same time, I needed an answer.

"Are You there?" I whispered in the still of the car.

The phone rang, and I jumped in my seat, then slapped a hand over my heart. I quickly answered the call, glancing over my shoulder to see if Ashlynn had awakened. Thank goodness her eyelids remained closed.

"Hello?" I opened the car door, exiting the driver's seat before softly shutting the door so I wouldn't bother Ash.

"Hey, it's Chris."

"Hi. What are you up to?"

"Just finished a visit from some middle school students interested in animal science." Chris cleared his throat. "Hey, I hope this doesn't weird you out, but I got the feeling God wanted me to call and pray with you."

"W-what?" My heart thumped in my chest. Was he serious? Was there really Someone listening to me?

I looked up, but the cloud-covered sky simply forecasted snow and gave me no glimpse into a higher power.

"Erykah, did you hear me?"

"Sorry." I shook my head, trying to clear my thoughts and listen to Chris. "I'm just stunned."

"Why's that? Should I not pray for you?"

"I literally just asked if God was there. I was wondering if He could see me, hear me. And then you called to offer prayer." I swiped at the salt tracks lining my cheeks.

"Then let me pray. He's listening."

I could feel sobs gathering in my chest. How could God really exist? How could the stories I'd been reading in the Bible be true? How could Someone who demanded holiness from the Israelites look at me and think I was worth anything? I couldn't follow the logic.

It's because it requires faith.

Goose bumps pebbled my arms. Where had that thought come from? Had I read that in the Bible? Had Chris uttered those words?

"Dear heavenly Father, I want to thank You for seeing Erykah. For hearing her prayers. For being willing to answer her questions. You love her beyond bounds and know how desperately she needs to be seen and loved. Please guide her in her care for her nieces. Please comfort her in the passing of her sister and brother-in-law. Please continue to show me how to help her as she searches out answers regarding You. In Jesus's name, I pray. Amen."

"Amen," I whispered, not knowing what else to say.

Just as in times before, Chris's words centered me. Settled the angst gathering like a blizzard. "Thank you," I added.

Seriously, I was so tired of thanking him. I hated being beholden to anyone, and I owed Chris in spades. Though I suspected I'd never be able to repay him for all the good he'd done for me and my nieces. I couldn't understand how he was still single. Why hadn't a woman snatched him up? All those complaints about wondering where the good men were, and I'd literally bumped into the best one at a restaurant.

Granted, bringing any romantic feelings into the situation would only muddy the waters. I needed to keep a clear head. I had to remember that remaining friends was in all of our best interests.

Still, when he flashed those baby blues my way, my stomach dropped, and I wanted to swoon like the starlets of old.

I rounded the car to grab Ashlynn. "I'm headed into the house. My boss told me to take another week of leave."

"Wow, really?"

"Yes." I winced. "Shoot, I should've stopped by and picked up Cheyenne and Charlie."

"Of course not. You have Ash, right?"

"Right."

"Then watch over her, and you'll see me and Cheye later. I'll bring dinner."

"Chris . . ." I tried for the same tone I used on Cheyenne.

He chuckled. "Okay. Fine. You can cook if you'd like. But maybe we can go and do something fun this weekend?"

"Fun?" What was that? Was fun even appropriate during grief?

"Yeah. A good hike."

I snorted. "Hiking isn't fun."

"Bet I can prove it is."

"What if it snows again?" The last snowfall had only just melted away.

"Snow won't kill us."

"Hypothermia is a real thing. As is losing a limb to frostbite."

"Okay, Dr. Doom. I'll make sure I take you to an appropriate place and have you dressed in appropriate attire for the weather conditions."

My lips twitched. "Sounds like a plan."

"See you later, Erykah."

The hairs on my neck stood up at the huskiness in his voice. How did he manage to say my name in such a way that my heart yearned? "Bye, Chris," I rasped.

I hung up the phone before embarrassment at my own vulnerable tone could echo in my head. What I didn't want to do was replay our conversation and analyze any undertones or hidden meaning in his words. Chris was a friend and would stay that way. I couldn't let myself hope for anything more. Not with the girls now in my care. They needed my full attention. I didn't need to distract myself with the little tiny crush that was developing.

No, I'd swat it away like a birdie in badminton. I just needed to get through this adjustment period.

And find a new place to live.

Maybe if I didn't see Chris's baby blues every day, I could keep him firmly in the friend zone. It was time to focus on a new place. Find something close to the hospital, in a good school district, and with a backyard for Charlie and the girls to play in.

Eighteen

Who said taking kids on an easy hiking trail was a good idea?

Chris thought the paved Perkins Central Garden Trail would be a nice, easy walk to get the girls out of the house. Change of scenery, so to speak. It didn't hurt that the Garden of the Gods offered some seriously stunning views. Walking alongside the sandstone monuments always made Chris think of God, and more specifically, Psalm 19. *"The heavens declare the glory of God; And the firmament shows His handiwork."*

Standing out in nature, Chris always felt like creation pointed to the Lord. He wanted the peace that came with that knowledge to fill Erykah and comfort the girls. Except Ashlynn apparently hated riding in the stroller and Cheyenne thought the rocks were boring.

"They're brown." Cheyenne folded her arms.

She looked just like Erykah doing that.

"I'd say more tan than brown. They've got that orange undertone."

The glare on her face should scare Chris, but he was determined to get on Cheye's good side. He'd thought they'd bonded over the past week with her coming with him to work. PathLight had done a photo shoot of Chris so they could promote the docuseries, and Cheye had been calling out poses with the photographer. Watching her had allowed Erykah to house shop during the day without the worry of the girls getting tired from going house to house.

Yet after a week of house hunting, she hadn't found a place that fit her and the girls' needs. Either the homes were too far away, not in a good school district, or too small. She'd found something wrong with each one.

"I think they're pretty," Erykah said. She reached out her hand, wiggling her fingers, as if to tell Cheyenne, *Hold my hand.*

The little girl slid her palm against her aunt's. "But this is boring."

"Charlie likes it." Erykah pointed to the pup on the leash.

"Because he thinks this is the biggest bathroom." Cheyenne spread her arms wide, then flopped them back to her sides with a groan.

The way she gave drama all day long, the girl could be an actress.

Erykah smirked, then met Chris's gaze. For a moment, his heart stopped, and his gaze lasered onto hers. Looking at the gentle smile that softened her features made him want to tug her into his embrace. He felt like a dad out with his kids and adoring wife.

It's an illusion. They're not yours.

Chris's steps faltered as he tore his gaze away. He'd been close to this before. He hated that Tracey had broken her word and left him with the fallout, but if she hadn't, he wouldn't be here for Erykah.

She needed a friend, and his thoughts were veering more and more away from that path. The best thing would be for her to find her own place. Then he wouldn't have to worry about the feelings that arose in him every time he looked at her smooth brown skin or smelled her intoxicating scent that begged him to draw closer.

No, they should've gone house hunting instead of coming to one of Colorado Springs' iconic landmarks.

They finished the trail and headed back to the parking lot. Maybe next time Chris would just take the kids to the zoo. Surely Cheyenne wouldn't be annoyed by looking at animals. She seemed to like hanging out with Kimble and the other animals at Gamble on Nature.

"Dr. Kennedy!"

Erykah stiffened as someone yelled her name across the parking lot. They both turned to face the voice. An older man walked toward them with a younger woman at his side.

"I thought that was you."

Erykah's lips contorted into some weird smile . . . or was that a grimace? Chris almost laughed at the discomfort covering her face. It reminded him of how she looked when Ashlynn blew out a diaper yesterday. However, the discomfort now came from these two people, which put him on edge.

"Dr. Cook. What are you doing here?"

"I enjoy a good leisurely stroll every now and then." His gaze flicked to Chris's, then back to Erykah. "I see you're relaxing, as I suggested."

Wait, this was the boss who gave her another week of leave?

"Attempting to." She bounced Ashlynn up and down, which was the baby's preferred method of being held. She hated being still.

"Who is . . . ?" Dr. Cook's voice trailed off.

Erykah's eyes widened, and she looked so startled, so uncomfortable, Chris had to step in. He offered a hand. "Chris Gamble. I'm a friend of Erykah's."

"Oh, how nice to meet you." Dr. Cook shook his hand enthusiastically. "Erykah is so quiet at work that it's hard to imagine her with friends."

Excuse me?

The man had the grace to look ashamed. "I'm sorry. That's not at all what I meant to say."

"Grandpa, stop talking," the young woman said. She flashed a sympathetic look to Erykah. "He doesn't know when to be quiet sometimes."

Erykah let out a hesitant laugh. "He does talk often at work."

Dr. Cook raised his hands in a *What can I say?* gesture. Obviously, he knew the comments were true.

"Are you guys just arriving?" Dr. Cook asked.

Erykah shook her head. "Leaving."

"Sorry to have missed you." He turned a curious gaze toward Chris. "Chris Gamble? You're not the YouTuber, are you?"

Chris could feel his neck heating. "I do have a channel there."

"He has a million subscribers now." Erykah smiled at him. "I think he's doing great things."

She knew how many subs he had?

"I want to be in his next video," Cheyenne spoke up.

Chris had almost forgotten she was there. He looked down at her. "I'm not sure that's a good idea." He was leery about the ramifications of minors on such a public platform. Then again, he could make one private, just for her to watch and know she was on YouTube.

"Charlie got to be in a video."

"Because he's a pup." Erykah had agreed to let Chris put up a video about what to do when you spot an animal in the wild when out with your dog.

"Your channel is fascinating." Dr. Cook gestured to the

visitor's center behind them. "Was it your idea to go for a walk?"

"It was."

Dr. Cook nodded his head. "Good exercise and a beautiful view."

"It is."

"Well, I've taken up enough of your time." He turned toward Erykah. "I hope you enjoy the rest of your day. And I apologize for sticking my foot in my mouth."

"It's okay, sir."

When they got to the car, Chris went to buckle Cheyenne, but she pushed his hands away. "I got it."

"Sorry."

Erykah peered across the car seats to meet his gaze. "He's right, you know," she said softly.

"Right about what?"

"I don't have friends."

He stared at her. "What am I? Chopped liver?"

"I mean at work." She smirked.

"Are you supposed to? Is it a requirement?"

She finished buckling in Ashlynn and straightened. "Why are you making things difficult? You know I'm not good at small talk and being kind." Her face contorted into self-disgust. "I've never been good at knowing what to say."

"You speak to me just fine." He shut Cheye's door and rounded the back of the vehicle to stand next to her. "Besides, what does it matter what Dr. Cook thinks? Doesn't it matter that I call you friend and think you're one of the kindest people I've ever met?"

Her chest rose and fell. "Really?"

He hated the uncertainty in her voice. "Truly." He tucked one of her twists behind her ear. "I think you're perfect the way you are."

143

She leaned her cheek against his palm.

Chris could easily cup the back of her head and press his lips against hers. In fact, the honey scent that often teased his senses made him want to do just that. Would the taste of honey sweeten her kiss?

"Chris . . ." Erykah's warm breath caressed his lips.

He leaned forward. This was a woman ready to be kissed. *Willing* to be kissed. How could he ignore that?

His phone chimed, and he jolted backward. Erykah almost crashed into him, but he gripped her upper arms, steadying her.

"Sorry. I need to get this." That ringtone only rang for one person. "Hey, Mom."

"Chris, how are you?"

He blew out a sigh, annoyed that he hadn't been able to kiss Erykah. He glanced at her, but she averted her eyes and opened the passenger door, getting in before he could mouth *sorry* or any other pointless platitude. Only he didn't actually know if he was sorry.

"I'm fine, Mom." He squeezed the bridge of his nose.

"Good. I was wondering what you'll be doing for Thanksgiving. Do you want to come up?"

And leave Erykah and the girls alone? "Um, I'm probably hanging with a friend. She's had a difficult time this year." He made his way slowly to the driver's side. "You could come down, though." Which she wouldn't.

"Well, I mean, I could."

He blinked. "What?"

"Come down. Are you having a meal at your place?"

Uh . . . He hadn't given it a thought. What would the girls want to do? "I suppose I could."

"Great. I'll be there. Can I come the night before and sleep in your guest room?"

"Of course." Surely Erykah would be in a new place by then. Thanksgiving was a couple of weeks away.

"Then I'll see you then. Bye, hon."

"Bye, Mom."

He stared at his phone. What had just happened? He looked into the car, and his breath hitched. What *hadn't* happened?

Nineteen

Chris's three-story home did *not* provide the amount of space I needed.

Everywhere I turned, his comforting scent followed. How did the man hang around animals all day and work outdoors but not stink? Talk about unreal. Instead, he smelled like pine or something woodsy. My senses went on high alert whenever I caught the aroma trailing him like a cartoon. Guess that made me a toucan, because I definitely wanted to follow my nose.

You're losing it, Erykah. Get it together.

Someone with my education shouldn't be having a mind melt whenever a certain man neared. I'd managed to get all the way to forty-one and not lose my cool over a man. But remembering the way he cupped my cheek, eyes darkening with intent to kiss . . . Well, there was a first time for everything.

But that's an event I refuse to think about.

I swallowed. I needed space.

Taking dinner out of the oven, I set the dish on top of the stove. A piercing scream rent the air.

"Cheyenne!" I dropped the oven mitts and raced to the living room.

Cheyenne held her left hand as tears streamed down her face.

"What happened, sweetie?" I dropped to my knees, trying to figure out what was wrong with her.

"Are you okay?" Chris huffed as he ran in from wherever he'd been.

"No," Cheyenne wailed. "There's a piece of wood sticking out of my finger."

I blinked. That 1970s horror scream had stopped my heart because of a splinter?

"Let me see." Chris knelt down before her. "Oh yeah, I see it. I can pull it out."

"No way!" Cheyenne jerked her finger, then whimpered. "It hurts too bad."

"Sweetie, if you let Chris take it out, it'll feel better."

The shade my niece tossed me would've shaken me coming from an adult. As it was, I had to bite down on my lip to keep from laughing. How had I never known how much of a drama queen Cheye was?

Tears pricked my eyes as I thought of Ellynn missing this.

"How about you hold Charlie while I take it out?" Chris asked. "That way he'll make sure you won't feel any pain."

"He's a puppy. He doesn't have powers like that."

Chris's lips twitched as if suppressing a smile. "Actually, holding dogs has been scientifically proven to make us happier. So if you're happy while I remove this piece of wood, you won't notice when it's gone. Well, you will because the pain will go away too."

"You promise?" she asked so quietly, I almost had to lean forward to hear her.

"Promise."

"O-kay," she drawled out.

Chris headed to his room to get tweezers while I went to find Charlie. I found him in the girls' room, guarding Ash while she lay asleep in the crib. How she hadn't woken up from a scream that would make Jamie Lee Curtis proud, I didn't know. But I was thankful. Ash had been extra cranky lately, and the internet searches I'd conducted told me she was probably teething . . . or grieving. I hated that I didn't know which was which.

"All right, Cheyenne. I've got my make-you-feel-better kit ready," Chris said.

This. This was why it was hard to keep my wits about me. How was Chris so kind, charming, and just downright sweet? The part of my heart I'd buried deep inside seemed to awaken with every act of kindness he performed.

Cheye wrapped an arm around Charlie, and he snuggled in closer. She squeezed her eyes tight and held out her fore-finger.

"Wow, you're so brave," Chris said.

I watched as he pulled the splinter out in one go. My heart swelled at how calm he was. Chris was an amazing man.

"Ta-da." Chris held up the splinter in front of Cheyenne. Her mouth dropped open. "But it's so tiny."

"I know. Sometimes it's the tiniest of things that really hurt."

Her brow furrowed, but she said nothing else.

I turned to Chris and mouthed, *Thank you.*

Of course, he mouthed back.

I let my cheeks curve upward in hopes that the feelings gathering steam in my chest would lessen. He just had to keep saving us over and over again. Surely this wasn't real affection filling my heart to the brim, but some kind of love-of-rescuer complex. I shook my head. Was that a real thing?

"Are you okay now?" I asked Cheyenne.

"Yeah."

"Hug?" I held out my arms, hoping this was the right next step.

Cheyenne launched herself at me, and I had to brace myself to prevent us from tipping backward. My forty-plus-year-old body did *not* like the catapult motion. Still, I wrapped my arms around her and murmured, "All better now."

It's what I imagined a mom would say, maybe even what Ellynn had said to soothe her daughter in the past. *I'll make you proud, Ell. The girls will know how much you loved them and how much I do too.* I swallowed.

"I miss Mommy and Daddy," Cheye whispered.

"I miss them too." I kept my tone low, not wanting to ruin the moment. She wasn't as vocal as I thought she should be on the subject. I didn't want Cheyenne becoming closed off like I had when my parents hadn't provided the care I needed as a child. Growing up to be the mother figure to Ellynn had taken a lot out of me. All I wanted was for Cheye to progress naturally and not have any disasters grow her up faster than necessary. Was that even possible?

"I'm glad you're here, Auntie Erykah."

"So am I, sweetie." I drew in a steadying breath. "I'll be here for a long time."

Please.

I didn't know who I was pleading to, but then again, there was only one entity I was trying to determine the existence of. If He was real, maybe He'd make sure Cheyenne didn't lose another person close to her.

Please.

Cheyenne drew back, and her brown eyes were luminous. "I'm hungry."

"Good, because dinner's ready." This I could handle. I

stood up and helped her to her feet. We walked into the kitchen, and Chris followed.

"How much longer before Ash wakes up?" he asked.

I glanced at my smartwatch. "Probably twenty or thirty minutes."

"Guess you'd better eat, unless you want me to grab her when she cries?"

"No." I shook my head. "My responsibility."

"But you have help." Chris gave me a pointed stare.

I could practically hear his thoughts. *"You don't have to do this alone. I'm here as long as you need me."* Or something else that ran a ten on the chivalry scale. Seriously, how *was* this man still single? I wanted to take a step closer and reenact that moment we had at the Garden of the Gods yesterday. *No you don't. You're essentially playing house right now. Of course your hormones are reacting. That's all this is.*

My face flamed at my thoughts. Did Chris think I was desperate? Had I imagined that look in his eyes?

"You okay?" Chris whispered. "You look upset."

"I'm just wishing I could shut my thoughts down for the night, or at least for the length of a bathroom break."

He chuckled. "You've got that many, huh?"

"Like you wouldn't believe." *And they're revolving around you.*

"Maybe we should do something after dinner to distract you."

"Like what?" Because wasn't an almost toddler, a five-year-old, and a puppy enough? If I got any more distracted, I'd need to check into the nearest hotel to remember who I used to be.

My gut clenched. *Oh my word.* That wasn't what I meant. I'd give anything for my sister to be alive and home with her kids again, but I didn't want to go back to being alone. What kind of monster was I that I wasn't thankful that people were around me, and I had a real purpose? I closed my eyes against the shame of the thought.

You had purpose before. You still helped people. Now you're helping family.

"How about a movie?" Chris asked, interrupting my self-reprimand.

I eyed Cheye. "For all ages?"

"Of course." Chris leaned forward to whisper in my ear. "I know how to stay in a kid-friendly lane."

With a jaunty whistle, he turned away from me and set about dishing up dinner. Yet my brain was still focused on his nearness. That low whisper raised every nerve ending along my entire body. Then there were his words. Was he being kid-friendly on purpose . . . with *me*? If so, what did that mean? I had so many questions and no answers. I wanted to ask . . . and yet I didn't.

"Can you grab the silverware?" Chris asked.

I blinked. "Right. Silverware." I glanced at the table. "And napkins."

"Thanks, Erykah."

Do not shiver at the way he says your name. Do. Not. I shivered.

This man was going to unhinge me. I had to get out of this house. "You know, maybe instead of a movie, I'll just take a walk around the neighborhood."

Chris's blue eyes pierced me. "By yourself?" There were many questions behind those two words.

I nodded. His gaze roamed my features, and sympathy replaced the worry. "Understood. You can go right after dinner, if you need to. I'll take care of the girls."

I really did need to. Because sitting here, knowing he would bless our food, then talk equally to me and Cheye would undo what little self-control I maintained. I wanted to gush how I had a crush on a guy I'd met by chance at a hamburger place and then at the governor's mansion. I've watched enough movies to know some people would call it fate or destiny. Apparently, we'd left coincidence at the first meeting when we ran into each other a second time.

Still, having a crush on a guy was a big deal for me. I didn't normally have any type of romantic feelings. Worse, I didn't have a sister who could advise me anymore. I'd been the first person Ellynn had called when she'd met Asher. I'd been the first person Asher had talked to before he'd proposed. Now I was a lone island. My nieces were too young to confide in, and Charlie, well, he kind of talked back, but I didn't think this conversation would prove to be in his wheelhouse. I needed someone real to talk to.

Are You there? Are You real?

But how did you talk to God? I knew prayer was the answer, because I'd seen Chris in action. But seriously, how did we communicate? Was there a back-and-forth action that happened between a human and a deity? That seemed so . . . so . . . *wild*. What made me think I was important enough to talk to *the God*? I wasn't. I was merely me.

But I needed to talk to someone . . . anyone. I was desperate.

Twenty

Chris stared out the window facing the backyard as Erykah navigated the tall pines with Charlie and a flashlight. He hated letting her go without company, but he fully understood the desire to be alone with one's thoughts.

Lord God, whatever is going on with her, please help her sort through it. May she find You and be able to understand how You're the answer to any question. Please comfort her. I'm not sure if she's stressed from all the changes or if something else is on her mind. Whatever it is, please guide the way for Erykah. Be the literal flashlight in her hand, if that's what it takes.

Because as much as Chris wanted to be out there trudging through the weeds with her, he had an equally important assignment: Ashlynn and Cheyenne. He didn't take the trust Erykah gave him regarding her two nieces lightly. He was thankful he could be there for them all, no matter how inadequate he felt.

Taking care of both girls for the length of a walk—or however long Erykah would be outside—shouldn't make him nervous. But it did.

Cheyenne asked so many questions, and her temperament

seemed to change with the wind. Ashlynn liked him well enough, but she fed off others' emotions and was prone to excessive crying.

He turned away from the window to see Cheyenne with her hands on her hips and her brow furrowed. *Uh-oh*.

"You okay, Cheye?"

"I'm hungry."

She'd just eaten a good-sized helping of the casserole Erykah had made. How did her stomach have room for more food? "Do you want seconds?"

"No." She tossed her curls. "I want an apple."

That was a good snack choice. "Okay." He grabbed one out of the fruit bowl and handed it to her.

"But . . ." Tears welled up in her eyes. "You didn't cut it."

Right. *You're dealing with little kids. Get it together.* Chris grabbed his bamboo cutting board and a knife out of the block on the counter. Speaking of which . . .

Chris pushed the block of knives against the wall, then eyed Cheyenne, trying to measure her arm span. No way he wanted to risk her being able to reach those and possibly injure herself. He sliced the apple into eighths, cutting right through the core, then dropped the slices onto one of the colorful plastic plates Erykah had brought from her sister's house. He set the dishware at the table in front of Cheyenne's booster seat.

"There you go, kid."

"You cut it wrong!" she cried. Her head tipped back, reminding Chris of one of the *Peanuts* gang.

All he could see was a wide mouth letting out a wail that would surely wake Ash.

He rushed to her side, hoping to hush her before Ashlynn started crying. "How? What did I do?"

"What's that?" Cheyenne pointed to the seed in the middle of the apple. "Mommy never put *that* on my plate."

"It's the seed."

"Is that like a baby apple?"

It was all he could do not to tease, but the seriousness in Cheye's gaze kept Chris quiet. He drew in a breath, trying to figure out how to keep her from rejecting the perfectly good apple.

"How about I just remove them?" He scooped up the few seeds that had landed on her plate.

He'd have to be more careful in the future. Weren't seeds a choking hazard? Even though Cheye was bigger than Ash, she could still easily choke. Come to think of it, so could Chris or Erykah for that matter.

"There. All better." He smiled at her. "I promise it'll still taste like an apple."

She shook her head. "I don't want it."

Chris ran a hand down his face. Of course she didn't. Cheyenne got out of the chair and stalked out of the kitchen like she hadn't just wasted a perfectly good apple. Though Chris would eat it. He couldn't throw it away without a perfectly good reason. *How about the fact you don't want it?* Yeah, not good enough.

Before he could reach for a slice, cries sounded on the baby monitor. Ash was awake. He headed down the steps to the basement and went straight to their room. The eight-month-old held on to the crib rail, tears rolling down her face.

"Hey, Ash. You okay? Need a diaper change?" *Please be dry, please, please . . . please.*

She held out her arms, so Chris picked her up. Her cries settled, and she nuzzled her head right under his neck. Holding her made him want a family. Was this what his friends were trying to get him to have? A life with a good woman and the kids who came from that relationship?

"You want a bottle?" Ash's bottom didn't feel soggy, thank goodness.

She whimpered and made a grabbing motion as if wondering where the milk was. He probably should've prepared one before coming downstairs, but he hadn't wanted her to cry long. Her cries went straight to his heart and ripped it to shreds.

"Let's go get a bottle," he murmured.

Instead of Ash making a happy noise, the longest, wettest sound of wind ripped the air and stopped him in his tracks. That wasn't just a normal sound of passing gas. Not when the arm that was tucked under her diaper had warmed.

"Oh no." He looked down at the cherub. "I thought we were friends? Why would you do this?"

Her bottom lip trembled, and her dark eyes filled with water like something out of a *Looney Tunes* episode. "Don't cry, don't cry, baby. I'll change you."

God, help me. Please don't let it be a blowout.

He still remembered the time that happened on their road trip.

Chris laid the baby on the changing table and wished for a bandana to cover his nose and mouth. He grabbed a fresh diaper to have at the ready, then unsnapped the onesie. As he peeled the flaps back, the full force of the smell smacked him in the face.

"Whew, Ash, you let that rip!" He wrinkled his nose and waved a hand in front of his face.

She giggled. The more he waved his hand, the harder she laughed. If that wasn't just the cutest thing, he didn't know what was. While he cleaned her up, he continued to make the stinky face—yep, he'd named it—and gained more laughter.

Cheyenne found them and glared at Chris from the doorway. "Why is she laughing?"

156

"I was making a face. It made her laugh."

"I want to see."

He did it again. Instantly, Ash laughed, but Cheyenne's glower only darkened. "You're not funny."

Chris bit back a sigh. "Do you want to do something fun?"

"Like what?" She eyed him warily.

Like what, indeed. Erykah was outside, walking who knew where, and he didn't want to encroach on her quiet time. "Want to watch a movie?"

"I want a tea party."

Chris stared at her as his thoughts stuttered to a halt. Had her father had tea parties with her? Would Chris if he had a daughter? Definitely.

He nodded. "'Kay. I'll be right up there." He held up the diaper. "Do you want to throw this out for me?"

"No way," she yelled as she raced toward the stairs.

"No running!"

Chris's phone buzzed. He grabbed it, checking to see if the notification was from Erykah.

Tuck
Chris, are you able to make the wedding or not?

Tuck
And I'm not being accusatory.

Tuck
Shoot, I should've called.

Lamont
Nah, this is entertaining.

Lamont sent a GIF of a foot going into a mouth. Chris had to laugh at the image.

Chris
I should be able to. I'll fly out day before and day after. I don't want to be gone too long.

Tuck

I hope you know Erykah and the girls are welcome.

Would that be a good thing to invite them to? Would she be able to get away from work?

Chris

I'll ask her. But pray for me. My mom is planning to visit for Thanksgiving.

Lamont

Is that not a good thing?

Chris

She never comes to me, so I can't help but worry.

Lamont

Never ever?

Chris

NEVER

Lamont

😔

Tuck

Then pray I will.

Lamont

Same. Also, don't forget our wedding is New Year's, and Erykah and the girls are definitely invited.

Man, his friends were in full wedding season. Chris thought back to his almost wedding and again felt relief that he hadn't married Tracey. Perhaps breaking your word wasn't always a bad thing. He knew now that they weren't meant to be, but even so, the trauma of the whole ordeal still clung a little too much.

Lord God, thank You that my friends found the right women. Please bless their marriages.

Chris

I'll invite her.

Tuck

Piper and I would love to have her there. We're keeping the guest list small to keep reporters away.

Piper's dad had confessed to using blood-doping agents on his horses early this year. It had been a huge scandal that'd broken out a couple of months before Piper's own horse—not associated with her father's thoroughbred farm—had won the Kentucky Derby. His confession had earned him a hefty fine, a lifetime ban from horse racing, and a five-year ban on betting. He'd missed jail time since the person who'd administered the drugs was the farm's veterinarian.

Chris

Bet. Ttyl. Gotta feed a hungry baby and have a tea party with the 5yo.

Lamont

#FamilyGoals

Chris smiled. Theirs wasn't the stereotypical family, but over the past couple of weeks, he'd come to feel like they *were* a family, though he didn't know if Erykah felt the same way or was merely tolerating his presence.

His mind reverted to the day before, when she'd leaned against his palm and stared up at him with big eyes that were signaling consent for a kiss. At least, that's what he'd believed until his mom had called and interrupted.

"What do you think, Ash?" he whispered. "Does your aunt like me?"

Ash looked at him like *Feed me.*

"Right. Sorry, baby girl."

As he prepared the bottle, Chris turned on the tea kettle. How could he pour the tea so it wouldn't burn Cheyenne's mouth? *Aren't tea sets plastic?* He needed to use a different liquid. Maybe Asher would've used apple juice since Cheye enjoyed it so much. He grabbed the bottle from the fridge, then made sandwiches.

"Cheyenne," he called.

Footsteps pounded. "Yes?"

"Do you have a tea set?"

"Yes," she said earnestly. "I'll be back." Her little arms pumped as she left the kitchen in a hurry.

Watching her was equal parts amusement and awe versus the very real tension of being exhausted from her energy. She quickly brought a tea set in.

"I'll get the tea and snacks ready, okay?" Hopefully he would cut the sandwiches to her liking.

"And I'll get the hats and feathers."

He frowned. *Feathers?*

By the time Cheye walked into the living room, Chris had the coffee table set up as the makeshift tea table. Sure enough, Erykah's niece walked into the room wearing a hat . . . and feathers. More accurately, she wore a neon pink feather boa. She placed a small hat on his head and gave him a green boa.

"Now you look like Daddy would."

He'd called it. Asher played dress-up and gave tea parties for his daughter. Chris could only pray he was doing the man proud and not disappointing him or his daughter. Stepping into the role of caregiver came with so many mixed emotions. No wonder Erykah needed a breather.

Chris pushed away his thoughts and smiled brightly for Cheyenne. "Should we take a picture?"

"Yes. We have to."

He grabbed his cell and adjusted Ash in his arms while she inhaled her bottle. "Say *cheese*."

"Cheese," Cheyenne yelled cheerfully.

Chris would have to show Erykah when she came back, but for now, he'd be present with her nieces and learn the ways of a successful tea party.

Twenty-One

I turned around the great room, looking at the house from this position. The home was three stories, brand-new, and in a good school district. Granted, the drive to the hospital from here would be longer than it was from Chris's house. Still, the place came with a Colorado Springs address and would provide a good environment for the girls to grow up in.

But something had me hesitating to give the Realtor the green light. What was it? The distance? The fact that I wouldn't be able to close on the house for another two months, meaning I'd be beholden to Chris for all that time? Or was it just not the right home?

My mind flashed to the image of Chris and the girls having a tea party. When I'd seen him wearing that green boa, I'd placed a hand to my heart, trying to suppress the ache in my chest. He'd worn a similar grin to how Asher looked when Ellynn had sent me a picture of my brother-in-law having a tea party with Cheye. I wasn't surprised that Chris was willing to play with my niece—the only surprise was how my heart reacted.

Looking around this house, somehow, I couldn't imagine

Chris and the girls having a tea party in here. *But that doesn't mean this isn't the right home.*

Only, how *was* I supposed to know which place was the right choice?

"What do you think, Dr. Kennedy?" Kate asked.

I gave her a brief smile. "It's certainly gorgeous."

"That it is. And brand-new, so nothing to fix."

True, but I'd heard of problems with new builds as well, usually due to shoddy workmanship. "Can I think about it before saying yay or nay?"

After spending time in the woods trying to talk to God, I still wasn't sure about my next course of action. I'd logically assessed everything in my life up to now and could make a debate for coincidence and science as the reasons for so many moments in my life that now could also be debated as a God thing. Yet I still wasn't sure if I fully believed in Him. I'd moved from skeptical to wanting to believe Someone cared for me and would watch over me. I just didn't know what I needed to see or hear to turn that final step into full-on belief.

"Of course," Kate replied, but the light was already dimming in her eyes.

I couldn't blame her. We'd looked at a lot of houses, and nothing screamed *This one*. Meanwhile, Cheyenne still wasn't enrolled in kindergarten.

She already knows how to read and write. She won't fall too far behind.

Yes, but . . . I wanted us all settled somewhere. We'd been in Chris's place for too long. Long enough for Cheyenne to depend on him, play tea party, and for Ash to coo and laugh whenever he was around. We'd skip on how much I depended on him through this whole ordeal. I needed to learn how to rely on myself and only myself once more.

"Dr. Kennedy, have you considered moving to other towns close to Colorado Springs?"

"Like where?"

Kate named a few cities and then said, "Maybe even Woodland Park."

My insides quaked at the mention of Chris's town. My mouth dried as I tried to formulate a response. "Um, I'm temporarily living there, but I'm not really sure I like the commute." Surely that was the reason I didn't want to live there any longer. It had nothing to do with the blue-eyed man who smelled like the woods in all the best of ways.

"I hate to point this out, but this house has an even longer drive than your current commute."

Something I already knew. "What are the pros again?" My gaze scanned the interior once again.

"There's a really good school district here." Kate studied me. "But if this isn't the home for you, I'm sure I can find something comparable in Woodland Park. You wouldn't have to uproot your kids."

I stepped back. This was too much. How was I supposed to plan Cheye's and Ash's futures? That was what Ellynn should be doing. If I uprooted them again, would that compound the trauma of losing their parents? *But you have to. You can't live with Chris forever.*

"Dr. Kennedy?"

I blinked, bringing my Realtor into focus. "I'll let you know what I decide soon."

"Fine." She sighed. "You know how to reach me."

I thanked her, then hightailed it to the car. Maybe I needed to take up running or something. Join a gym and get some restless energy out of my system, then I'd be able to focus on what mattered. *Or maybe consider grief counseling or a single-parent support group.*

164

As much as I tried to work through the pain of losing my sister and brother-in-law, some days the grief overwhelmed me. Looking in the mirror showed I'd aged. If it weren't for the girls, I'd probably still be lying in bed in a puddle made from my tears. But I knew what it was like when a parent checked out. The girls deserved the best of me. At least the support from Chris helped me not to feel like a true single parent.

But something's gotta give.

Because lately my emotions were too much. Taking care of the girls exhausted me. Ignoring the feelings I had whenever Chris was around made me panic, like that almost kiss. But the homes I'd toured . . . I just didn't *love* any of them. There was no feeling of rightness or a magical yes moment in my head. Only a heap of indecision and the pressure to pick a place in order to move on.

My condo had already sold, so moving back there wasn't an option. And surely Chris wanted his space and privacy back, but he had made it clear there wasn't a rush for me and the girls to find our own place. *I* was the one putting pressure on myself. I hated owing a person, and the amount of good deeds Chris had imparted on me . . . Frankly, it would take me a lifetime to pay him back.

Maybe if I took the step of enrolling Cheyenne into the school in Chris's district, I wouldn't feel like such a failure.

For now, I'd make the drive back to Woodland Park, hang out with the girls, cry myself to sleep for the umpteenth time, then drive to work the next day. I wasn't sure how my extra week off had flown by so fast. I'd looked into the leave act Dr. Cook had mentioned, but going unpaid for three months wasn't something I found helpful. What would help was screwing bones back together and inserting a new knee or hip. Solving my patients' problems would take my mind off my own.

As I drove down the interstate, my cell rang. I glanced at the NAV screen to read the caller ID. I didn't recognize the number, but the area code was Lexington. The auto accept connected the call.

"Hello?"

"Dr. Kennedy, it's Linda Simmons."

"Yes, how can I help you?"

"A court date has been set for you to be deemed a permanent guardian for Cheyenne and Ashlynn. They are willing to allow you to be present via video chat. Are you able to do so?"

"Yes. Thank you so much for the accommodation." I still wasn't sure if I could go back to Ellynn's house, knowing she wasn't there, and pack everything off for good.

Chris had informed me Piper and Tuck were willing to oversee an estate sale if need be. Everyone was so . . . accommodating. I didn't know how to handle that. Sometimes, I wanted to curl up in a ball and forget that this was my reality. I wanted my baby sister back. I wanted my goofy brother-in-law, who made my sister laugh more than I'd ever seen growing up with her. I wanted my beautiful nieces to have their loving parents. How could I be a substitute? I was married to my work and had only just now found a friend.

"Then I'll mark you down as video chat and confirm your date."

"Thank you, Ms. Simmons."

"If you don't mind me saying, I'm praying for you and the girls. God will see you through."

My breath hitched. Why did this feel like the brightest neon sign flashing in a desert showing me exactly where water was? I wasn't sure why that image popped in my head, but it resonated deep within.

"Thank you," I whispered before disconnecting.

I wasn't sure how many times I'd say those words, but

they might turn bitter in my mouth if I didn't remember that I'd gone from being completely alone to having someone I could talk to. I had someone who would comfort me if I needed it. Chris had become one of my dearest friends in this whole ordeal. He'd understand how I felt about being named permanent guardian. Plus I could talk to Charlie. He comforted me at night when no one else could.

At times I still felt like Dr. Erykah Kennedy, but having people when I used to be alone made me feel like a new species. I'd never been completely comfortable in solitude, despite how awkward I was around others. Even though being excluded and looking from the outside on every part of life had drained me, I was used to that song and dance. Social anxiety had been my companion long before Charlie whimpered in the bushes.

Even now I found myself seeking solitude from the constant attention of my nieces, a dog, and a YouTuber. In fact, Chris even asked me to be in an upcoming video. He'd already planned out his online video content for next month, wanting holiday-inspired shorts he could upload once Thanksgiving was over.

Somehow I'd gained a family when Ellynn had lost hers.

"Why?" I whispered. It made no sense. Why did this have to happen?

The silence in my car continued. There was no answer, and I had a sinking feeling I'd never get one.

I turned on my music, desperately trying to drown out the thoughts in my mind as I traveled the rest of the way home. By the time I parked behind Chris's gas guzzler—talk about irony—I was ready to be done with the day. But I still needed to cook dinner, hang out with the girls, and pretend like seeing Chris do domestic chores didn't give me tachycardia.

When I walked through the front door, chaos greeted me.

Cheyenne lay on the floor, arms and feet swinging as she screamed at the top of her lungs. Ash's wails were intermixed in the cacophony as Chris looked helplessly between the two.

I sniffed. Something was burning.

I placed my purse on the hook, hung up my jacket, then immediately took Ashlynn from Chris's arms. She tucked her head underneath my neck, hiccups shaking her little body.

"Something's burning. Did you attempt dinner?" I asked with a smile.

Chris muttered under his breath and raced into the kitchen. Knowing he had that alarm taken care of and Ash had now quieted, I knelt beside my other niece.

"We don't do that," I stated firmly.

Cheye halted her kicks and screams and stared at me. "Do what?" She sniffed as salt tracks marred her cheeks.

"Throw tantrums. That's not kind, and we always try to be kind." Flashes of a memory with Ellynn peeked through to the present, when I had to impress upon my sister the importance of acting completely differently from our parents. She too liked to throw a good tantrum, similar to the ones our mom did when she ran out of drugs.

"Chris won't let me have a snack."

"Probably because dinner is almost ready, Cheye. You can't eat both."

"Then I won't eat dinner!" Her voice ended on a yell.

I simply arched a brow and stared her down. When she huffed, I asked the question she knew must be coming. "Was that kind?"

"I don't have to be kind," she whined.

"Would your mama say the same thing?" I hated to ask. Her mom was gone. My sister wasn't here to navigate this or any other storm. But I knew Ellynn's heart, and no way she wanted her child to act like this.

"Mama's gone," she whimpered.

"I know. It hurts." I patted my heart. "Very much."

Cheye nodded.

"But don't you still want to make her happy?"

"Yes."

"Then please be kind. It would also make me happy, and I'm sure Chris would appreciate it as well. He's been such a huge help to us, hasn't he?" Poor man probably needed a walk outdoors.

"He fixed my baby."

Cheye had a baby doll she slept with that was beyond tattered. "How did he do that?"

"Gave her a dress!" She sat up, tears forgotten and a smile on her face. "He gave her a new dress, fixed her hair, and she looks almost new."

Had Chris sewn something? I turned to glance at the kitchen, and he gave me a thumbs-up. Guess that meant dinner was salvageable and we could eat.

"Did you thank him?" I asked, once more studying my niece.

Her head bobbed vigorously.

"Good. Now go apologize to him for acting that way and sit so we can eat dinner."

"O-kay." A petulant expression covered her face.

Guess she was like me in that department, found apologizing way too difficult to do. But remembering my childhood and all the ways our parents failed me and my sister, well, I wanted to be an adult who could apologize. I could only hope I'd raise the girls in a similar manner.

Twenty-Two

What was worse than attending a wedding with a woman who wasn't your wife and two kids who were slowly wrapping you around their fingers? Easy, attending a wedding by yourself.

"Come with me to the wedding. It'll get the girls out of the house. It'll be nice." Chris had smiled, hoping Erykah could sense how much he wanted her company.

"I think it's best if we stay here. We don't want to bother your friends more than we already have."

"They could be your friends too," he'd offered.

"I'm fine with how my life is now."

That last comment had sunk his stomach faster than an anvil in an ocean. He didn't know what happened on her night walk the other day, but ever since, she'd been pulling away. Pulling back from their movie sessions, from random texts throughout their day, and from those moments they'd been having that had been laced with more but remained unspoken. Like that almost kiss.

He blew out a breath. In a short while, Chris would watch Tucker and Piper exchange vows, and he had to do so knowing he was truly the fifth wheel in the group. Erykah wasn't an option, not with all that was on her plate. If he could accept the fact, maybe the pressure weighing his breaths down would ease.

He made his way down the white aisle to a seat on the groom's side. The sun shone, and the absence of clouds reminded him of another wedding—and how there had been no pronouncement of husband and wife. Instead of angst, he felt only irritation that he'd stayed in a relationship longer than necessary. *But you gave your word.*

He swallowed. Today wasn't about him or the fact he was here alone. Today, he'd celebrate Tuck and Piper, then go back home to the girls. For however long they'd be there. Maybe he should've offered to bring the kids with him and give Erykah a break.

No. She said she wanted you to have the break.

But in the short amount of time that Erykah and the girls had been staying with him, his heart seemed to have synced to theirs. Was Ash giggling over a face Cheye made? Did Erykah finally sign Cheye up for kindergarten, or would she put her in the hospital daycare? And Erykah Kennedy . . .

Well, there were too many thoughts for Chris to sort through, like how soft her cheek had felt against his palm.

Instrumental music pierced the air, and the attendees stood. Chris glanced at Tuck, who had a sappy grin on his face. Chris would've laughed if it weren't for the awed expression on Piper's face as her dad walked her down the aisle. As much grief as Chris liked to give Tuck for keeping his feelings hidden for so long, he couldn't deny that the wait seemed to be worth it for both of them.

He listened as the officiant led them through the vows, ring exchange, and then finally . . .

"It is my honor to introduce you to Mr. and Mrs. Hale."

Chris clapped with the rest of the guests as he stood. He

gave Tuck a slight punch to the arm as they passed down the aisle. His friend glanced over his shoulder with a grin. If Chris remembered correctly, the newlyweds would be doing pictures after the ceremony. They'd even asked Chris to participate, despite his absence from the limited wedding party.

"Hey, man. You look lost in thought." Lamont patted Chris on the back of his shoulder.

He pushed away the loneliness beckoning to him. Just because Erykah hadn't come didn't mean Chris was truly alone. Besides, he tried to live a life of singleness with gratitude, believing God had saved him from what would've been the wrong marriage. *Pull it together, Gamble.*

"Yeah, a little." Chris turned to the movie star. "Guess you're next." He forced his mouth upward. *But what's in store for me, Lord?*

"I can't wait." A huge grin covered Lamont's face. "I'd say yes today if I could."

"Really? Nothing about marriage scares you?" They moved to the arbor set up to the side like an outdoor photobooth.

"Of course it does. I'm human. But my fears stem from my inadequacies rather than any issue with Nevaeh. I wholeheartedly believe she's the right woman for me, but I'm worried I'll fail her when it matters most."

Chris could understand that. Right now he wondered if he'd failed Erykah by not convincing her that she had a place here. Would she retreat into her shell once more or, worse, go away?

He swallowed. "How do you think you'll fail Nevaeh?"

"Being the spiritual leader in our home." Lamont shrugged. "Sometimes I feel like I'm not good enough in my own faith walk."

"Man, that's the enemy talking. I know for a fact you're in

the Word every day. You pray multiple times a day. You make sure to rest once a week. You seek God's wisdom often." Lamont was a great example of discipline. Chris had no doubt he'd be on his knees for the duration of his marriage.

"I do do those things." Lamont slowly nodded.

"Then trust that God will equip you to be the leader of your family. Trust you know what to do if a trial comes against you, your marriage, or whatever." He nudged Lamont with his elbow. "God's been showing you how to walk with Him in your singleness so you'd be prepared for leading another in marriage."

He sighed. "Pretend I didn't say this, but I feel better now."

Chris laughed. Telling another guy what you felt inside wasn't always easy. But Tuck and Lamont always kept it real and made vulnerability easier to swallow. *Tell him what you're dealing with.* Only right now wasn't about him.

He clapped a hand on Lamont's shoulder. "You'll be just fine, young buck."

Lamont laughed. "Oh man, that sounds like something they'd say in those 1970s TV shows."

"Way to make a man feel old," he groused, but he wasn't offended.

"Middle age isn't so bad, is it?"

Chris thought about it. "Actually, it's really not. I'm at a place in my life that I'm mostly content."

"Mostly, huh? Is that why you looked introspective when I walked up?"

"Yes."

"Thinking about Erykah?"

"Something like that." Chris slid his hands into his pockets. With just that one question, all the thoughts he'd managed to ignore while focusing on Lamont came hurtling like a battering ram.

"Want to talk about it?"

Did he? Chris rubbed his chin, jolting at the smooth skin. He'd forgotten the clean shave he'd done for the wedding. "I feel like she's pulling away, and I don't know why. Is it grief? Something more?"

"Is she snapping at you, or has she gone silent?"

"Mostly silence. Sometimes I think my help has been more hurt."

Skepticism drew Lamont's brows downward. "How can that be true? Didn't you say she started reading the Bible and seeking God?"

"Yes."

"Then looks like you're helping." Lamont gave him a point-blank stare. "Remember that grief looks different on everyone. She may not be able to articulate what she needs from you. She's been through so many changes since she met you."

He was right. Chris had been so struck by her show of strength that he forgot that was sometimes another defense mechanism. Inside, she may be curling up ready to wave a white flag of surrender. "I should've known better," Chris murmured.

Lamont arched an eyebrow, but before he could say anything, the photographer called out to them. She gestured for them to join Tuck, Piper, and Nevaeh at the arbor. Lamont took his place next to his fiancée and Chris stood at the end of the happy couples. When the photographer said, "Cheese," Chris pasted on the brightest smile he could manage.

His phone buzzed in his pocket, and he itched to check it. Was it Erykah? A YouTube notification? Did Cameron need something back at the center? Whatever it was would have to wait until his cheeks could resume their normal position on his face.

As soon as they were excused from pictures and allowed to head to the reception, Chris had his phone out, scanning the many text messages.

> **Erykah**
> A polar bear's hair is not white. It's colorless.

> **Erykah**
> A chameleon's tongue is as long as its body.

> **Erykah**
> The lion has the loudest roar.

> **Erykah**
> Water bears exist.

He laughed at that last one. Why was Erykah texting him random animal facts?

> **Chris**
> Are you looking up animal facts for Cheye?

> **Erykah**
> No. She actually asked me to text you them. She found Wild Kratts on streaming and has been glued to the screen. I'm thankful because she was complaining of being bored earlier.

That made sense. He didn't think the good doctor suddenly cared about every animal on the planet. Though she liked to pretend she wasn't curious, he'd seen her teaching Charlie tricks and taking interest in Chris's own work.

> **Chris**
> Maybe read her one of the library books you checked out.

> **Erykah**
> She refused.

> **Chris**
> Build her a fort?

Erykah
How?

Had she never had the opportunity to do so? He knew her childhood hadn't been the best, but somehow her missing out on blanket forts saddened him. Chris searched the internet for a good video, then sent the link to her.

Chris
Here's how to do it. You can use your blankets, and there are some more in the closet next to the guest room. You have free rein of all the house amenities.

Erykah
I'll text you the results.

Chris
Please do.

He tucked his cell back into his interior pocket.

"You look happy," Piper said, coming up to give him a side hug.

"And you look beautiful, Ms. Piper." Her gown was simple in its design, but the pure joy on her face brought to mind the old adage of the person making the clothes, not the clothes making the person.

"Thanks," she said. "I'm so glad you came out. I know you probably wanted to be near Erykah and the girls."

Understatement. "They could stand to have me out of their hair." But the thought choked him up. Was he holding them back? He'd promised to be there for Erykah, but what if she didn't want him to be?

Déjà vu.

"I'm sure they miss you."

"Well, I miss them."

"I wanted to tell you to give Erykah my number. I'm not sure if she needs or wants another friend, but I'd happily be one."

"Thanks. I'll give her your number." Piper was a loyal friend to have, and Erykah would be blessed to have her in her corner.

"How is she doing? The girls?"

"About as well as can be expected. Cheye has a hard time and throws tantrums regularly. But I'm sure a lot of kids would throw them for less. Ash is fussy, though I think she's beginning to adjust." Probably didn't have to fight memories as hard as Cheye and Erykah were.

"I'll keep praying for y'all."

"Appreciate that."

Tuck stepped up next to Piper, placing a kiss on her cheek. "Thought I'd come ask my wife to dance."

She grinned. "I'm all yours."

Tuck guided her to the dance floor, and a song came on that had them both grinning and melting into each other's arms.

Chris was thankful he was going home on a flight tomorrow. As glad as he was to be here, the absence of Erykah was stark in the midst of the love fest. The only question was, Would she be happy he was under the same roof once more, or would she want more space?

Twenty-Three

I gripped the steering wheel as I waited for Chris to put his luggage into the trunk. Should I get out and give him a hug? *No.* We weren't *together* together. Still, it felt rude to just sit in the car waiting for him to hop in as I idled in the airport pickup line. Before I could come to a conclusion, the passenger door opened, and he climbed in.

Immediately, his woodsy scent greeted me as if to say, *Did you miss me? Did you forget what I smelled like?* Not likely.

"Hey," he murmured.

I tried for a smile, but my trembling lips probably made it look like a spasm. "Hi," I croaked.

"Chris!" Cheye shouted from the back seat. "I missed you. Why did you leave?"

"I went to a wedding."

She frowned as if this were the first time she'd heard such a story. Never mind that was our repeated refrain while he was gone for two whole nights.

"I want to go to a wedding," Cheye said.

"I'll let you know the next time I go to one," Chris replied smoothly.

Airport security caught my eye, so I put the car in gear and followed the signs to get us on the road home.

"How was it?" I asked. "I'm sure Piper made a beautiful bride."

"It was great. I've never seen two people so perfect for each other."

Really? How did he know that? Was that something people merely said, or did they truly mean the sentiment?

"Chris, Ash missed you too. She can't talk, but I know," Cheyenne said in a superior tone.

I equally loved and hated the fact that the girls missed him. How would they respond when we finally moved into our own place? Maybe pulling back was the right decision. Then I could guard my—*the girls'* hearts. Being their guardian also meant I had to protect them from life.

"Are they going on a honeymoon?" I asked, trying to keep the adult conversation going.

Cheyenne would interrupt us again, but Chris and I were used to that. This was how we talked at home. *Home.* Had Chris's place so quickly been labeled as *home* in my heart and head?

Stop thinking so much. Just enjoy him as a friend who's been on vacation and now returned. It should be that simple, right?

I glanced at Chris only to find him studying me. The strength of his gaze weakened my shields, so I swallowed against the urge to spill my guts and turned my gaze to the road. "Do I need to stop, or should I head straight h—to your place?" I asked. *Phew, that was a close one.*

"You can head home." His cell rang. "Hold on a sec."

I tried not to listen to his conversation, but it was kind of hard to ignore in the confines of the Rover. Apparently an animal needed assistance, and Chris was the closest staff member to help.

"Hold on, Cam. Hey, Erykah, could you swing by the center? Cam said someone's coming with a displaced animal."

"Sure." I took the next exit, instinctively knowing how to get to Gamble on Nature.

As soon as he ended his call with Cameron, Cheye piped up, "What does *displaced* mean?"

"An animal could no longer stay at its current location and needed to be moved." He sighed, running a hand through the soft curls on his head. His hair was just long enough for me to notice them and wonder what they felt like.

I tried hard not to stare at his smooth jawline, but whenever he shaved, my eyes were drawn to the warm brown skin. My fingers desperately wanted to trace the ridged outline of his jaw or, better yet, cup a palm to his cheek. My hand still remembered the last time it made contact with Chris Gamble.

That's not very friendly of you, Dr. Kennedy. Definitely not, but now the thought was lodged in my mind like a bone spur on a heel.

"It could also mean they found the animal at someone's house, and we're the only ones available to take care of it tonight."

"Did Cameron say what kind of animal?" I asked.

"Auntie Erykah, where are we going?" Cheyenne interrupted. "This isn't the way home."

Wow. How fast my niece had figured out the Colorado Springs area. "We're going to Chris's work so he can help that animal."

"Yay." She clapped her hands.

I glanced in the rearview mirror to see Ash's car seat mirror. She still slept. *Thank goodness.* I blew out a breath.

"I'll know more once I get there and am able to assess the situation," Chris said.

"It's not dangerous, is it?" We came to a light, and I stopped, turning to stare at my housemate. Only his expression was closed off.

But why? Usually he was so open with me. *But have you been open with him? Aren't you guarding your heart?*

Yes, but now the thought seemed ridiculous. This was Chris. The one who'd befriended me with no strings. The one who'd arranged a private flight from Colorado to Kentucky in the blink of an eye. Not to mention the way he'd helped me with the funeral arrangements when I'd been overcome with tears and unable to articulate Ellynn and Asher's desires. Chris was always there . . . and that was probably what scared me the most.

"It won't be for you. You and the girls can stay in the car while I'm in there." He rubbed his face. "Actually, maybe just drop me off. I'll get a rideshare home."

"Chris, that's too much money. I don't mind waiting for you."

I wouldn't leave him stranded—he'd never do that to me.

"Let's just play it by ear."

I nodded in agreement, then stepped on the gas as the light turned green. We said nothing more as Cheyenne took over the conversation. She and Chris played an animal game the rest of the way there, naming animals that represented each letter in the alphabet. By the time Cheye yelled, "Penguin!" I'd pulled into Gamble on Nature's parking lot.

"Are we going inside?" Cheye unbuckled her seat.

"Cheyenne," I huffed. "What did I tell you about that? You need to ask me first before you unbuckle."

"But we're here, and Chris needs our help, right?" Her big brown eyes looked so hopeful.

Chris rubbed his chin, then looked at me. I motioned with my hand as if to say, *The ball is in your court.* He nodded, seeing the motion.

"Yeah, Cheye. I could always use your help."

She grinned. "Good. Let's see what kind of creature this is."

"*Creature*, huh? Where did you learn that word?"

"*Wild Kratts*."

Chris chuckled.

I grabbed Ash from the car seat, swung her diaper bag over my shoulder, then followed the other two into the wildlife center. As soon as I stepped inside, the smell of animals hit me. I wasn't sure I'd ever get over that smell, but it wasn't exactly horrifying. However, the quiet of the evening surprised me. I'd never come here when there was no one else around.

An animal made a noise, and Ash's eyes rounded. I repressed a chuckle and nuzzled my cheek against hers. "It's okay, baby. Probably the ferret."

I'd seen videos of Chris and Kimble. The black-footed ferret made noises I'd never imagined an animal could make. Maybe they scared off predators in the wild. Ferrets weren't the biggest animal, that was for sure.

"Will the person come through the front door?" I asked Chris.

He was turning on lights left and right. "We actually intake animals in the back. I'm just lighting the way, so we don't bump into anything. Gotta make sure the girls are safe." He looked over his shoulder and made a face.

Ash immediately giggled, tilting her head to the side. This was her new way to laugh, and it filled me to the brim. She was such a happy baby, and the way she laughed chased away my sadness and brought joy to my life. I'd always loved my nieces—how could I not? But taking care of them had changed my love in a way I didn't know how to describe. I would die for them, but I wanted to live for them more.

If only I could figure out exactly what that looked like. Parenthood seemed to be a fluid concept that required daily change, and the person inside me who loved routine struggled with the notion I couldn't predict each day. Sure, I could say I'd go to work, drop Ash at daycare, et cetera, but that was it. I didn't know if Ash would have a blowout diaper one day or upchuck the next because she thought a jar of snap peas was repugnant. It certainly smelled bad enough to induce projectile vomiting.

Regardless, not knowing what would come my way threw me off and made me want to retreat, but I had to continuously show up for the girls. Plus, I didn't want Chris taking on more responsibility. Cheyenne and Ashlynn were mine, not his. How could I expect him to give up so much for nothing in return?

Maybe that was why he was so quiet today. Maybe being with his friends had reminded him of how his life was before me, and he missed it. But of course he was too nice to say anything.

Will you say something?

Wasn't that a good question.

I shifted Ash to my other hip, giving my right side a break. She'd grown and was probably ready to be in twelve-month clothing even though she hadn't turned one yet. Chris's phone rang, then he headed down the hall.

Chris's gaze darted to me, then away. "I'll be right back."

"Can I come?" Cheye asked.

"Not yet. Let me see what kind of creature it is first." His blue eyes twinkled as he stared at her.

I tilted my head, studying them as silent communication passed back and forth between Chris and my niece. Their interaction wasn't unusual. It looked just like it would at his house. So why was he being more close-lipped with me? Had I done something wrong? And if so, what?

Twenty-Four

Chris opened the back door, trying to push aside the image of Erykah's confused face. She must've picked up on his altered behavior. Not that he could really feign surprise. He'd decided on the airplane to give her the space she desired, but judging by the look on her face, that's not what she wanted. Or at least, if he was interpreting it correctly, she wasn't feeling gratitude but hurt.

"Hey, you Chris Gamble?" the animal control officer asked.

"I am." Chris stuck out a hand. "What do we have here?"

"Someone found a female black-footed ferret in their garage. Called animal control, and now here we are."

Chris examined the small crate the animal was in. "Is she hurt?"

"Negative."

"All right." Chris signed the transfer paperwork.

Then he got one of the clean crates from the bottom shelf and opened it so that the man could transfer the ferret with ease. She quickly moved to the other enclosure, and Chris closed the crate doors. After locking up behind the man, Chris turned to the ferret.

"Welcome to Gamble on Nature. I'm Chris," he said,

peeking into the crate. "You're going to be okay. I might even introduce you to Kimble if you're well-behaved."

She chucked at him, and he laughed.

He didn't think she was someone's pet. There was a look about her that spoke of the wild, but the quickness with which she'd traveled from crate to crate spoke of domestication. Maybe she'd recently been released from a breeding farm.

He turned on the laptop in the in-processing room and pulled up their standard questionnaire. Grabbing some gloves, he opened the crate into an enclosure that would allow him to examine the new ferret and ensure she was physically okay.

After going through the checklist, Chris determined she was fine. Probably got turned around and found herself in the garage. He should've asked the animal control officer if the ferret came from a rural neighborhood or suburban one. That's something he could do tomorrow morning. He sent himself an email detailing that and added a note to check for chipping, so he wouldn't forget to do so tomorrow, then slid his phone back into his pocket.

"Hey, you wanna meet Kimble?"

Actually, this would be a good thing for Erykah and Cheyenne to witness. He wasn't sure if Ash would care, but it was safe for them to watch. He coaxed the ferret into her crate, then slid off the gloves.

He walked down the hall and found the girls in his office.

"What is it?" Cheyenne asked.

"A ferret."

"Like Kimble?"

He nodded.

"Can I see?"

Chris glanced at Erykah, asking the question with his gaze. She nodded.

"Sure. Do you want to come too, Erykah?" Chris asked.

Her mouth parted, and he smiled, trying to show that he wasn't totally closed off. But he was going to need clearer direction from her. Did she want the ease and friendliness that was normally between them, or did she want space and less of him?

He swallowed against the indigestion that question raised in his insides.

"Yes, that sounds like fun."

Chris motioned for them to follow him. Cheye slid her hand into his and started chatting animatedly as they headed toward the back. Apparently she'd been researching ferrets, rereading the book Erykah had checked out of the library for her.

"Do you think she'll like Kimble?"

"I hope so."

"Are you going to name her?" Cheye asked.

"Probably not. We have to find a new home for her."

"No!" Cheyenne squeezed his hand. "Keep her. Don't send her away."

He drew in a breath. Chris stopped walking to kneel before her. "I want the best for every animal I meet. You know that, right?"

She nodded, but her lip remained poked out.

"So it may not be best to keep her here. There might be a better place for her. Plus, if she has a chip saying she belongs somewhere else, I'll have to give her back."

"Would you ever give me back?" Cheye whispered.

Chris froze. He wanted to look toward Erykah, but he had no idea if she could hear their conversation since Ash had started babbling when Cheye first started talking. *Lord God, please give me wisdom.*

He looked her in the eyes. "Cheyenne, we're friends, right?"

She nodded vigorously.

"Since we're friends, that means I will always be here for you, even if we don't live together." The words had his stomach in knots, but he had no idea why.

Sure you do. Erykah and the girls will move. They'll no longer be in your life on a daily basis.

But until he was hauling boxes, he'd forget that bit. He was needed now, and that had to be his primary concern. Besides, the Lord wouldn't want him to turn into a ball of worry thinking about the future.

"Okay," she murmured.

He stood.

"Everything okay?" Erykah asked, coming to stand next to him.

"Tell you later," he mumbled.

"Got it."

They continued to the back room. He pointed to a spot they could watch, then went to retrieve Kimble. The little guy was playing around in his enclosure. Probably came out to eat the dinner that was left for him before the last person clocked out. Kimble happily climbed up Chris's arm and onto his shoulder.

"Want to meet a lady friend?" Chris asked.

Kimble chucked at him. Chris prayed the animals would be okay. He was hoping they'd play together and enjoy seeing one of their kind, especially considering the species was endangered.

Cheyenne cheered when he walked in with Kimble, while Erykah's mouth dropped in surprise. He stopped near her, and Ash's eyes widened.

"Erykah, Ash, this is Kimble. Kimble, meet the ladies." Kimble chucked, never leaving the perch of Chris's shoulder.

"You have a real-life animal on your shoulder," Erykah said.

"No different than Charlie lying on my lap."

She snorted. "Likely story."

He loved when her snarky side came out. She kept it so close to her vest it was easy to forget sarcasm was one of her love languages.

"How about we put Ash in the floor seat and let you hold Kimble?"

"Yes!" Cheye clapped her hands. "Can we make a You-Tube video too? I'll direct." Cheyenne made a shooing motion to her aunt.

Chris bit down on his tongue, trying to keep his laughter in.

"Uh, I don't know," Erykah said.

"The floor seat is in my office."

"I'll get it."

Cheyenne took off before he could say otherwise. "Walk," he shouted after her, then turned back to Erykah. "He's harmless. He'll love you."

Determination coated her brown eyes. "Okay. I can do this."

"You sure can." He grinned, and all of a sudden, she was looking at him like she had before. No guardedness in her eyes, just pure ease.

Erykah set Ash in the little baby seat while Chris got his phone set up on the tripod so Cheye could direct their video. He doubted it would be good enough to upload, but if it excited her, he'd let her play around.

"Hey, guys, I'm Chris Gamble, bringing you another Gamble on Nature video. Today I've got a special guest, Dr. Erykah Kennedy." He turned toward her, and she waved at the camera. "Dr. Kennedy isn't an animal doctor. She's actually an orthopedic surgeon and one of my good friends. It's her first time meeting Kimble." He paused. Maybe he should've thought this through.

"Hold hands so Kimble can go across your arm onto her shoulder," Cheyenne suggested.

Chris laughed. "Great idea, Cheye."

"I don't know." Erykah's voice shook.

"It'll be great." He laced their fingers together, ignoring the way his body seemed to relax with relief. Never mind the way his senses came alive under her touch.

He sidestepped, then lifted their hands. "You ready?"

"Um . . ." She bit her lip.

"Do you trust me?"

Her gaze met his. "Yes." She paused. "I'm ready."

"Kimble, go."

The ferret went down his shoulder across his arm, then scrambled up Erykah's. She squeaked out an unintelligible sound that had the girls laughing. Kimble stopped on her shoulder, curling up.

"You did it, Auntie Erykah." Cheyenne clapped with glee.

"I knew you could," Chris said. Hearing his voice drop down an octave had his throat drying out. Was holding her hand really affecting him that much?

"I think you can call him back now," she said.

Chris blinked. "Right. Kimble, come."

The ferret reversed his course and made it safely back to his shoulder. Cheyenne squealed with happiness, then yelled, "Cut! I saw that in a movie once."

He laughed out loud.

Erykah let go of his hand, and an expression he couldn't catalog flashed in her eyes before she moved away, picking up Ash from the baby seat. Chris moved to his phone to stop the video.

"I stopped it," Cheyenne said.

"How?"

She rolled her eyes. "You just press the red button, and it stops."

"Oh, she knows how to record videos," Erykah said wryly. "Ask me how many videos I've found on my phone of her and Ash."

He chuckled. "Two or three?"

"I stopped counting. Some were good, and I saved them."

"Kids these days are surprisingly smart with technology."

"Agreed." Erykah came to stand by him. "Will you introduce Kimble to the other ferret now?"

"I will."

"Can I record?" Cheyenne asked.

"Sure." He handed her his cell phone. She moved to the end of the plexiglass enclosure, holding his phone horizontally.

Chris set Kimble in the enclosure, then picked up the female ferret's crate to let her into the enclosure. She and Kimble stared at each other, then ran closer, and a second later, they were playing.

Ash giggled as she watched, and his heart filled. He loved these girls. If he and Erykah ever dated, well, he could imagine a life very much like this one but with the affection that was currently lacking between him and Erykah.

"I think you should name the ferret Phoebe if you change your mind about letting her stay," Erykah suggested.

"Like the detective in *Kindergarten Cop*?" he asked.

She smiled. "Yep."

"Why not Joyce? After all, that's who he fell for."

"I'm pretty sure the ferrets are siblings."

He threw his head back and laughed. Immediately Cheyenne began questioning what was so funny. Knowing she wouldn't understand, he put her to work helping him close the center once more.

Twenty-Five

*Be strong and of good courage, do not fear nor be afraid
of them; for the* LORD *your God, He is the One who
goes with you. He will not leave you nor forsake you.*

I stared at the words, trying to make sense of them. I could
understand God offering the encouragement to be strong
and courageous. Anybody could encourage anybody. But
the idea that He would never leave me . . . That forced me to
look back to my childhood, when I had felt very much alone.

My parents had checked out of life, leaving me to grow up
without their guidance. And though I'd had Ellynn to lean
on, I'd ended up in the role of her caretaker, not the other
way around. A sharp pang went through my chest at my loss.

*I'm alone now. If You never leave nor forsake, then why do
I feel both so keenly? Ellynn and Asher are gone. My parents
are who knows where. I'm without people.*

You have Ash and Cheye. Chris. Even Charlie.

I bit my lip at my thoughts. Chris and Charlie came into
my life right before the loss of Ellynn. In fact, Chris had
been in my condo when I'd received the horrifying news.

I wasn't alone when Officer Pratt gave me the report that changed me forever.

I continued to think back and reflect. I tilted my head, remembering one of our neighbors who used to offer us food. Occasionally, she would bring Ellynn and me hand-me-downs, stating her own children could no longer fit in the clothes. Was God's hand in that as well?

A lump formed in my throat, and I dropped my head on the Bible resting on my desk. I wished Ellynn were here so I could ask her all the questions. She believed for some reason, and I wished I had thought to ask why instead of discounting her beliefs because they didn't fit mine.

I picked my head back up and rubbed my eyes. It was about time for my workday to start. Chris had been surprised when I'd asked him to handle the girls this morning, but I'd wanted a little quiet and had known he'd agree. I hoped that didn't mean I was taking advantage of him. I just needed some time to think before a day of surgeries.

Whatever weirdness had existed when I'd picked him up from the airport had dissipated by the time we said good night to each other. I was so thankful, because being around Chris made everything better. There was peace in his presence, and he was plain fun. Not in an outlandish way that turned me off and had me wondering if he knew how to be serious. But in witty banter or playing with the kids or trying to pull me into the great outdoors and simply rest.

I swapped my street clothes for scrubs. The blue uniforms the hospital made us wear had its name stamped over the left breast pocket. I pulled my twists into a bun at the nape of my neck and slipped on my blue satin–lined scrub cap. Just as I put on my lab coat, a knock sounded at my door.

"Come in," I called.

I folded my clothes and slid them into the bag leaning against my desk.

Dr. Ann Collier stepped in. "Good morning, Dr. Kennedy. I'm here for the rundown of your day."

"Good morning to you too, Dr. Collier. Go ahead."

I sat down and listened as she listed off the surgeries for me to perform today. A few times I interrupted to ask clarifying questions. Not because I needed clarification, but Dr. Collier was only a second-year resident, and I wanted to make sure she knew who was getting what and why. Occasionally I asked an obvious question just to see how she'd respond. After getting satisfactory responses, I returned to the patient up first.

"All right. Is the first patient all set?"

Dr. Collier checked the hospital iPad for his status. "Mr. Gordon just checked in."

"Great. Please ensure everything goes smoothly with his check-in process. Page me five minutes before you need me. I've got some emails to get through real quick."

"Of course." Dr. Collier studied me.

"Yes?" I asked, trying not to fidget under her scrutiny. I could only hope the next words out of her mouth were work related.

"Um, I just wanted to let you know that I'm praying for you. I know how hard it is to lose a sibling." She swallowed. "My older brother died when I was eighteen. Car crash. It was his fault." She closed her eyes. "Um, what I'm trying to say is I hope God surrounds you with His comfort. I know how bleak those earlier days are."

My mouth dropped. This was the most Dr. Collier had ever shared with me. And for it to be so personal . . . Something in my heart cracked. I swallowed against the lump in my throat. "I'm sorry for your loss." How I hated those words, but I actually meant them. Felt a connection with them that I wouldn't have had before. "Thank you for thinking of me."

We'd never had a personal relationship, but at this moment, I regretted keeping my residents at arm's length. Shouldn't I want to form some kind of personal relationship with the people I guided in the OR?

"Of course. How are your nieces?"

I thought a moment. "Ashlynn, uh, the baby, she's eight months." *That's not what she asked*. "When the accident first happened, she cried so much." I stifled my own tears. "Now she's babbling and giggling. She seems happy to see me." I didn't know if that meant she didn't miss Ellynn anymore, and I didn't want to contemplate that fully.

"And your other niece? You have two, right?"

I nodded. "Cheyenne's a pistol. The girl's a diva at five but so smart."

Both Ellynn and I had intelligence in spades, so that didn't surprise me. But being with Cheyenne in person every day showed me much more of her personality than I'd ever gotten over video chat.

"How's she dealing with the grief?"

"We've cried together. She also has a lot of tantrums. I've read that's normal because of the loss."

"Have you considered finding her a child therapist? To help?"

I blinked. I actually hadn't ever thought of that. *Why haven't you? How could you have overlooked that?*

Something must have showed on my face, because Dr. Collier quickly spoke. "I mean, you don't have to. I just know it helped me greatly, and I can only imagine a five-year-old would have a tougher time than I did."

Hadn't I considered grief counseling for myself? Why

not Cheyenne? "No, it's a good idea. Something I should've thought of sooner."

"I'm sure this has all been overwhelming. I had the comfort of my parents to see me through. You've had to become a mom." She sighed. "Just remember God's got you, and He's watching over you. You're not alone."

Tears pricked my eyelids. If someone had given me a comment like that before, I would've scoffed. But after reading my Bible and trying to figure out prayer, the words seemed like validation that He was watching me, listening to me, answering the questions I had for Him.

"Thank you, Dr. Collier."

She nodded, then stood. "I'll get to work."

When the door closed behind her, I dropped my head to the desk and let the tears fall just a little bit to release the tension holding me captive. These weren't bad tears, despite having spoken about Ellynn and how the girls and I were handling her and Asher's absence. These were tears of relief. Someone greater than me saw me, heard me, and kept sending people to pray for me.

How many signs do you need to believe, Erykah?

That was a question I'd asked myself before, but today, it hit me. I didn't need any more signs. He was real. God saw me. He was with me. He had been watching over me my whole life.

I believe You're real. But I don't know what to do next.

I raised my head and grabbed a tissue, blotting at the tears on my face. Chris had told me that when I believed in God the act was called *salvation* or *getting saved*. But I didn't fully understand what that meant. I pulled up my web browser and typed a question into the search engine: *How do I get saved by God?*

I clicked on a result and read the contents. It seemed

straightforward. The webpage outlined a salvation prayer. My heart pounded as I read the prayer. I could say this for myself. I could give my heart to Jesus and confess my sins.

So what's stopping you?

Was it nerves? Talking to Dr. Collier had tipped me over to belief. Seeing the signs of God's care in my past had primed me, as well as all the reading I'd been doing in the Bible Ellynn had given me.

I closed my eyes.

Ellynn, I don't know if you can hear me. I don't know if that's how heaven works. But I want you to know I've been reading the Bible. Thank you for always thinking of me and for giving it to me. I want you to know I believe in God. I'll do right by the girls and teach them about Him as well.

Which probably meant I should accept one of Chris's invitations to attend church.

I love you, Ellynn. I miss Asher. I miss your family. I promise Cheyenne and Ashlynn will never feel alone. I'll continue providing a stable home like you and Asher gave them. I'll tell them about you two, how you met, how you fell in love, how you made a beautiful family. I promise.

I sniffed.

Um, God, it's me. I'm sure You heard my conversation with Ellynn. Maybe You think that's silly, but I hope You understand. I believe in You. I believe that You won't forsake me or leave me. That You never have, even though I've spent a lifetime feeling alone. I know that's because I haven't acknowledged You before now. I bit my lip, trying to figure out what else I wanted to say. I peeked at the salvation prayer.

I confess that I've lived a life apart from You and sinned. Please forgive me. I believe that Jesus Christ is Your Son, who died for my sins and rose again.

There wasn't much else to the prayer, but that seemed so inadequate.

Thank You for giving me signs of Your presence. Thank You for Chris, Charlie, and the girls. Please show me how to be a good guardian and make You, Ellynn, and Asher proud. In Jesus's name, amen.

My heart felt lighter. Somehow, I knew the rest of my day would be better for it.

Twenty-Six

Chris stared out into the night sky. He drew in a deep breath, then slowly let out the air, willing the band holding his head in a vice grip to let go. With each deep breath, tension seeped out of his upper back. However, the tension squeezing his brain wouldn't recede. How long would it take the over-the-counter meds to kick in? It had been a while since he'd had a headache this bad.

The sound of a doorknob turning broke through his relaxation attempts. He eyed the door as it opened. Erykah stepped out into the backyard and gave him a sympathetic look.

"Your turn for some air?"

"Something like that."

She sighed and sat on the vacant seat next to him. "I'm sorry. We've taken up so much of your space and turned your home into a whirlwind. It's no wonder you need peace."

"Don't." He shook his head, barely hiding a wince. "You know I'd do it all over again. There's no way I wouldn't be here for you." Being away from them while he'd seen Tuck and Piper marry had proven that much. And it had also shown him his fear was Erykah wouldn't be there for him.

Her brown eyes studied him, as if he were DNA under a microscope. "You have a headache."

"Uh . . ." Not what he'd expected her to say. "I do."

"Feels like your head is in a boa constrictor's death grip?"

He snorted. "Oddly specific."

"You're an animal guy. I'd figured you'd know exactly what I meant."

Cute. "You're right, so I do get it."

"Okay. Time for Dr. Erykah to fix you up." She rubbed her hands together with a mischievous grin plastered on her beautiful face.

Why does she have to be so breathtaking even when teasing me? "What are you going to do?" he asked suspiciously. He had to act normal, whatever she had in store. He couldn't let on to his growing feelings.

She rolled her eyes in the same fashion Cheye often did. "I'm going to get rid of your headache." She came to stand behind his chair. "Do you trust me?"

"Of course." Without a doubt. Erykah wouldn't hurt him . . . *intentionally.* It wasn't in her nature.

"Good. Lean back."

Chris did as he was told, startled when his head met the softness of her puffer jacket. He tensed, waiting for instructions.

"Relax," she murmured.

How could he when this was the first time they'd been so close, besides the occasional comfort hug here or there?

Her warm hands glided down his face, and his eyes closed instinctively. The pads of her fingertips trailed up the sides of his face and settled at the temples. She began making circular motions with the softest touch. Relief crept into his temples, into his whole body. His shoulders dropped from his ears.

As Erykah's fingers rotated in circles, she slowly increased the pressure. A low moan left his lips before he could contain it. Her hands paused.

"Did that hurt?"

"Complete opposite." How was his headache already easing away?

She continued the massage.

Chris wasn't sure how long she worked on his temples, but by the time she stopped and stepped back, his head felt like jelly—in the best of ways.

"Thank you so much." Chris stretched his neck left, then right, a satisfying crack sounding at each point.

"That's gross." Erykah faked a shudder as she sat back in her chair.

"Are you telling me the orthopedic surgeon can't handle a little neck cracking?" He smirked.

"I can't stand to hear knuckles cracking either." She shuddered again. "The sound incites the same reaction as nails on chalkboard."

"Yet I'm pretty sure you drilled a hole through Tuck's bone."

"Couldn't be helped." She smiled prettily.

Chris laughed, thankful when the action didn't set his head off again. "What are the girls up to?"

"Bed. The house has complete silence if you want to sit somewhere warm." She tugged her jacket closer around her.

Here he was enjoying the balmy temps with just a sweater. Granted, his headache had made him feel overly warm.

"Is it too cold out here for you?"

"Nah." She shook her head as if she hadn't just exhibited a sign of being cold. "It's only forty degrees. We'll talk about cold when it drops into the twenties with that howling wind. Then I want to take a page out of Baloo's book and hibernate."

"Baloo?" He blinked, trying to figure out why that name sounded familiar.

"*Jungle Book*?"

"Right. 'Bear Necessities.'"

"Exactly."

"What made you think of that movie?" He hadn't seen that since he was a kid.

"The girls were watching it after dinner. They love the live animation makeover."

He'd been hiding in his room then, hoping the headache would go away. *You missed movie time. Couldn't you have been in pain some other time?* "Wait? What?" Erykah's comment about live animation caught his attention.

"Do you live under a rock?" Erykah's mouth dropped. "All the great movies of our childhood are getting remade with real people and everything."

He vaguely recalled that. "I don't stream a lot of movies." He'd rather be outdoors.

"I know. Remember Cheye's meltdown when she discovered you didn't have Disney Plus?"

"She's terrifying." He rubbed the back of his neck.

They shared a look. "Truly," Erykah conceded, "but I love her." A soft smile graced her lips. "I never imagined loving her more than I already did."

They were silent for a moment. Chris wondered how the dynamic would change when his mom came to town. Would Erykah go into hiding in the basement? Would the girls like his mom? Would *he*? He couldn't remember the last time they'd celebrated a holiday together.

"My mom is coming to town in a couple of days."

"Right. Thanksgiving." Sadness filled her voice.

Lord, help me help her. I can't imagine how hard this holiday will be. "Do you want me to take her out for dinner? Give you and the girls some space?"

"No. Please. I don't really want to spend the holiday alone." Pleading filled her eyes.

"Then you won't. However, I do have to apologize in advance for anything my mom says."

Her eyes gleamed. "Will she embarrass you? Tell stories of you as a kid?"

"More like lament my bachelor ways and try to plan our wedding."

The smile fell right off Erykah's face. *Ouch.* Did she have to look so horrified at the thought? Chris rushed to explain. "I haven't dated in years. My mom is always asking me about when I'll find someone new. The fact that you're staying here with the girls might have her thinking something more is going on than just a friend helping a friend."

"How long?"

How long for what? "What do you mean?"

"You said you hadn't dated in years. Quantify that for me."

Yikes. Why had she narrowed in on that? "Um. Thirteen."

"*Thirteen?*" Erykah's eyes bugged out.

Chris prepared himself for her follow-up questions. He'd hinted at his past to Lamont and Chris, but not even they knew the full scope.

"What happened?" Erykah asked.

"She left me standing at the altar."

"As in she didn't show up at all, or she was there, then changed her mind?"

"You want the whole story?"

"If you don't mind sharing it."

He closed his eyes for a second, remembering that day and

the events that led up to the end of it all. He sat up in his chair and turned his gaze to Erykah. "I met Tracey in college."

"Was it love at first?"

Chris shook his head. "Not at all. I thought she was out of my league. She was a year ahead of me and went to school on a cheerleading scholarship. I admired her looks but didn't really know a lot about her."

"Then what happened?"

"We ended up in the same science class my sophomore year. She was struggling with the material, and the professor asked if I would tutor her. So I did."

"Oh, a nerd-jock romance?"

Chris cocked his head. "Do you read romance books, Dr. Kennedy?"

"Maybe." Her face flushed. "Ellynn actually liked them a lot. She'd leave different ones all over our apartment when I was in college. One day when I was stressed over an exam, she put one in my face and told me to chill out."

"It worked?"

"Yep. I read those sweet ones that give off Hallmark vibes, maybe one a month. I'm selective, so it takes me a long time to choose."

He liked knowing that about her.

"Back to your story." She pulled her legs up underneath her, her attention rapt on his face.

"We started talking in between classes. I expected her to ignore me and pretend she didn't have a tutor, but she said hi the next time we ran into each other in one of the student cafeterias. Then she started emailing me in between tutoring sessions. Just random items that interested her, but they had a joking undertone. Then, with the urging of one of my classmates, I asked her out."

He paused. "Oddly, we fit. She was popular, I wasn't. But

we could stay up all night talking and laughing. She encouraged my dreams, and we dated until I graduated from college." He swallowed. "I proposed graduation night, and she said yes."

"So that made you, what, twenty-two?"

"Right."

"But you said thirteen years?"

"She didn't want to get married right away." He shrugged. Now he could see that was a red flag, but then, he'd thought she was just really cautious with their future. "I had plans for grad school, and she had another year left in her own program. We both agreed we'd set a date when I graduated with my master's degree.

"When she graduated, she moved to Utah. We talked every night on the phone and took turns visiting each other. When I graduated, I got a job near her, but she still wasn't ready to have the wedding. It wasn't until all of her friends started to get married that she finally wanted to settle down. By that time, Tracey wanted to move back to Colorado as well."

And his own doubts had begun to surface. But being engaged for so long had caused its own form of self-doubt. Were his feelings simply because they'd waited so long to plan the wedding? Or were his feelings valid? He'd never talked to her about it, and he should've.

"So did you?"

He nodded. "It took a year to plan our wedding and get new jobs, but we did it. We settled in Denver, and I was excited we were finally taking steps forward." Despite his apprehensive thoughts. "But then she started picking fights. There seemed to be no rhyme or reason to them. Every time I asked if she was okay, she would apologize, blame it on a bad mood, then promise to be better. Claimed she was turning into a bridezilla."

Chris had desperately wanted to believe the lie. Didn't want all their years together to have been a waste, even though God was showing red flag after red flag. He never truly consulted the Lord about his feelings, just tried to work everything out on his own so he could say he kept his word. He winced inwardly and glanced at Erykah.

She bit her lip as if nervous where the story would go. Since she already knew he'd been dumped, it really couldn't get that much worse, in his opinion.

"This continued until the night before the wedding. We had the worst fight ever. She said some things that really shook me and made me want to call the whole thing off."

"But you didn't?"

"No. I'd made a commitment and wanted to see it through." *Stupid, stupid, stupid.*

Erykah blew out a breath. "But she changed her mind?"

"Everything was fine until she was walking down the aisle. It was like a bad version of *Runaway Bride*."

"She ran?" Erykah gasped, placing a hand over her heart.

"Tore up the aisle trying to get away. Her bridesmaids chased after her, but it was a lost cause. She was a really fast runner." He could see the humor in it now, but back then . . .

"I'm so sorry."

So was he. He should've gone with his gut instinct and called things off the night before. But he'd been afraid of what the guests would say, of being accused of going back on his word.

"The whole mess showed me I couldn't trust myself in the relationship department. I've been too chicken to try again since then."

"Or maybe you just needed time to heal."

"Thirteen years' worth?" His brows raised.

Erykah shrugged. "Could be. Besides, who am I to judge?"

"Go ahead. I'm sure many people would."

"No." Erykah shook her head. "I meant what I said quite literally. I've never dated, so I have no right to judge someone in that area."

Had he heard her right? "You've never been on a date?"

"Never."

"But you're so smart! Not to mention gorgeous. How come a guy hasn't asked?" And did those comments sound ridiculous now that he'd voiced them out loud?

"Oh, I didn't say I've never been asked. I said I've never been on a date." She paused, a look of concentration on her face. "Growing up with parents who were addicts made me crave stability. Studying for school to get good grades to get into med school to have a reliable job was vital to me. Taking care of Ellynn until she graduated from high school and giving her a stable environment was essential, because I didn't have that when I was growing up. Once I devoted myself to my career, I figured my job was too unpredictable in the beginning to start a relationship. There just never seemed to be a right time to jump into the pool."

Chris wanted nothing more than to ask her out. The words were on the tip of his tongue, except now she was grieving the loss of her family.

Still not the right time.

Twenty-Seven

Chris's mom was here.

I stood on the last step before reaching the main floor, watching as she and Chris shared a hug. Indecision had me rooted to the spot. If I went to the main landing and introduced myself, would she find it weird? Intrusive? Could I somehow get to the kitchen to prepare Ash's bottle before his mom even saw me?

As if he could hear me thinking, Chris stepped away from his mom and caught my gaze. He tilted his head, an invitation for me to come closer, but I couldn't move. Meeting someone's parent seemed like next-level relationship stuff. Even though we were only friends, I couldn't ignore the what-ifs that lived rent-free in my mind. What if I had changed my to-go order and sat down with Chris instead of leaving like a coward? What if I had flirted intentionally at the governor's dinner and let him know I was interested? Or what if we had kissed in the parking lot of the Garden of the Gods?

It was all too much for my mind to process. Considering I was living in his basement, it seemed like crossing an imaginary line to tell him I wanted to see if we could move past friendship. Nothing about our timing felt right . . .

Ever.

Did that mean it was just supposed to stay a friendship? And if so, wasn't it totally normal to know your friends' parents?

I walked onto the landing and into the living room.

"Mom, this is my friend Erykah."

His mom spun around so fast I was surprised she didn't just keep spinning. The look on her face was so comical I had to bite the inside of my cheek to keep the laughter in. I wouldn't say she had stars in her eyes, but I could practically hear her thoughts: *A woman!*

I held out my hand. "Nice to meet you, Mrs. Gamble."

"And how nice it is to meet you." She held my hand between both of hers, glancing over her shoulder at Chris. "Are you . . . are you *living* here?"

Yep. She was trying not to have a fit. "Temporarily. Chris is letting me and my nieces stay in his basement while I house hunt." What kind of relationship did she have with Chris that he hadn't shared this fact yet?

"Oh, are you new to the area?"

"She lives in Colorado Springs, Mom. Her place was too small for her needs, and she's searching for a bigger place."

"Seems like she found one," Mrs. Gamble murmured.

Chris rolled his eyes. I guess he hadn't shared about my tragic circumstances. My nose scrunched. I shouldn't think of my life that way, but that's exactly how it felt. I kept waking up each morning hoping I would find out it had all been a dream.

"Mom, Erykah is a friend."

"He's right, Mrs. Gamble. I don't date." Though Chris certainly had me entertaining the idea more and more.

"Ever?" she asked, as if to say, *Yeah right.*

"Ever," I replied firmly.

"Auntie!" Cheyenne yelled at the top of her lungs as she stormed up the stairs. "Auntie, come quick."

"What?" I rushed over to her, eyes already scanning her for injuries.

"Charlie found a spider. It's as big as his face."

"What color is it?" Chris asked.

"Brown."

Chris took on a pallor that had my nerves ratcheting up. "I'll go check everything out. Is Ash still down there?" he asked.

"Yes, should I be worried?" I whispered.

"I'm sure it's okay." He tromped down the stairs. I leaned over the rail, watching him go, but Cheyenne tugged on my hoodie hem to get my attention.

"Yes?"

"Who's that?" She pointed right at Chris's mom.

I guided Cheyenne over to his mother. "Mrs. Gamble, this is my niece Cheyenne. Cheye, this is Chris's mom."

"Whoa. How old are you? You have gray hair!" Cheye pointed.

Kill me now. "Cheye!" I snapped. I knew kids said the darndest things, but could they be a little less embarrassing? At what age could I expect her filter to kick in?

"Well, Cheyenne, I'm sixty-five. Is that ancient?"

Cheye's eyes bugged, and her head bobbed up and down. "But I like your hair. It's straight and shiny. Mine's not." Her bottom lip poked out.

"Oh, this ol' thing isn't my real hair." Chris's mom patted her bob. "But I love your braids. You look beautiful."

"How do you have fake hair?"

I wanted to clamp a hand over Cheyenne's mouth before she could utter another word. Fortunately, Chris came up the stairs with Charlie bounding behind his heels and Ashlynn in his arms.

"What was it?" I whispered.

"Hobo spider. I'll check and make sure there's no more in a bit."

Weren't those . . . *venomous*?

"A baby," Mrs. Gamble gasped, holding her clasped hands underneath her chin. "Isn't she utterly precious." She glanced at me. "May I?"

I nodded, but Ash would have none of it. She curled under Chris, shrinking her body away from his mom.

"Oh, okay. Perhaps not. I don't want you to feel shy with me, sweetie." Mrs. Gamble looked at Ash, then me. "Your niece as well?"

"Yes, ma'am."

I could see the questions in her gaze, but Chris shook his head at his mom, staving off the interrogation.

"How about I get them a snack, and you catch your mom up on everything?" I asked.

I took Ash from him and then told Cheyenne to follow me. She was always hungry. After cutting up a string cheese and adding some apples to a small plastic saucer, I placed it in front of Cheyenne. "Where's your water bottle?"

She had a small princess water bottle that she usually kept with her.

"Downstairs with the spider."

"Chris got rid of it." But were there more? No way I wanted to go down there and attempt to sleep knowing there could be more spiders of that ilk. Where was a flame thrower when you needed one?

"Did he kill it or take it outside?"

I flinched at Cheye's choice of words, suddenly thinking of Ellynn and Asher. My breath came in spurts, and my vision darkened.

Breathe. What's going on with you?

210

Had they been scared when they realized they'd be hit by a car going the wrong direction? I could only pray that God saw fit to take them quickly. The thought of my baby sister and brother-in-law struggling at the end had been in too many of my nightmares.

"Erykah? You okay?"

I swallowed, then blinked. Chris's concerned gaze came into focus. "Uh, yes."

He grabbed a cup, filled it with water, then thrust it at me. "Drink. Sit. I've got this."

I followed his instructions and sat down. His mom joined me at the fourth seat, watching her son. Did she know this table once held only two chairs, but Chris had bought two more to accommodate the girls? He'd added a plain booster seat for Cheye and a portable high chair that fit on top of the seat for Ash. Right now, I was technically sitting in Chris's spot.

"You know how to make a bottle?" Mrs. Gamble's voice held surprise.

"Yeah. Unfortunately, we ran out of breast milk last month. But Ash seems to like this formula now." He handed the bottle to Ashlynn, who immediately put her two chunky hands on each side and held it. "Do you want me to grab a jar of baby food for her too?"

"No." I shook my head. "She won't be hungry for that until dinnertime."

"I can't believe my ears. You sound fully domesticated, son."

"It's the girls." He cracked a wry grin at his mom. "They change a man."

"Mm-hmm. The little ones, you mean, and not the big one?"

My face warmed under the heat of Mrs. Gamble's pointed

stare, but I refused to turn her way. Let her think what she wanted to think. I knew Chris was just a friend. We would probably never move on from that. Could you move out of the friend zone, or was it like quicksand sucking you under?

"And exactly where am I staying since you have house guests?"

Chris pointed toward the hall. "They're downstairs, so the guest bedroom is still available."

"I guess it's a good thing you bought this big ol' place."

I leaned forward. "Have you seen the backyard? He's got a compost bin, rain shelter, and everything." I'd honestly never seen anything like it.

"Oh, this isn't my first time visiting, but it has been a while. I'm surprised he uses the internet."

I laughed. "He kindly bought a few streaming packages so that some people wouldn't melt down without that convenience." I rolled my eyes toward Cheye.

"I believe it. I almost had my own meltdown the first time I visited here and realized he expected me to take combat showers."

"Doesn't he realize that's not enough water to wash hair?" I cried. Chris and I had briefly talked about water usage. I agreed to use less on a daily basis but informed him of the struggle that was a Black woman's hair.

She harrumphed. "He does not. Don't get me started on his toilet."

"What's wrong with that?" Chris leaned back against the island. Amusement made his blue eyes dance, and I could feel the corners of my own mouth lifting in response.

He really was so very pretty to look at. Not that he was pretty in the feminine sense, but . . .

I bit back a sigh. Hadn't I told myself to stop swooning over him? This was just some sort of rescuer complex because he said I didn't owe him, and I had no way to repay him back for his kindness.

People are kind for kindness's sake, Erykah. You know this.

I did, but I didn't. It was something I lived by, but not something I necessarily believed other people did too. But Chris went above and beyond. No way I could categorize all he did for me and my nieces as mere kindness. This was heroics.

Ugh, don't use that word.

Right, because this wasn't a romance book, and I certainly wasn't a heroine. Heroines in the books Ellynn read were teachers, nurses, or even single moms. I couldn't remember ever picking up one with a doctor or surgeon. Come to think of it, an animal conservationist who also happened to be a YouTuber was missing from the mix as well. Proof my feet were firmly planted in reality.

Now to get my head and heart on the same page and remember that Chris was not for us. None of my current circumstances were permanent. I'd find a new place and learn how to parent alone.

I suppressed a shiver. That made me want to curl up and cry, but I'd save that for later. Later when the clock struck midnight, and I was avoiding sleep because of the nightmares or crying myself to sleep because this would be my first time not visiting Kentucky for the holidays. Maybe one day, when the wound wasn't so fresh, I'd go back and visit the cemetery where Ellynn and Asher lay. But not this year.

Twenty-Eight

The next morning, Chris had somehow found himself kicked out of the kitchen. He and Erykah had come up with a menu that both the adults and the children would enjoy. Yet Mom had taken one look at the sleep-deprived expression on Erykah's face and Chris's usual comatose-but-awake face and told them they were off kitchen duty this Thanksgiving. Erykah had mumbled a thanks, then gone right back to sleep.

Cheyenne sat in the living room, watching TV, and when Ash woke up, he took her from the crib and fed her since he'd offered to watch the girls so Erykah could get more rest. Now Ash sat near her big sister, safely in her Pack 'n Play, eyes glued to the TV.

He really needed to try to get the girls outdoors again. Yes, it was cold, and Colorado had already seen several winter storms, but there was so much to enjoy outside. Maybe a ski trip would be fun. The docuseries had paused filming because of Thanksgiving and would pause the last two weeks of December, too, so there was plenty of time before the new year to head up to the mountains.

He grinned. Seeing Erykah on skis could be interesting. He

didn't know if she'd ever gone before or if she was someone who preferred to remain indoors by a fireplace, sipping hot chocolate.

Chris splayed out on the couch and closed his eyes. He just needed to rest them for a moment, then he'd go back in the kitchen and see if Mom needed help.

"Chris. Wake. Up."

Someone shoved him, and he blinked his eyes open. Cheyenne's small face frowned at him. He heard Ash crying. He jumped up. *Crap!* How could he have fallen asleep on kid duty?

"What happened?" he asked.

"She's hungry. Or she stinks." Cheye shrugged her shoulders. "I don't know."

"Right." He rubbed the back of his neck. "Okay."

Ash held out her arms as he neared, and he scooped her up. She snuggled closer, but if the soggy diaper weighing on his arm could talk, she needed a change.

"Sorry, baby girl," he murmured. "Let's go get you changed."

He headed down the basement stairs, then froze. Quiet sobs reached his ear. Erykah wasn't asleep. She was grieving. He squeezed his eyes shut, mentally kicking himself in the rear. Why hadn't he checked on her this morning? When the girls were occupied, he should've made sure she really was sleeping and not sobbing her heart out.

Chris quickly changed the baby's diaper, went back up the stairs, and deposited her in the Pack 'n Play.

"I'm going to go talk to your aunt. Be back, Cheye."

"Can I have a snack?"

"Come on in here," his mom called. "I'll get you something."

Cheyenne ran into the kitchen, and Chris took his cue. He had to make sure Erykah knew she wasn't alone.

He tapped on her door. "Erykah?"

There was a slight pause in her cries. He wasn't sure if she heard him or not, because the sounds coming from the room told him she was still hurting.

Chris twisted the knob. "I'm coming in."

Every emotion tugged within him. Erykah lay there, curled up in a ball, tears pouring down her face. Chris said nothing. Instead, he rounded the bed and got on the opposite side. He lay on his side and scooted until he could curve an arm around her and pull her back against his chest. Spooning her close, he held her silently, letting her cry with the assurance she wasn't alone.

Instead of her tears quieting, they seemed to get louder, as if she was allowing her emotions to freely escape now that she wasn't by herself. Chris said nothing, simply continued to hold her. He wasn't sure how long they lay there, but eventually her weeping ceased.

When Chris thought he couldn't take the silence anymore, Erykah rolled over, then scooted back so she could look at him.

"Thank you," she whispered.

He swallowed. "I don't know if I should be thanked for that."

"Chris, I have a feeling I'll be thankful for you for the rest of my life. Not because I want to embarrass you or because I think you need to hear it. But the feeling inside my chest is so overwhelming I have to let it out. And that comes out as thank-yous. Thank you for not saying anything. For not telling me it'll be okay or any of those other platitudes that make me want to scream at the top of my lungs." She huffed. "You just let me cry, and that's worth more than anything you could have ever said."

"I hate that I can't take your pain away. But the least I can do is let you know you're not alone." Growing up with his mom so focused on surviving and dealing with her own grief, he'd often felt overlooked and forgotten . . . *alone*.

Erykah stared into his eyes. Was she searching for something or thinking of what to say next?

"When were you alone? When your dad passed away, or when your engagement broke?"

He nodded slowly. "When the engagement ended, my friends didn't know what to say so they slowly stopped calling and then disappeared altogether. My mom has never been one to really talk about emotions, which left me to wrestle with them by myself growing up. Now that I have friends I can truly count on when I need them, I know just how valuable having a community is. I never want another person to feel like I did in those dark times."

"There is so much more to you than I realized."

"Yeah? Like what?"

She tucked her hands under her cheeks, her gaze steady on his. "Like you're kind to your very core. I've never seen anything like it before."

"You know I'm not always kind, right?" Surely she didn't think he was a saint.

"Of course not." She snorted. "You're only human. But even at your worst, I see that you still choose kindness. That amazes me. *You* amaze me."

He needed to leave, walk out of this room, and catch his breath. The way Erykah looked at him, the way he already felt about her, nothing good would come if he stayed a moment longer.

"Let's go get you some lunch." He sat up, swallowing as he stared at the blank wall. *Lord, please don't let her think I'm rejecting her. Please, I just need to get out of this room and to where the kids are.* His hold on his emotions was slipping

217

precariously. Because all he wanted to do was turn around and kiss Dr. Erykah Kennedy until the sun went down or one of the kids started screaming. More than likely it would be the kids to interrupt, and right now he prayed Cheye would come stomping down the stairs or Ash would alert them for something.

"Chris?" Erykah asked softly.

He squeezed his eyes shut. "Hmm?"

"You know it's Thanksgiving, right?"

He nodded.

"Then we can't eat. Your mom hasn't finished cooking."

"True," he rasped. "But I'm sure we can find a snack. The girls might need one."

"You're right." The resignation he heard in her voice almost made him want to turn and face her. Instead, he willed one foot, then the other to move him from the bed and out of her room. Once in the basement's open area, he let out a breath, then raggedly drew in the next. He repeated the technique until his heart felt calm and his emotions under control.

By the time he was upstairs in the main living area, Erykah was right behind him. They didn't speak. Didn't say anything about the moment he chose to ignore. Chris could only pray that one day he'd get the chance to explain why he'd done what he'd done.

But that would *not* be today.

Not when grief was fresh and her living situation up in the air. He needed to walk a fine line of helping while keeping himself accountable.

His phone buzzed in his pocket.

Lamont
Happy Turkey Day!

Tuck
Happy Thanksgiving, fellas!

Chris
Happy Thanksgiving, guys. Tell the ladies the same.

Lamont
Will do. Maybe one year we'll get together for the holiday.

Chris
That would be great.

Maybe by then he wouldn't be alone. He glanced at Erykah, who was kneeling next to Cheyenne and playing with some dolls. Wouldn't it be amazing if this was his life? If Erykah and the girls were a permanent fixture he wouldn't have to say good-bye to? People he'd see every single day until the girls graduated from high school and went off to college, Erykah still by his side?

Thinking of the future didn't help him keep his present self in control. Chris bit back a sigh and glanced back at the text thread.

Tuck
We need to get that planned, then.

Lamont
Next year?

Chris
Let's make that happen.

Tuck
Hey, Piper wanted to know if you passed on her number to Erykah.

Uh-oh. It had totally slipped his mind.

Lamont
This is Nevaeh. Pass mine along, too, please.

Chris
I forgot. I'll tell her right now.

He slipped his phone into his back pocket, then sat on the couch. "Hey, Erykah . . ."

"Yes?" She turned and stared into his face. But her closed-off expression gave him a hint of her feelings.

His neck heated. "Um, Piper wanted me to give you her number in case you ever wanted a woman to talk to."

"Really?" Her eyes widened.

"Yes. And Lamont's girlfriend offered the same." He rubbed his neck. "I know you've never met Nevaeh, but the offer stands. I meant to tell you when I got back from the wedding, but . . ." He didn't know what else to say. The awkwardness from earlier weighed on him.

"I appreciate that. I might take Piper's offer. She seems really kind."

"She is. She and Tuck are some of the best people I know."

"With the movie star being the other?" She smirked.

Joking with her, he could do. "Sometimes the Lord puts you in front of people you never imagined you'd ever meet."

"Do you think maybe . . ." She paused. "Do you think maybe we could go to church this Sunday?"

Something inside him stilled. "Of course." What did that mean? Did that mean—

"I want to go to church!" Cheye's head swiveled away from her dolls, and she raised up on her knees. "Do you have a Bible like my mama? She would read to me."

Erykah's eyes teared up, so Chris spoke to Cheye. "What did her Bible look like?"

"It was pink. She colored in it."

Was she talking about a journal Bible? "That sounds cool. Mine doesn't have pictures. No lines to write on."

"Oh. What about you, Auntie Erykah?"

She sniffed. "Mine is like Chris's, but your mama bought it for me, so it's extra special."

"Wow," Cheye whispered.

"Maybe I can find one for you," Chris offered. "Do you want one you can color in?"

She nodded.

"Then I'll find you one."

"Thanks, Chris."

Erykah looked at him. She didn't say *thank you*, but he heard it clear as day. He smiled and said nothing more. There was no need to.

Twenty-Nine

Yesterday's events wouldn't leave my mind. Even as I came into work, signed on to my computer, and responded to emails, the imprint of Chris's warmth surrounding me like the very best electric blanket on a winter's day kept replaying in my mind. That one moment had inexplicably tethered me to the man.

I didn't know whether to cheer over that or cry.

Probably cry because when I'd taken the chance to tell him exactly what that meant to me, he'd evaded. He'd brought up mealtime and then left my room. But why?

I thought we were having a moment. I *thought* he liked me . . . even if his feelings were only a smidgen of mine.

Now I found myself on my lunch break, staring at Piper Hale's number in my contacts. Could I reach out to her without it being awkward? Would I sound inept just like every time I attempted to talk with my coworkers socially?

Just give it a try. Isn't being in your forties supposed to free you from being shy?

I had no idea, but maybe it would be better to text instead of call. The thought immediately relieved the stress mounting in my gut.

> **Erykah**
> Hi. This is Erykah. Chris told me I could reach out.

> **Piper**
> Hey, Doc! I'm so glad you did. I've been thinking about you and praying for God to bring you comfort.

I bit my lip as tears smarted. How could a woman who was practically a stranger take the time to pray for me? That made no sense, but then again, I'd seen Chris do the same thing.

> **Erykah**
> I appreciate that.

> **Piper**
> Can I call you? Is that okay, or are you busy doctoring?

A chuckle escaped before I even recognized the sound. When was the last time I'd genuinely laughed at something?

> **Erykah**
> Yes, please.

The phone immediately rang.

"Hello?" I winced. Okay, so maybe answering the phone like I didn't know who it was wasn't the smartest thing to do. *But that's what people who grew up before caller ID do.*

"Hey, Erykah. Hope it's okay to call. I know some people don't like talking on the phone."

Pretty much, but I was willing to try. "No, it's fine. I'm on my lunch break."

"How's house hunting?"

"Terrible." I let out a groan. "Nothing fits right. It's either too far away from my work or in an awful school district. Meanwhile, Cheyenne hasn't started kindergarten, and I don't know if that means I'll have to homeschool her after all or hold her back a year." Though Colorado didn't mandate kindergarten attendance, I still felt like I was restricting her by keeping her from going. But Ellynn was homeschooling her, so there wasn't a vast difference, other than the fact I wasn't actively teaching her anything. At least she learned about animals when at work with Chris.

"Why don't you call a school in Chris's school district and see if there's a time limit on enrolling her? That might make your decision easier."

"I had the same thought. I'm not sure why I haven't yet." I scribbled a reminder on a sticky note—that way I wouldn't procrastinate any longer.

"Also, I'd love to talk to you about God sometime . . . if you want, that is."

"Actually, that would be lovely." Should I tell her I'd prayed the salvation prayer? My face heated up. Would she think a simple prayer in my office inadequate? "Do you pray like you're talking to a friend like Chris does?" Maybe I could ease into the conversation.

Piper laughed. "More like whine like I'm talking to a parent. I love that you've seen Chris pray. He seems like he's pretty secretive. Not like in a bad way, just that he doesn't let others get to know him very well."

I had that thought before as well, but now that I did know him better, I realized he was being protective of all parties involved when he finally did share. What did it mean that he'd shared things with me he hadn't with his other friends?

"Can I ask . . ." I bit my lip. Maybe I better not.

"Ask anything. Go ahead."

"How long have you known Chris?"

"A couple of years. Why?" Piper paused. "Are you . . .

interested in him?" Her voice held a girlish quality, as if she were holding back her glee.

I don't know why that amused me, but it did. When I allowed myself to think of Chris like that, I wanted to act like a teenager myself.

"Define interest." I played innocent. Who knew if this conversation would circle back to him.

"Look, whatever you tell me stays with me. Just because I've known Chris longer doesn't mean I'll go running to him. That's not how I work, nor does Nevaeh, if you choose to invite her into our conversations."

"How can a perfect stranger want to meet me?" I asked. I thought Chris mentioning Nevaeh was just a nicety, but hearing Piper say it made me think otherwise.

"We don't have a lot of friends, so we covet true friendships. Plus, she and I have been praying Chris meets the right woman. I actually mentioned you back when we went to a gala for the Derby. But I had no contact information for you. Imagine my surprise when I found out you were the woman Chris was flying to Kentucky with."

Piper had thought I'd be a good fit for him? I had so many questions, but no clue what to actually ask.

"Are you still there?"

"I am." I sighed. "I like him, Piper. But this whole living arrangement has made things awkward." A light bulb flickered to life above my head. *Oh man*. I got it. That was what bothered Chris yesterday. We'd been in my room, lying on my bed, and he was someone who had religious morals. *You do too*. I wasn't yet fully sure of all the ways God expected me to follow Him, but having a man in my bed seemed quite the opposite of His expectations.

My mouth dried.

I owed Chris an apology. Maybe he'd thought I was

propositioning him when that was so not my intent. I squeezed my eyes shut as waves of embarrassment washed over me.

"I think Chris likes you as well. He's a really, *really* good guy. If he hasn't asked you out, it might be your living arrangement, like you already mentioned."

"Then I need to find a new house as soon as possible." Because I couldn't put either of us in that situation again.

Piper laughed. "I'd offer to help, but I'd have no clue what to do from so far away."

"Not to mention I need to sell Ellynn's house."

"I'm still willing to help with that," she said. "I could go through the items in the house and figure out if you want them shipped to you or donated, or I could do an estate sale and get it all sold for you."

"You'd really do all that?"

"I'd be happy to."

"Yes, please." I wrote that on the sticky note as well. "Now, if only the right place would flash like a neon sign when I scan real estate listings." I shook my head. Like that was possible.

"You know," Piper started, "the Bible does talk about wisdom. How if you ask God for it and believe Him, you'll receive it. It's in the book of James. I can text you the verse later. I know you're exploring questions about Christianity, so feel free to ask me anything. I love talking about God."

I opened my mouth to tell her about the salvation prayer but stopped. Even though we were getting to know each other, I wasn't ready to divulge that information. "Thanks. I really appreciate it."

We hung up, and I blew out a breath. It hadn't been *too* awkward talking to her. It'd almost seemed like I'd known her for a while. What was it about Chris and his friends that made them genuinely welcome me? Was it the God thing?

My phone chimed, showing a text from Piper.

Piper

"If any of you lacks wisdom, let him ask of God, who gives to all liberally and without reproach, and it will be given to him. But let him ask in faith, with no doubting, for he who doubts is like a wave of the sea driven and tossed by the wind. For let not that man suppose that he will receive anything from the Lord; he is a double-minded man, unstable in all his ways." James 1:5–8

Erykah

Thank you.

I read the verses over and over. How could I ask God for wisdom when I had only just accepted He was real? And what did it mean to not doubt? Not doubt He heard? He'd answer? I sighed. The last thing I wanted was to be deemed unstable. The thing I actively ran from. Every decision I'd ever chosen was on the side of stability, not instability. Ever since I'd been old enough to realize my parents were addicts and not able to parent Ellynn and me as we needed.

"God?" I paused, wishing this didn't feel so awkward. I believed He heard me, but why did my words have to feel so stilted? I drew in a steady breath, remembering how Chris prayed to Him. "Um, I need wisdom for where to live, what school Cheyenne should go to, and help removing any doubt that You won't answer or help me."

I winced. That sounded so bad, but I had to be honest. He'd shown me He listened, but I could still hear a voice telling me all the ways I'd been alone as a child. All the times I'd gone without. The hard days of parenting my sister before she graduated.

Speaking of honesty, maybe I just needed to tell Chris how I felt. Tell him I wasn't trying to proposition him, but that I very much wanted to go on a date—*after* I moved. Then maybe this awkwardness between us would fade, and we could go back to before.

There's no turning back. Ellynn and Asher are really gone.

I inhaled deeply, trying to keep the tears at bay. I didn't want to cry at work.

My phone chimed, and I looked at my texts.

Chris
Want to go on a ski trip?

He always reached out at the right times.

Erykah
Skiing? With the girls?

I bit my lip as I waited for the dots to stop doing the wave and the words to appear.

Chris
Yep. Cheyenne is old enough to take lessons.
We can put Ash in a baby sled.

Despite mending the bones of Olympic skiers, I'd never experienced the sport myself. Did I want to be out in the cold, going down the mountain, knowing people broke bones doing the same thing? Then again, I did want to do something with Chris, even if this wasn't actually a date. *But it sounds like one.*

People don't take their kids on dates.

Or did they, and I just didn't know because I'd never had the care of small children before?

Erykah
I'll look at my schedule.

I pulled up my calendar. The week before Christmas and week of Christmas were already blocked off with the note *Fun with Ellynn and fam!*

My eyes watered. Could I go skiing, knowing Ellynn and Asher were missing out?

Maybe it's the distraction you need.

I wasn't sure of that, but what else did I have to look forward to? Making a decision, I sent my availability to Chris.

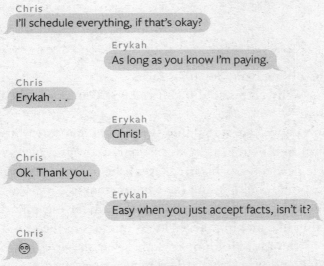

Chris
I'll schedule everything, if that's okay?

Erykah
As long as you know I'm paying.

Chris
Erykah . . .

Erykah
Chris!

Chris
Ok. Thank you.

Erykah
Easy when you just accept facts, isn't it?

Chris
😳

I laughed. We definitely needed to have a talk when I got back home.

Thirty

Chris ran a hand down his face.

"Why is this so difficult today?" Cameron asked him.

"I don't know." He stared into the camera that was waiting to film him being funny as he shared about a pygmy rabbit. He needed to be his usual YouTube persona, but for some reason he couldn't find the wherewithal to care.

He sighed and sat down on the stool. "I'm having a hard time feeling like making these videos matters in the grand scheme of things." Holding Erykah when she cried, that mattered. Planning a ski trip to keep the girls occupied, that mattered. Okay, so maybe not so much the ski trip itself, but the fact the sport was an activity all of them could participate in and make memories . . . *together.*

Performing for a camera in the hopes that someone would be convicted to take better care of the planet and the animals within . . . well, would they? Or would it just come off as entertainment value? The PathLight docuseries was more in-depth and could potentially do more than his YouTube channel, but Chris no longer believed his involvement to be a good idea. The director seemed to want to commercialize

Colorado for tourist reasons, not to help save the world. Shame on Chris for thinking he could convince anyone to be a better steward. The odds of that were like one in a million.

Jesus would go after that single one.

Chris let out a breath. "I'm sorry. Give me a second to get my head on straight."

"Want to talk about it?" Cameron gave him a sympathetic glance.

"I wouldn't even know where to start."

"With the words making the loudest noise."

That actually made a lot of sense. The thing that had been echoing in his head since Erykah's breakdown was the idea of being there for someone. How could Chris physically be present for someone in need? His mom didn't seem to need anything from him, never had. Though there was the strange interaction Thanksgiving Day. She'd cooked for them all, cooed over the girls, then exited without an *I love you*. But that was all beside the point.

Erykah needed a friend, the girls needed guardianship, and the world . . . Well, the world was too big for him to hold in his hands. So he'd been thinking about his personal circle—which encompassed Erykah and the girls, the guys and their ladies, and Cameron and the people at work. Was his circle supposed to be that small?

"I'm not sure if what I'm currently doing is what I'm supposed to be doing. Am I making any sort of effective change, or am I just chasing numbers to get more subscribers?" He ran a hand down his face. "I believe God wants me to show the majesty of His creatures and creation. That I'm supposed to challenge people in a kind way to care for the earth and everything in it. But the board wants to show progress, and having a million subscribers is proof, but am I actually making a difference? I just feel so . . ."

"Helpless?" Cameron supplied.

"Yes." His shoulders sagged. "That about sums it up."

"Chris, I think everyone goes through that. Not only do we all come to that crossroad, but you have to remember, you're grieving."

He blinked. "Come again? I'm not the one who lost a sister and brother-in-law. Erykah did."

"I know, and her grief is different from yours because of all the shared memories she has. Plus, she's a single parent all of a sudden. But you're grieving with her. I know you. You don't do things halfway. Your heart hurts for her and those girls. That's grief. It's actually known as *disenfranchised grief* because society's rules on grief make us feel like we can only lament for people we knew personally."

"Disenfranchised grief? Where did you even hear that?" He stared at Cam in amazement.

"A podcast on grief." Cameron gave a soft smile. "I'm realizing that I'm an empath, so I've been doing my research so that my emotions don't tank because of another person's. Anyway, they did an episode on this type of grief. It's why millions of people can mourn the loss of a celebrity even though they didn't personally know them. The celebrity still touched our lives. Whether it's because we grew up watching them on a show that gave us special memories, or we sang every song they ever recorded. It doesn't matter why we grieve. Erykah's family has impacted you. You are grieving, and as your colleague and friend, I'm telling you it's okay."

Chris let her words sink in. "I keep thinking of Erykah's nieces. Ash will have no memories of her mom or dad whatsoever, and Cheye . . ." He ran a hand through his hair. "I'm not sure what she'll remember when she's older. My heart breaks every time I see them."

"Grief."

He let out a chuckle. "Fine. I get it. I'm grieving because of the impact they have on me currently, not previously."

"In a nutshell."

Wow. Something to mull over later.

"And if you think about it, God made us to be a community. You and I are the body of Christ, so what affects me affects you. We may not look at it like that because we don't share the same home, but if someone in my family passed away, wouldn't you grieve for me?"

"Well, yeah. But I've also known you for a decade." He winced. "Yikes. Makes me sound old."

"You are old."

He folded his arms. "Not you too."

"You're not shocked." Cameron smiled. "Just remember that God wants us watching over each other and being concerned for one another. Just look at how many *one another* statements are in the New Testament. To me, it sounds like you're doing exactly what He's asked you to do."

She paused. "The board wants you to do these videos. As a good steward, I know you'll give them what they want." She drew an imaginary circle with her pointer finger in the air. "Full circle."

"All right, all right. I get it. I'll make this video."

"Yes. Then go home, hug the kids, and maybe ask Erykah to tell you about her sister and brother-in-law."

Had he even thought to do that before? That was something he definitely needed to rectify. He stood. "Let's get this done, then."

"Is YouTube Chris ready?"

He smirked. "As ready as I'll ever be."

"Then on my mark." Cameron held up three fingers, then two while the other hand hovered on the camera, then one.

"Hey, guys. It's your pal Chris here. I wanted to interrupt

your busy day to give you a shot of something happy." He pointed to the wooden box in front of him. A lot of the animals he filmed liked to hide in there before he pulled them out to showcase them to the world. The box was well ventilated thanks to holes positioned all around it.

"What I'm about to show you might make you go awww." He mimicked the way Cameron usually said it, and she rolled her eyes. "But that's exactly what you need to get you through hump day. You ready?"

He stared at the camera and waited a beat. "Before I show our mystery guest, let me tell you the poll results." He always posted a poll on socials and had people comment with a guess for the following week. "The three most popular guesses were a rat, a snake, or a rabbit. Now to unveil our mystery creature . . ." He slid the cover back, knowing Cameron would be zooming in.

The animals shifted as light hit them but otherwise stayed snuggled together. He reached for one, then the other.

"If you guessed rabbit, you were pretty close! These two pygmy rabbits just want to brighten up your day." He held them up to the camera. "These little guys like to sleep cozied up. They're not considered native to Colorado as they're mostly found in the Pacific Northwest. However, more and more of these little guys are popping up in Colorado, enough to get our attention. These two guys will be transported to a Washington wildlife rehab center as soon as we're able." They were so soft, live stress balls, really. He could feel the uncertainty fall away as he took in part of God's creation.

Chris set them back in the box, knowing Zach would get them back in their proper spot soon. He smiled at the camera.

"Well, that's your 'get over the hump day' animal spotlight. Leave your guess for next week's mystery box and don't forget to hit Like and Subscribe and check out my longer videos."

"And done," Cameron said, once the red light went away. "Good job."

"Thanks for talking with me, Cameron."

"What are project managers for?"

"You mean friends?" He stared at her pointedly.

She smiled. "Exactly. Now go home. We'll get everyone settled and lock up the place."

"You sure you don't want to leave early and meet Felix for an early dinner?" When her engagement had been fresh, she'd talked a lot about her fiancé. Now she seemed quieter. "Everything okay with him?"

"Yeah, of course. We're going to be doing the seating arrangements for the reception later. So staying won't ruin any plans." She waved him away. "You need to get home for Cheye. Go."

He nodded.

Erykah had enrolled Cheyenne into the school in his district, and today was her first day. The office had seemed quiet without her.

He glanced at his watch. If he left right now, he'd make it back home in time to see her get off the bus at 3:30 p.m. He whistled, and the sound of a dog collar tinkling reached his ears. Charlie came to stand in front of him.

"Ready to go home?"

Charlie barked.

"Attaboy. Let's go."

The pup was fully potty trained now but still had a lot of puppy energy, so Chris always brought him to work. This was probably the best place for him to roam free and not get into trouble.

Once Chris parked in front of his house, the sound of

brakes from a bigger vehicle sounded. He looked at the rear-view mirror and saw the school bus a few houses down. He got out of the car, putting Charlie on a leash before heading down the street.

A little girl with two French braids who looked like Cheyenne hopped off the bus. He cupped his mouth. "Cheye!"

She turned and scanned the area, then spotted him. She ran down the street, looking like a marshmallow in her puffer jacket. Where was her hat? Surely Erykah hadn't dropped her off at school without a beanie. Chris knelt down.

"Chris!" Cheyenne wrapped her arms around him. "I don't like school."

"What? Why?" He pulled her back to look into her face.

"The kids said I talk funny."

Well, she did have an adorable country accent, but considering she'd grown up in Kentucky, Chris hadn't given it a second thought. Unfortunately, he'd temporarily forgotten how cruel kids could be.

"What else did they say?"

"They just kept laughing every time I talked."

Oh man. How could he fix this for her? "Did your mommy talk like you?"

She wrinkled her nose as if thinking. "No, but Daddy did."

"Then you guys have the same accent."

"Accent?"

Chris faked a New York accent, then a country one.

Cheyenne giggled. "I get it."

"See? You talk like your daddy. And your mommy talked like your aunt, right?"

She nodded.

"Then you have nothing to be upset about. Just tell them you're from Kentucky."

"Okay. Maybe tomorrow won't be so bad."

"I'll pray it's not."

Cheyenne petted Charlie. "I missed Charlie. How come he can't come to school with me?"

"Pets aren't allowed at school. They don't want you to be distracted while you learn."

"You have pets at your work."

Trust her to try to find a parallel. "Remember, most of the animals at my job are wild. They're not pets. Do you know what I mean?"

She blew out a breath. "They're not domesticated," she enunciated slowly, as if trying to remember how he told her to pronounce the word.

"Right." Erykah was lucky Charlie hadn't been wild.

He stood to his feet and held out his hand. "Did you learn anything exciting today?"

"Did you know that turtles can live for a long time? Mrs. Vega has a turtle as a class pet." Cheyenne's brow wrinkled. "We can't take him home with us, but we're allowed to take breaks and talk to him. He's fifteen. That's old, but not as old as your mom."

He could only imagine what Cheyenne would think if she knew his age. "Did you know turtles can't outgrow their shell?"

"No," she gasp-whispered. "That's so cool. My backpack is like a turtle shell."

He glanced at the bright pink Barbie backpack. "I don't know. It's pink."

"I'm a girl turtle."

Chris had to hold back laughter. Life around Cheyenne was never dull. "You need a snack?"

"Yes. I'm starving." She groaned dramatically. "Can I have apples and cheese?" She tilted her head to the side.

"I can do that."

"Cut them right this time." She pointed a finger as if reprimanding him.

But that wasn't necessary. He'd learned his lesson from her last meltdown. "Yes, ma'am."

"I'm not a ma'am. I'm a little girl."

A bossy one at that . . . but so adorable. He hated that Cheyenne and Ash had lost their parents but was so thankful that God had allowed Chris to play a small part in their lives. He knew they had impacted him in ways he'd never expected.

With Tuck married and Lamont soon to be, Chris could see why his friends wanted more for Chris. *He* wanted more, just in God's timing.

Thirty-One

The kids were asleep. Now was the best time to walk up to Chris, tell him how I felt, and see what happened.

But I couldn't get the words past my lips. In fact, my mouth seemed to be clamped shut. Every time Chris had asked me a question or said something, I responded with a shrug or a *mm-hmm*. I was sure he thought I was acting weird. I *was* acting weird, but I didn't know how to carry on a normal conversation when these feelings were swimming in my gut like leaky bacteria. I mean, how was I supposed to just walk up to him and say *I like you* when I'd never done that to any other human being on planet earth before?

Ugh, I really shouldn't have been so addicted to studying. *You were focused.* I'd had Ellynn to worry about, not to mention my own desire for success. And I had succeeded. There were accolades shoved in a box in Chris's home office. None of which would help me speak to the man I actually wanted to talk to.

"Erykah, are you okay?"

My throat dried as I turned to look at Chris.

He'd been working on his laptop in the living room, approving videos post-edit and looking over a schedule

Cameron had created. He hadn't moved except to grab a cup of tea half an hour ago.

"Yeah. Why?" *Congrats. You spoke. Now say what you need to say.*

"You seem quieter than usual. You'd talk to me if you needed to, right?"

Why did he have to ask that? Could he see inside my brain to all the jumbled-up emotions within? "Of course. You're my friend."

Something flickered in his gaze. Wait, I used the word *friend*. Even I knew that was taboo, but Chris *was* my friend. It was part of the reason why I liked him so much. How could I not when he'd done everything to make me feel comfortable?

Chris was a friend, but he was so much more.

"Chris . . ." I swallowed. I could do this. *Just say it.*

"Yeah?"

"I . . ." I swiped my hand down my yoga pants. Why did my palms have to get so clammy all of a sudden?

I knew the physiology behind the action, but emotionally speaking, my hands needed to dry quickly.

Chris rose to his feet and sat next to me on the couch, where I'd been attempting to read a book. A good book, but the million thoughts occupying my mind meant I hadn't turned a single page since I'd sat down after tucking Cheyenne into bed. Ash had been asleep for an hour already.

"What's going on?" He placed a warm hand on my kneecap.

Every nerve ending came alive. I could either gather the courage to say what was on my heart or kiss him.

Oh, great idea. Kissing him would be easier. You wouldn't have to say anything. Just lean forward and pucker your lips like they do in the movies.

Right. I could do that. I licked my lips just in case they were as dry as the Sahara expanding in my mouth. Nope. Didn't feel too bad. I stared at his mouth, then froze. I had no idea how to start this other than making duck lips. Why hadn't I watched a movie to get some tips?

I filtered through some rom-coms. *Never Been Kissed* could be a blueprint, but there's no way I was passing for a high school senior. Not to mention she chickened out and wrote a letter telling the guy about her feelings.

Use your words.

"There's something I want to say." Not really, but hadn't I decided this was the best course of action? Could I backtrack and ask him if I could just text him? Then I wouldn't have to stare into his beautiful blue eyes while I gathered my wits about me.

Seriously, how could this man be so good-looking? Was it the warm gaze he studied me with? The brown skin that made me want to run my finger down the length of his forearm? Or was it the kindness in every single action? Then again, it might be those nerdy black glasses he broke out when his contacts irritated his eyes.

"Tell me. I'll listen to anything you have to say."

Which was probably why my heart beat as fast as one experiencing sinus tachycardia. My heart even palpitated, which surely wasn't normal.

You're not a cardiologist, so stop freaking yourself out and get this over with.

"Chris, I l—"

"Aunt Erykah!" Cheyenne yelled as she stomped up the stairs.

Chris and I both jumped and swiveled to look at the stairs.

"What's wrong, sweetie?" I tried to get my brain to switch gears. But I honestly didn't know whether I was annoyed by

241

the interruption or relieved. *Probably the latter. See how your heart rate has already slowed down?*

It was true, despite the scare Cheye gave me with her vocal cords working overtime.

"There's something in the basement."

Judging by that furrowed brow, Cheye would have deep lines in her forehead well before she hit middle age.

"What's in the basement?" Chris asked.

"I don't know." She threw her hands up in the air. "You have to come there and look. What if it's a monster?"

"Are you sure it wasn't Charlie making a noise?" I asked. The dog snored louder than anyone in the house.

"He's sleeping next to Ash. I checked." She walked up to Chris and wrapped her hands around his arm. "Come on. Look."

He flashed me a look that said *You coming with?* I nodded, trying to hold in a smile at the way he allowed Cheye to pull him to standing. I knew she didn't have that much strength because she'd tried that maneuver on me, and I hadn't budged.

"All right, we're coming," Chris assured.

"Aunt Erykah doesn't have to. You're the one with muskles."

I slapped a hand over my mouth, my shoulders shaking as I held in the laughter.

"You mean *muscles*?"

"That's what I said." She stopped midway down the flight of stairs and turned around, a finger on her lip. "Shh. We gotta catch him. He's in the bathroom."

"Oh. Right."

Chris made a motion with his arm, but I couldn't see what he did since I was behind them. I assumed he zipped his lips, and the thought had my mind cataloging all the ways Christian Gamble made my heart flutter. He was just so good.

Chris walked into the bathroom and flipped on the light. A winged creature fluttered and made some kind of noise. I screamed. Or was that Cheyenne? As if trying to figure out the same thing, she looked at me and screamed again. Higher. Longer. Then she lunged for me. I swung her in my arms and immediately went to the girls' room. I hurried in, then shut the door.

"What was that?" Cheye asked.

I turned to stare at Ash, who hadn't moved. How she slept through the screaming was beyond me.

"Whisper, 'kay?" I spoke in a low tone to Cheyenne.

"What was that?" she loudly whispered.

"A bat?" It was dark, shrieked, and flapped. Then again, I guessed it could've been a bird.

"Ew. I don't like bats."

Neither did I, but I couldn't exactly explain why I didn't like them. I just didn't. They were creepy, and one should definitely not be in the house. I stifled a gasp. Did that mean there was an infestation? I'd seen a few episodes of *Infested* before I could no longer take watching the many ways wildlife had overtaken people's homes. First it was the random hobo spider, now a bat? *Save us, God.*

If Chris had a horde of bats—What were a group of bats called? A swarm?—then I would be packing up and stuffing my nieces into the nearest hotel.

Calm down. It may not come to that.

I blew out a breath.

The doorknob twisted, and Cheye yelped, squeezing her arms around my neck tighter. "It's coming for us."

"Shh. It can't open doors."

Chris stepped inside. "You two just left me." He shook his head, feigning displeasure. "I could've been attacked by a swarm."

243

Ha! I was right.

"But you're strong," Cheyenne said.

See, even she understood the power of having a man in the house. I didn't know what that said, but I completely sided with her. He was a modern Dr. Dolittle.

"Did you get him?" I asked.

"Not even going to ask if I'm okay? If the monster tried to get me?"

"It was a bat, not a monster," Cheyenne said primly.

Chris and I both chuckled.

"Fine. Don't care. But yes. I caught him. He won't disrupt your beauty rest any longer, little miss."

Cheyenne slid from my arms. "Good. I'm tired. You can go now." She shooed Chris away and climbed back in the bed.

When I closed the door behind me, Chris said, "That girl is going to be *trou-ble* when she gets older."

"Thanks for that. Just what I look forward to."

"I'll start praying for her future husband now. He'll need all the prayer he can get."

I laughed. "Thank you for getting the bat. Is he okay?"

"Nothing a little visit to Gamble on Nature won't help with."

"Then I'll turn in so you can handle that." I motioned to my room.

"But we didn't get a chance to talk." He studied me.

It took all my willpower to keep my face neutral as I feigned unimportance. "It can wait." I even waved my hand as if to suggest it was immaterial. Who was I kidding?

And let's remember, this makes you a coward once more.

Maybe, but I was going to be an unembarrassed coward who didn't have to get rejected after seeing a live bat. I could sleep peacefully knowing I wouldn't look foolish in Chris's eyes.

Though part of me still wanted to come clean.

"You sure?"

I nodded, reverting back to clamped-lips status.

"Then good night."

"Good night," I murmured.

I watched him leave, then slapped my forehead. "Coward," I groused.

Thirty-Two

Driving from Kentucky to Colorado had taught Chris that road trips with kids were full-on events. Packing up a car for a measly drive to Keystone Resort should've been much easier. Yet Erykah had stuffed item after item into her car until he informed her there was no more room for anything else. They were only going to be at the lodge for a week, having both agreed it would be better to spend Christmas at the house than at a ski lodge.

Plus, he'd managed to arrange for Lamont and Tuck to join them. They were bringing Nevaeh and Piper, and for once, Chris wouldn't be the odd man out. He hadn't told Erykah yet, but hopefully she'd enjoy the surprise. He had it on good authority that she and Piper had connected well and were messaging on a daily basis. He wasn't sure if they actually talked on the phone or stuck to texts, but Tuck seemed to think Piper couldn't wait to come to Colorado. That had to be a good thing, right?

"We're here," Erykah announced.

Chris put the vehicle in park, thankful Cheyenne would finally stop asking, "Are we there yet?"

"I'll go check in."

Erykah nodded.

He went inside and checked in, opting to use the hotel app instead of getting keycards to cut down on waste. As he turned to walk outside, someone called his name.

Lamont strolled across the lobby toward him. A few people did double takes, but when they saw Chris and recognition failed, they went back to their personal conversations. Most likely they'd assumed they weren't really looking at *the* Lamont Booker simply because they didn't recognize Chris.

Lamont gave Chris's back a slap. "Hey, man. I didn't realize you guys were here already."

"I just checked us in. I'm about to lug everything to the rooms. You won't believe how much Erykah packed."

"Well, y'all do have a baby with you." Lamont smirked.

"Wait until you meet the kids. They're great."

Lamont studied him. "You like her."

"What do you mean?" Chris resisted the urge to shift back and forth on his feet.

"Erykah. You *like* her, like her."

Chris could feel the back of his neck heating up. "Maybe."

"I know you two haven't gone out. We would've heard something. And it's not like you to keep something like that a secret. So what's the issue?" Lamont folded his arms. "Is it the kids?"

"No, of course not." Chris removed his beanie, running his hand over his hair. "She's grieving. Her life's been turned upside down."

"Hmm. Have you prayed about asking her out?"

Chris blinked. He'd talked to God about it. God *knew* Erykah was grieving. The whole instance at Thanksgiving showed that. Not to mention Cameron pointing out that Chris was on his own journey with grief. But what specifically had he told the Lord? Basically what he'd told Lamont.

"I mean, everything I just told you I told Him."

"Were you asking God to give you wisdom, intervene, or just telling Him how it is and how you'll respond?"

Why did something like conviction prick at him? "The . . . latter?"

Lamont arched a brow.

"Okay. We'll pick this up later." After he could ask for forgiveness and not feel shameful for not asking God for direction. "I gotta help Erykah."

"Let me come with you."

"Sure. The more hands the better. Plus, I'm sure she'll love to meet you."

"Does she know we're coming?"

"Nope." Chris smiled. "I wanted it to be a surprise."

"Does she like surprises?"

"I think so."

Lamont chuckled. "Good luck."

They walked outside just in time to see Erykah get out of the vehicle. Her eyebrows shot up when she spied Lamont walking next to Chris. He could feel a grin wanting to escape, but he maintained a pleasant expression.

"Surprise," Chris said when they drew close enough for her to hear him. "Dr. Erykah Kennedy, meet my friend Lamont Booker. Lamont, this is Erykah."

"Nice to meet you," he said, offering his hand.

"And you," she replied. She turned to Chris. "Is this why you were so antsy today?"

He chuckled. "I should've asked if you like surprises."

"I don't know that I've ever been surprised."

"Does now count?" Lamont asked.

"Maybe?" she replied hesitantly.

"What if I told you Piper and Tuck are here too?" Chris asked.

Her mouth dropped, then she nodded. "Okay, it counts."

Lamont laughed. "Glad to hear it. Chris said you needed help unloading. Point me in the right direction."

Chris's phone made the notification sound. He grabbed the device and saw a message from Tuck.

Tuck
Lamont disappeared. Should I assume he found you?

Chris
Yep. He's helping unload the car.

Tuck
Should I grab a luggage cart?

Chris
If you wouldn't mind.

Tuck
Coming right out.

"Tuck's coming with a cart, so maybe you won't have to stress your muscles too much, Lamont."

He snorted. "Good, because I have no idea what I'm supposed to do with a Pack 'n Play or floor mobile."

"Who are you?" Cheyenne called from her seat.

Chris could see through the back windows that she was trying to contort in her car seat and stare at Lamont.

"I'm Lamont, Chris's friend."

"You look familiar."

Even a five-year-old recognized the movie star?

"How can he when you just met him, Cheye?" Erykah went around to the passenger door and unbuckled her.

Ash must have seen, because she squealed like she wanted to be let out too. Erykah took her out next, then used one of those wrap things to secure the baby to her front.

Cheyenne came around to the back of the car and squinted at Lamont. Then she reared back and gasped. "You're Mr. Quick!" she shouted.

"Cheyenne, not so loud," Erykah scolded.

"But, Aunt Erykah, he's Mr. Quick."

"Who?"

Lamont's face flushed, and Chris burst out laughing. He'd never thought Lamont would ever look uncomfortable about a film he'd acted in. However, the movie had been considered a flop by box office standards, similar to Ryan Reynolds's portrayal of Green Lantern. Lamont had played Mr. Quick, aka Tad Thomas, the man with super speed.

"It's a movie I was in," Lamont answered Erykah, then squatted before her niece. "I'm an actor. I'm not really Mr. Quick."

"So you just pretend?" Cheyenne tilted her head to the side.

"I do."

"Isn't that lying?"

God bless Cheye. Chris couldn't wait to tease Lamont later.

"No. Pretending is my job. So kids like you can have something to watch."

Chris could tell Cheye was mulling all the information over.

"You get paid to lie?"

Lamont's face flushed again, and it was all Chris could do not to add in a comment or two.

"Something like that," Lamont muttered.

"I will pray for you," Cheyenne said primly.

Erykah and Chris both laughed. Chris clutched his side, slapping a hand on Lamont's back. "The things kids say, huh?" He huffed, trying to keep his laughter under control, but it was tough.

Chris glanced at Erykah to see her wiping tears from her eyes. She caught his gaze, and her grin widened. *Kids*, she mouthed.

He nodded. *Cheyenne*, he mouthed back.

He had never met a kid like her. Then again, probably most parents thought like that.

He blinked. Was Cheyenne like a daughter to him?

You do pick her up from the bus stop, feed her, wash her clothes, and put a roof over her head.

No. It was different. She was Erykah's niece and responsibility. Chris just helped. Yet he couldn't help but wonder what Cameron would have to say about it. Had she listened to some podcast that talked about who could feel like a parent and who couldn't?

"Got the cart," Tuck called. He stopped the luggage cart next to the vehicle, and Lamont began loading it up. Tuck said hi to Erykah as Chris grabbed the last item out of the trunk.

"You got everything?" Erykah asked.

"Yep."

Erykah closed the passenger door. "Do you want to hand me the room key?"

"It's on the app." He unlocked his phone, opened the app, and showed her.

"Got it."

They all walked into the lobby. "Is this going to be weird for you?" Chris asked Erykah.

"No. I'm really excited to see Piper in person again and to meet Lamont's fiancée." She squinted. "She is here, right?"

"Yeah. Probably talking to Piper. Guess Tuck didn't tell them we'd arrived."

"I actually did." Tuck looked back at them. "They're trying to be nice and not overwhelm y'all. Said they'll wait a couple of hours so y'all can settle in."

"That's so sweet." Erykah looked pleased at that information.

And Chris could now officially breathe. She didn't hate the surprise. They were going to have fun, and he got to do it with the woman he liked and his friends.

Thirty-Three

Chris's friends were great.

Nevaeh was giving Cheyenne a miniature spa experience, and Piper was getting baby cuddles from Ashlynn. And me, well, I was chatting with both of them as they lobbed questions at me.

"So you've never felt queasy at all? I don't think I could handle seeing blood or body parts." Nevaeh shuddered.

"As bad as this might sound, it becomes . . . clinical," I mused. "Logically I know the patient is a human, but when I'm operating on them, I see the medical issue. My focus becomes lasered on the bone and all the surrounding parts." I took a sip of water. "That's why surgeons don't operate on someone they know personally. It becomes impossible to separate your knowledge of the person and what they mean to you from just their anatomy. So for the safety of the patient, another surgeon will step in." I rocked back in the recliner.

We'd been sitting in Lamont's hotel suite, which was simply stunning. My hotel room wasn't as nice, but it wasn't too shabby either. By Chris's request, I'd gotten connecting doors so that he could help with the kids. My side had two queens, and his had one king. There was plenty of room for the Pack 'n

Play to act as a crib. He'd offered to take the baby at night so I could rest, but he was already doing so much so I declined. All we were missing was Charlie, whom we'd boarded near home.

"Have you found what you were looking for?" Piper asked, her gaze flicking to Cheyenne with a question in them.

I shook my head. Cheyenne knew we needed our own place, but she'd begun to call Chris's house home. I wasn't quite sure she understood he wouldn't be moving with us, and I wasn't prepared to rock the boat. Since then, I'd been looking at houses without her or anyone else's input.

"I'm still looking." I grimaced. "Cheyenne started school." That I could talk about.

"You did?" Nevaeh asked. "What grade are you in?"

"Kindergarten. And I'm smarter than everyone."

"Cheye . . ." I used my warning voice.

"But I *am*. Ms. Vega said I was too smart for her to teach."

I frowned. Did she mean in temperament? Because let's face it, Cheye had some of my younger self's sass, before life stomped it out. Or did she really believe Cheye needed to skip a grade?

"I'll talk to her and see what she means."

"Sure." Cheye shrugged and faced forward once more.

Nevaeh was now polishing Cheyenne's nails, since her hair was all done. I'd said no to the makeup because five just seemed too young, even for play.

"Uh-oh." Piper grimaced. "I think Ash needs a change."

"Did you make a stinky?" I asked my youngest niece.

She giggled.

"Yep. That means she totally did." I took Ash from Piper. "I'll be right back."

"Okay."

I went to my room and unlocked the door now that I'd downloaded the hotel app to my phone. Chris had given me his login info. How wild to think we were sharing app info like a regular couple.

You could've made a step in that direction had you not chickened out.

Probably so, but I also could breathe easier knowing I'd dodged the bullet of confession. Being vulnerable and taking a chance he felt the same way made me sweat. I unlocked the door, grabbed the diaper bag, and pulled out the mat to lay Ash down on. Before I could put her down, Chris knocked on the connecting door.

"Yes?" I called.

"You okay?"

I unlocked the bolt and opened the heavy door. "Yep. Came back because Ash obliterated her diaper."

Chris grinned. "Better you than me."

"Oh, do you want an opportunity to change her? I know it's your favorite thing."

He took a step back. "How about I grab the wipes and a clean diaper for you?"

"What, you're not going to tell me how I need to use a towel and a cloth diaper?" I could barely contain my mirth at the chagrined expression on his face.

The first time Chris saw me using a disposable diaper, he'd gone on about how it was affecting our carbon footprint. There were words like *waste*, *pileup*, and others I'd ignored. Instead, I'd held up the offensive material in front of him so he could get a good whiff of Ash's healthy bowel movement.

He quickly changed his tune and was now the first one to throw soiled diapers in the trash.

A great convert.

Still, I was willing to compromise in some areas, just not diaper duty. No way I wanted to wash poo out in the sink, bathtub, or anywhere I would put my clean body.

"No."

"Where are the guys?" I wrapped up Ash's dirty diaper.

"They went to see if the ladies want dinner soon." He held out a hand. "I'll take it."

"There's a trash can on my side of the room."

"But you'll be so distracted by the kids you won't take it out. Plus, it's cold, and you don't have a jacket on."

True. "Thank you." I handed him the offender. "What time is it that we're talking about dinner already?"

"Six." He set the diaper near the trash can, then leaned against the doorjamb. "I'm surprised Cheyenne hasn't asked you about food yet."

"She's eating goldfish and getting pampered by Nevaeh. Her needs have already been met."

Chris chuckled. "I love that kid."

My heart warmed in my chest. "Chris, I . . ." Yikes. Now was *not* the time to bare my soul. We were surrounded by his friends—*yours too*—and on vacation. Surely now wasn't the time to get brave and confess how interested I was in a romantic relationship with him. I bit the inside of my cheek, indecision tugging at me like tweezers pulling on threaded stitches.

"Yeah?" Something shifted on his face, and he leaned closer, still miraculously leaning. But now leaning against the doorjamb and leaning forward. Was that like leaning squared? Because I'd watched *While You Were Sleeping* more times than I could count. Leaning equaled wanting according to the rules of Jack Callaghan.

Just say it! He's leaning!

Ash yelled. I whipped my head around to make sure she hadn't fallen off the bed or anything. How could I have forgotten about her? What was *wrong* with me? My niece was now my responsibility until she turned eighteen and left my house but never my heart.

I grabbed her off the bed, thankful she hadn't decided to roll off or attempt a vault landing. She'd simply been frustrated trying to grab hold of her sock. Keeping the baby between us, I looked at Chris, who now stood straight. Guess the moment was over.

That's a good thing. You don't want to tell him on vacation anyway.

Only the disappointed feeling in my gut said otherwise.

"How about something in the resort so that we don't have to leave?" I suggested, getting us back on normal footing.

"Sounds good to me. Let's go find everyone else and see if they came to the same conclusion."

We said nothing as we walked down the hall to Lamont's suite. Just like we never spoke about the moment at the Garden of the Gods or all the countless times I thought my feelings could possibly be reciprocated. Was the timing simply not right?

Chris knocked on the door, and Lamont quickly opened it.

"Come on in. So far the vote is eating in the lodge restaurant. How do you two feel about that?" he asked.

"That's what we were thinking, so sounds perfect," Chris said.

"Great. Do you need to grab anything for the kids?" Lamont asked me.

I pointed to the strap on my shoulder. "Already got the diaper bag."

"Great. Let's go eat."

We walked down the hall toward the elevator. We had no problem getting on or arriving at the restaurant without a wave of visitors. Soon we were seated in the back, after the staff pushed multiple tables together. I got a highchair for Ash, who sat happily at the end, playing with the puff snack I'd taken out of the diaper bag. Our server placed fresh bread and butter at the table for a complimentary appetizer. Chris sat across from me, and it took all my strength not to stare into his gorgeous eyes.

"So we hit the slopes tomorrow?" Lamont asked.

He and Nevaeh sat at the end, but across from each other so that our table was naturally boys across from girls. *So grade school.*

"Nah," Tuck said. "I'll be hanging in the lodge in front of the fireplace."

"Come on, man." Chris looked at his friend. "You can ride a jumping horse but can't go down a hill in some skis?"

"Some things were not meant for man to try."

Nevaeh snorted. "I never thought I'd agree with you about something like this, but you are so correct. There's no way I'm sliding down a hill willingly."

"Babe, it'll be fun." Lamont smoldered at his fiancée.

Smoldered! Did that work? Judging from the demure expression on Nevaeh's face as her eyes practically shot out hearts, it did.

"Okay. I'll try it once."

"Yes." He placed a kiss on the back of her fingers. Then Lamont remembered the rest of us were at the table. "Piper, you going?"

"I'll try once like Nevaeh."

All heads swiveled to me. "I think I'm with Tuck on this one."

"Oh no." Piper shook her head. "Tuck is coming whether he realizes it or not."

I hid a smirk while Chris made a whipping noise. I bit down on my lip, trying to keep silent, but Lamont laughed with abandon.

Chris met my gaze. "Piper and Tuck have been friends since they were about Cheye's age. He'll do anything for her."

"That's sweet," I said.

"Thank you, Doc." Tuck glared at Chris. "Just wait. It'll be your turn one day."

"One day?" Nevaeh laughed. "I'm sure that ship sailed."

Lamont and Tuck stared at Chris, then looked at me. My face heated. They all seemed to think Chris was gone over me. My breath hitched. Was it true? Did he feel the same way? I wasn't just a passing fancy but something more? I wasn't sure what to think since I'd been keeping my feelings close to me, and Chris had said nothing. It wasn't real unless it was spoken, right?

Chris changed the subject, and I let out the breath I hadn't realized I was holding. I remained quiet as the others joked back and forth. Observing their dynamics was pretty interesting. Fortunately, they didn't let me stay completely silent. Each made sure to ask me a question here or there.

By the time we finished eating and Cheye had a dessert, I was ready to close my eyes. Driving up here had taken a lot of my brain power between Ash crying from being stuck in her car seat and Cheyenne's endless "Are we there yet?" I just wanted to lay my head down and sleep before one of the kids woke me.

We waved bye to the others as we neared our hotel rooms.

"Give me Ash," Chris murmured.

Ashlynn held out her hands the minute he said her name, and I let her go from the wrap I had around her. She snuggled against Chris. Guess she was as tired as I was.

I said nothing as Chris followed me into the room and got Ash ready for bed while I wrestled Cheyenne into pajamas. Soon the room filled with tranquility as the kids surrendered to sleep. Chris opened the connecting door, then turned to look at me.

"Erykah?"

"Yes?" I watched him in the dim lighting.

"Could you come in here so we can talk a moment? I don't want to disturb the girls."

I nodded. "Sure." But immediately my stomach churned. Was something wrong?

Chris gestured toward the chair in front of the desk. He sat on the couch near it and leaned forward, elbows resting on his thighs. "I think it's time we talk about the subject you've been avoiding."

I swallowed. *Lord, help.* "W-what do you mean?"

"I can tell there's something you want to tell me, but something's holding you back."

Hurt flashed so quickly in his eyes, I almost missed it. *Almost.* "I know I can talk to you about anything," I rushed out.

"Do you?"

"Of course. You've been there for me since day one." I bit my lip, trying to grasp the words. "I simply don't know *how* to tell you."

"If I turn around so you can't see my expression, would that help?"

Would it? I shook my head. "No, that feels too weird."

He studied me, then his lips slowly curved into a smile, his blue eyes darkening with excitement. He pulled out his cell phone, not saying a word, and began to type.

I startled when my phone chimed but breathed a sigh of relief when I realized what was going on.

Chris
How about this way?

I got up, walked into my room, and sat on the nearest chair before typing my reply.

Erykah
This is perfect.

Chris

Good. I'm all ears.

I could do this. Just admit how I felt and let the chips fall where they may, or however that expression went. *Lord, please help me be brave.*

Erykah

I like you. Not just as a friend, though you make the very best one. But I want more than friendship with you.

I blew out a breath, then hit send. Immediately the dots waved in a dance as I waited for Chris to respond.

Chris

I feel the exact same way.

Erykah

Really?

"Really." Chris's soft whisper reached my ears.

I turned and saw him standing in the doorway of our connecting rooms. Slowly my foot took a step before the other finally followed. I stopped right in front of him. "I've wanted to tell you so many times before."

"Same, but I didn't want you to think I was being disrespectful as you grieved or taking advantage of you since we're sharing a house."

I sighed. He was so good to me. "I wouldn't have taken it that way."

"Then can I . . ." He trailed a finger down the side of my face and down my arm until our fingers were entwined. "Take you on a date tomorrow?"

"Please."

And we stood there doing nothing but holding each other's hands and grinning like two fools.

Thirty-Four

The fresh powder made for a perfect day of skiing. Nevaeh had only tried once, then confirmed she belonged in the lodge with Erykah. Tuck and Piper had decided they loved skiing almost as much as they loved riding horses. And Lamont was apparently a pro.

"Ready?" Lamont called.

"Let's go." Chris pushed off.

Ever since the text conversation he'd had with Erykah, he'd been riding on a high. Knowing Erykah cared for him just as he cared for her had him elated. Nothing could bring him down.

He started as a bird dipped too low and aimed for his face. Chris jerked right and overcompensated. Before he could panic, he fell right off the side of the mountain.

Lord God!

A scream ripped from Chris's throat.

His body jarred from the impact of the fall, but that wasn't what had him screaming and praying to God. No, the piercing pain in his right leg stole his breath. Something was wrong. Catastrophically, if he had to guess from the pain that had him begging the acid to go back down into his stomach.

Carefully, he lifted his head to look at his legs. He groaned and flopped back onto the snow.

"Chris! Chris! Can you hear me?" Lamont yelled.

Chris opened his eyes to see his friend peering over the mountain ledge. It took a herculean effort to hold up a thumb to let Lamont know Chris still lived. His hands shook as he tried to keep from vomiting.

"Help's on the way, man. Hang in there."

"I don't think I can," he mumbled.

Lamont probably couldn't see how bad Chris's injury was from his vantage point. *Stupid bird*. Not the first time he'd had a run-in with an animal, but the first time the result laid him flat. Heat pricked the back of his eyelids, so he attempted to blow out a breath.

Wrong thing to do. He quickly turned his head and lost his breakfast.

"Chris, you all right?" Tuck called.

Chris's arms shook, but he managed to stick a thumb up again.

"Do you think something is broken?"

Think? He *knew*. He kept his thumb up.

Chris could hear them mumbling. Then he heard the sweetest words ever.

"Help is here, man. They're sending someone down."

He heard the rappel system and opened his eyes in time to see a rescue worker and basket being lowered.

"Sir, I'm gonna get you up and to the hospital."

"Compound fracture," Chris gritted out.

"I see that, sir. We'll get you taken care of."

"Erykah," he rasped.

"Is she your wife?"

"Tell my friends . . ." He breathed, trying to keep the nausea at bay. "Get Erykah *now*."

"Take it easy, sir." The man spoke into his radio. "He's asking for someone named Erykah."

"Roger that," the radio crackled.

Knowing that Erykah would come, Chris closed his eyes and let the dark soothe him.

"Chris? Chris? Wake up for me."

A soft hand rubbed the side of his face. He didn't want to wake up, because then the pain would attack him again, but the voice sounded so worried. He willed his eyes to open, and light shined right into his retinas. He winced and closed them again.

"No. Open them again for me. I'll shade you."

He did as the voice instructed and stared right into Erykah's beautiful eyes. "Erykah," he murmured.

"I'm here."

"Leg's broken."

"I saw. We're almost to the hospital. I called ahead since I have a license to operate there."

Of course she did. She was amazing. "Save my leg."

"It won't come to that. No one's losing a leg tonight."

He tried to grin, but it took too much effort. "You operate."

"I . . ." She sighed. "They may not let me. We know each other, we . . . we *like* each other." Nervousness shined in her gaze as if she wasn't assured of his feelings yet.

He'd worry about that later. "But you're the best."

She stroked his face, saying nothing. Chris didn't know if that was a yes or if she was thinking. Either way, he kept quiet.

Lord, please don't let anyone else operate on me. I know I'm asking a lot of her, but I want a chance to heal from this, and she's the best. Please, God. Help me. Help her.

"I'll see what I can do. Don't worry about anything right now."

He frowned. "The girls?"

"Piper and Nevaeh have them. The guys are following behind the ambulance. Don't worry."

She was adorable in protector mode. "I'm sorry."

"For what? You have nothing to be sorry for."

"I ruined our vacation," he groused.

"Shh. It's okay." She placed a kiss on his forehead.

His entire being heated. He'd seen a forehead kiss in movies, but the man had always been the one to place it on the woman's head. There was something to be said about receiving one. Chris wished he was in the right frame of mind to turn the kiss into one of promise. The ambulance hit a pothole, and a groan tore from his throat.

He barely felt Erykah's touch against his forehead, but he heard her prayer. His body immediately stilled as if his being knew the importance of this moment.

"God, please bring Chris comfort. Please help relieve the pain. Please give him the best surgeon for the best recovery. Um, amen."

"You prayed." He tried to lick his lips, but his mouth had completely dried out from the last wave of pain. Did that mean he was going into shock or just that everything hurt?

"I should've said something earlier, but I-I believe. Though I'm not sure I would call that a prayer. I'm not eloquent like you are."

"It . . . was perfect." He swallowed down the acid. "Going to be sick."

A plastic bag was thrust under his mouth just in time.

This had to be the most humiliating *and* agonizing experience of his life. To vomit in front of the woman he loved. *Love?*

His heart stopped, then received a jolt. When had his more-than-friendly feelings turned to love? Hadn't he just thought it was romantic interest being tortured by a friend zone he couldn't escape from? Only the stabbing pain in his leg kept distracting him from his thoughts.

The ambulance stopped.

"We're here," Erykah murmured. "They're going to move you. It'll hurt, but I'm here. I won't leave your side."

"Operate . . . please."

She bit her lip. "That's not allowed when you know the person."

"*Please.*"

Tears filled her eyes, and his gut clenched. As much as he wanted the best doctor, he never *ever* wanted to make her cry.

"I'm sorry. Forget it," he gritted.

Doctors swarmed around him, and Erykah went into her element. The tears that had been there a moment before dried as she began speaking in a jargon that sounded like something straight out of *ER* or *Grey's Anatomy.* He'd never been prouder. All Chris could do was watch in awe as the other doctors responded to her authority.

After getting images, they wheeled him down to the surgery prep floor. He talked to the anesthesiologist and another orthopedic surgeon. Erykah walked into the room, hair in a scrub cap and scrubs on her body. He blinked, afraid to hope.

"Are you . . . ?"

She shook her head. "I can't. But they did agree to let me in the room to make sure everything goes according to my satisfaction."

Relief filled him. He wouldn't be alone. She would protect him.

He grinned. "I'm so happy."

"Ah, the drugs finally kicked in, huh?" She chuckled, but the line between her brows didn't smooth out like it usually did when she laughed.

"I think they upped the dose." He stared at the IV hooked to his arm. What had they given him, again? Morphine?

"They did. You were still in too much pain."

"I don't like drugs."

She cupped the side of his face. "You need it to relax. Soon you'll be waking up again, and it'll be all over. You'll be on your way to healing."

"And you'll be here?"

"I'm not leaving."

He closed his eyes. Obviously she was referring to this whole ordeal, but Chris liked to hope that there was a double meaning to her words. That she wasn't just interested in casual dating but wanted a relationship that was made for the long haul. That she wouldn't leave and abandon him like his ex. That Erykah would put in the work to make their relationship a great one, recognizing Chris would give his all for the same goal. Even if she only meant for today, the words gave him peace. Knowing she was by his side allowed him to close his eyes and succumb to the meds running through his veins.

Thirty-Five

My stomach was in knots. My center of gravity had shifted, leaving me off-kilter. Seeing Chris on that stretcher when they raced him off the slopes had slowed down time and pitched my heart to my feet. Even now, watching as the on-call surgeon performed the emergency surgery, I still couldn't make time speed up to normal. Couldn't get us to the other side of Chris's recovery.

I could only watch helplessly as another surgeon performed the repair I'd won awards for. I'd checked his credentials when they first informed me of the doctor's name. He had adequate training, and this wouldn't be his first compound fracture.

That did *not* comfort me at all.

I wanted to be the one repairing the fracture, but knowing I'd be working on Chris made me want to burst into tears. Having a surgeon who couldn't stop the waterworks would be more harmful than a doctor I found subpar. So I watched from a place where I could be as unobtrusive as possible . . . and prayed.

Please, don't let this surgery go awry. Please fix Chris.

Please give him miraculous healing. You do miracles, right? Because I need a miracle.

What would I do if something happened and Chris didn't recover?

Don't think like that.

The thought had been cycling in the back of my mind from the moment I'd received a phone call from Lamont telling me Chris had fallen off the mountain and was being rescued. My heart had literally stopped for a couple of beats.

Not another person.

I couldn't lose another person I called my own. Not one more. And that was what I kept telling God over and over. Not one more. I wasn't sure if He was listening in this instance, but I wouldn't stop praying until I had an answer.

The doctor began screwing the tibia together. So far, he'd done everything to my satisfaction. But standing in the corner watching the dance that was the operating room made me realize just how disconcerting everything was to an outsider. I glanced at the monitors, checking Chris's heart rate and blood pressure. Everything looked as it should. Thankfully, I'd had a copious amount of practice standing in surgery, because I wasn't moving from this spot unless I was forced to or the surgery was complete and considered successful.

Chris wanted me here. He *needed* me. For once our relationship wasn't about me taking, taking, and taking some more. He'd asked for me, kept hold of my hand the entire ride here. Though if I really thought about it, he probably hadn't been cognizant of me holding his hand.

Still, I would be here until he said otherwise. Even through all the pain and rehab he still had to face. I blinked. *Oh my word.* How was he going to film the rest of his docuseries while on crutches? Did he get sick leave from his nonprofit? And why didn't I know more about how his business worked?

Was I so caught up in myself that I couldn't ask about a friend?

I snorted.

Who was I kidding? I'd passed friendly feelings like passing Go and collecting two hundred dollars. I was so completely in love with Chris. How could I not fall for a man of his caliber? He was the gold standard. I regretted not expressing those exact words to him before. Sure, he knew I wanted a romantic relationship, but . . . would that all change now? How could I expect us to move forward when he'd literally taken a step backward? Like a bad move in Chutes and Ladders, Chris was at the beginning of this journey. *Don't focus on that right now. Wait until he's out of the woods before you figure out the next steps.*

By the time surgery was over and Chris was wheeled out of the room, I felt like crumbling. I thanked the doctor for his hard work and went to the nearest bathroom . . . and lost all composure. I cried as quietly as possible while also allowing every pent-up emotion out. Chris could've died today. Something could've gone wrong in surgery.

But he didn't die. Surgery was textbook. Your prayer was answered.

I hiccupped. Chris was alive. He was on his way to healing. I hadn't lost another person.

I blinked at the reflection staring back at me. God had answered my prayer. As much as I could credit the resulting miracle to modern medicine and the EMTs who'd rushed him to the hospital, I couldn't discount the fact that I'd been praying from the moment I knew Chris had been hurt.

Knowing Lamont and all of them like I did, they'd been praying too. God heard us. God answered us.

"You love me," I whispered.

Goose bumps broke out across my arms as the hairs on my

body raised in awareness. I wasn't spooked, but right then, in that moment, I did *not* feel alone, even though there was no one else in the bathroom with me.

God is the Spirit, right?

I licked my lips. I couldn't explain what I felt. There were no adequate words to describe the way my heart hammered and the way my skin prickled in recognition. I just *knew* I wasn't alone.

God had been taking care to show me all the ways He was real. And even though I fully believed, He still showed up. Still answered my prayers. He saw me and knew I still needed confirmation when I doubted. How astonishing it was He cared enough to answer my prayer and not take Chris away from me.

Tears fell in relief. Gone were the ones of heartache; now I cried in pure gratitude. I bowed my head, letting myself pour out my thanks.

Thank You for the way You've revealed Yourself today. You saved Chris. You heard me. You provided a path to healing.

My breath shuddered. Knowing the many ways God continued to show up for me humbled me to my core. Never—well, besides Chris—had I had someone show up for me without question. The irony in that thought had me snort. *I'd* questioned God repeatedly until I'd accepted all the ways He'd blessed me. A little part of me thought He'd stop then. He'd gotten me to admit I was wrong and He existed, and that would be the end.

But God showed up . . . *again*.

Chris needs you.

Right. There was a man on the way to recovery who I wanted to be there for. I wanted me, not the nurse in recovery, to be the first person Chris saw when he woke. I turned on the water, splashing my face. Thank goodness I hadn't put on makeup. Cheyenne hadn't cared that my face was natural, and neither had Chris when he'd looked at me earlier. He'd been thankful for my presence. So I would go and be present.

I hurried to the recovery room and breathed out a sigh of relief. He hadn't roused from the anesthesia yet.

"Dr. Kennedy?"

I turned and saw a nurse striding toward me. "They said I could give you an update. I'm Sam."

"Nice to meet you." I shook her hand. "Everything looking good?"

"Yes, ma'am. He should be coming out of it in a half hour if my guess is accurate."

I grinned. "I'm sure it is."

"Well, I have been doing this for twenty years, so I'd say I have it down to the minute. Do you need some water? Crackers?"

I couldn't eat anything right now. I just wanted to see Chris's blue eyes staring back at me. "A cup of water would be great. Thank you."

"Of course. I already put a chair by his bedside."

I walked to Chris's bed and sat in the chair next to him. I ran my hand down his arm and covered it with my palm. Would he feel the warmth? Would he know he was safe? I hoped so.

"You did fantastic in surgery," I whispered. "I'm so proud of you."

I ran my hand through his hair. It was thick at the top, holding a slight curl at the ends. I'd been wanting to touch his hair forever but didn't want to be that girl.

Then don't. Soothe but don't explore.

I stifled a chuckle. Maybe the relief at the knowledge he'd made it through surgery made me a little batty.

I gasped. The guys! They must be frantic. I pulled out my cell and opened a new text thread, adding everyone to the chain.

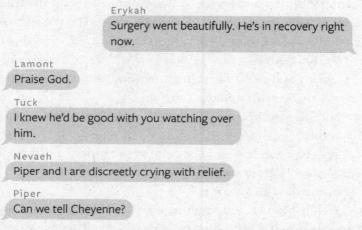

Erykah
Surgery went beautifully. He's in recovery right now.

Lamont
Praise God.

Tuck
I knew he'd be good with you watching over him.

Nevaeh
Piper and I are discreetly crying with relief.

Piper
Can we tell Cheyenne?

My poor niece! People kept getting hurt around her. This had to have scared her, if not scarred her a little. I'd have to let her new therapist know about this recent development. But I was glad Cheye had an outlet. Her tantrums had calmed some.

Erykah
Please. Tell her he's going to be okay, and I'll be home after dinner.

Because I wouldn't leave before that. I was sure the guys or even the girls would be willing to maintain a rotation at the hospital, so Chris wouldn't be alone. Should I call his mother? *You don't have her number.* I'd have to remember to ask Chris about that once they moved him to a permanent room.

A low moan came from his lips. I turned my attention from my thoughts and focused on him. I ran a hand across his forehead.

"Are you hurting? Do you need some water?" I asked quietly.

Recovery rooms were always quiet, and I didn't want to talk loudly and disturb another patient coming out of surgery and back into reality.

"Erykah?" he rasped.

"I'm here." I'd never go anywhere if he'd let me stay next to his side forever.

"I'm okay?"

"You're great." I placed a kiss to his knuckles and squeezed his hand. "I'm so proud of you. You did it, and the surgery went perfectly."

"Thank God."

"Amen." I smiled. I'd get a handle on the lingo. I'd actually looked that word up and found out *amen* was merely an agreement. Since I'd been thanking God earlier, I didn't mind thanking Him once more.

"You prayed? Or am I misremembering?" Chris studied me, his gaze becoming clearer as the fog of anesthesia slowly lifted.

"I did, and God answered." I smiled. "I'm so glad you're okay." I brushed his hairline. "Do you want some water? I'm sure I can get something cold. It'll feel good on your throat." I'd since finished the cup Sam had left for me.

"Please."

I hurried to the watering station and filled a Styrofoam cup, then stopped at the nurses' station. "Hey, Sam, can I get a straw for Chris?"

"Of course, Dr. Kennedy." She handed me one. "I saw his vitals picked up but knew he was in good hands with you there. If he needs some pain meds, just let me know."

"Thanks, Sam."

"Sure thing."

I held the straw steady for Chris as he took a sip.

He let out a sigh. "You're right. That works wonders." He took another swallow, then let his head drop back on the pillow. "How are the kids? Are the guys here?"

"Yes. Lamont and Tuck are in the waiting room. They want to see you once your room is ready. Then the plan is for them to hang out with you until visiting hours are over. I'll go back with one of them to relieve Nevaeh and Piper and reassure the girls, though the ladies already told them you're okay."

"You must have been filled with worry." His gaze assessed mine.

"That might have crossed my mind."

A somber expression filled his face. "I'm sorry."

"You have nothing to apologize for. I'm just glad you're okay."

"Healing is going to suck, isn't it?"

I didn't want to lie, but I didn't want to make him feel defeated before he even began the recovery process. "Let's not worry about that right now. Just recover from surgery. 'Kay?"

"Okay."

Thirty-Six

When Chris was a teen, the thought of using crutches seemed kind of cool. Lean on something and let it take your weight, then you just propel your body forward. Fun.

But at forty-two, he could say crutches were for the birds. He hated them with every fiber of his being. They annoyed his arms, his armpits, and that soft skin no one talked about that covered the side of his ribs. But without the devices, the pain of putting his body weight on his right leg would be unbearable.

Next week, he'd start in-person rehab. But it seemed too late. Sure, he recognized that logically his body had suffered a traumatic event, and he needed to recover. However, being laid up meant he'd missed his friend's wedding. Lamont had sent Chris a recording of the ceremony, but it wasn't the same. Their wedding had been small and intimate but obviously with glitz and glam. Nevaeh dazzled in some kind of lace dress that reminded him of leaves. Lamont had cried, and Nevaeh couldn't stop grinning.

He hated that he'd missed it. Chris had been in a funk since the ski resort, so to keep himself from taking it out on the girls, he'd remained holed up in the guest bedroom on the main floor—because he did *not* want to navigate the stairs going up to his bedroom. Christmas had come and gone, and the flip of the calendar had brought a new year.

Happy New Year to me.

This wasn't how he'd imagined he'd be ringing it in. This year was supposed to be about new beginnings and things to look forward to.

You'll look forward to the use of your leg without crutches.

Without a doubt, but he had to get through recovery first. The thought of dealing with this over the span of four to six months made his throat raw with unshed tears—the shed ones were saved for showers and rain. He prayed there would be no lingering limp afterward, but that wasn't a guarantee. Chris didn't have the kind of money it took to tip the odds in his favor. If his insurance determined after a certain point that he didn't need more rehab and his leg didn't heal the way he prayed . . . then his life would forever be altered in ways he didn't want to even contemplate. *Yet still you do.*

PathLight had been less than pleased to hear of his injury. The docuseries was on a definite pause since Chris couldn't exactly go out on excursions and showcase the beauty of Colorado and native wildlife anymore. The thought of hiking or even climbing onto the back of an ATV made him wince with pain.

His coworkers at the nonprofit were more than happy to pick up his slack and post on YouTube for him. After all, his profile was the nonprofit name, not Christian Gamble. Still, he felt like dead weight. He was useless to his coworkers, unless answering the phone and applying for grants counted. That he could do at home, and he forced himself to do it so he didn't become panic-stricken from all of the what-ifs.

Chris couldn't even help Erykah the way he wanted. Cooking dinner had become an Olympic event because of the crutches impeding his movements. He couldn't pick up Ash and balance both her *and* the crutches. Just the walk to meet Cheye at the bus stop was agonizing. Still, he made himself do so. He didn't want to be completely useless.

Heat pricked the back of his eyelids, and he looked up at the ceiling, hoping the threat of any emotions would recede. Instead, liquid ran down his temples and onto the pillow. *It's not raining outside. Get it together, Gamble.*

But being flat on his back had messed with his emotions more than he cared to admit. Chris couldn't remember the last time he was this still. There'd always been something to do or somewhere to be. Now he couldn't go anywhere at the pace he wanted, so why bother moving?

In everything give thanks.

Was this a situation Chris was supposed to thank God for? And if so, what exactly would he be thankful for?

Not being dead, for one.

He winced. Okay, that was a concession he could make.

That an artery wasn't hit.

Right, because then being dead would've been a surety.

That Erykah has done everything to help your recovery.

His heart warmed at the thought. Erykah had been a rock star since he'd been injured. Even Cheyenne had been sweeter to him. Offering to bring him a snack or just sit and watch TV with him—when he decided to move from the bed to the couch. And little Ash was comfortable just curling up in the crook of his arm. The ladies had given him more reasons to smile than he'd have if he were recovering all alone.

Then that's another thing to be thankful for. You're not doing this by yourself.

Even now with Erykah at work, Cheyenne at school, and Ash at the daycare, Chris wasn't alone. Charlie lay at his

277

feet as if his mere presence would bring comfort to Chris. *Which it has.*

Lord, You're right. I'm sorry for throwing myself a pity party. I do have a lot to be thankful for. Thank You for all those things I begrudgingly thought of at first. I can see the true blessing of each and every one. You took away my loneliness by bringing Erykah and her nieces into my life. And now You're with me and have ensured I'm not going through this by myself.

Tuck and Lamont continued to text and check on him. Even Piper and Nevaeh had sent him care packages. Nevaeh sent an ice pack made specifically for legs, along with an elevation pillow. Piper had sent a lavender candle to soothe his nerves. Of course the guys threw in gag gifts. Tuck had sent an *Oh snap* gingerbread shirt while Lamont had gifted a shirt that had an image of a man kicking a bear with the words *I was fighting a bear.*

All the gifts had moved him in some way. The biggest blessing of all was Lamont paying for his hospital bill. You know, the part the insurance *wouldn't* pay. He'd tried to offer to pay his friend back, but Lamont had been adamant about not wanting Chris's money. Apparently he'd done the same thing when Tuck had broken a shoulder earlier last year.

You have much to be thankful for, Gamble. Get out of this bed and walk around. The doctor wants you to do so a little each day anyway.

If he didn't use both of his legs, the possibility of atrophying and losing muscle mass increased. Apparently that would only delay healing.

"Charlie, want to go outside?"

The dog barked, his ears moving forward.

"Let's go, boy."

The little dog jumped off the bed and ran to the doorway,

turning back to watch Chris reach for his crutches and maneuver them under his arms. He stood, then hobbled after the dog, who moved quickly through the living room to the kitchen area and sat by the back door.

Chris twisted the lock, and the dog ran outside, barking at the sunshine. Charlie rolled around in the grass that had just been cleared of snow, thanks to the abundant sunshine and slightly warmer temps. Would he find the first mud patch?

Chris waited out there until the pain begged him to head back inside. He whistled for Charlie, and the dog came trotting toward the house.

"Wipe your paws." A quick peek told him the dog had stayed out of any mud patches. *Good.* If he could avoid the extra work of bathing a dog, Chris would.

Charlie did as asked, then ran inside, straight to his doggy bowl, lapping up water. Chris grabbed a tube of crackers, holding the bag in between his teeth, then crutched his way to the living room. By the time he got his leg situated just right on the couch and YouTube running Michael Jordan highlight reels, his phone rang.

Mom flashed on the caller ID.

Since his accident, Chris's mom had called every day to check on him. In the early days following the surgery, he hadn't been surprised. After all, breaking a bone and getting screws inserted was considered major surgery. That phrase probably concerned her on some level, but then she kept calling. She'd even started texting Erykah. For the first time in . . . *ever*, his mom appeared to be interested in what was happening to him.

"Hey, Mom."

"Hey, son, how are you feeling?"

Sad. Morose. Discouraged. "Fine."

"Are you in a lot of pain?"

How was he supposed to answer that? There was a constant ache that had failed to go away. When it rained a couple of days ago, he'd wanted to curl into the fetal position. He didn't want to take narcotics any longer than necessary, so he was left with your basic OTC pain reliever. But he could watch TV without lamenting the pain so . . .

"No." But he was counting down the two hours left until his next round of pain meds.

"Have you started rehab?"

"Not until next week, like I told you *yesterday*." He pinched the bridge of his nose. *Didn't that sound curt?* "Mom, what's going on? Are *you* okay?"

"I'm not the one with the broken leg."

"But you're the one who visited me for Thanksgiving and have called consistently for the past couple of weeks." He paused, his brain trying to make sense of it all. Every time she called, he was floored, then he tried to figure out why. Experience told him she didn't care about the intricacies of his life. Her part ended when he'd turned eighteen.

His gaze narrowed. "Are you sick? Are you . . . *dying?*"

"What! No. Why on earth would you think that?"

"Tell me when's the last time we talked so much before I got injured?"

Silence greeted his ears. *Exactly.* She couldn't tell him when they last communicated so much because that *never* happened. Not when he went off to college. Not when he'd gotten a job out of state. Not when he returned to Colorado. With every major event in his life, his mom had given him radio silence unless it was his birthday or a major holiday.

"Chris . . ." She sighed. "I'm trying to do better. *Be* better."

"Then you're not sick or dying?"

"No." She chuckled.

"Is this some kind of strange New Year's resolution, then?" No, the weirdness had started at Thanksgiving.

"Son, I want us to have a relationship where we talk to each other. Where we share what's important to us."

"Since when?" He winced. Okay, even he could hear the skepticism and a stronger coat of bitterness than he'd realized existed within.

Was he . . . *mad* at his mom?

He'd always figured he loved her for who she was. A single mom who fed him, clothed him, and put food on the table. The fact that she didn't do anything else wasn't a shock to his middle-aged system. Only now he could feel anger stirring in the depths of his heart, and he didn't like that one bit.

Whether it was because he didn't want to be angry or because he'd have to deal with the source of his anger remained to be seen.

Get her off the phone first, then contemplate the phone call and her motives later.

"You're right in thinking a sickness started it. But wrong that I'm seriously ill or dying." She cleared her throat. "They found a lump in my breast, but after some biopsies and removing it, they determined the mass to be benign and not a threat to my health. Nevertheless, the whole ordeal put some things into perspective."

Yeah, like how he had no clue his mom had gone through anything like that.

"When did you have the surgery?" he asked.

"Last September."

"It's January, Mom."

She sighed. "Hence the reason I've been trying to connect more. I would've come to visit for Christmas, but you said Erykah wanted a quiet Christmas. When you got hurt,

I wanted to come up and help, but you said you didn't need it. So I'm calling instead." She sounded almost hurt.

Despite hearing every word and listening to the tone of her voice and what she hadn't said, Chris was having difficulty processing it all as true. "I'm not sure what to say."

"How about we start with how you *really* feel?"

Could he? Could he accept the step forward she offered? "About the leg or the phone calls?"

She let out a short laugh. "Pick one."

"All right." He paused. "I hate being dependent on crutches and that I can't move as freely as I want."

"That's understandable. You've always moved about, even as a child. I used to discipline you by telling you to sit still." She chuckled. "You couldn't stand it, and I'm not ashamed to admit that amused me."

They were sharing memories now? He didn't actually remember his mom disciplining him. Yet he'd known as a kid and teen that he'd better not break a rule his mom had put in place. Guess that meant he'd have to have been disciplined to understand that. Cheye liked to test Erykah's boundaries on a daily basis. That kid had to apologize so many times throughout the day it wasn't funny. . . . Okay, yes, it was.

"I believe that, because this feels like torture." He waffled between wanting to move and help out and wanting to crawl right back into bed and complain about how painful this all was. *Mentally, spiritually, and emotionally.* He was exhausted in all the ways.

"Are you allowed to walk?"

"Not without the aid of the crutches. Still, my leg just hurts. I'm not sure if I'm not used to the crutches, or if this is all part of the healing process."

"Did you know you can buy cushions for the crutches? If they're bothering you so much, add more foam to them."

"Really?"

"Yeah, I'll text you a link. I used some when I broke my foot a few years ago."

"You broke your foot?" His mouth dropped open. "When? Where was I?"

"You were in Wyoming for some work thing, so I didn't want to bother you. All I had to do was wear a boot and get through the pain. Now I'm simply waiting for arthritis to show up. It will, as old as I am."

This was too much. He'd *missed* so much. "Mom, are you going to call tomorrow?"

"I am."

Chris bit his lip. "You know, you're always welcome to come and visit again. Just give me notice so I can make sure you have clean sheets to sleep on."

"Thank you." Her voice sounded shaky, like she was suppressing tears. "How is Erykah doing? The girls?"

"Cheyenne is in school and Ash at daycare. They all have good and bad days. Erykah is trying to find a place to live but now doesn't want to leave until I'm on my feet."

Could he add that to the list of things he couldn't stand? He felt like he was holding her back from starting a life that would benefit the girls. Cheye's therapist mentioned how important a good home environment and routine was. She was a little concerned that Erykah would be moving soon, and Chris had finally begun to see the merit of her comment.

After all, his offer to share his home had always been a stepping stone. Would Cheye feel like she was losing someone all over again—no matter if he'd still come to visit? And Ash? She was used to seeing him every day and snuggling in his arms at least once. What were they going to do when that bridge arrived?

"Chris . . ."

"Yes?"

"I'd be happy to come and help you all. If Erykah is putting her life on hold for you, then my arrival means she can maintain her house search. Once she secures a place, I can stay with you until you're able to do everything on your own. I think I'm perfectly capable of watching over my own son."

His breath stuck in his chest.

Having his mom move in temporarily was a dynamic Chris had never thought he'd face. However, if she was serious about the olive branch and wanting to deepen their relationship, then this was a good time to do that. It wasn't like he could go anywhere.

Only now there would be nothing stopping Erykah and the girls from finally moving on to the next step. Cheye needed to be able to heal from the trauma of losing her folks, though she'd most likely grieve for the rest of her life. Every day the girls lived in his house cemented the idea of permanence in Cheyenne's mind. The last thing Chris wanted to do was hurt that precious little one simply because she changed addresses.

What am I going to do?

Thirty-Seven

Lamont
Is Chris really fine?

Tuck
Right? If he uses "fine" one more time, I'll have to fly up there and see how he's doing myself.

Nevaeh
Guys are never fine when they're injured. You'd think after dealing with women, you'd realize no one is when using that word.

Piper
Erykah, feel free to ignore us until you're able to chat. We know you're busy.

Tuck
Totally. I had a break in my own schedule, which is why I replied.

Lamont
Same. I didn't mean to bombard you, just concerned for him.

Erykah
He's not fine, but I don't know how to help. Most of the time he pretends to work on the computer but really just stares out the window looking lost.

Nevaeh
Praying for him! Should I send another care package?

Tuck
Guess sending a gag gift didn't help.

Lamont
Yikes. I sent one too.

Erykah
It made him laugh, so thanks. And I know you all are praying.

Piper
Without ceasing! That's in 1 Thessalonians 5:17.

Nevaeh
Ooooh. You reading the Bible, girl?

Erykah
I am. I'm finishing up Ruth.

Lamont
The Psalms are my favorite. Check that out next.

Tuck
No! Book of James is the best.

Piper
How about we pray God leads her?

Lamont
Even better.

Tuck
We'll leave you alone now, Doc. We'll be praying God gives us wisdom on how we can best help Chris.

Erykah
Amen

I put away my phone and stared out of the hospital window. Though the office didn't have the views Chris's living room offered, the snow on the rooftops certainly gave me a little peace.

Yesterday when I'd arrived home, Chris had been in a sour mood. He'd seemed so withdrawn. Yet when I asked him if anything had happened, he'd been curt in his reply and refused to give any more information. I wasn't born yesterday. I hadn't lived four decades on this earth not to realize when something more than a broken leg was going on. *But what?*

Could he be depressed? Had the trauma of the event taken a hidden toll my eyes couldn't see? I wanted so badly to fix what ailed him, but I couldn't if he wouldn't open up and tell me what was wrong.

God, please show me what to do. Please help Chris see I'm trustworthy and can share the weight of his burden. Please.

I bit my lip, not knowing what else to say. At least talking to God was becoming easier. It felt weird to bow my head, clasp my hands, and voice my problems as if Someone were really listening. But He'd shown me He *was* listening. Lately, when I prayed, my body felt warm. Almost like I was being wrapped in a hug.

Of course I'd researched on the internet to find out if others had felt the same sensations. There were articles saying that God sometimes physically touched a person, but I wasn't sure what to think. Was my desire to be seen and heard just manifesting these sensations?

No. Don't fall into unbelief again. God has shown He's real, and He's watching over you. He'll continue answering your prayers in some way.

I had to keep my thoughts from straying to unbelief, but, boy, that was easier said than done. My gaze drifted to the sticky note I'd placed on the edge of my monitor. Piper texted me Scriptures that she thought might help me, and some hit me right in the heart. I'd taken to writing those down, placing them where they'd be visible so I could reread them. I even had some on the bedroom mirror at Chris's house.

Maybe I needed to place some verses for him to read to keep him from being so . . . unhappy. I simply wanted to see him smile again.

My computer chimed, a new email popping up from my Realtor. I clicked on her name, then read the message.

> Dr. Kennedy,
>
> I found the perfect place. Good school district. Not too far from your work. The current owners want to close by the end of the month. Here's a link to the listing. Let me know if you want to view it. I have availability this evening or tomorrow evening.
>
> Sincerely,
> Kate

I clicked on the link and then the photos. As I scrolled through them, excitement coursed through me. This was the best listing she'd sent. Though I'd obviously change some of the wall paint colors—who used neon yellow in the living room?—and I would have to update some of the appliances. I definitely wanted to see it in person.

Could I leave early to look at it this evening? I clicked on my calendar. All clear. It would allow me to grab some dinner on the way home so that no one had to starve either.

I quickly typed up a response, and Kate confirmed our time for viewing. I grinned. If all worked out well, we'd be in a new place by February. I couldn't wait to tell Chris.

My grin fell. *Chris*. How could I leave him? His mobility wasn't the best, and I'd promised him I would stay until he was on his feet. Surely the physical therapist would give us a better idea of recovery time when he attended the evaluation appointment next week. Though that wasn't my biggest worry.

I'd been so excited to know that Chris had romantic feelings for me. Knowing I wasn't the only one in that boat had been comforting as well as exciting. But since his accident, we'd almost reverted to pre-confession. I didn't know if it was because we were still living together or because of his injury. Regardless, Chris stayed holed up in his room most of the time, and when not in his room, he put all his focus on the girls. It was almost like he was avoiding me, but I had no idea why.

When I moved, would that make him retreat even further?

"What do I do, God?" I whispered.

The intranet system beeped, alerting me to a message request. I clicked on the bubble and read the message. There was an emergency that required a consult. I replied, then opened the patient's info on my iPad. After studying the images, I agreed with the radiologist. Spiral fracture.

I responded with my assessment and informed them the scheduler would reach out to make the necessary appointments. Since it wasn't a compound fracture, the patient would have to wait for an opening in the orthopedic schedule. Most likely they'd get in in the next couple of days. My next few surgery days were already booked, so odds were another doctor would be tagged.

I continued the rest of my paperwork day until I was able to clock out and head to the property. By the time I pulled up to the for-sale sign, my nerves had me feeling like I'd drunk one too many cups of coffee. I walked up the sidewalk and checked the doorknob. Unlocked. I stepped into the foyer. *Huh*. The neon yellow didn't look as horrid as it had in the pictures, but only because the light from the windows softened the shade somehow. Guess you really could paint a living room that tint.

"Dr. Kennedy, you made it." Kate beamed at me. "Have a look around, then let me know if you have any questions."

"Thanks, Kate."

I walked through the place, taking my time to observe the amount of space in each room. I searched for any cracks, water stains, and other deformities. Chris had given me that tip. Yet nothing looked suspect. Even the bold colors on the walls grew on me as I lapped the house to view everything for the second time. If this was the one I went for, I wanted to make sure I didn't miss a thing.

Satisfied, I went back to the kitchen, where Kate stared at her phone.

"This will work."

Her eyes widened in surprise, then she beamed. "Fantastic. Does that mean you want to put in an offer?"

"Yes, please."

We talked about the particulars and then split ways. Kate had to go to the office to work up the documents. She would email them to me so I could sign the offer electronically. I placed an online to-go order at a restaurant near Chris's house, then put my car in drive. By the time I made it to Woodland Park, the order would be ready.

I headed to the daycare and picked up a happy Ash. She was babbling more but had yet to say *auntie*. I figured chanting that in her ear on a daily basis was easier than getting her to say Aunt Erykah.

She grabbed my face and pressed her cheek to mine. "Mama."

Tears pricked my eyes. All this time I'd said *auntie* in her ears, and she skipped right over that. My love for her grew daily, but my heart hurt for Ellynn. Still, I lingered in the hug, embracing the moment, before moving her into her car seat.

Kid music streamed through the speakers as we drove

home. At least Cheyenne wasn't here to demand we listen to "Baby Shark." Chris was still triggered from our road trips. When I caught sight of his house, my lips drifted into a smile. When I'd first moved in, I'd been a little horrified at the log-cabin style. Not my thing. But now . . . now I was filled with anticipation, knowing I'd get to see my people. This had become home. If only I could cheer Chris up and remind him he would heal.

I parked the car, then grabbed Ash and the paper bag holding our dinner.

I'd sanded the steps earlier this morning. (Chris had informed me salting steps only added to water pollution.) Thankfully, no snow had fallen. I wasn't ready to shovel another layer anytime soon.

Charlie barked a greeting when we walked into the living room, and Cheyenne cheered.

"Did you bring dinner?" She peeked into the bag.

"I did. Think you're strong enough to carry this to the kitchen?"

Cheye gave me a *Girl, please* look.

"Right. I'll do it."

"I'll take Ash." Chris looked at me from his spot on the sofa.

I handed the baby over, discreetly trying to figure out his mood. He wasn't curt like yesterday, so maybe that had been a bad pain day. *Please let him be feeling better today, God.*

"Welcome home," he murmured in a husky voice.

Chills went up and down my spine. What I wouldn't give to turn and place a kiss on his lips and *really* be welcomed home. "Thank you," I whispered.

I drew back, hoping my face didn't look flushed and my expression didn't say *Kiss me, please.* As much as I wanted to finally find out how his lips would feel, I needed to get him to let me in. If he was worried about his recovery or if yesterday had simply been too overwhelming, I needed to know. I wanted us to work, and communication was key.

Are you going to tell him about the house?

My heart skipped a beat. I'd definitely wait until the girls were in bed.

Cheyenne kept up most of the chatter as we ate our meal. Ash babbled as if adding to the conversation. A few times, I saw a ghost of Chris's smile. Not the full-blown one that made my heart flip and made me want to clasp a hand to my chest and flutter my eyelashes like Tai from *Clueless*. No, this one sparked hope that the Chris I knew would make it out of this. Whatever *this* was. I just wished he'd talk to me.

Then ask him how he feels.

Right. I could do that. Walk up to him and try to get down to the heart of the matter.

All through the bedtime routine, my brain kept preparing for the upcoming talk. For finding out what made Chris so sad and me trying to figure out how to tell him I'd found a place. Surely he would be happy I'd no longer be freeloading. He'd have his house back to himself and would be able to enjoy the quiet once more.

Now that Charlie was crate trained, I could safely leave him by himself while I went to work. *Right?* The backyard at the new place would be perfect on the warmer days, but until then, Charlie could stay in the crate while I was away. I'd be able to drive home for lunch to let him run around a bit.

I'd just have to remember those points in case Chris worried about the girls and the pup. *But will he worry about me?*

I changed into a hoodie and sweats and put my twists in a bun on top of my head. Then I went to the living room. Chris still sat in the same position I'd left him in when I took the girls downstairs for their baths. Instead of the TV playing a show, it showed a caption that read *Are you still watching?*

Chris stared at the screen as if the words hadn't penetrated. A lost expression I was growing all too familiar with resided on his face.

"Chris, please talk to me." I sat down, scooting close enough to lay a hand on his arm. "Please tell me what's wrong."

He turned his head and looked at me. His gaze seemed to catalog every feature on my face before his chest rose, then fell. "Erykah, I think you should leave."

Thirty-Eight

The words tore from his gut.

Chris hated to say them, but he'd been thinking about his mom's offer since yesterday, and the only conclusion he'd come to was for Erykah to leave. He'd offered space in his place so she'd have time to find adequate housing, not to mention his desire to help her. But now he was an added burden when she'd already dealt with so much. How could he have her helping him around the house when she had Ash and Cheye, who required her attention unless they'd managed to sleep peacefully? She was literally doing everything by herself right now. For heaven's sake, she'd shoveled snow and sanded the sidewalk before leaving for work this morning. What kind of man did that make him to have the woman he . . . *loved* shoveling snow?

If he gave her notice to move out, surely she'd be able to find something for her and the girls. He didn't want to hold them back or make their life any more difficult than it already was.

"What do you mean? Where do you want me to go?" Erykah asked.

"You need to find another place to live." He drew in a

breath. "Preferably by the end of the month." He couldn't stand seeing her doing everything in this house another day. If she was going to do so much, she'd be better off living in her own space without a daily reminder of Chris's uselessness. But he needed to ensure they had someplace to move to.

"Are . . . I . . ." She licked her lips. "Have I done something wrong?"

"Of course not. I'm the one . . ." He looked away.

The crestfallen expression on her face was like a shard to his heart. *I'm not kicking her out.* This was for the good of her and the girls. Cheye would finally get a new path for healing, and Erykah wouldn't have to live in the basement any longer. He knew his place was not her idea of *home sweet home.* Besides, his deductible for physical therapy would make a dent in his pocket. Not to mention PathLight would be severing their contract with him and requiring a payback on the advance they'd given. He'd basically be paying for them to find a new star for their show.

But that's a good thing, right? You don't actually like working for them.

That was beside the point. His income would take a hit. The leg, the money, worrying about overwhelming a woman who already had so much on her plate . . . all the things that had kept him from sleeping soundly. He never wanted to be a burden, and honestly, sometimes a person had to reassess their promises. Discover when it was time to back away— like Tracey had when she ended their relationship—and find a new plan.

"You guys will be better off without me." His throat cracked on the sentence, but he had to show her he meant every word.

"Better off without you? Are you suggesting we'll never see you again? Aren't we friends?" Shock coated every word.

Being her friend wouldn't change, but he was failing in that department. "Of course the girls can visit, and you'll always be my friend. No matter what." Whether she remained his was another story.

"And that's it? Just a friend?" Her brown eyes bored into his.

The desire to pull her close and into his arms swelled within him. But just as quickly, he batted the feeling away. As much as he wanted to take her on a date like he'd asked weeks ago, he couldn't. Legit couldn't. He couldn't drive, couldn't even cook her dinner. With the uncertainty surrounding the docuseries and his financial troubles, Chris couldn't figure out what he could possibly offer her. She was a world-renowned orthopedic surgeon. Chris would be foolish to offer his heart only for her to return it like Tracey had when she'd seriously considered forever.

He swallowed. "We'll always be friends."

"Okay, then." Her head dropped, and the next words were muffled as she spoke into her chest. "I guess you'll be happy to know I found a place." Her head shot up, and the fakest smile he'd ever seen plastered itself on her face. "My Realtor is putting in an offer, and if they accept, I'll close by end of month. We'll be out of your hair."

"Uh . . ." His mind blanked.

Erykah held up a hand. "No need to say anything more. You've made your position perfectly clear." She stood up. "Do you need anything? If not, I'm gonna hit the sack."

"No." Didn't matter that there was an awful cramp in his calf. He wouldn't ask one more thing of her.

"Good night," she said curtly.

He winced and said nothing as she walked away and down the stairs. As soon as she was out of sight, he closed his eyes.

Lord, that hurt. Please don't let that have hurt her as

much as it hurt me. I want nothing but the best for her. The
girls will finally get to a permanent place and won't have to
worry about me on top of everything else.

And as for closing the door on a future romance . . .

Well, she was beautiful *and* smart. She'd find someone else worthwhile.

Maybe he should take a page out of her book and go to sleep. No need to think over this ad nauseam. He grabbed the crutches and pulled himself up, keeping his weight on his left leg. Still, that didn't stop the pain radiating in the back of his calf. Why did that area even hurt when the screws were holding his bones together, not his calf muscles?

He placed the crutches forward, and stepped on his left leg, moving the right one slowly. Footsteps pounding against the stairs drew his attention. Erykah stormed back toward him, anger furrowing her brow and narrowing her eyes.

She stopped short, her feet an inch away from his. *Uh-oh.* His pulse drummed in his ears.

"How dare you." She pointed a finger until it jabbed his chest.

"What—"

"Don't talk. You're done talking. It's my turn to talk." She punctuated each sentence with a jab as if dotting it with a period.

Chris had enough clarity to see the proverbial steam rising from the top of her head. He'd never seen her this upset. All he could do was gape.

"You can't just make a decision without me. We're friends, but we've become more than that these past few months."

He couldn't disagree with any of that.

"So for you to try some high-handed, fall-on-your-sword action is bull! We're a team, Christian Gamble."

"You're so beautiful when you're angry."

She stepped back and propped her hands on her hips. "Excuse me?"

Abort! Retract statement now. "Uh, I meant . . . nothing. Forget I said anything."

"No." She shook her head. "No. What did you mean?"

Was there no way of escape? If he weren't dependent on these crutches, he'd try the avoidance tactic. "I meant just what I said. You look beautiful when you're mad. There's fire in your eyes that gives you a glow that's different from the one that lights up your smile."

"Urgh!" Erykah threw her hands up, then pointed back at him once more. "That. That is exactly what gets on my nerves about you. You haven't said two things to me regarding our relationship. Obviously dating while we live together is taboo, but you could've said, 'Erykah, as soon as I get better, we'll dine the night away.'"

Did his voice really sound like that? Slow and strangely low-pitched? At least he had enough sense not to ask that as she continued her rant.

"But no," she elongated. "You've been all withdrawn and broody. I told myself you were simply hurting, that breaking your leg the way you did was traumatic. That eventually you'd talk and confide in me as I have done with you these past few months. And when I finally think you're going to do so, you pull the rug right from underneath me by kicking me and the girls out."

"I'm not kicking you out. You just said you found a new place. You're *moving* out."

She snorted. "Yeah, because you knew that when you got it in your thick skull that I needed to remove myself from your life so you can wallow in pity."

"I'm not." *Aren't you?*

The look she gave repeated the sentiment.

"Then what's the real reason you want me to leave?" she asked calmly. "Don't give me that bull about being better off without you."

"It's *true*." He drew in a breath, trying not to let his frustration overtake him.

"How can you think that?" Her eyes flicked back and forth, studying him. "Seriously, how could you ever think that when you're the reason we're doing as well as we are?"

"You were shoveling snow this morning. How is that doing well?" He'd just compounded her burden, and that was the last thing he wanted.

"Chris . . ." She breathed out. She cupped a hand against the side of his face. "You're injured. The least I can do is help you after all you've done for me."

"I didn't do anything that anyone else wouldn't have."

"Truly?" She eyed him skeptically. "You would really do all that you have for me and the girls for anyone?"

Hadn't he admitted moments before that he loved her? Maybe he wouldn't have been able to put a label to the emotion when he was seeing her for the first time or having that second-chance meeting at the governor's mansion. But it was quite obvious he'd passed *like* long ago and had fallen head over heels for her.

"Probably not."

"And do you really want to stay just friends?"

Why was she bringing this up? He was trying to be the better person. If she attached herself to him through the mess with PathLight and his useless leg . . .

"Erykah . . ."

"Be honest," she whispered. "Remember?"

"I love you," he rasped.

"And I love you."

His mouth drew up into a smile for the first time in weeks. He rested his forehead against hers. "For real?"

"Yes, but you need to tell me what's going on. Don't shut me out."

"PathLight is terminating their contract with me. I have to pay back the advance. My YouTube views and follows are dropping, which means less income on that front. I can't help around the house. I'm in agony just picking up Cheyenne from the bus. I'm . . . a burden to you."

She drew back. "There is so much to unpack in that statement, but let's start with the agony. Why does it hurt walking to the bus stop? You're not putting your weight on your leg, are you?" She looked down at the offender.

"Of course not. But my calf hasn't stopped hurting."

A mask slid over her face, and standing before him was *Doctor* Kennedy. "Since when?"

"Since we left the hospital." Why were his senses tingling like he was Peter Parker? "Why?"

"Why didn't you say anything before now?"

"I literally just had surgery. What was I supposed to say? 'Ow, my calf hurts, give me more meds'? Oh, wait, they prescribed me some and sent me home."

She huffed. "Chris, you need to go to the hospital right now."

"What? Why?" The very thought had him breaking out into a sweat. What did she think was wrong?

"You might have a blood clot."

"Tell me you're joking." He groaned.

She gave him a pointed stare. "I'll get the girls and then drive you there."

"No. Don't wake them up." He pinched the bridge of his nose. "Um, Rebecca, down the street. Maybe she can watch the girls. And if not, I'll take an Uber. I don't want to disturb them."

"Are you *serious*? Did we not just have a question about you acting like you're a burden when clearly there's someone who cares for you and is *happy* to help?" She placed her hands on her hips once more.

"Erykah, do you actually want to wake Ash up?"

She bit her lip. "Which house is Rebecca's?"

"Blue one."

"Got it. Be right back." She grabbed her coat, slipped her feet into her boots, and disappeared.

Chris pulled out his cell phone.

Chris
Erykah thinks I might have a blood clot. Omw to hospital.

Tuck
Praying. Please keep us posted or have her do so.

Lamont
Yeah, that's nothing to mess around with.

Great, everyone seemed to know that but him. He stared at the door, then back at his phone. Should he tell them about his convo with Erykah?

Chris
Also need prayer about my relationship with Erykah. She knows how I feel.

Lamont
You admitted you love her? Wow.

Tuck
I thought you'd take at least another month or two.

Chris
Not surprised you were wrong.

Lamont
Did she not say it back? Is that the issue?

Chris
She loves me too.

Tuck
Then what gives?

Chris
I might have kicked her out before I confessed.

Lamont

Tuck

Lamont
You need so much prayer, it's not even funny.

Chris
I think I hear her coming back. We'll continue this later.

Tuck
Wait until the other ladies find out.

Lamont
Truth.

Thirty-Nine

G reat catch, Dr. Kennedy. He does indeed have a blood clot."

My stomach clenched. "It's still in his calf, right? No other clots anywhere else?"

"No. But it is a big one, so we'll need to keep him to monitor it as we start him on blood thinners. We want to ensure it doesn't travel."

"Understood." Because the deadliest thing that could happen was for that clot to travel and end up in his lungs, heart, or brain. He'd suffered enough—having his oxygen blocked in his lungs or suffering a heart attack or stroke was too much.

"I'll go check on the status of his room transfer. The nurse will assist you from there."

Chris wasn't out of the woods yet. I hated that, but at the same time, the hospital was the best place for him if the clot did in fact travel upward.

Please heal Chris. I don't care if You use medicine or a miracle. Just don't take him away from me.

Though the man was beyond stubborn. How could he try to send us away, but then confess to loving me? *Ahh! He* loves *you*. I wanted to hug him close to me and shake him all at the same time.

I squinted my eyes at Chris.

"What?" He held his hands out. "I've literally said nothing since the doctor walked out of the room."

"You do know you're not Jesus, right?"

"Of course I'm not." His eyes widened. "What are you even talking about? What does this have to do with the blood clot?"

"No one's talking about the clot." I waved a hand in the air. "I'm talking about the way you tried to push me away. You really think I expect anything from you since you broke your leg? You think I expect you to go shovel the driveway or scrape the snow from my windshield?"

"I *should* be the one to do those things."

"Oh, I see. So when I got sick that one week, and you had to care for the girls, you were really expecting me to get up out of the bed and ensure I didn't fumble my responsibilities? How thoughtless of me to just lie there and recover. You must have been so furious with how lazy I was being."

An exasperated groan fell from his lips. "I know what you're doing."

"Do you? Because trying to point out your foolishness without calling you a fool is taking every ounce of verbal skill I possess. Remember, I went to school to become a doctor, not an orator."

"I feel so useless sitting there doing nothing while you and the girls pick up my slack. I can't help you with Ash or Cheyenne."

"Yes, you can. You do every single day. You pick up Cheye from the bus, with a broken leg and a blood clot, I might add." I pursed my lips. "And Ashlynn is only happy and calm when she's curled up next to you, which allows me to decompress from work and take care of dinner."

"At least let me make dinner."

"With *crutches*?" Was it wrong to shake a grown man until sense fell into his noggin?

"I can dump something in the multicooker. Maybe buy something that can cook slowly all day. But watching you come home after a long day and cook tears me up."

I blew out a breath. "Have you ever been still and simply rested? You think maybe God wanted you to slow down because you've been running ragged between the nonprofit, Path-Light, and my complicated life? I haven't seen you rest yet. Not even on the weekend, because you're at church volunteering and attending service when you're not wrangling animals."

Chris grimaced. "Maybe you're making some sense."

"You don't like being still, do you?"

"Not at all."

"Is that what prompted that farce of a conversation?" I held my hands out wide.

"Actually, my mom offered to stay with me and help me recover. Said there was no reason you needed to stay here if you were halting your house search because of my injury." He cleared his throat. "I then came to the conclusion it would be best if I stopped holding y'all back from the next step."

I took a chance and walked to his side of the bed, then bent my head until our foreheads touched. "Silly man. I've stayed this long because I want to be near you. I feel safe. I feel cared for. I feel . . ." What was the word that could adequately describe all these feelings? "Cherished."

Chris cupped the sides of my face with his warm palms, and my heart melted at the care shining in his eyes. "I'd like nothing more than to show you exactly how I feel."

Our breath mingled as my lips hovered above his. Did I dare initiate a kiss?

A throat cleared, and I jumped backward. A knowing grin

pulled the nurse's mouth upward. "Sorry to interrupt. But I just wanted to go over your room transfer. Your escort is here."

She pointed to a woman wearing red scrubs, a sweater, and a lanyard with her picture on it. She waved but avoided looking us in the eyes.

My own cheeks were hot. I'd almost kissed Chris. We'd been *so* close, but now, still so far away. Had we actually resolved anything? Were we together now? Did we need to have a DTR discussion, as the residents would say, to define the relationship? Surely Chris knew I was all in for this relationship, no matter *where* I lived. If he needed me to leave, I would, I just didn't want the door closed on our future.

I kept my thoughts to myself as I followed the escort down the halls, into the elevator, and through more hallways. Finally, Chris's bed was wheeled into his new room on the med-surg floor.

I pulled out my cell and read a text from Piper.

Piper
How is he? Is it a clot?

Erykah
It is. They're keeping him overnight and starting blood thinners. It's big, so they want to keep an eye on it and make sure it doesn't travel.

Nevaeh
We're praying.

Lamont
Without ceasing.

Tuck
Tell the ol' man he's not a single wheel anymore.

I frowned.

"What's wrong?"

I looked up at Chris's question only to see it was just the

two of us once more. "Oh, Tuck wanted me to pass on a weird expression."

"What did he say?" Chris adjusted the back of his bed, sitting up more.

"That you're not a single wheel anymore."

Chris dropped his chin to his chest, and a soft chuckle left his lips. He looked up again. "Tell him I get it. I won't be thick-headed any longer."

"O-kay." I typed up the message, then slid the phone into my bag. "You gonna tell me what that's all about?"

"Are you going to come closer?"

I walked to his side and stopped. "Okay. I'm close. Now what?"

"You're gonna have to help a brother out, since I'm kind of stuck sitting in this bed."

"Are you finally going to kiss me, Chris Gamble?" I sat on the edge of the bed.

He slid his hand around the back of my neck and tugged me closer. "Every day, if you'll let me."

"Yes, please." I slid my arms around his neck and held my breath in anticipation.

Warmth filled me at the first brush of lips. My breath shuddered as he grazed his full lips against mine once more. If he was trying to fan the flames, he succeeded. I tugged his head closer, pressing our lips fully against each other, and let out a sigh.

Chris groaned and deepened the kiss, twisting the edge of my shirt between his hands. All thoughts ceased, and I could only feel. Feel how much I wanted to kiss this man for the rest of my life. Never ever had I felt so much from one contact. From comfort to safety to feeling like every pore was on fire. I couldn't get close enough. I needed to get far away.

We broke apart, and I ran my hands down the back of

his neck and patted his shoulders. "Um, yes. That was . . ." I inched backward, my gaze never leaving his.

I'd never seen his eyes such a brilliant blue, and that made me want to erase the distance. *You're in a hospital*. Despite him having a private room, I did *not* behave this way in a hospital. This wasn't *Grey's Anatomy*.

"You really do love me," I said, just to reassure myself. "So much."

I grinned. "And you take back kicking me out?"

"Erykah . . ." Chris ran a hand down his face. "After that"—he pointed between us—"don't you think it's even more imperative that you move out? I don't think I can stay in the same place with you now that we've kissed."

I bit my lip. I wasn't going to lie. I loved the look he gave me as if he couldn't get enough. At the same time, I loved that he didn't want to live with me for *that* reason. "I'll move out as long as you retract the ridiculous reason you suggested."

"Yes, ma'am." He chuckled. "I was a fool. I retract that reason and offer up your virtue and mine as the valid one."

My virtue? He cared about my virtue? How sweet was this man? "Um, do we need to have an exclusivity conversation?" Why was this so awkward? I should've just used *DTR* confidently instead of acting like a geriatric millennial.

"Exclusivity? You're it for me, Erykah Kennedy."

I couldn't keep the joy from showing on my face. "And you're it for me, Chris Gamble."

As I curled up next to his side, I wished I could tell Ellynn that I'd finally found someone. She'd probably break out singing the Barbra Streisand and Bryan Adams song. And though I couldn't tell her, knowing how she'd respond gave me the comfort I needed in this moment.

Forty

Chris stared up at the ceiling. He'd been talking to God for the past half hour as the machine next to him showed his vitals. The room lights had been turned off long ago as it was currently five in the morning. He should be asleep, but after the tech had checked his vitals, his eyes had remained open, and his mind had begun thinking.

Erykah *loved* him. His heart filled with some kind of euphoria he couldn't describe. Not that he needed to. It was enough knowing how she felt. But now he was stuck. Did he let her move out with the girls when that was the last thing he actually wanted?

After they'd talked for a couple of hours last night, she had returned to his place. Though she'd offered to take off work today, he didn't want her whole schedule to be rearranged when he wasn't going to be doing anything but recovering. She would bring the girls to visit after work, and that was perfect.

But back to the larger issue at hand.

Chris had had enough time to think. What he'd come to realize was one, considering the girls moving out created a hole in his heart that he wanted to close back up as quickly as possible, and two, he didn't actually want Erykah to move out . . . *ever*. Which left him with the question, Could he actually let them leave?

The thought of him and Erykah sharing the same place now that they were in a romantic relationship gave him pause. It pricked at his sense of propriety and what God would think. But if marriage was his endgame, did it make sense for her to buy a house, only for them to marry down the line and move back in together? Not that he was suggesting they shack up either.

But does she even like your house? It's too ecofriendly for her.

Well, no, she called it home. Other than the earlier adjustments, Erykah had adapted to his way of life, or they'd found a compromise that they could both be satisfied with. She fit perfectly in his home, in his arms, in his heart.

Lord, I don't want her to leave. I don't want the girls to leave. I'll miss them so much.

Still, could he honestly say he was ready for marriage this instant? Was he just looking at the situation with his limited worldview? The last thing he wanted to do was jump into marriage simply to keep them from leaving. He wanted to walk in God's will for this relationship. Something he hadn't done for the last one.

Lord, I just want the best for them. You know how much I love Erykah. How much I love Cheyenne and Ashlynn . . . like they were my own children.

Watching them grow over these past few months had given him pure joy. He couldn't recall when he'd been so happy to go home and find people there. No, not just *people*, but specifically Erykah and the girls. *And maybe that's why you never wanted to rest before.*

His mom had shown him the importance of working.

She'd barely had time to grieve the death of his father before she'd had to return to work. And other than the week he took to wallow in pity after Tracey jilted him, Chris didn't take a lot of vacation days.

But being a family with Erykah and the girls had fulfilled something in him. Sharing his love of animals, nature, and conservation efforts throughout his home had warmed his heart. Cheye even knew exactly which bins to throw items into. She liked seeing the snow melt and go through the purification system he had. He couldn't wait to share what the garden would look like come spring. They'd become his family as sure as anything.

Lord, what do I do? Do I propose to Erykah or wait?
And what does Erykah want?

The thought stood out in his mind. Here he was trying to prevent her from exiting, and he hadn't even asked her what she wanted. Sure, she'd admitted to wanting to be near him, but to what end? Had she thought about marriage? Or did she want to take their relationship slowly?

He blew out a breath. That conversation would have to wait until she stopped by after work. All he could do was tell the Lord what he wanted and submit to His will. Chris may or may not get the desire of his heart, but he *knew* God would give him a perfect gift. Whatever that might be.

Be patient. Be still and let God work everything out for your good and, more importantly, Erykah's.

The thought cheered him up. God would take care of all of them—that was a promise. Chris closed his eyes and prayed he could get some more sleep.

Unfortunately, the next shift woke him before he could fall into a deep sleep. He didn't have his laptop, so he couldn't work on that. All he had was his cell phone.

Chris
I'm bored.

Tuck
Nothing good on hospital TV? 😂

Chris
No

Lamont
You can stream on your cell. Surely there's something to watch that way.

Tuck
I found a couple of your movies on streaming when I had surgery.

Chris
Oh, I can watch one and provide commentary.

Lamont
This should be good, ol' man.

Tuck
Did you and Erykah make up?

Lamont
Yeah, is she moving out?

Chris placed a group call, keeping the video option off. He didn't want them seeing him in the hospital. That was too weird.

"Well?" Lamont asked instead of saying *hello*.

Chris told them about asking her to move out, her finding a place, them making up and agreeing to date. Just hearing the whole thing repeated exhausted him. "Can we honestly live together *and* date? That seems . . ."

"Against God's rules?" Lamont asked.

"Well, yeah. What will people say? Erykah's just getting to know everyone at church."

"Has anyone said anything up until this point?" Tuck asked.

His neighbors probably assumed they were married, and the people at church didn't come over his house. "No, but still."

"Look," Tuck said. "Your situation is a little different. Erykah needed a place for her and the girls, and you provided that. She stays in the basement and you on the top floor. There's a whole common area separating y'all."

"Didn't you say she's moving out at the end of the month?" Lamont asked. "Voilà, problem fixed."

"But I don't want them to move out," Chris said quietly. The very thought made the bands on his chest tighten.

"Whoa. You don't?" Lamont asked.

"You thinking marriage or something else?" Tuck's question came next.

"I want marriage. I'm just unsure if I want it now."

"I know how people's perception can create an alternate reality," Lamont said. "What matters is that you and Erykah know the truth of the situation. However, I will say if temptation is going to be an issue, then you might want to let her move out as planned."

Chris heard him, but he wanted Tuck's opinion as well. "What do you think, Tuck?"

"I don't know. I believe you won't cross the line. Plus, the girls are there. But what if you don't marry until a year later? Now it becomes messy. Saying those three words changes everything."

"What makes you hesitate about marriage?" Lamont asked.

Chris swallowed. "I was engaged before."

"What?" they cried.

He told them about the relationship and about being left at the altar. Occasionally they'd chime in with questions, but finally, Chris finished his story.

"So you're afraid," Tuck said.

"But how long are you going to let fear keep you from happiness with someone who genuinely loves you back?" Lamont asked.

"I don't want to fail her. It's more than how I feel about Erykah. I have to consider the girls as well."

"Then maybe take things slow." Lamont sighed. "I feel for you. I'm sure you all have bonded, but she might want to experience what dating is like, don't you think?"

Chris *would* be the first man Erykah had dated. "What do you mean?"

"Talking on the phone until you fall asleep." Lamont chuckled. "My favorite thing with Nevaeh."

"Oh, first date," Tuck said. "We did a picnic for ours."

Chris could get behind a first date. "Thanks, fellas. You guys have given me a lot to think about."

"That's what we're here for," Lamont stated.

"And to keep you humble. We know being the old *and* fifth wheel was too much. Glad you only have to suffer middle age now."

"I can't wait until you hit forty, Tucker Hale." But Chris's lips twitched as he said it.

"You'll be even older then," Tuck shot back.

Chris appreciated the good-natured ribbing. It made him feel a part of something. These two were the constants in his life, and he wouldn't take that for granted.

"Send a text our way when you get released. We're still praying," Lamont added.

"Yeah, make sure it's the group text with the ladies. I know they'll want to know," Tuck said.

"Will do."

Chris hung up and stared back up at the ceiling. *Thank You for their friendship and wise counsel.*

The more Chris thought about his situation with Erykah,

the more he considered going slow might be part of their journey. If that was the case, they definitely shouldn't be in the same house. When she moved into her new place, he could take Erykah on dates. Do outings that included the girls, because he'd miss them with a deep ache when they left, but also ones that were just the two of them. And maybe then he'd know the right time to propose.

As long as it goes according to God's plan. And don't forget to include Erykah in the conversation.

He couldn't spend all his time solving the issue. He'd already done that and caused unnecessary hurt between them. Chris needed to make sure he was opening up to the love of his life.

Forty-One

We were home.

The girls were so happy that Chris was no longer in the hospital. I'd picked them up after work so they could visit, and when we got there, the doctor informed us that his clot had shrunk, and he was comfortable sending Chris home on blood thinners.

So here we were.

Ash sat tucked under Chris's arm as he watched an animated princess movie with Cheyenne. They were all glued to the screen, not that this was surprising. Curling up on the couch and watching a movie had become part of their evening routine. Even dinner had carried on as usual. Everything was the same.

But *I* was different.

I wanted to talk to Chris about what happened yesterday. What was next in our relationship? Could I call him my boyfriend? Granted, I'd thought about these questions all day long. I knew what I wanted, but I wasn't sure what Chris Gamble wanted.

I clapped my hands as the end credits rolled. "Bath time."

"Do I have to? Can't we watch another movie?" Cheye asked.

"No, ma'am. It's bath time."

She poked her bottom lip out and crossed her arms.

"Cheye, you're going to listen to your aunt, right?" Chris asked.

She studied him, then turned to me. Finally, she stood and went over to Chris, giving him a hug. "Good night."

"Night, sweetie." He patted her back as her little arms attempted to hug his shoulders. Chris looked up at me. "You coming back for Ash or taking her now?"

She curled back into him. "Dada."

Chris's and my gazes widened. My heart dropped. I wanted to cheer, I wanted to cry. Instead, I cleared my throat. "I'll come back. She took a bath yesterday, so I'll skip one tonight."

"'Kay. She likes watching old basketball reels anyway."

I stifled a laugh.

Cheyenne held on to my hand and the railing as we descended into the basement. She went to get her bath toys as I ran the water, checking to make sure the temperature stayed perfect for a five-year-old.

"Aunt Erykah?"

I turned, looking at my niece over my shoulder. "Got your toys?"

She bobbed her head.

"Ready to get in?"

"Yeah. Are we gonna wash my hair too?"

That might take a little longer than I'd like, but we also hadn't washed it in a while. "Sure. Want two braids?"

"Yes." She beamed.

She undressed herself, but I helped her into the tub, making sure she didn't slip. I sat down on the toilet lid as she played with her water toys. I was tired from the day, yet anticipation went through me at the thought of alone time with Chris after the girls went to bed.

"Aunt Erykah?"

"Yes?" I blinked, focusing on my niece.

"Can I ask a question?"

"Sure, sweetie." I leaned forward.

"Mommy and Daddy are gone forever, right?"

I wanted to grab my heart. "Yes, but remember they're in heaven. One day we'll be there with them."

"Ash called Chris Dada."

I'd wondered if she'd caught that. "She's a baby. They just babble." Though it sure didn't feel like nonsensical words when it sounded very much like *daddy*.

"I also heard her call you Mama yesterday."

Uh-oh. Was Cheye mad at me? I couldn't make Ash stop babbling *dada* and *mama*, but eventually she'd learn to say words like *auntie* and *Chris*, right?

I held back a sigh. "Does it upset you?" I asked quietly.

"A little."

My poor sweet girl. I'd give her a hug as soon as I retrieved her from the bath. "Just so you know, I've been trying to get her to say *auntie*."

"I know." Cheye's bottom lip poked out. "But Ash won't remember Mommy and Daddy when she's old, will she?"

"She probably won't have any memories of her own since she's so young."

"Will I forget them too?"

Tears pricked my eyes. "Sweetie, I'll do everything to help you both remember them and how amazing they were."

I'd already made photo albums for each of the girls. I'd hung family pictures in their rooms, as well as individual ones I'd found of Asher and Ellynn. I even told them stories about when Ellynn and I were younger.

"Can I call you Mama?" Cheye's voice was so small. "Ash-lynn does."

My breath hitched. How did I navigate this? "Do you really want to, or do you think you have to because Ash did?"

Cheyenne's brow furrowed. "I don't want to be different."

I cupped her face. "I would be honored, but please, *please*, know you don't have to if you don't want to. Eventually Ash will learn to say *auntie*." But a part of me cherished the words from Ash. I'd probably never have kids of my own, and hearing *mama* melted me.

"Regardless of what you call me, I'll always be here for you, 'kay?"

Cheye nodded, and I kissed her cheek.

She went right back to playing.

I wasn't sure if doing so was a coping mechanism, but I envied her. I'd like nothing more than to grab my phone and pretend like something held my attention while my inner self fell apart. Still, we had the rest of her bath time routine to get through.

Soon Cheye was tucked into bed, and Ash lay in her crib.

The only question was, Should I cry now or fall apart in Chris's arms? *Door number two, please.*

I raced up the stairs and sat gingerly on the couch so as not to jostle Chris's legs. "I need a hug."

He opened his arms. "I'm sorry Ash called me Dada. That had to have been a shock."

I sighed. "Yes and no. She's called me Mama, but I chalked it up to her just practicing the sounds she can make now."

Chris studied me. "Did you really, or did you have mixed emotions?"

"Mixed emotions, of course." Tears welled in my eyes. "Cheye thought she had to call me Mama because Ash did."

"Oh wow." He said nothing so I listened to his heartbeat,

thankful I didn't have to carry this burden alone. "But you reassured her?"

"Yes. I just hate that she's going through this at five. I hate that Ellynn and Asher aren't here."

"I imagine you always will." Chris placed his chin on top of my head. "But the girls couldn't be in better hands. You love them like they're your own and not merely your nieces. That's probably why Ellynn and Asher wanted the girls to be in your care."

I sniffed. "Thank you."

"Anything else bothering you?"

"Well, I was wondering how this is going to work out."

"Us?"

"Yes," I breathed.

"Well, you'll move into your new place. Then I'll call on you and take you on a date."

"I'm still waiting to hear if the seller accepted my offer." But part of me didn't want to leave. Now that I knew how much he loved me and I loved him, my mind had immediately conjured up ideals of weddings and saying *I do*. *Too soon, Erykah.*

Wasn't it? "A date sounds nice, though."

"But not the moving?"

"Is it ever fun?"

Chris chuckled.

"But really, I'd be happy if I didn't have to leave this spot." My face heated. Great, did that hint at forever, or would he take it to mean I was comfortable in his arms?

"But neither one of us wants to be tempted to cross the line." Chris spoke in a low voice.

That made so much sense, because even now I wanted to kiss him to my heart's content. "You're right," I groused.

"I feel the same way." Chris held me tighter.

"I need to tell the girls."

"Definitely. Do you want me to be there with you? I can reassure Cheye that she'll still get to see me often."

Despite the offer, his voice seemed sad. Would he miss our daily interactions as much as I would? And poor Cheye—she might revert to her pre-therapy days and throw a tantrum.

Moving out might bring up feelings of losing Ellynn and Asher all over again. Part of me wanted to plead my case and ask Chris to consider letting us stay. But the only way I could see him agreeing to that was if we considered marriage.

"*Mawage?*" The *Princess Bride* quote reverberated in my head.

But yes.

Chris was it for me. I didn't need to date anyone else to know that. I was forty-one years old and knew myself, knew my heart, *knew* Chris. Honestly, I didn't *need* him to take me on an actual date to know how I felt. I wanted a lifetime with him.

So tell him!

Of course. It was that simple. He didn't have to be the one to set the pace every step of the way. I *loved* him. And I didn't want to move out just to move back in whenever he decided to propose. Unless, in fact, he *didn't* want that with me. I wouldn't know unless we discussed it.

I pulled back, moving to a sitting position. "I have something to say, and I want you to think everything over before saying something. I also want us to pray together and separately about it."

"O-kay." His gaze darkened with concern. "What's wrong?"

"Nothing's wrong." I smiled. I felt good about this. "I want to talk about our living arrangement."

"I'm listening."

The words bolstered me. *Say what's on your heart. He*

loves you and won't ridicule you. Right. "I don't think I should move out." I waited for him to say something, then realized I was supposed to be making a speech.

"I love you. You love me. We're already a family. We've been living like one for months now. Our feelings were just a little slow to . . ." *To what? Admit? Recognize?*

"Voice?" Chris offered.

I nodded. "Exactly. I know we both want to honor God, and I'm not suggesting we do away with that. But maybe, just maybe, the answer isn't in me moving out." I licked my lips. Could I really suggest this? *Breathe.*

"Maybe we get married instead."

Forty-Two

Married?

Hadn't he had the same thoughts? But hadn't he also wondered if it was too soon to propose and if he was actually ready?

Chris stared into Erykah's beautiful eyes. "I'll pray about it."

"Oh good." She let out a breath. "I was afraid you'd think the suggestion was out of left field or . . ."

He shook his head. "No. I've had similar thoughts but haven't come to any conclusions yet."

"Great minds?" She chuckled, then laid her head back down on his chest. "I don't know if it's the right answer. I don't know if the idea is strictly because I don't want to part from you, even if it's temporary and *one day* we get married."

Hadn't he contemplated the same thing? "I completely understand. Do you want to pray now?"

"Yes." She sat up. "Want to hold hands?"

"Definitely."

She placed her soft hands in his, and Chris bowed his head. He loved that she trusted him to pray and suggested it first.

"Lord, we come to You today asking for Your divine wisdom and guidance. Please give us ears to hear, eyes to see, a heart that's understanding, and a spirit that's willing. We want to obey Your direction, whatever it may be."

He paused, gathering his thoughts. "We love each other, Lord, and we know that's a blessing from You for both of us. We've become a family and want to stay united not just for us, but for Cheye and Ash as well. What would You have us do? Are we jumping the gun?"

Chris really didn't know which direction to go. He didn't want to think he was at a fork in a road with only two choices. God was so good at straightening a path. On their own merits, people had chosen to marry for less than love and kids. On the flip side, couples had stayed together in a loveless marriage for kids. Chris needed to clear his mind of what others did and focus on what God wanted for them.

"God," Erykah said quietly, reverently, "You've shown me You hear us and You answer prayers. All we're asking is that You show us what the answer is in this situation. Please help our love for each other and our own desires not impede us from hearing You. And if You ask us to separate, please help us express to Cheyenne how that's not a permanent solution but one that offers more time for all of us."

"Amen," Chris whispered.

"Amen."

He opened his eyes. "Guess now we just wait."

"Right." She sighed. "How's your leg feeling?"

"Much better. I feel foolish now thinking that pain was from the broken bone."

"How were you supposed to know when no one told you what to watch for?" She huffed. "I should've done so and not depended on them to relay the correct information."

"It's okay." He squeezed her. "I'm okay."

324

"But you almost weren't," Erykah whispered, then cleared her throat. "Fortunately, God answered my prayer and healed you."

"Is that when you decided He was real?" Chris couldn't be happier that she'd developed a real relationship with Christ.

"He's been showing me that He sees me in many different ways. It was actually a conversation with a coworker that tipped me over." She smiled at him. "I felt a little naïve about saying the salvation prayer. So I kept quiet and just continued to do the work to understand Him. I feel like my past has a purpose now."

"Yeah? In what way?" Chris rested his chin on top of her head.

He wanted to close his eyes and go to sleep. Holding her, listening to her talk, it all relaxed him. Being with Erykah allowed him to let his guard down and truly . . . *rest*.

I get it now. Why You had to slow me down. I was letting life pass me by.

But not anymore. He was blessed by having the girls, by this time to sit and be, like God spoke of in Psalm 46:10 when He said, "Be still, and know that I am God."

"I don't think it's just one thing. I can look back and see taking care of Ellynn was one purpose. Going to medical school and then helping others heal was another. Being here and in a position to raise Cheye and Ash is also a reason." She looked up and smiled at him. "And loving you is an added bonus."

He placed a kiss on her cheek. "I love all of those reasons. They helped shape you into who you are today."

"Exactly." She snuggled closer. "Can we just sleep here?"

"As much as I would love to fall asleep with you in my arms, my forty-two-year-old back would object vehemently."

She laughed. "I hear you. For me, it's my shoulders. If

I sleep on my side, I wake up feeling like my collarbone is broken."

"The beauty of aging."

"When do you turn forty-three?"

"Next month."

"Really? What day?"

He stilled, swallowed. "Uh . . . the fourteenth."

"February fourteenth? Are you serious?" At his nod, Erykah smirked at him. "That must be annoying."

"A little bit."

She sat up. "Should we celebrate, or do you prefer a low-key day?"

"Will we be together?"

She nodded.

"Then nothing else matters. It's all icing."

"I love you." She wrapped her arms around his neck.

"I love you too."

Erykah beamed. "Okay, I'm off to bed. I've got an early surgery tomorrow."

"Night, beautiful." He placed a kiss on her forehead.

"Night, handsome."

Chris grabbed his crutches and hobbled to the guest bedroom. Even though he and Erykah had already prayed, he would do as she'd asked and pray by himself. The thought of marrying her settled something in his insides. When he'd questioned whether he was moving too fast earlier, he'd thought about his last jaunt down the aisle, and something quaked in him. Not that he had any residual feelings for Tracey. He'd forgiven her, and he'd forgiven himself for not ending their relationship sooner when he'd felt that prompting. It was more that Chris hadn't known exactly how Erykah felt about the subject.

Knowing she wanted to marry shifted his insides into alignment. The thought of marrying *her* didn't fill him with trepidation. Like she said, they were already a family. The guys had told him to ask her what she wanted, and she'd delivered.

Thank You, Lord. I'm amazed. I feel loved. There's just no other word for it.

• • •

The next morning, Chris spent an hour pouring out his heart and finding Scriptures to read to keep him focused on the end result: hearing from God. Just when peace settled in his heart at the assurance that God *would* answer, his cell phone rang.

He reached for the device, glancing at the caller ID. Today, seeing *Mom* flash across the screen didn't surprise him, and it spoke of the promise that they both would continue to strengthen their relationship.

"Hey, Mom."

"How are you feeling, son?"

Chris removed his leg from the elevation pillow Nevaeh had gifted him. "My leg is a lot better."

"And you're taking your meds for the clot?"

He smiled. Hearing her care about his life . . . well, he'd thought he was past needing his mom's attention, but maybe not. "I am. Erykah is also double-checking."

"Speaking of Erykah . . ." She trailed off, then stayed silent.

"Is everything okay?"

"I was cleaning out some old boxes yesterday. It's a new year, and I want to declutter."

"Good idea. Don't forget to donate the items that can still be used, or even sell them if you prefer." He could never turn off the sustainability portion of his brain.

"Oh, of course. I have a donation pile and a to-sell pile."

"Good." Reusing stuff really did help the earth.

"However, that's not the purpose of this call."

His brows rose. "It's not?" Was this just a distraction from the real issue? Had she and Erykah exchanged words or something?

"No." She laughed. "Well, kind of. It's all related. You'll see if I can just figure out the right words."

"Breathe, Mom. No need to rush through the conversation."

"Okay." Her inhale was audible. "I found something while I was cleaning and wondered if you might have any use for it."

"What is it?"

"My mother's wedding ring."

Chris stilled. "Her wedding ring?"

"It's circa 1930s if I remember correctly. It has that whole art deco vibe. I'm not sure if it's your thing or if Erykah would like it." She paused. "Am I overstepping? Are you guys dating, or is her being a friend really the end of the story?"

"Actually, I'm in love with her." He swallowed. Had he even said those words to his mom when he got engaged to Tracey? "You're not overstepping at all, and I'd really like to see a picture of it."

"Hold on." He heard a muffled sound, then her voice once more. "I just texted a picture of it."

"Thanks." He put her on speaker, then went to his text messages to pull up the image.

Perfect.

Not only was this something old, but he had a feeling Erykah would absolutely love the ring. The idea of a family heirloom made him feel connected to his past in a way he didn't normally experience. His mom didn't normally share stuff like this with him.

She's trying, remember that.

"Are you sure you don't want to keep this, Mom? It's your mother's."

"I'm sure. I think you and Erykah have something really solid."

Was this God's answer? Even if it wasn't, he knew one day he'd put this on Erykah's finger. "Thank you so much."

"Of course. I'll bring this with me when I come visit at the end of the month."

"I can't wait." And he couldn't. He was actually looking forward to the visit.

Chris hung up the phone. *Lord, is this You?* Before he could think any further, his phone rang again. *Cameron* flashed on the caller ID.

"Hey, Cam, what's up?"

Sniffles met his ear. "Hey, Chris. Um, I was calling to ask for a day off."

He'd never seen Cameron cry, and he couldn't remember the last time she called in unexpectedly. "Are you okay? Are you sick?"

"I ended it."

His mouth dropped. "With Felix?"

"Yes," she cried. "I realized that I was more in love with the wedding than I was with him. And though it feels like I'm a terrible person for ruining his life, I also feel . . ."

"You feel?" Chris asked cautiously.

"Relief. Awful, right?" She blew her nose right in his ear. *Oh, Cameron.* "Did you pray over this?"

She sniffled. "Yes. But it doesn't make this feel any better."

"Did I ever tell you I was left at the altar?"

Cameron gasped. "What? No!"

"At the time, I hated that she left me there to pick up the pieces. But, Cameron . . ." He closed his eyes. "It was the best decision she could've made."

329

"Really? You're not just saying that?"

"If it's not right, it's not right." He paused. "What did Felix have to say?"

"He said he sank a ton of money for nothing. He told me to get back as much as I could, so I've been making phone calls since yesterday."

Chris winced. He knew what that was like. "I'm sorry, Cam."

"It's okay. But I do have a problem."

"If I can help, I will."

"My honeymoon is nonrefundable. The only thing they said I could do was change the dates. Obviously since I'm not getting married, I don't want to go on a honeymoon by myself or with anyone else."

Got it. He still had no idea what that had to do with—

"Do you want the honeymoon? I mean, I know you keep saying you and Erykah are just friends, but there are some very serious nonfriend vibes going on between you two. That video y'all did together with Cheyenne directing was so adorable. You two *fit*, you know?"

He'd forgotten he'd shared that with the crew.

"I thought to myself, 'Cam, one day they're going to get married.' Which means, if you do, you'll need a honeymoon. So how about it?" She finally breathed.

At this point, Chris had goose bumps on his arms. *Okay, Lord. I'm listening.* "Cameron, that actually would be amazing." Because now he had a ring and a honeymoon. If that didn't seem like a sign to marry the woman he loved, he didn't know what would. "Wait, where is it?"

Not that he really cared, but he'd like to know how to prepare for it if Erykah agreed this was the right move.

"I got a one-bedroom suite at the Sonnenalp resort in Vail. The current reservation dates are February fourteenth to the twenty-first."

His mouth dropped. "Can you change the name the reservation is in?"

"Yes."

"I tentatively say yes, but I need to talk to Erykah first. If we take it, we can refund you."

"Does that mean you stopped ignoring your feelings and finally admitted them?" Cameron sounded gleeful. Her earlier sounds of crying vanished.

"I did."

She squealed. "I'm so excited. Are you going to propose?"

"I've been thinking about it." More than thinking.

"Stop thinking and do it already. You two are perfect for each other."

He grinned. "Thanks, Cam."

He already owned a tux. A quick internet search showed going to the county clerk's office and signing a license automatically made them married. They didn't even need an officiant if they didn't want one. All they really needed was a venue, but surely that wouldn't be hard to find.

Lord, You are amazing. He couldn't wait to tell Erykah.

Forty-Three

I stared down the hall, my mind focused on Chris and the would-we or wouldn't-we dilemma we faced. When I thought of Chris, my thoughts immediately turned toward his goodness, the gentle care he exhibited, and his baby blue eyes—my kryptonite. The man was as good-looking as his personality. *Husband-potential jackpot.*

"What are you grinning about, Dr. Kennedy?"

I blinked and met Dr. Collier's gaze. "Um, just thinking."

"About a guy, right?"

After Dr. Collier had told me she prayed for me, we'd started talking more and more when we met. I wouldn't go so far as to call her a friend, but she was certainly more than my resident.

My cheeks heated. "Maybe," I replied hesitantly.

She giggled. "I totally understand. I've been dating this guy for a couple of months, and he already has me thinking of weddings and married life."

"Really?" Didn't most people think two months was too soon for that?

"Mm-hmm." She pulled out her cell. "This woman I follow on Insta has an awesome job of modeling wedding dresses. She picks a theme and then gives you tips on how you can recreate something similar or make it your own."

Dr. Collier scrolled through the woman's profile, showing all the stunning photos of her in different gowns. "Wow." What must it be like to make money modeling dresses?

"Yesterday she modeled a dress that her sister wore. This was just one she did for fun, not sponsored or anything. Their mom passed away when they were young, and since their mom didn't have a traditional wedding, there was no wedding dress to pass on." Dr. Collier waved a hand. "Anyway, her older sister bought one with the intention of letting the other sisters wear it if they ever married. They plan on passing the dress down to the next bride-to-be in the family."

My breath caught as I thought of Ellynn's wedding dress. Piper had shipped it to me, because I'd intended to pass it down to Cheyenne or Ashlynn. But what if I wore it whenever Chris and I chose to marry? I bit my lip as the idea took root.

"The woman said that knowing she had something of her sister's and would be sharing the heirloom with future generations meant a lot to her."

I could feel my own tear ducts welling up.

"Don't cry, Dr. Kennedy!" Dr. Collier sniffed. "I'm sorry. Maybe this was a bad idea to share with you."

"No." I shook my head. "Continue."

"There's not much else to share. I sobbed like a baby when I read this yesterday. Such a beautiful moment, right?"

I nodded. "A priceless memory."

"Right? I hadn't thought of it like that before. Maybe I'll see if my mom still has hers."

"I'm sure she does. What mother doesn't want to pass on a dress to her kids?" At least, keeping a dress seemed like something people my age and older did, but I could be wrong.

My mother never had a wedding, but I had no idea if she was even alive to ask had I wanted to go that direction.

Was it bad that the thought didn't faze me? She had long since been a nonfactor in my life. I just went through living like I didn't have a mother.

He's a Father to the fatherless.

I thought of the Scripture Nevaeh had sent me. Did that include motherless as well? Though I didn't know where my dad was either. Both of my parents had checked out of the parenthood department.

"What kind of wedding would you want?" Dr. Collier asked.

Great question. What *did* I want? I mulled over the question and instantly knew. "Something simple. Something with my family and closest friends. I don't need to invite tons of people or go all out on décor. Just knowing I'd be marrying the person God sent me would be enough."

"Aww, Dr. Kennedy, you're a romantic at heart." She nudged me with her shoulder, then froze. "I'm so sorry. I did it out of habit. I know you're my superior and . . ." She gulped. "I'm sorry," she squeaked.

"It's okay, Dr. Collier." I huffed out a laugh. "I never thought of myself as a romantic, but I think you might be right." I pointed to her phone. "And the idea of wearing my sister's wedding dress would mean the world to me."

Sympathy crossed her face. "I can imagine your sister would be happy to be connected with you on that special day in that way."

"I think she would too." My throat felt raw, but my heart was full.

Now all I wanted to do was rush home and try on Ellynn's wedding dress. Would it fit me?

Dr. Collier and I parted ways, but my mind constantly

went back to the dress hanging in the back of my closet. This felt like a sign from God. Had Chris woken up and had a similar thought? I stopped in the corridor and pulled out my phone.

> Erykah
> Thinking of you.

> Chris
> You beat me to the punch. I just opened our thread to text you the same thing.

> Erykah
> Now I can get through the rest of the day knowing you're thinking of me.

> Chris
> I won't stop.

> Erykah
> ♡

"Dr. Kennedy, I've been looking for you."

I looked up at the sound of my boss's voice. "Everything okay, sir?"

"Yes, yes, just fine." Dr. Cook studied me. "Uh, I have something in my possession I wondered if you had use for."

"What's that?" I straightened.

"My dad's wedding ring. Something kept telling me this should be yours." He winced. "I'm not trying to get into your business. I try to be professional but also as personable as possible, so please don't take this the wrong way. And if you have no use for it, I completely understand."

I bit my lip. Every time God showed me He saw me, He heard me, overwhelming gratitude consumed me. How could the God of the universe care enough for me when my own parents never had? *Maybe that's why His love is such a balm.*

"May I see it?"

"Yes." Relief smoothed his brow. He dug through his pocket, pulled out a little black box, and passed it to me.

With a flip of a lid, I stared at the simple wedding band inside. The silver band had a cross in the center and two anchors hanging from it. It was the most beautiful thing I'd ever seen.

"I love it," I whispered.

"Then it's yours if you want it."

"How much would you like for it?" I looked up to meet his gaze.

He waved a hand. "Nothing. It's free."

"Dr. Cook, I couldn't." We weren't family. I couldn't just take his family ring without offering some form of compensation.

"Please, Dr. Kennedy. You've been through a lot these past few months. If this brings you any measure of happiness and can be used by you, keep it."

I wanted to hug him, but I'd never done that. *Ever.* "Uh, may I . . ." Why was this so awkward? "Hug you?" I rushed out.

A smile covered his face. He gave me a side hug, squeezing my shoulder firmly. "It's been a joy to watch you blossom. Even your residents have noticed."

"They have." I smiled, thinking of my earlier conversation with Dr. Collier. I guess love softened my rough edges.

After I placed the ring box into my office drawer for safekeeping, I locked it, then pocketed the key. My cell rang, and my brow furrowed at the unknown number.

"Hello?"

"Dr. Kennedy, this is Governor Jankowski."

"How are you?"

"Just peachy. Hey, listen, I have a venue that I'm no longer able to use and was wondering if you or the hospital had use for it. Not sure how often you have conferences and whatnot."

"What kind of venue?"

As the governor spoke, my wheels turned. This had to be the answer to our prayers. After thanking the governor for thinking of me and accepting the use of the venue, I turned to my email. A message from my Realtor informed me the seller had *not* accepted my offer. I assessed myself. I didn't feel sad but a little relieved. Life felt like it was actually going in the right direction.

Love from the Father, love from Chris, and the sweet, pure acceptance and love from my nieces. Piper and Nevaeh had welcomed me with open arms, and Dr. Cook and Dr. Collier had taken a chance to look past first impressions. God had surrounded me with people who could help me thrive and who accepted me for me. He'd answered the deepest desire of my heart: to belong. Something I'd stopped hoping for long ago.

Thank You so much. I'll forever be grateful.

Forty-Four

Y ou ready, man?" Lamont asked.

Chris grinned. "Absolutely. The way this came together is nothing short of a miracle." He checked his bow tie to make sure it looked fine.

"Stop fidgeting," Tuck said. "It was fine the last time you checked."

"Can't help myself. Too much energy, gotta get it out somehow."

"This has to be the fastest wedding I've ever seen come together, and definitely one for the books." Lamont sat on the couch in the sitting area.

The governor had paid for a space at The Broadmoor he'd no longer needed. Chris was still amazed he'd offered it to Erykah but felt like it was the biggest God wink of the decade. Now they were about to say their vows in one of the wedding venues located at the hotel.

Erykah would be wearing Ellynn's wedding dress, and she, too, had come into the perfect wedding band—her words. Chris had yet to see it since they'd agreed to exchange rings on their wedding day.

Chris had bought a cane—doctor approved—so he didn't have to crutch his way down the aisle. And after they said *I do*, his mom would babysit Cheye and Ash so that he and Erykah could go to Vail for the honeymoon. Cam had been relieved that Chris was able to fully reimburse her, but he couldn't help but feel like he'd come out on the better side of things.

How did I get to be so fortunate?

"I can't believe how well this came together either." Tuck stroked his beard. "It's definitely a God thing."

"Right? Erykah was in tears when we started comparing notes." He sighed.

Chris was so thankful that today was the first step to cementing them as a family.

"Did you write vows?" Lamont asked.

"Yes. We both wanted to."

"You nervous?" Tuck asked.

Chris shook his head. "Eager more than anything."

"I'm not going to lie." Lamont smirked. "I thought you'd be the fifth wheel forever."

They all laughed.

"So did I, man. So did I." A knock sounded on the door, so he called out, "Enter."

Nevaeh stuck her head in and grinned. "Don't you guys look all snazzy. We're ready to head in." She snapped her fingers. "Places," she said with a grin.

"Oh, I'll be waiting." Chris thanked the Lord he had no jitters and felt no triggers. There were no flashbacks of standing alone at the altar. Chris was secure in knowing that Erykah would never do that. She was the one God wanted him to marry, and this was the right time.

Tuck slapped him on the shoulder, and Lamont slapped him on the other one.

"Let's pray real quick," Lamont said.

Chris bowed his head.

"Lord God, we thank You for this union. These two people found their way to each other by Your grace and divine plan. We ask that You give them the love they need each day to cherish and respect each other. Please give them the wisdom they need to parent, and the joy they need to serve You individually and as a family."

"Amen," Chris whispered.

"And, Lord, we ask that when times get rough, they turn their attention to You and then to each other. We pray the love they feel today only continues to grow throughout the years," Tuck added.

"In Jesus's name, we pray," Lamont said.

"Amen," they chorused.

"Now let's go get you married," Tuck said.

They filtered into the event room, and Chris took a minute to look at their family and friends in the seats. His mom held Ash, whose dress matched Cheye's flower girl dress. Cameron and his other coworkers had also shown up. Erykah had invited Dr. Cook and his wife, along with a few of her residents.

Music began to play, and Cheyenne walked down the aisle tossing petals. She looked adorable in her red dress with white tulle peeking out. It had been his idea to get married on his birthday. He'd never really cared to celebrate it and didn't see that changing in the next forty-plus years. *God willing.* So marrying Erykah on Valentine's Day would give him something to celebrate.

Nevaeh came down the aisle next in a red dress that fell to the floor. Piper followed her, wearing a matching style. Then the music changed, and everyone stood. Chris held on to the cane as his heart beat faster, waiting for Erykah to appear.

When she did, his breath hitched in his chest. She was stunning.

Her twists had been contorted into some updo that made her look absolutely radiant. Ellynn's dress fit her perfectly. The sleeveless gown followed her curves and flared out at her knees. The only adornment on the dress was a bow at the neckline that was held in place with a cluster of jewels. But that's not what kept his attention. The way she smiled at him as she walked down the aisle made Chris's heart pound with fervor.

Lord God, I know You saved me from a wedding that was never meant to be so I could experience this moment. Thank You.

When Erykah neared, Chris took her hand. "You look gorgeous," he whispered.

"As do you," she murmured.

Chris's pastor had agreed to officiate the wedding. Thankfully, he hadn't been busy this Valentine's Day. Chris listened, and when the time to read their vows came, suddenly nervousness struck him. He wasn't an English major and couldn't write poetry to save his life. He'd prayed over the words and had asked for wisdom, but what if they still failed to adequately explain how he felt?

Trust. Breathe.

Right. He had this because God was in this.

"Erykah Kennedy, I vow to love you until I draw my last breath." He stared into her eyes, hoping she knew how seriously he took this commitment. "I vow to love Ashlynn and Cheyenne as daughters of my heart. I vow to cherish you and lay down my life for you, whether it's as simple as taking your needs into consideration before my own or literally. I vow to be the spiritual leader of our household and keep my faith submitted to God. I vow that no other woman or thing will come between us."

"Christian Gamble, you are a gift from God, and I promise to remember that in good times and bad. I promise that I will respect you as God asks wives to do. I promise that I will be your biggest cheerleader and always be a safe place for you to rest. I promise to let no other thing or person come between us. I vow that I will love you all the days of my life."

Why was his cheek wet? He wiped at it, then smiled at Erykah, whose eyes looked as watery as his were.

Lamont handed him his grandmother's ring, and Chris followed the pastor's guidance until Erykah wore it, a beam on her beautiful face. After she placed the gifted ring from Dr. Cook on his finger, Chris glanced at it. Both of their rings were vintage. The original wearers had worn them until the day they'd died. Chris liked to think it was a foreshadowing of his and Erykah's life to come.

Before he knew it, the pastor gave the famous line, "You may now kiss the bride."

Chris shifted forward, careful to keep his weight to the left. He slid his right hand along Erykah's cheek and kissed her until the cheers of the crowd penetrated the haze that accompanied the feel of her lips.

"I'm happy to introduce to you Mr. and Mrs. Christian Gamble."

EPILOGUE

FIVE YEARS LATER

Cheyenne! Ashlynn! Let's go!" I shouted.

I tapped my foot as I waited for the girls to come upstairs. Chris had already stowed their suitcases in the car, so that was an item crossed off my list. Still, they were taking their precious time coming to the door.

"Mom, Ash took my earbuds." Cheyenne came running up the stairs, a pink backpack on her shoulders.

My ten-year-old was gangly and reminded me so much of how Ellynn used to look. When she'd first called me Mom, I'd had to keep the waterworks under control until I had a quiet moment alone. A slight pang hit my chest, but I took in a deep breath and blew it out. *You're always in my heart, sweet sis.*

"I did not!" Ash came running after Cheyenne. "Daddy won't let me have my own, so why would I take yours?"

Ash looked like a perfect blend of Asher and Ellynn and had the same wild hair Cheye had at five years old.

Chris walked up the steps and stared at the two girls bickering. "What's going on?" he asked, sliding an arm around my waist.

I leaned into him, loving the fresh scent that clung to him. I wanted to turn my nose into the crook at his throat and settle in there forever. Instead, I placed a quick kiss there.

"Gross. They're kissing again," Cheyenne whispered, not quietly at all.

Chris leaned down and placed a soft kiss against my lips. "Give them something to *ew* about."

I laughed, wrapping my arm around his neck.

"Come on, Mom. Please stop," Cheyenne begged.

I pulled back and looked at her. "Kissing your husband is the best thing invented."

"Sure." She rolled her eyes. "My earbuds?"

"Cheye, don't roll your eyes at your mother. It's disrespectful." Chris's tone was stern, but I could hear the love in his voice for our girls. "And I have your earbuds. I placed them in the car when I loaded it up earlier."

Relief sagged her shoulders. "Thanks, Daddy." She hugged him around the waist, then ran to the car.

Ash walked toward us. "*I* want earbuds."

"Are you responsible enough to not lose them?" Chris asked.

"Uh-huh." Ash nodded.

He pulled a little case out of his pocket. "I'm trusting you, Ashlynn."

"Thank you, Daddy!" She grinned and hugged his legs.

We walked outside, and Chris pulled out the keys and locked the front door. "Ready for some fun?"

"So ready."

I couldn't wait to see the gang all together again. We'd taken to doing annual vacations together. Each year, we picked a different place, ensuring it was family friendly. Cheye and Ash always wanted to come. They adored the fact that Lamont was a famous actor and that Tuck and Piper regularly made the news as Derby-winning trainers.

Of course, Chris still had his YouTube channel, which continued to grow. Now he showed how families could help animals and the earth, and sometimes the girls got to be in a video with him. Ashlynn loved it more than anything, but Cheye was already hitting that preteen stage where she liked to pretend we didn't exist at times.

I buckled my seat belt as Chris started the car and backed out of the driveway. Soon we were at the airport, and then we were up in the air. This time we'd agreed to meet at Disney World. The girls were super excited, having never been. Chris and I were excited to see friends again as well as experience the magic of Disney.

After the plane landed, a shuttle from our hotel picked us up, carting us and the luggage. We quickly checked in. I jumped in the shower, needing to wash the travel off me. By the time I got out, the girls and Chris had changed. I grabbed my cell, stopping the playlist and opening a text message.

> **Erykah**
> We're here.

> **Piper**
> Yay! Want to come to our room? Nevaeh's already here.

> **Erykah**
> The whole crew?

> **Piper**
> Yep

"Chris, they're gathering in Piper and Tuck's room. You ready?"

"Definitely." He turned to the girls. "Come on, ladies. Let's go see everyone."

"Can I hold the baby?" Cheye asked.

"I don't see why you can't. Make sure you listen to instructions, 'kay?" I said.

We walked down the hall and knocked on the door at the end. Lamont had managed to get us all rooms on the same floor.

Piper opened the door, holding her six-month-old daughter in her arms. "Erykah!"

"Oh my word. She's so precious," I gushed. "Can I?"

"Of course!"

Chris and I had tried to get pregnant for a couple of years, but nothing happened. We then agreed that the girls were enough, and I put the dreams of having a baby away. Didn't mean I didn't love the chance to hold one. Remy was such a cutie.

"Where's Quade?" I asked. Besides the baby girl, Piper and Tuck had a three-year-old son who kept them on their toes.

"I think he's playing with Faith," she said.

"Can I hold Remy too, Ms. Piper?" Cheye asked.

"Of course, Cheyenne. Why don't we sit so you can hold her more easily?"

I transferred the baby to Cheye's arms, then looked around the living space. The guys had already gathered in a corner, laughing. Judging by Chris's expression, they had just teased him. Ash sat in front of the TV next to Faith, Lamont and Nevaeh's daughter. Quade and Monty—actually Lamont Jr.—were in another area crashing their trucks into each other.

"I'm so glad we could all meet up. This is going to be an awesome vacation," I said.

"Better than Niagara Falls?" Piper asked.

I laughed. "Well, at least drier."

"Hey, Erykah." Nevaeh walked out of the kitchen area and came to sit on the couch with us.

We hugged.

"Your twins are getting big."

She grinned. "I know. I equal parts love it and want to keep it from happening."

Cheyenne gave Remy back to Piper, then went to go stand by Chris. She was a true daddy's girl, even if she wanted a little independence now.

"I so know what you mean. I can't believe Cheye is double digits now."

"She'll be graduating from high school before you know it," Nevaeh said.

"I hope not." I looked at the kids, then turned to the ladies. "Are y'all planning on having more kids?"

Piper shrugged. "We don't really have a plan. We're seeing where God leads."

"I like that."

"Me too, girl. But I'm a slightly neurotic parent, who knew?" Nevaeh chuckled. "Having the twins wiped me out, and I'm not sure I'm ready for what a second round of pregnancy could bring."

I could totally understand that. Nevaeh's pregnancy with the twins had been rough. She'd been hospitalized a couple of times to get her the nutrients her body lacked.

"What about you?" Piper asked. "Are you and Chris still convinced you don't want to have any more? Not even through adoption?"

That was a great question. We'd ended up adopting Cheye and Ash because they wanted to have the same last name. But adopting another kid hadn't even entered my radar until earlier this year. "Actually, that word keeps popping up in my mind lately. I'm not sure if we'll go that route, but I'm listening to whatever God wants to tell me."

"Well, you already know you're great parents and have a huge capacity to love," Piper commented.

I watched Chris. Knowing him had enriched my life in so many ways. He'd taught me to love with abandon, and God gave me the courage to do so. Maybe adoption could be something we considered.

"I'll pray about it."

"We'll pray for you too," Nevaeh said. She sighed. "Lamont gets better looking every year. It's not fair. He'll probably go into his forties and fifties without anyone knowing he's aged. Meanwhile I'll—"

"You'll be beautiful," I interrupted. "Remember the Bible says beauty is fleeting. The fact that we all love God with all of our heart, mind, and soul means we radiate His light, and that is a beauty money can't buy and cosmetics can't emulate."

"Preach, Dr. Erykah." Piper smirked.

"Oh my goodness, you smirked just like Tuck," Nevaeh said.

My mouth dropped. "Yeah, you did."

"Well, they say eventually you'll look like your significant other." Piper shrugged. "I figure growing hair on my chin will be the next step."

We laughed, and our conversation morphed to the effects of aging.

Soon we were loading up our families as we left the room in search of food. I wasn't sure what would happen in my future, but I thanked God for giving me friends who had become family. They would walk this journey with me and be there in a minute if I needed them.

Thank You for always seeing and hearing me. For knowing exactly what I need before I even do. I love You, Lord.

DISCUSSION QUESTIONS

1. Erykah has been career-focused since she was in grade school. Why do you think it's important to have a work-life balance?

2. Grief is a theme presented throughout the book. Have you ever walked that path personally or with someone? What is something you would want others to understand about your grief?

3. Chris was jilted at the altar and let that experience color the rest of his relationships. Did he handle it correctly? Why or why not?

4. Friendships are an important theme in the LOVE IN THE SPOTLIGHT series. How do you think their friendships helped each of the characters?

5. What was one of your favorite scenes in the book? Why did it stand out to you?

6. What surprised you most about the book? Did you feel there were any significant plot twists? If so, what were they?

7. What lesson impacted you the most while reading *The Nature of Love*?

8. Did the book challenge some of your opinions on family, grief, or offering support? How so?

9. How did the novel explore themes of found family?

ACKNOWLEDGMENTS

I can't believe another book has been written. Every single time I reach the end and get a beautiful paperback in my hands, I feel blessed. This book could *not* have been written without help from some amazing people.

Thank you to my Book Troop! Special shout-out to Susan Atkinson for Cheyenne's name. Katie Combes for Ashlynn's name. Candy Vanhoose Holbrook for Charlie's name. Heather Lancaster for Linda Simmons's name. Octavia Mason for Harold's name. Y'all are the best!

Thank you so much to Sarah Monzon for all the help you gave me critiquing. I value your friendship so much!

Many thanks to my agent extraordinaire, Rachel McMillan, for championing my books. I appreciate your guidance in my writing career.

Of course I can't leave out the awesome people at Bethany House. Working with all of you is a dream come true. Thank you to Kate Deppe and Jessica Sharpe. Also many thanks to the marketing team, cover design team, and all the other people I don't get to work closely with but know have a hand in this book. Keep doing what you do!

Last but not least, I'd like to thank my husband and two boys. Glenn, thank you for keeping me on schedule, supporting me through the tears, and reminding me who I am writing for. Not to mention answering my questions about the male psyche and simply being my champion. To my boys, thank you for thinking I'm famous and wanting people to know I write books. I love y'all so much!

For more from

Toni Shiloh

read on
for an excerpt from

To Win
A Prince

Fashion aficionado Iris Blakely dreams of using her talent to start a business to help citizens in impoverished areas. But when she discovers that Ekon Diallo will be her business consultant, the battle between her desires and reality begins. Can she keep her heart—and business—intact despite the challenges she faces?

Available now wherever books are sold.

one

EKON

I padded out of my bedroom, stopping in the hallway to peer through the floor-to-ceiling windows overlooking the hills of Etikun. For some reason, my alarm had sounded instead of the soft voice of my personal assistant to wake me. Nazum had worked for me since I turned eighteen, and my alarm had only been a backup in case I chose to sleep in. Where could he be?

I continued toward the living area. "Nazum?"

Nothing.

The only noise reaching my ears was my slippered feet. Not a single servant ran about. The place appeared to be empty. Had something happened? I checked my mobile for any missed messages and found none. The seventy-inch TV beckoned me.

My black leather couch was perfectly positioned in front of the entertainment center. Surely the local news would explain where my servants had disappeared to. With a press of a button, I had it up and running . . . and gaped. There stood Father in his princely dress, talking to a reporter. The headline read *Prince Iseoluwa Diallo denounces son's actions.* I turned up the volume.

"His mother and I are deeply ashamed. We cannot express our regret enough for his involvement with Ms. Layeni. As far as we are aware, there was no intimate relationship between them."

I shook my head. *Disgusting.* No one but the council and queen knew Ms. Layeni was my half-sister. To insinuate anything else was deplorable, but that was Father's way. Keep all misdeeds secret so he could continue the façade of the humblest prince in Etikun. But I knew the truth, the stain of his infidelity against Mother.

"Prince Diallo, do you think the punishment should have been more severe?"

Father's brow furrowed. "I do not go against my queen or the council's decisions. However, I have seen fit to add my own form of penance to their sentencing."

What? I slowly looked around my empty penthouse flat, stomach souring as realization came to me.

"What sort of reprimand will you enact?"

"I have removed all servants from Ekon's employ, transferring them to other jobs within Diallo Enterprises. They should not suffer for his gross misjudgments. I have also removed his vehicles from his ownership in order to sell them and transfer the earnings to a charity of my wife's choice."

A primal roar tore from my lips as I flipped over the coffee table. How *dare* he remove my servants! Did he expect me to do everything myself like some commoner? Simply because the council stripped me of my title did not mean I had to live like the lower class.

How was I supposed to prepare for my first day of business

consulting without breakfast and clothes to wear? How would I get there? *Public transportation?*

A shudder coursed through me, and I sank onto the sofa cushions, head in my hands as I rocked. My breath came in spurts as the implications of Father's actions sank in. I was barely cognizant of the reporter asking more questions.

Until one stood out.

"Do you still consider Mr. Ekon Diallo your son?"

My gaze rose as I held my breath.

"If he can turn his wayward ways around."

Enough of that. I turned off the news, throwing the remote to the floor. The clatter of it hitting the marble tiles made me wince. I better not have chipped them. Who knew if I had the funds to replace them, considering I was no longer a Diallo employee. Would Father cancel my bank membership as well? Could he?

I paced back and forth, chest heaving. Part of me was not surprised Father did not have the decency to explain these repercussions to my face. Learning about them on the morning news like the rest of the country was par for the course. I could only imagine the comments filling social media right now. Something I had purposely ignored since I walked out of council chambers as a nobody.

"Ahhhh!" But shouting did not make me feel better. It only made the vein in my forehead pulse all the harder.

I stomped across the room and into the kitchen. Since I apparently no longer had a personal chef, I would have to make my own breakfast. A quick glance at the stove clock showed an hour before my report time. Normally, I would eat an omelet prepared by my chef. Now I would, what . . . make it *myself*?

Unfortunately, I had no time to voice my complaints. I could not show up late and have the council's opinion of me worsen—or Father's. I shook my head and pulled up a YouTube tutorial for making the perfect omelet. After watching the video a few times, I removed eggs, bacon, and cheese from my refrigerator. There were some *akara* balls left over from the day before the sentencing. I could heat those up to make a complete meal. It should be simple enough.

I turned the knob to start the flame as shown on the video, then moved it to the middle setting as recommended. The fire lit the stove. I smiled. Clearly cooking was not as difficult as Chef had always made it seem. I grabbed an egg and tapped it on the counter like I had seen the cook do in the video. The insides splattered on the counter, making a slimy path down the cabinet before the yolk landed on the floor.

I bit back an oath.

A quick glance located the materials to clean up the mess. The feel of the snotty yolk in the paper towel made me want to retch. Relief filled me as I managed to place the mess in the trash.

At least I had more eggs. I would simply use less force than before. A small smile shifted something inside me as I successfully cracked the egg before pushing my thumbs inside to make a hole to open the shell.

The egg exploded, sending clear and yellow liquid down my nightshirt.

The oath left my mouth this time. I glanced at my watch. How had thirty minutes passed so quickly? If I was to meet Ms. Blakely on time, breakfast would have to be postponed. I put the ingredients back in the refrigerator, then removed my shirt and tossed it into the laundry room.

That chore ranked low on my priority list. As long as I had clean clothes, I would not have to worry about learning how to operate the washing machine. I flipped through the dress shirts hanging in my walk-in closet and opted for black. It matched my growing irritation as my stomach complained about not being fed.

No servants. No cars. No title of prince. Instead, I would now answer to *mister*. What more could happen to me? The hairs on the back of my neck rose at the question, and I shook off the unnerving feeling. I needed to find a driver. My mouth curled. A taxi, even?

A few minutes later, I grabbed my wallet and stuffed it into my back pocket. A quick look in the mirror showed my smooth chocolate skin. My hair was close-cropped and freshly lined, thanks to a trip to the barber before the council sentencing. My shave this morning had maintained my clean look. The only thing I added was a black beaded necklace, interspersed with a few golden beads. I was now ready to meet Ms. Blakely and get my business consultant hours under way.

Three hundred and twenty hours!

The amount was pure ridiculousness. Yet if I worked an eight-hour day, then forty days later would see an end to my servitude. What if Ms. Blakely scheduled me for less than a full day's work? Then the torture would be endless. I had a jewelry business I was desperate to return to. But wait. Would Father allow me to return? Somehow, I needed to get back in his good graces.

Clearly, Father wanted to wash his hands of me. How could I remove the stain of conspiring against the queen from the Diallo name? Reversing such monumental damage seemed impossible.

I could still remember the rage on his face when he discovered I had been talking to my half-sister. But that was because my relationship to her was a taboo topic. No one in Etikun knew that Dayo and I shared a *màmá*, because the woman I called Mother was known as my biological mother. In reality, Dayo's mother was my biological mother, as Father had

had an affair with her. I had not known this until my teens, when Dayo showed up unannounced at our house, wanting to meet me. Father forbade it, but when I turned eighteen, I reached out to her.

Now she was imprisoned. My biological mother deceased. All I had was the woman I had always known as Mother.

I shook the morose thoughts from my mind and headed toward the penthouse elevator. It led to the lobby, where everyone would see me step into a taxi instead of my chauffeured Porsche.

A taxi!

At least I would not have to drive myself around Ọlọrọ Ilé.

Fortunately, the taxi waited at the curb when I arrived on the lobby floor. I kept my eyes straight ahead, avoiding any eye contact with my neighbors and the concierge at the front desk. I could not bear to see the looks of condemnation or pity I had been receiving since first becoming headline news. There was nothing like seeing your face plastered on the screen with the words *house arrest* scrolling underneath.

The moment I stepped outdoors, reporters swarmed me, yelling my name. I pushed through the throng, ignoring the questions regarding my feelings on my father's earlier interview. I opened the back door of the taxi, slamming it shut as I slid across the cloth seats.

"Drive now," I spat.

"Yes, *ògbéni*. Where to?"

I flinched inwardly at the title of *mister*, hearing the derisive tone of Alàgbà Ladipo instead.

"Uh." I peered at the note on my phone listing the address of Ms. Blakely's business. I relayed it to the driver.

"Got it, *ògbéni*. I will get you there quick as possible."

Thank goodness Ọlọrọ was not prone to traffic jams like

other parts of Africa. The island boasted a small population of less than a million.

I focused on the scenery passing by as the driver took me to Aṣọ, Ms. Blakely's business. Once I arrived, the first thing I wanted to ask was why she chose that name. Aṣọ meant *clothed* in Oninan and seemed a simplistic name for a fashion company. Granted, my experience was in the jewelry industry, but still.

Hopefully she had not submitted paperwork denoting the name and a trademark for the logo. Certainly I could brainstorm much better options than Aṣọ. Business was in my blood and went along with the degree hanging on my home office wall. Another requirement from Father.

He had been grooming me to take over Diallo Enterprises one day, but with this setback, I wondered about my future there. Out of all the changes I had experienced this past month, not working at the family business made me the most nervous. I could not lose my position as COO of Diallo Enterprises. *I cannot.*

I would call Father this evening. Inform him how much of an asset I would be to Ms. Blakely. Father would have to reconsider stripping everything from me then. *Right?*

This was not my life, and the upsets had me shaken. Still, I had an image to protect regardless of my current infamy. I would become a prince once more, and this would all be relegated to a minor detour in my life.

"Are you okay, òigbéni? You are awfully quiet back there."

I peered at the rearview mirror. "Simply thinking, *monsieur.*" *Mister* sounded better in French. Plus, speaking the language reminded me of my superiority over the taxi driver.

I was accomplished. Held an MBA, spoke six languages, and was heir to the Diallo empire. I was no *commoner,* despite the royal council's pronouncement that I could no longer be titled. I had led a princely life, been raised in privilege from birth. I did not know how to be anything else.

Despite this, I was sure the royal council expected me to accept my new identity. The queen had even mentioned that I needed to learn what it was like to serve. Helping Ms. Blakely with all my business knowledge was a service in itself. Why must I demean myself in front of the community as well? At least that torture did not start until next week.

One thing at a time.

"I will leave you to think, then." The driver turned on the radio and began bobbing his head to the rhythm of the music.

"I appreciate that, monsieur." I glanced at my watch. I was due at Aṣọ in five minutes. "Will we arrive soon?"

"*Bééni, bééni,* ògbéni."

His assured *yes* would not help me if he did not apply a little more pressure to the gas pedal. It would not look good if I showed up late on my first day. I sighed. This day was off to a horrible start.

The taxi driver stopped behind the vehicle in front of us and began shaking and singing at the top of his lungs.

"Ah, do you listen to this, ògbéni?" he yelled out.

"No, I have not heard this song before." Despite my obvious disdain, the driver continued his serenade. Father had always played instrumental music. Back in my university days, I had been familiar with popular songs, but that style was not something I gravitated to.

I wanted to lower myself from view in case anyone saw me with the driver exuberantly singing at full volume. Why did he have to roll his window all the way down? He looked ridiculous. Did that make me so by association?

"Monsieur." I pointed ahead when he turned to look at me. "The car has moved."

"Ah, yes. I apologize. This is my jam!"

I glanced at my watch. Two minutes to arrival and a few more miles to drive.

I was going to be late.

Eleven minutes later, security escorted me to Ms. Blakely's office. She stood behind her desk, a look of irritation on her very pretty face.

I blinked. I remembered her. She had been at the welcome ball for the queen during our Independence Day festivities. She had worn an emerald dress. I remembered because the matching jewelry had made her skin glow like a brown axinite.

"You're late," she snapped in an American accent similar to the queen's but less cultured. No, that was not the right word. Less guarded.

I clenched my hands. If I had had my Porsche or even the Mercedes to drive, I would have been on time. Something told me the queen's best friend would not care about my plight. So I offered the truth. "My taxi driver got distracted dancing instead of driving."

Her mouth dropped open. "What?"

"It was quite embarrassing. He sang loudly—and *badly*, I might add. He would break out dancing at traffic lights only to realize traffic had commenced upon my reminder. He insisted that almost every single song that came on was *his jam*."

She folded her arms across her chest. I saw the slightest twitch of her lips.

"Fine. I'll make an allowance this time. But I expect you to be on time in the future, Mr. Diallo."

Ugh. I cannot bear that label. "That is my expectation as well, Ms. Blakely. It was my first time in a taxi, and I did not know what to expect."

Her mouth parted again, eyes wide with shock. It was quite obvious she had not been raised in a life of privilege if she thought taking a taxi a common practice. But that was none of my concern.

I slid my hands into my pockets. "I am ready to begin. Am I to work an eight-hour day?"

Her nose wrinkled as she pushed her curly mane away from her eyes. How did one woman have so much hair?

"We'll see. I'm in the early stages, but I've gotten a lot completed." She frowned, her ruby-red lips turning downward. "And unfortunately, still have too much on my plate."

"I am here to help in any way I can." And to prove to Father that I deserved the things life had afforded me, and maybe even to convince the council to rescind their decision and restore my title.

"Yes, well, have a seat." She gestured to the white chair in front of her glass desk.

I sat down and held my breath. Whatever happened in this meeting would determine my future. I could only hope Ms. Blakely would put me on a path that led me back to the top.

Toni Shiloh is a wife, a mom, and an award-winning Christian contemporary romance author. She writes to bring God glory and to learn more about His goodness. Her novel *In Search of a Prince* won the first ever Christy Amplify Award. Her books have won the Selah Award and have been finalists for the Carol Award and the HOLT Medallion. A member of American Christian Fiction Writers (ACFW), Toni loves connecting with readers and authors alike via social media. You can learn more about her writing at ToniShiloh.com.

Sign Up for Toni's Newsletter

Keep up to date with Toni's latest news on book releases and events by signing up for her email list at the website below.

ToniShiloh.com

FOLLOW TONI ON SOCIAL MEDIA

Toni Shiloh, Author   @ToniShiloh   @ToniShilohWrite

More from Toni Shiloh

Piper McKinney dreams of her horse winning the Kentucky Derby, and with the help of her best friend, horse trainer Tucker Hale, that hope starts to become reality. Then her parents are embroiled in a scandal, and Piper is implicated. She and Tuck will have to survive the onslaught to find their way to the winner's circle—and each other.

A Run at Love
LOVE IN THE SPOTLIGHT

Hollywood hair stylist Neveah loves making those in the spotlight shine. But when a photo of her and Hollywood heartthrob Lamont goes viral for all the wrong reasons, they suddenly find themselves in a fake relationship to save their careers. In a world where nothing seems real, can Neveah be true to herself . . . and her heart?

The Love Script
LOVE IN THE SPOTLIGHT

Brielle Adebayo's simple life unravels when she discovers she is a princess in the African kingdom of Ọlọrọ Ilé and must immediately assume her royal position. Brielle comes to love the island's culture and studies the language with her handsome tutor. But when her political rivals force her to make a difficult choice, a wrong decision could change her life.

In Search of a Prince

BETHANYHOUSE

 Bethany House Fiction

 @BethanyHouseFiction

 @Bethany_House

 @BethanyHouseFiction

 Free exclusive resources for your book group at BethanyHouseOpenBook.com

 Sign up for our fiction newsletter today at BethanyHouse.com